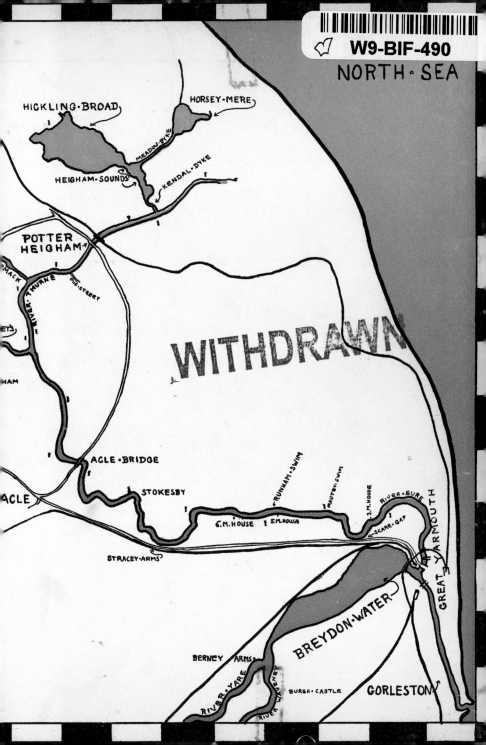

COOT CLUB

Also by Arthur Ransome

SWALLOWS AND AMAZONS

SWALLOWDALE

PETER DUCK

WINTER HOLIDAY

PIGEON POST

WE DIDN'T MEAN TO GO TO SEA

SECRET WATER

THE BIG SIX

MISSEE LEE

THE PICTS AND THE MARTYRS

GREAT NORTHERN?

RACUNDRA'S FIRST CRUISE

ROD AND LINE (FISHING ESSAYS)

OLD PETER'S RUSSIAN TALES

AUTOBIOGRAPHY

(ed. Rupert Hart-Davis)

FIRST NIGHT IN THE *TITMOUSE*

COOT CLUB

by

ARTHUR RANSOME

JONATHAN CAPE
THIRTY BEDFORD SQUARE
LONDON

FIRST PUBLISHED 1934
REPRINTED 1934, 1935, 1937, 1938, 1940, 1941, 1942 (twice), 1943, 1944,
1945, 1946, 1948, 1949, 1951, 1955, 1958, 1964, 1969, 1976

JONATHAN CAPE LTD, 30 BEDFORD SQUARE, LONDON WCI

ISBN O 224 60635 2

PRINTED IN GREAT BRITAIN BY
LOWE AND BRYDONE PRINTERS LIMITED, THETFORD, NORFOLK
BOUND BY G. AND J. KITCAT LTD, LONDON

CONTENTS

BOOK ONE
COOTS AND FOREIGNERS

BOOK TWO
IN SOUTHERN WATERS

CONTENTS

LIST OF ILLUSTRATIONS

LIST OF ILLUSTRATIONS

COOTS AND FOREIGNERS

FLASH

NOTE

Throughout Book One, readers who want to know where they are should use the map of the northern rivers which makes the first end-paper.

CHAPTER I

JUST IN TIME

THORPE STATION at Norwich is a terminus. Trains from the middle of England and the south run in there, and if they are going on east and north by way of Wroxham, they run out of the station by the same way they ran in. Dick and Dorothea Callum had never been in Norfolk before, and for ten minutes they had been waiting in that station, sitting in the train, for fear it should go on again at once, as it had at Ipswich and Colchester and the few other stations at which it had stopped. The journey was nearly over. They had only a few more miles to go, but Dorothea, whose mind was always busy with scenes that might do for the books she meant to write, was full of the thought of how dreadful it would be if old Mrs. Barrable, with whom they were going to stay, should be waiting on Wroxham station and the train should arrive without them. She would go back to her boat, for she was living in a boat somewhere down the river, and Dick and Dorothea, even if they did manage to reach Wroxham by some later train, would never be able to find her. So when Dick had wanted to get out of the carriage and go along the platform to watch the engine being coupled on at the other end of the train, Dorothea had been very much against it. If Dick were to get out, she would have to get out too, lest one should be left behind and the other carried on to Wroxham alone. And if she got out, why then the train might go on without either of them and their luggage might end up anywhere. She looked at the two small suit-cases on the rack ("Don't let them bring much luggage;

there isn't room," Mrs. Barrable had written). So Dick and she had wasted ten whole minutes sitting in the carriage, looking out of the open window at the almost empty platform.

A whistle blew, and the guard waved a green flag.

"Bring your head in now, Dick," said Dorothea, "and close the window."

But before Dick had time to pull the window up, they saw a boy come hurrying along the platform. He was heavily laden, with a paper parcel which he was hugging to himself so as to have that hand free for a large can of paint, while on the other arm he had slung a coil of new rope. He was hurrying along beside the train, looking into the windows of the carriages as if he were searching for someone he knew. And Dorothea noticed that, though it was a fine, dry spring day, he was wearing a pair of rubber knee-boots.

"He'll miss it if he doesn't get in," said Dick.

"Hurry up, there, if you're going," a porter shouted and at that moment, just after he had passed their window, the boy stumbled over a rope's end that had fallen from his coil. Down he went. His tin of paint rolled on towards the edge of the platform. His parcel burst its paper. Some blocks and shackles flew out.

The train had begun to move. A porter far down the platform was running towards the boy, who had jumped up again almost as if he had bounced, had grabbed his blocks and crammed them in his pockets, and had stopped the escaping paint-tin with his foot just before it rolled between the platform and the train. In another moment he had the tin in his arms and was running beside the carriage.

"Don't try that now," shouted a ticket inspector.

"Wait for the next," shouted the porter, who was running after the boy.

"Heads!" called the boy.

The next moment the paint-can came flying through the

open window between Dick and Dorothea. The coil of rope
whirled round and shot in after it. The door was opened and
the boy flung himself in head first and landed on all fours.

Dorothea pulled the door to. Dick said: "They always like
it shut," and reached out and closed the handle.

The porter, left far behind, stopped running.

"Just in time," said the boy. "I didn't want to miss it.
Lucky for me you had your window open."

"Haven't you hurt yourself?" said Dorothea.

"Not I," said the boy, dusting his hands together, hands that
looked so capable and hard-worked that Dick, at the sight of
them, wanted to hide his own.

Dorothea looked at him while he picked up his paint-can,
badly dinted but not burst, took his blocks and shackles and
a packet of brass hinges and a bag of brass screws out of his
pockets, to see that he had lost nothing by his fall, and then
carefully re-coiled his shining new rope on the seat. He
looked, she thought, most awfully strong, and his hands, and
the blue knitted jersey, and those boots and rope and things
made her almost think he might be a sailor, but his jacket
was quite like Dick's own, and his flannel shorts . . . hundreds
of boys wore flannel shorts.

The train pulled out of Norwich, and Dick, looking from
the window, noticed a bit of a ruin, with a narrow arch in it,
left at the side of the line.

"Pretty old," he said to Dorothea.

Dorothea, somehow feeling that this needed explaining to
the strange boy, said, "Our father's an archæologist."

"Mine's a doctor," said the boy.

And then the train was running close beside the river, and
they saw a steamer going down from Norwich. They crossed
a bridge, and there was a river on both sides of the line, the
old river on the left curving round by the village of Thorpe
with crowds of yachts and motor boats tied up under the

gardens, and, on the right, a straight ugly cutting. In another minute they had crossed the old river again, and the train was slowing up at a station. Close by, across a meadow, they could see a great curve of the river, and three or four houseboats moored to the bank, and a small yacht working her way up.

"Interested in boats?" said the boy, as the others hurried across the carriage.

"Yes, very much," said Dorothea. "Last holidays we were in a houseboat frozen in the ice."

"They're always getting frozen in, houseboats," said the boy. "Done much sailing?"

"We haven't done any at all," said Dick. "Not yet."

"Except just once, on the ice, in a sledge," said Dorothea.

"It wasn't really sailing," said Dick. "Just blowing along."

"You'll get lots of sailing at Wroxham," said the boy, looking up at the big black and white labels on the two small suit-cases.

"We're going to live in a boat," said Dorothea—"She isn't at Wroxham. She's somewhere down the river."

"What's her name?" said the boy, "I know most of them."

"We don't know," said Dorothea.

"Mine's *Titmouse*. She's a very little one, of course. But she's got an awning. I slept in her last night. And she can sail like anything. This rope is for her. Blocks, too. And the paint. Birthday present. That's why I've been into Norwich."

Dick and Dorothea looked at the blocks and fingered the silky smoothness of the new rope. It certainly did seem that they had come to the right place to learn about sailing.

Dorothea already saw herself and Dick meeting Nancy and Peggy Blackett and the Walkers, too, with whom they had spent a happy month on the shores of a wintry lake, and surprising them with the news that she and Dick could count themselves sailors more or less. After that winter holiday they had set their hearts on learning, but it was no good going north at

Easter, for the Blacketts were away with their uncle, and the Walkers were in the south with their father, who was home in England on leave. They had given up all hope of getting any sailing before the summer. And then, half-way through the Easter holidays, the letter from Mrs. Barrable had come in the very nick of time. Mrs. Barrable, long ago, had been Mrs. Callum's school-mistress, but she painted pictures and was the sister of a very famous portrait painter. And she had written to Mrs. Callum to say that her brother and she had chartered a small yacht on the Norfolk Broads, and that her brother had had to go off to London to paint portraits of some important Indians, so that she was all alone in the boat with her pug-dog William, and that if Dick and Dorothea could be spared she would like to have their company. Just then they could very well be spared, as their father had to go to a conference of archæologists upon the Roman wall and, of course, wanted their mother to go with him. Everything had been arranged in a couple of days, and here they were, and already, before they had got to Wroxham, they had met this boy who seemed more of a sailor even than John or Nancy. Things were certainly coming out all right.

"Hullo," said Dick, soon after they passed Salhouse Station. "There's a heron. What's he doing on that field where there isn't any water?"

"Frogging," said the strange boy, and then, suddenly, "Are you interested in birds, too?"

"Yes," said Dick. "But there are lots I've never seen, because of living mostly in a town."

"You don't collect eggs?" said the boy, looking keenly at Dick.

"I never have," said Dick.

"Don't you ever begin," said the boy. "If you don't collect eggs, it's all right . . . you see we've got a Bird Protection Society, not to take eggs, but to watch the birds instead. We know thirty-seven nests this year. . . ."

"Thirty-seven?" said Dick.

"Just along our reaches. . . . Horning way. . . ."

"Our boat's near there," said Dorothea.

"By the way," said the boy, "you didn't see two girls in this train—twins? No? They were in Norwich this morning, but I expect they drove back with their father. Otherwise they'd have come this way. We always do. Going by bus, you don't see anything of the river worth counting."

"There's a hawk," said Dick.

"Kestrel," said the boy, looking at the bird hovering above a little wood. "Hullo! We'll be there in a minute."

The train was slowing up. It crossed another river, and for a moment they caught a glimpse of moored house-boats with smoke from their chimneys where people were cooking mid-day meals, an old mill, and a bridge, and a lot of masts beyond it. And then the train had come to a stop at Wroxham station.

The strange boy was looking warily out of the window.

On the platform he saw an old lady looking up at the carriage windows. He also saw the station-master. He chose his moment and, slipping down from the carriage with his paint-can and coil of rope, was hurrying off to give up his ticket to the collector at the gate. But the station-master was too quick for him.

"Hum," he said, "I might have guessed it was you, when they rang me up from Norwich about a boy with a ticket for Wroxham jumping on the train after it had fairly got going. Told me to give you a good talking to. Well, don't you do it again. Not broken any bones this time, I suppose?"

The boy grinned. He and the station-master were very good friends, and he knew that the railway officials in Norwich had not meant him to get off so easily.

"I was on the platform in time," he said. "Only I was looking for Port and Starboard, and then I slipped, and the train started, and I simply had to catch that train."

"Port and Starboard?" said the station-master. "I saw them go over the road-bridge with Mr. Farland more than an hour ago. They'll have had their dinners and be on the river by now. . . . Yes, madam. Let me give you a hand." He was talking now to Mrs. Barrable, the old lady, who had just found Dick and Dorothea. The station-master reached up to help Dorothea down with her suit-case.

"Well, and here you are," said Mrs. Barrable, kissing Dorothea and shaking hands with Dick.

"And who was that other boy?" she asked.

"We made friends with him in the train," said Dorothea. "He knows a lot about boats."

"And birds," said Dick.

Mrs. Barrable watched him as he hurried through the gate and down the path to the road. "Haven't I seen him before?" she said. "And who are the Port and Starboard he was asking about?"

"That's Tom Dudgeon, the doctor's son from Horning," said the station-master. "You'll maybe have seen him on the river in his little boat. He's not often away from the water in the holidays. And Port and Starboard, queer names for a couple of girls. . . ." But there was the guard, just waiting to start the train, and the station-master never finished his sentence.

"Busy man," said Mrs. Barrable. "Come along, Dick. Written any more books, Dot? You really have done well in keeping your luggage down. We'll easily find room for these. I've got a boy with a hand-cart to take your things to the river. We're going down by water. Longer but more fun. There's a motor-launch going down to Horning, and the young man says he'll put us aboard. The *Teasel's* lying a good long way below the village. But we must have something to eat first, and I must get you some boots like those that boy was wearing. You'll want them every time you step ashore."

CHAPTER II

DISAPPOINTMENT

NEVER in all their lives had Dick and Dorothea seen so many boats. Mrs. Barrable had taken them shopping at a store that seemed to sell every possible thing for the insides and outsides of sailors. She had taken them to lunch at an inn where everybody was talking about boats at the top of his voice. And now they had gone down to the river to look for the Horning boatman with his motor-launch. The huge flags of the boat-letters were flying from their tall flag-staffs. Little flags, copies of the big ones, were fluttering at the mastheads of the hired yachts. There were boats everywhere, and boats of all kinds, from the big black wherry with her gaily painted mast, loading at the old granary by Wroxham bridge, and meant for nothing but hard work, to the punts of the boatmen going to and fro, and the motor-cruisers filling up with petrol, and the hundreds of big and little sailing yachts tied to the quays, or moored in rows, two and three deep, in the dykes and artificial harbours beside the main river.

"Why are such a lot of the boats wearing dust-covers?" asked Dorothea.

"Rain-coats, really," said Mrs. Barrable. "Those are awnings. Everybody rigs them at night to make an extra room by giving a roof to the steering well. And, of course, when the boats are not in use the awnings keep them dry. Lots of the boats are not let yet. Luckily for us it's early in the season. Later on people come here from all over England, and in the summer Wroxham must be like a fairground."

DISAPPOINTMENT

"It's rather like one now," said Dorothea, listening to the gramophones and the hammering in the boat-sheds. "Oh, look. There's someone just starting. Do all the big boats have little ones like chickens hanging on behind?"

"Dinghies," said Mrs. Barrable. "Suppose you're in a yacht and want to fetch the milk or post your letters, you just jump into your dinghy and use your oars."

"We *have* rowed once," said Dick, "but only for a few minutes."

And then Mrs. Barrable saw the boatman waving to them.

IN·WROXHAM·REACH

A minute or two later they were off themselves, in a little motor-launch, purring down Wroxham Reach. In the bows of the launch were the two small suit-cases, and the parcels that had been sent down to the river by the people at the village store. Dorothea looked happily at one large, awkward, bulging parcel. Mrs. Barrable had bought them cheap oilskins and sou'westers as well as sea-boots. There was no excuse for wearing such things on a fine spring day, with bright sunshine pouring down, but just to look at that bulging parcel made Dorothea feel she was something of a sailor already.

Once round the bend at the low end of the reach, they had left all the noise and bustle of Wroxham behind them. Tall trees were growing on either side of the river. There were quiet little houses among the trees, and green lawns at the water's edge, with water-hens strutting about on the grass as if they were pigeons or peacocks. A man with long thigh boots and a yachting cap was busy with a lawn-mower.

"Look," said Dorothea. "There's a sailor mowing the grass."

"Most people here have got at least one foot in the water," said Mrs. Barrable, "and they do say a lot of the babies are born web-footed, like ducks."

"Not really?" said Dick.

"I'm not so sure," said Mrs. Barrable. "Every infant in this place seems able to sail a boat as soon as it can walk."

"Were you born here?" asked Dorothea, glancing, in spite of herself, at Mrs. Barrable's neat, rubber-soled shoes.

"At Beccles," said Mrs. Barrable. "On another river. Not very far away."

Not everybody, thought Dorothea, could be born on a river, but at least she and Dick would do their best to make up for lost time.

The houses came to an end. Here and there, looking through the trees, Dick and Dorothea caught the flash of water. Through a narrow opening they saw a wide lake with boats sailing in a breeze, although, in the shelter of the trees, the few sailing yachts they had passed had been drifting with hardly enough wind to give them steerage way. A little further down the river they caught a glimpse of another bit of open water. Then again they were moving between thickly wooded banks. Suddenly they heard a noise astern of them, and one of the big motor-cruisers that they had seen at Wroxham came roaring past them, leaving a high angry wash that sent the launch tossing.

"Just like real sea," said Dorothea, holding on to the gunwale and determined not to be startled.

"They got no call to go so fast," said the boatman. "Look at that now. Upset his dinner in the bilge likely."

The boatman pointed ahead at a little white boat tied to a branch of a tree. It was very much smaller than any yacht they had seen, hardly bigger, in fact, than the dinghies most of the yachts were towing. It had a mast, and an awning had been rigged up over part of it, to make a little shelter for cooking. The wash of the big cruiser racing past sent the little boat leaping up against the overhanging boughs, and a great cloud of smoke poured suddenly out.

"It's Tom Dudgeon," said Dorothea.

"It's the *Titmouse*," said Dick. "There's the name."

The boatman slowed up the launch for a moment as they went by.

Tom Dudgeon, who had been kneeling on the floor to do his cooking, looked out with a very red face. They saw that he had a frying-pan in his hand.

He nodded to the boatman. "Bacon fat all over everywhere," he said. "Oh, hullo!" he added, seeing Dick and Dorothea.

"Shame that is," said the boatman as he put on speed again. "Proper young sailor is Tom Dudgeon. Keeps that little *Titmouse* of his like a new pin."

"Ah," said Mrs. Barrable. "Now I dare say you can tell us who are the Port and Starboard he was talking about to the Wroxham station-master...."

"The station-master said they were queer names for girls," added Dorothea.

The boatman laughed. "Port and Starboard," he said. "We all call 'em that. Nobody call 'em anything else. Mr. Farland's twins. All but sisters to young Tom, they are, what with Mrs. Farland dying when they was babies, and Mrs. Dudgeon, the doctor's wife, pretty near bring them up with

25

her boy. She'll not have time for 'em all now, with a new young 'un of her own. Been as good as a mother to them two girls has Mrs. Dudgeon. . . . Steady now! . . . Did ever you see the like o' that?" He swung his launch sharply aside to avoid a sailing yacht that was tacking to and fro and had suddenly gone about in mid-stream just after he had altered course to keep out of her way. "Probably never in a boat before," said the boatman, "and in a week they'll be laughing at the new-comers. A good nursery for sailing is the North River." [1]

Dorothea looked happily at Dick, and Dick at Dorothea.

They left the trees. The river was beginning to be wider, flowing between reed-fringed banks with here and there a willow at the water's edge. A fleet of five little yachts was sailing to meet them, tacking to and fro, like a cloud of butterflies.

"Racing," said Mrs. Barrable.

The boatman looked over his shoulder. "If it's no hurry, ma'am, I'll pull into the side while they go by."

"Of course."

He shut off his engine and let the launch slide close along the bank until he caught hold of a willow branch to hold her steady. Dick caught another.

And then, as the first of the little racing boats flew towards them, spun round, and was off for the opposite bank, the boatman turned to Mrs. Barrable.

"There's Port and Starboard, ma'am, if you want to see 'em. Fourth boat. Mr. Farland gener'lly do better'n that."

The second boat shot by and the third. The fourth came sweeping across the river. "Ready about!" they heard the helmsman call, and the little boat shot up into the wind, with flapping sails, so close to the launch that Dorothea could have reached out and shaken hands with one of the two girls who were working the jib-sheets.

[1] This is another name for the River Bure.

"He've a good crew, have Mr. Farland," said the boatman, "though they don't weigh as much as a man, the two of 'em together."

"I don't believe they're much bigger than us," said Dorothea delightedly.

"You'll be seeing 'em again," said the boatman starting up his engine. "They'll be going down river past your boat and back again before they finish by the Swan at Horning."

"Your boat," he had said. How long now before she and Dick were pulling ropes like those two girls, and listening for the word from Mrs. Barrable at the tiller? Dorothea was planning a story. Why, if only she and Dick could sail like that, almost anything might happen. She looked at Dick. But Dick was busy with his pocket-book. In the winter holidays it had been full of stars, but with the year going on and nights getting shorter, birds had taken the place of stars. Heron, kestrel, coot, water-hen, he had already added to his list of birds seen, and just before meeting those racing boats he had seen a bird with two tufts sticking out from the top of its head, and only its slim neck showing above the water. He had known it at once for a crested grebe.

*

On and on they went down the river. They were coming now to another village. The launch slowed up. They were passing wooden bungalows and a row of houseboats. The river bent sharply round a corner. There was an old inn at the bend, the Swan. Then there was a staithe [1] with a couple of yachts tied up to it. Beyond the staithe were big boat-sheds, like those they had seen at Wroxham.

"This is Horning," said Mrs. Barrable.

"Our boat's not far now, is it?" said Dick.

[1] A staithe in Norfolk is a place where boats moor to take in or discharge cargo : much what a quay is elsewhere.

"This is where Tom Dudgeon lives," said Dorothea, "and those two girls."

The launch stopped for a moment at one of the boat-sheds, and Dick and Dorothea looked eagerly at the yachts tied up there, wondering which of them was the *Teasel*. But they had stopped only to pick up the dinghy in which Mrs. Barrable had rowed up to the village that morning. They were off again, down a reach of the river that was almost like a street, with little old houses on one side and boats moored on the other.

"That's the doctor's house, isn't it?" Mrs. Barrable asked the boatman. "The one we're just coming to, with the thatched roof. I remember my brother pointing it out to me."

"The one with a fish for a weathercock?" asked Dick.

"He's a fisherman, Dr. Dudgeon," said the boatman, with a chuckle. "Put up that old bream himself. No much time for sailin', I s'pose, bein' a doctor, but you often see him fishin' off his garden end when the season come on. And Mr. Farland live in the house next to it, t'other side of the dyke."

Mr. Farland's house was further from the river, and Dick and Dorothea could see only the upper windows above the trees. But they saw his boat-house, and caught just a glimpse of the dyke between the two houses, a glint of water behind reeds and willows. There were more houses, some of them quite new, a windmill that had lost its sails, a ferry where a horse and cart were being ferried across, and an old inn close by the ferry with a boat or two moored beside it. Dorothea pointed to one of these, but Mrs. Barrable shook her head. That was the end of the village, and the launch put on speed once more. They passed a little church and a big house on the slope of a hill, with crowds of water-hens and black sheep feeding together by the waterside. Here, too, was a boat tied up in a dyke. But it was not that boat either.

"It can't be much further," said Dick.

"THE LAUNCH WAS SWINGING ROUND"

"Mother said it was at Horning," said Dorothea.

"Keep a good look-out," said Mrs. Barrable.

And the river went on bending and curling and twisting, and every other moment they thought they would be seeing their boat.

They came in sight of her at last and did not know her, a neat white yacht, moored against the bank, with an awning spread over cabin and well, as if she were all ready for the night.

"Oh, look, look!" cried Dorothea. But it was not at the yacht that she was looking. Working up the river was an old black ship's boat, with a stumpy little mast and a black flag at the masthead. Two small boys were rowing, each with one oar. A third, standing by the tiller, was looking through an enormous ancient telescope at something on the bank. The three small boys had bright coloured handkerchiefs round their heads and middles as turbans and belts. The launch was racing down the river to meet them, and in a moment or two, Dick and Dorothea were reading the name of the boat, *Death and Glory*, not very well painted, in big white letters, on her bows.

"You hardly expected to meet pirates on the Bure, did you?" said Mrs. Barrable.

The boatman laughed. The steersman of the *Death and Glory* waved his big telescope as the launch went by, and the boatman waved back. "Horning boys," he said over his shoulder. "Boatbuilders' sons, all three of 'em. Friends o' Port and Starboard an' young Tom Dudgeon."

But what was happening? The noise of the engine had changed. The launch was swinging round in the river towards that moored yacht. The loose flaps of the yacht's white awning stirred. A fat fawn pug clambered out on the counter and ran, barking. up and down the narrow side-deck.

"It's William!" cried Dorothea.

"Hullo, William!" said Dick.

"Here we are," said Mrs. Barrable. "Poor old William must be tired of taking care of the *Teasel* all by himself."

*

"She's ever so much bigger than she looks," said Dick.

The parcels and suit-cases had all been put aboard, the little dinghy had been tied up astern, the launch had gone, and Dick, who had been standing rather unsteadily on the counter of the yacht, had climbed down into the well to find himself in a comfortable sort of tent, full of light which poured through the white canvas of the awning.

"Here are your sandshoes," said Dorothea. "Mother said we were to wear them on board. I ought to have got them out in the launch."

Putting on sandshoes instead of their walking shoes was itself enough to make them feel that their sailing had all but begun.

"There'll be much more room when we've got rid of the parcels," said Mrs. Barrable. "All the stores go into the lockers you're sitting on. Come in now, and bring those suit-cases. No. You won't have to duck your heads if you keep in the middle. This is the main cabin, and through here is yours."

They wriggled round the table, and through the little folding door into the cabin that was to be their own. On each side was a bunk spread with thick red blankets.

"May we lie down, just to try?" said Dorothea.

"Of course."

"There's lots of room," said Dick.

"And if you joggle you can feel the boat move," said Dorothea.

"And electric light," said Dick, turning the switch on and off. "How do they manage it in such a little boat?"

"Batteries," said Mrs. Barrable. "We get them charged once a week or so, and they last out very well unless someone does too much reading in bed."

They unpacked the suit-cases and stowed most of their things in the drawers under their bunks. They looked out at a world of reeds and water that seemed somehow different when seen through a port-hole. They went back into the main cabin and tried what it felt like to be sitting on bunks at each side of a table. After that, of course, they climbed out through the flaps of the awning, and worked their way unsteadily along the narrow side-decks, leaning against the awning to feel less insecure. They took hold of the shrouds and looked up at the masthead and tried to believe that it would not take them very long to learn the names of all those ropes.

Presently Mrs. Barrable lit a Primus stove in the cooking locker in the well and put a kettle on to boil. Dick and Dorothea were watching the kettle, and Mrs. Barrable was in the cabin, putting some paint brushes to soak, when the noise of water creaming under the forefoot of a boat made them look out just in time to get a second view of the yacht race, as the five little racers sailed by. Port and Starboard and their father were now third.

"They've got time to win yet," said Mrs. Barrable.

Twenty minutes later they saw them again, on their way back up the river. The folding table had been moved into the well, tea had been poured out, and Dick had been sent into the cabin to get William's chocolate-box from the little sideboard, when Dorothea, peeping out from the stern, saw the white sails moving above the reeds. In another moment the boats themselves were in sight, and Dorothea, Mrs. Barrable and Dick hurried out on deck.

"They've done it," cried Dorothea.

"Very nearly," said Mrs. Barrable.

32

DISAPPOINTMENT

"*Flash*, their boat's called," said Dick, and *Flash* was second, and the steersman of the leading boat kept looking anxiously over his shoulder.

"Go it, go it!" cried Dorothea, and almost fancied that Port . . . or was it Starboard? . . . one or other of them, anyway . . . smiled at her as the *Flash* foamed by. All five boats were out of sight in no time round the bend of the river above where the *Teasel* was moored.

And then, just after Dick and Dorothea had settled down to enjoy their first tea afloat, suddenly and altogether unexpectedly, the blow fell.

"When are we going to start?" said Dick, asking the question that had been for some time in both their minds. "I suppose it's too late to do anything to-night."

"Start?" said Mrs. Barrable, puzzled. "Start what?"

"Sailing," said Dick.

"But, my dears, we aren't going to sail. . . . Didn't I explain to your mother? We can't sail the *Teasel* with Brother Richard away. . . . I can't sail the *Teasel* by myself. . . . And you can't, either. . . . We're only going to use her as a houseboat. . . ."

There was a moment's dreadful silence. Castles in Spain came tumbling down. It was all a mistake. They were not going to learn sailing after all.

Dorothea made a tremendous effort.

"She'll be a very splendid houseboat," she said.

"And there are lots of birds to look at," said Dick.

"My dear children," said Mrs. Barrable. "I am most dreadfully sorry."

CHAPTER III

WHAT'S THE GOOD OF PLANNING?

LATE in the afternoon Tom Dudgeon came sailing home. He was later than he had meant to be. He had spent some time at Wroxham, talking to Jim Wooddall, the skipper of *Sir Garnet*, the business wherry that was loading by Wroxham Bridge. Jim Wooddall had kept an eye on the *Titmouse* while her skipper was shopping in Norwich. Then, there had been that trouble when he was cooking his dinner. After that he had been watching a kingfisher until he had found where it was nesting, in a hole in one of the few bits of really hard bank. There had been a good many other nests to inspect, and by the time he came to the Swan at Horning, people were waiting there expecting to see the finish of the race. He had seen the little racers earlier in the afternoon and knew that Port and Starboard were sailing. They would be finishing any time now, and he had a lot to do before they came.

He sailed past the staithe and the boathouse till he came to a little old house with a roof thatched with reeds, and a golden bream swimming merrily into the wind high above one of the gables. A narrow strip of lawn ran down to the river between the willow bushes. Just below the lawn was the entrance to a dyke hardly to be noticed by anyone who did not know it was there. Tom turned in there between reeds and willows that brushed the peak of the *Titmouse's* sail. This was the *Titmouse's* home. Once inside it, she could not be seen from the river.

On the south side of the dyke was a row of willows, and

beyond them the house in which the twins, Port and Starboard, lived with their father and an old housekeeper, Mrs. McGinty, the widow of an Irishman, though born in Glasgow herself. On the north side, leaning against the doctor's house, was a low wooden shed. Here the doctor kept his fishing tackle, bait-cans and mooring poles, and the old fishing boat that lived under a low roof at the end of the dyke by the road. Here Tom did his carpentering work. Here were the doors for the lockers that were being fixed under the bow thwart and stern-sheets of the *Titmouse*, waiting for the screws and hinges Tom had brought from Norwich. Here the Coot Club held its meetings, and Tom and the twins met on most days whether engaged in Coot Club business or not. Tied up to the bank just beyond the shed was the first boat Tom had owned, a long flat-bottomed punt that had been made by Tom himself. Its name was *Dreadnought*, and unkind people said that it was well named because, whatever happened to it, it could not be worse than it was. It carried no sail, of course, but it was an old friend, and Tom still found it useful for slipping along by the reeds on a windless evening in the summer, watching grebes have swimming lessons. Tom drove it along with a single paddle, like a Canadian canoe, and he took some pride in being able to keep the *Dreadnought* moving at a good pace without making the slightest sound. The tall framework in the bushes beyond the *Dreadnought* was a drawbridge, the work of the last summer holidays. This made it possible for Port and Starboard to slip across to join Tom in the shed without taking their rowing boat from the Farland boathouse in the main river, and without having to go into the road and in at the front gate as if they were patients coming to see Doctor Dudgeon.

Tom lowered his sail, and tied up the *Titmouse*. Then he went round the house towards the river, and in at the garden door, listening carefully. Asleep, or awake? Awake. He heard a chuckle, and his mother's laugh in the room that these holidays had become the nursery once again.

"Hullo, Mother," he called, racing upstairs from the hall. "How's our baby?"

"Our baby?" laughed his mother. "Whose baby is he, I should like to know? The twins were in at lunch-time, and they seemed to think he was theirs. And your father calls him his. And you call him yours. And he's his mother's own baby all the time. Well, and how was it last night? Very cold? Very uncomfortable? You look all right. . . ."

"It just couldn't have been better," said Tom. "It wasn't cold a bit in that sleeping-bag. And it wasn't uncomfortable really except for one bone." He gave a bit of a rub to his right hip bone which still felt rather bruised. "Anyway," he said, "nobody expects floor-boards to be like spring mattresses. And there was a snipe bleating long after dark. The awning works splendidly. Any chance of seeing Dad? I'd like to tell him how well it worked. That dodge he thought of for lacing it down was just what was wanted."

"He's awfully busy. Half a dozen still waiting."

"I saw some of the victims hanging about as I came upstairs."

"You really must stop calling them that," said his mother. "And he may have to run into Norwich about some man with a stomach-ache who thinks appendicitis would sound better. Don't you go and be a doctor when you grow up."

"I'm going to be a bird watcher," said Tom. "I say, Mother, our baby's going to be a sailor. Look at him. He simply loves the smell of tar."

"Don't let him suck that dirty finger," said his mother.

"It's all right to let him smell it, isn't it?" said Tom, who was holding his hand close to the baby's face, while the baby, opening his mouth and laughing, was trying to put a tarry finger in.

TOM CAME SAILING HOME

"Don't let him get it in his mouth. Go on. You haven't told me anything yet. Where did you sleep?"

"In Wroxham Hall dyke."

"And you went to Norwich this morning?"

"I got rope and paint and hinges and blocks, and there's about half a crown left, and they gave me the screws for nothing."

"River pretty crowded coming down? Hardly yet, I suppose, though the visitors do seem to begin coming earlier every year."

"Not an awful lot," said Tom. "There was one beast of a motor-cruiser made me slosh the bacon fat all over the place when I was cooking my dinner."

"There was one yesterday," said his mother, "going up late in the evening, upset half Miss Millett's china in her little houseboat. She was talking of seeing the Bure Commissioners about it."

"Probably the same beasts coming down again," said Tom. "Most of them are pretty decent nowadays, but these beasts swooshed by with a stern wave as if they wanted to wash the banks down. I've got to get some hot water and clean those bottom-boards at once before the twins come."

"Coot Club meeting?" asked his mother. "Like a jug of tea in the shed?"

"Very much," said Tom. "That'll save boiling two lots of water. It'll take a good deal to get that grease off. Hullo! There they are! All in a bunch, too. There's *Flash*." He had caught a glimpse of the white sails of the racing boats coming up the river.

Tom's mother held the new baby up at the nursery window to see the white sails go by. She and Tom stood listening at the window after the sails had disappeared. Higher up the river they heard two sharp reports, "Bang! Bang!" almost at the same moment.

"Pretty close finish, anyhow," said Tom. "I'll dash down now, if you don't mind. They'll be along in a minute or two, and there's that water to boil, and I want to get the hinges on one of the locker doors just to show what they'll be like."

"Important meeting?" asked his mother.

"Very," said Tom. "It's to plan what we're going to do with the last two weeks of the holidays."

He took the first short flight of stairs at a jump, but remembering the victims in the doctor's waiting-room, took the next more soberly, and then, after a word in the kitchen about that promised jug of tea, hurried round by the garden to make ready for the gathering of the Coots.

*

The twins had never yet seen the *Titmouse* with her awning up, for the awning had only yesterday been given its finishing touches by old Jonas the sailmaker, and Tom had sailed away above Wroxham Bridge for the night, partly because he had laughed so often at the struggles of visitors with the awnings of the hired yachts that he did not want even the twins to be present when he was experimenting for the first time with his own. Now, of course, he was bursting to show it them. He was sure that once they saw how well it worked they would manage something of the sort for their own rowing boat. Then anything would be possible, and they could spend the last weeks of the holidays in going for a real voyage. But it was no good having the awning up with the bottom-boards still so greasy that if the twins were to sit on them there would only be trouble with Mrs. McGinty later on. And if they were to see just how good those lockers were, he must manage to fix a door on at least one of them.

He began by unloading the *Titmouse*, bringing rope and blocks and paint and screws and hinges into the shed. Then he brought in the little oil-stove that he had got from a boy at school in exchange for a pair of rabbits that were really not well fitted for voyaging in a small boat. He filled a kettle at a tap in the back kitchen, brought it round to the shed and put it on the oil-stove to boil. Then he took one of the locker doors, lying unfinished on the bench, and set to work chiselling out beds for a pair of hinges and making the holes for the screws, listening as he worked for the voices of the twins coming down the river.

Presently he heard them. Well, he had known he could not get much done before they came. One door, and that not fixed.

"Now then. Hop out, you two, and give her a push off. I'll put her to bed." That was Uncle Frank (Mr. Farland), who must for a moment have brought the *Flash* alongside the foot of the doctor's lawn.

"All right now?"

"All right."

"Push her off then. And don't be late for supper. Mrs. McGinty'll be asking what I've done with you as it is."

"Eh, mon, dinna tell me ye've droon't the puir wee bairrns." That was Port's voice, talking Ginty language.

"Tell her we won't be late. Macaroni cheese to-night. Specially for you, A.P." That was Starboard talking to her Aged Parent.

"Tell her the bairrns'll be hame in a bittock." That was Port again.

"I'll tell her to lock you both out," laughed Mr. Farland.

Tom heard the running footsteps of the twins, and, in another moment the two of them were at the door of the shed.

"Hullo, Tom!"

"Hullo! Who won?"

"We were second," said Starboard, "but it wasn't Daddy's fault. We had to go about and give them room just as we were getting level."

"What about No. 7? Hatched yet?"

"Still sitting. At least I think so. She was when we went down. Coming up we were in the thick of things just there and we'd passed her before I could see."

No. 7 was for two reasons the nest that mattered most of all those that the Coot Club had under its care. It belonged to a pair of coots, one of which was distinguished from all other coots by having a white feather on its wing in such a place that it could be seen from right across the river. Coots are common enough on the Norfolk Broads, but coots with white feathers where there ought to be none are not common at all, and ever since it had first been seen, this particular coot had been counted the club's sacred bird. Then, too, it had nested unusually early. It had begun sitting on its eggs long before any other coot on the reaches that the Coot Club (when not busy with something else) patrolled. Any day now its chicks might hatch out, and every member of the Coot Club was looking forward to seeing the sacred coot as the successful mother of a family, and to putting down the date of the hatching against nest No. 7 on the map they had made of their reaches of the river.

"The Death and Glories'll have seen all right," said Port. "They've been on patrol down there."

"They do know there's a meeting, don't they?" said Tom. "It's no good having one for plans with only half the club."

"We told them, anyhow," said Starboard. "They ought to be here by now. They were well past Ranworth when we passed them last."

"We won't wait tea for them," said Tom. "And it's pretty late already. Mother says we can have it here. You just jig round to the kitchen. . . ."

"What about the Coot Club mugs?"

"I took one in *Titmouse*," said Tom. "The others are all here."

"Pretty clean, too," said Port, looking into them as she unhooked them from a row of nails. "Considering the hurry there was in washing up last time."

"What do we want from the kitchen? Just grub?"

"Jug of tea," said Tom, who was having a hard task to get a screw in straight.

"Aren't you boiling the kettle here?"

"That's for something else."

At last he got rid of them. Port and Starboard went off to the kitchen, and were back again in a few minutes with a huge jug of hot tea (sugar and milk already mixed in it) a loaf and a pot of marmalade. They were not gone long, but the moment they were out of the shed Tom was hurrying down to the *Titmouse* with the first of the doors, and, by the time they came back with the tea, he was able to call them to the side of the dyke, to show them a closed locker, and, when he opened it, a spoon, a knife, a fork, and a plate stowed away inside.

"Fine," said Starboard.

"You just wait till they're all done," said Tom. "There'll be a partition here, to keep the stove from dirtying the awning. Then there'll be two lockers on each side here, and one on each side of the mast under the bow thwart. Can't have them under the rowing thwart, because of sleeping."

"Let's put the awning up now. . . . What's all that mess on the bottom-boards?"

"That's what I'm hotting up water for," said Tom. "We'll get it off with soap and soda." He unfastened the bottom-boards and hove them ashore. "One of those beasts of motor-cruisers joggled things up and sent the bacon fat all over the place. *Margoletta*, it was, one of Rodley's. A new lot of people in her, of course. The last lot were quite decent."

"We saw them this afternoon, too," said Port. "Real Hullabaloos. They crashed right through the middle of the race, calmly hooting to clear us all out of the way."

"Narrow bit of river, too. Lucky nobody got run down."

"Real beasts," said Tom. "Look here, it's no good putting the awning up till we've got the grease off those boards. We'll have tea first while the kettle boils."

In a few minutes the three elders of the Coot Club were busy in the shed, with the jug of tea and the loaf. Tom sat on an old empty paint-drum. The other two swung their legs, sitting on the edge of the high carpenter's bench, talking about the afternoon's racing.

"What about these plans?" said Starboard at last.

"Wait till you've been inside the *Titmouse* with her awning up," said Tom.

"Was it jolly cold last night?" asked Port.

"Just right," said Tom. "As good as any cabin."

"Oh," said Starboard. "I wish it was the summer holidays and the A.P. was taking us cruising again, like all these lucky beasts of visitors."

" Just you wait till we've cleaned those bottom-boards," said Tom, gulping down his tea in a hurry to get those boards clean, set up the awning, and let Port and Starboard see what they thought of it. Sitting in there, afloat, in a tent as good as a cabin, he was sure that they, too, would be stirred to action. After all there were two weeks of the holidays left. And you can do a lot in two weeks.

But Port and Starboard were not hurrying. The Coot Club had met to discuss plans often enough. No doubt Tom had something in his head. There had been the building of the drawbridge last summer. That had been pretty good fun while it lasted and the drawbridge was still useful. Then there had been bird protection, which was still going very strong. Piracy had been a good plan once, but it had had its day except among the younger Coots, who refused to be weaned from it. Whatever the plan was, Tom would spit it out sooner or later, and the twins, tired and hungry after their race, drank their tea and ate bread and marmalade until Tom could hardly bear it, and was glad when the kettle boiled over and made them think of something else.

There was a rush for it, and Starboard, using an old towel for a kettle-holder, picked it up and carried it outside, spluttering under its lid. All three of them set to work on those bottom-boards, and with hot water, soap, and hard scrubbing they soon had them free from grease, clean and dry enough to sit upon, if one didn't sit too long.

Tom fitted the boards in the *Titmouse*, and then, with the others watching, went carefully about the rigging of the awning. First there was the crutch, a thin bar of iron with a fork at the top of it, fitting into two rings in the transom. Then boom and sail, neatly rolled up, rested in the fork at one end and were hoisted a foot or two up the mast at the other. The folded awning was laid across the boom close by the mast and partly unrolled. The front part was neatly laced round the bows. Then, fold by fold, the awning was unrolled from the mast towards the stern, each fold being laced down at the edges to very small rings just outside the boat. The last two folds were left unlaced, to make it easy for getting in and out, and the twins were asked to step aboard.

"Jolly good," said Starboard.

They wriggled down under the middle thwart, one each side of the centre-board case that cut the boat in half down the middle. Tom rocked the *Titmouse*, just a little, to make them realise what it would be like to be asleep in her and afloat.

"Now do you see the idea?" he said. "It works with the *Titmouse*. It would work just as well with your rowing boat. The Death and Glories could manage it, too. Let's make more awnings at once and really go somewhere. . . . What about *that* for a plan?"

"Let's," said Starboard, and then stopped. Of course they couldn't. Why that very afternoon. . . . "We can't though.

Anyway not the last week of the hols. They've fixed up a private championship. The usual five boats. . . . They're going to have five races, counting points for Firsts, Seconds, and Thirds. That last week the A.P.'ll be racing *Flash* practically every day."

"Oh bother racing!" said Tom.

"And he's racing the day after to-morrow. Ordinary practice race, and again another day, I forget which," said Port. "It's a jolly good plan, but it's no good just now. We must think of a plan that we can manage without having to go off anywhere. . . ."

Tom's face fell. That plan had been glowing brighter and brighter ever since first his awning had been ordered from old Jonas. But it was no use struggling. The twins, because they had no mother, felt that they had to look after their A.P. It had always been like that, ever since they had been babies. Tom had long ago given up trying to persuade them. There it was. Nothing would stir them. If their A.P. had fixed up a lot of races for his little *Flash*, never for a single moment would they think of letting him get some other crew.

"We'll do it next hols.," said Starboard. "There'll be masses of time then. We'll only have a fortnight properly cruising. The A.P. can't get away for more. That's the worst of his being a solicitor. Think of some other plan for now. Quick, before the Death and Glories come along."

But Tom had no other plans.

"Perhaps the Death and Glories'll have something in their heads," he said.

"Not they," said Port. "We must think of something and think of it quick."

"Where are the little brutes?" said Starboard. "They ought to have been here ages ago."

They went ashore from the *Titmouse*, and back to the shed.

"There isn't going to be much tea left for the Death and

Glories if they don't buck up," said Port, looking deep into the jug as she filled the mugs again.

"It's not much good having a meeting," said Tom, "with no plans to propose."

●

"Here they are," said Port.

There was a splash of oars, a rustling of reeds, and the old black ship's boat came pushing her way into the dyke. Under their gaudy handkerchiefs the faces of her crew looked much more worried than ever pirates' faces ought to be.

"You're jolly late," said Starboard.

"Look here," said Tom, "what's the use of fixing up a Coot Club meeting if you three go off pirating and don't come back till nearly dark?"

"No, but listen," said Joe, at the tiller. "It ain't pirating."

"It's B.P.S. business," said one of the rowers, Bill. "It's No. 7. . . . Something got to be done."

"What?"

"No. 7?"

"What's happened?"

All thoughts of plans proposed or rejected were gone for the moment. No. 7 nest. The club's own coot. The coot with the white feather.

"Everything was all right when we went by," said Port.

"It's since then," said Joe. "One o' them big motor-cruisers o' Rodley's go an' moor right on top of her."

Tom ran into the shed for their plan of the river, which hung from a nail on the wall. There was no need of it, for every one of the six members of the Coot Club knew exactly where No. 7 nest was to be found.

"What did you do?" Starboard asked.

"We let Pete do the talking," said Joe. "As polite as he know how. 'If you please' and 'Do you mind' an' all that."

46

"Well?"

Pete, a small, black-haired boy, the owner of the enormous telescope, spoke up.

"I tell 'em there's a coot's nest with eggs nigh hatching," he said. "I tell 'em the old coots dussen't come back."

"We see her scuttering about t'other side of the river," said Bill, forgetting his handkerchief was a turban and taking it off and wiping his hot face with it. "She'll never go back if that cruiser ain't shifted."

"And didn't they go?" said Starboard.

"Just laugh. That's what they do," said Peter. "Say the river's free to all, and the birds can go nest somewhere else, and then a woman stick her head out o' the cabin and the rest of 'em go in."

"What beasts!" said Port.

"I try again," said Joe. "I knock on the side, and some of 'em come up, and I tell 'em 'twas a beastly shame, just when eggs is going to hatch."

"And I tell 'em there's a better place for mooring down the river," said Bill.

"They tell us to clear out," said Joe.

"And mind our own business," put in Peter.

"I tell 'em 'twas our business," said Joe. "I start telling 'em about the B.P.S."

"They just slam off down below. Makin' a noise in them cabins fit to wake the dead," said Bill.

"Let's all go down there," said Starboard.

"I'll deal with them," said Tom. "The fewer of us the better. Much easier for one." He looked at the *Titmouse* in her neat awning. "I'll take the punt."

"Can't we come, too?" said Joe.

"We could skip across and tell Ginty we're going to be late," said Port.

"What about the meeting?" said Bill.

"No," said Tom. "Meeting's closed. Plan's gone bust, anyhow. I'm going down the river at once."

Already he had untied the old *Dreadnought*, pulled her paddle free and was working her out of the dyke.

"Look here," he said. "If it's as bad as you say, I may have to do something pretty tough."

"We did try talking to 'em," said Bill.

"Well, if there's a row about it, you'd better be out of it. All Coots off the river. Go and do some weeding for someone in the village. Slip along with them, Twins, and make sure someone sees them doing it."

The *Dreadnought* slid out from the dyke into the open river. The last of the tide was running down, and Tom, with steady strokes of his paddle, sent the old home-made punt shooting down the middle of the stream to get all the help he could from the current.

The two elder Coots and the three small boys hurried to the edge of the doctor's lawn.

"I wish we could all go," said Joe, as they watched the punt vanish round the next bend of the river.

"We can't," said Starboard. "Those beasts have seen you three and talked to you, and you've just got to be somewhere else. Tom knows. He's counting on you to be properly out of the way."

"He'll deal with them all right," said Joe.

"I knew he would," said Bill.

"Pitch your tea in quick," said Port, and the pirates finished up the cold tea in the jug, and were given huge marmalade sandwiches to cram in as fast as possible. Meanwhile, there was the *Titmouse* with her new awning. They looked at her, and munched.

"Don't see why we shouldn't all rig up like that," said Joe, and Tom would have been very pleased to hear him.

"Hurry up," said Starboard.

All five of them embarked in the *Death and Glory* and pulled up-river to Horning Staithe, to make it as sure as possible that everyone should know that the three smaller Coots, at least, had had no hand in whatever Tom, away by himself down the river, should find he had to do.

CHAPTER IV

THE ONLY THING TO DO

WITH steady strokes of his paddle, a long reach forward, a pull, and then a turn of the blade at the right moment, Tom drove the old *Dreadnought* down the river. Everything was going wrong. First the twins getting tied up for the last week of the holidays and now these wretched Hullabaloos mooring on the top of No. 7. If only it had been any other nest, he told himself, it would not have been quite so bad. Horrible anyway for any bird to be cut off from her nest by a thing like that. He remembered what he had just heard of a cruiser charging through a little fleet of sailing boats instead of keeping out of the way of them as by the rule of the road she ought to do. He remembered little Miss Millett in her houseboat with the china rocked off her shelves. He remembered the smell of burnt fat and the spattering grease as that cruiser roared past the *Titmouse*. And these people had refused to move even when Pete had explained to them what they were doing. Well, move they jolly well should. Even if he had to wait till dark. Tom found it somehow easier to forget his own disappointment in the thought of the enemies of No. 7. Yet, already, he was a good deal bothered in his mind. "Don't get mixed up with foreigners." That, he knew, was the safe rule of parents and the Coot Club alike. But the thing couldn't be helped. Not if they wouldn't move when they were asked. There was only the one thing to do, and he would have to do it. Lucky that so few people seemed to be about. And then, just as he shot past the Ferry, he saw George Owdon leaning

GEORGE OWDON WAS LOOKING DOWN AT HIM

on the white-painted rail of the ferry-raft and looking down at him.

If George had been any other kind of larger boy, Tom might have asked his advice and help. But he knew better than that. George might be Norfolk, like himself, but he was in his way more dangerous even than the cruiser. George was an enemy. He had much more pocket-money than any of the Coots but was known to make more still by taking the eggs of rare birds and selling them to a man in Norwich. He would be ready to go and smash the nest on purpose if he guessed that Tom and his Bird Protection Society were particularly interested. So Tom padded steadily on.

"You're in a hurry, young Tom."

Tom, by instinct, paddled rather less fast.

"Not particularly," he said.

"What's the secret this time?" jeered George Owdon.

Tom did not answer. He was soon round the bend below the inn and out of sight from the Ferry. He could not tell what was going to happen, but he wished George Owdon had not been there.

He paddled faster again, and presently heard a strange jumble of noise from farther down the river. Faint at first, two tunes quietly quarrelling with each other, it grew louder as he came nearer until at last it seemed that the two tunes were having a fight at the top of their voices.

Suddenly he knew that all this noise was coming from one boat, a big motor-cruiser, that same *Margoletta* that had upset his cooking for him in the *Titmouse*. So that was the enemy. There it was (Tom could not think of a thing like that as "she") moored right across the mouth of the little bay in which the coot with the white feather had built her nest. A narrow drain opened out here into the river. There were reeds in the entry, and among these reeds, just sheltered from the stream, was No. 7. Members of the Coot Club had watched every stage of the building. The Death and Glories had found it almost as soon as the coots had begun to lay one bit of pale dead reed upon another. That was a long time ago now, in term-time, when Port and Starboard were away at school, and Tom could get on the river only at week-ends. Joe, Bill and Pete had each in turn played truant in order to visit it. There had been those days of great rains and Tom had feared that the rising river would have drowned the nest or even swept it away. But the coots had not let the floods disturb them. They had simply added to their nest, and, when the water had fallen again he had come down the river just as he was coming now, to find the coot with the white feather sitting on her eggs on the top of a broad, high, round platform made of woven reeds.

And now was all that to go for nothing? The bows of the big cruiser were moored to the bank above the opening. The stern was moored to the bank below it. "So that the lazy brutes can go whichever way they like on shore without having to use their dinghy," said Tom to himself. But he could hardly hear himself speak for noise. There was nobody to be seen on the deck of the *Margoletta*. All the Hullabaloos were down below in the two cabins, and in one cabin there was a wireless set and a loud speaker, and in the other they were working a gramophone.

Tom let his *Dreadnought* drift down with the stream, close by the *Margoletta*. Should he or should he not try to persuade those Hullabaloos to move? If one of them had been looking out of a porthole he might have had a try. Not that he thought for a moment that persuading would be much good with people who on a quiet spring evening could shut themselves up in their cabins with a noise like that. And anyway the Death and Glories had tried it and had told them about the coots.

The coots made up his mind for him. There they were, desperately swimming up and down under the bank opposite

the little bay that the cruiser had closed to them. Up and down
they swam, giving small sharp cries of distress quite unlike
their usual sturdy honk. They hardly seemed to know what
to do, sometimes taking short flights upstream, spattering the
water as they rose, flopping into it again, and swimming down.
And Tom knew just why they were so upset. Close behind
the cruiser and the dreadful deafening noise was the nest that
they had built against the floods, and the eggs that must be
close on hatching. Something had to be done at once. How
long had the coots been kept from their eggs already? It was
no use trying to talk to those Hullabaloos. If he did it would
only put them on their guard and make things much more
difficult.

Tom paddled quietly in to the bank below the *Margoletta*,
landed, tied the *Dreadnought* to a bunch of reeds, and then
crept along the bank until he came to the stern mooring rope
of the cruiser. He stopped and listened. Those two tunes went
on with the battle, each trying to drown the other. He heard
loud, unreal laughter. Bending low, Tom pulled up the rond-
anchor,[1] coiled its rope as carefully as if it were his own, and
laid anchor and coiled rope silently on the after-deck. A single
glance told him that the nest and the eggs were still there.
They might so easily have been smashed during the cruiser's
mooring.

So far, so good. Bent double, he hurried back along the
bank and, in a moment, was afloat in the *Dreadnought*. There
was no sign that anybody in the *Margoletta* suspected that anything was happening. He paddled upstream past the cruiser
and landed again. Creeping down along the bank he pulled
up the bow anchor, coiled its rope, and laid it on the foredeck. There was such a noise going on in both cabins that he
need not have been so careful. Then he leant lightly against

---

[1] A rond-anchor is a stockless anchor with only one fluke for mooring to
the rond or bank.

the *Margoletta's* bows. Was she going to move, or would the stream itself keep her where she was? She stirred. She was moving. The stream was pushing its way between her and the bank. In a moment Tom was back in the *Dreadnought*, pushed off and with a hard quick stroke or two set himself moving downstream, away from Horning and home and the Coot Club's private stronghold in the dyke below his father's house.

He had made up his mind about that before ever he had touched the *Margoletta's* anchors. Supposing the Hullabaloos should see him going upstream they would be sure to think of the Death and Glories who had gone that way after asking them to move. That would never do. He must lead them downstream instead. With luck he would be round the bend and away before they saw him. He would leave the *Dreadnought* somewhere down the river, and slip back to Horning by road. Lucky it was that it wasn't the *Titmouse* he had taken.

He paddled swiftly and silently downstream. The *Margoletta* was adrift and moving. He could see into the little bay. He glanced across at the troubled coots. Another few minutes and they would be back at the nest. Unless, of course, they had been kept away too long already. He passed the cruiser and settled down to hard paddling. What a row those Hullabaloos were making. They still did not know they were adrift. And then, just as he reached the turn of the river below them, he heard an angry yell, and, looking back over his shoulder, saw the *Margoletta* out in mid-stream, drifting down broadside on, and on the open deck between the two cabins a man pointing at him and shouting, and, worse, watching him through field-glasses.

The thing was done now, and the hunt was up. Tom wished he had oars with outriggers in the *Dreadnought*, to drive her along quicker than he could with his single home-made paddle. He forced her along with tremendous jerks, using all the strength in his body. He had been laughed at for making that paddle so strong, but he was glad of it now. Already he was out of sight of the *Margoletta*, but she would be round the bend in a moment as soon as they got their engine started, and in this next reach there was nowhere to hide. He must go on and on, to make them think that the boy who had cast them loose had nothing to do with Horning, but had come from some- where down the river. If only a nice bundle of weeds would wrap itself round their propellor. But it was too early in the year to have much hope of that. Yes, there it was. He heard the roar of the engine. They were after him. And then the roar stopped suddenly and there were two or three loud separate pops. Engine trouble. Good! Oh, good! He might even get right down to the dyke by Horning Hall Farm, where he had friends and could hide the old *Dreadnought* and know she would come to no harm.

On and on. He must not stop for a moment. He paddled as if for his life. Whatever happened they must not catch him. Mixed up with foreigners? Why, that would be the very worst kind of mixing. For everybody who did not understand about No. 7, he would be entirely in the wrong.

He thought of landing by the boat-house with the ship for a weather vane, startling the black sheep, and leaving the *Dreadnought* in the dyke below the church. But supposing the Hullabaloos were to see her, why, the first person they asked about her would tell them to whom she belonged. No, he must go much farther than that.

He was close to the entry to Ranworth Broad when he heard again the loud drumming of the *Margoletta's* engine away up the river. Too late to turn in there. The dyke was so straight. They would be at the entry long before he could get hidden. He paddled desperately on and twice passed small dykes in which he could have hidden the punt and then dared not stop her and turn back. Louder and louder sounded the pur-

THEY HAD SEEN HIM

suing cruiser. Would he have to abandon ship and take to the marshes on foot? And with every moment the thing he had done seemed somehow worse.

And then he rounded a bend in the river and caught sight of the *Teasel*. That yacht had been lying in that place for over a week. He had noticed her several times when sailing up and down inspecting nests for the Bird Protection Society. There was nearly always a pug-dog looking out from her well or lying in the sunshine on her foredeck. Tom had noticed the pug, but had never seen the people who were sailing the *Teasel*. At least for some time now they had not been sailing. Just living aboard, it seemed. And to-day it looked as if they had gone away and left her. The dinghy was there, but that meant nothing. There was no pug on the foredeck, and the awning was up over cabin and well. Perhaps the people were away on shore. And, at that moment, Tom had an idea. He could abandon his ship and yet not lose her. He could take to the reeds and yet not leave the *Dreadnought* to be picked up by the enemy. All those yachts were fitted out in the same way. Every one of them had a rond-anchor fore and aft for mooring to the bank. Every one of them had an anchor of another kind, a heavy weight, stowed away in the forepeak, for dropping in the mud when out in open water. . . .

Tom looked over his shoulder. The cruiser was not yet in sight, but it would be at any moment. Things could not be worse than they were whatever happened. His mind was made up. With two sweeps of the paddle he brought the *Dreadnought* round and close under the bows of the moored yacht. He was on deck in a flash with the painter in his hand. Up with the forehatch. There was the heavy weight he wanted. Tom lay down and reached for it and hoisted it on deck. He made his own painter fast to the rope by which he lowered the clumsy lump of iron into the punt. He wedged his paddle under the seat, and stamped the gunwale under, deeper, deeper, while the water poured in. The *Dreadnought*, full of water, and with that heavy weight to help her, went to the bottom of the river. Tom scrambled to his feet, jammed the hatch down on the anchor rope, and took a flying leap from the *Teasel's* foredeck into the sheltering reeds.

ROND-ANCHOR

CHAPTER V

ABOARD THE *TEASEL*

W<small>ILLIAM</small> was not aboard the *Teasel*. He had had a rather upsetting day, what with being left alone in the boat in the morning and having to make room for these newcomers in the afternoon. For some little time after tea he had lain as usual on the foredeck, catching the last of the sunshine and knowing that he made a noble sight for anybody who might be sailing up or down the river. But the short spring day was ending. People were settling down for the night. There was no one to admire him. He went back into the well and heard Dorothea say what a handsome pug he was, but those new-comers seemed unable to do their washing up without splashing. He went on into the cabin. Mrs. Barrable was writing a letter and took no notice of him. He was annoyed to find some of her paint-brushes soaking in a jam-pot half full of turpentine, left on the floor just where he could not help coming across it. If he had not been prudent in sniffing, that turpentine might have ruined his nose for a week. How careless people were. Thoroughly sulky, William went out again through the well, getting dreadfully splashed as he did so, climbed on deck, and went off along his private gang-plank to the shore to dig up and enjoy anew one or two treasure smells that he had hidden, some little distance away, on the strip of firm ground that lay behind the fringe of reeds.

*

Mrs. Barrable was making little drawings in the margin of her letter and on her blotting-pad. This was a habit of hers and, when she was writing to the mother of Dick and Dorothea, it did not matter. Writing to strangers, she often had to copy her letters out all over again, because of the illustrations that had somehow crept in. Once she had had to pretend she had lost her butcher's bill and ask him to send her another because, without thinking what she was doing, she had decorated it with a row of three cats with black mourning bows, weeping large tears at the sight of a string of sausages. But writing to her old pupil, Mrs. Callum, Mrs. Barrable could send her letters just as they were, no matter what drawings she had scribbled in the margins. To-day the margins were full of small sailing boats, because Mrs. Barrable was still seeing those little white-sailed racers, and because she was still thinking of the disappointment of Dick and Dorothea. They had been very good about it. Dick was busy making a list of birds seen, and Dorothea, on hearing how Mrs. Barrable and her brother had had to give up their plan of sailing round to the southern rivers where they had spent their childhood, had almost seemed to forget her own disappointment as she saw scene after scene in the woeful story of the returning exile wrecked almost within sight of the ancient home he had hoped to see once more before he died. . . .

"Very nice children they are, my dear," Mrs. Barrable had written, "and Dorothea is very like the little girl you used to be, but, you know, I should have been afraid to ask them here if I had known they both had such a passion for sailing. . . . They have told me now about those children they met in the north, those mumpy children" (here was a picture of a child with mumps) "who seem to have got it into their heads that sailing is . . . what it really is, my dear, as no one knows better than I. And, of course, they want to learn and I fear they will find it very dull to be cooped up in a yacht that is moored to the bank and really no better than a houseboat with only an old woman like me to keep them company." (Here she had let her pen run away with itself and there was a picture of a pair of lambs and an old woman in a poke bonnet all frisking together.) "Now, if only my brother were here instead of painting his Begums and Ranees, we should be sailing all over the place, though then, of course, there would be no room for Dick and Dot. I really had not thought how tempting it would be for them to see the other boats going by. There was one they saw to-day with two little girls. . . . Poor Dot! I ought to have remembered that windmills and reeds and slow rivers plaiting reflections and just asking to be painted may be enough for me but not for the ambitious young. But there's no one to come with us and sail the *Teasel* and tell them the names of the strings. . . . I know them myself, my dear, but she's a hired boat, and I don't know what brother Richard would say if I were to go sailing away without some expert hand to pull me out of scrapes. No, my dear, it's a pity, but Dick and Dorothea will have to be content . . ."

Mrs. Barrable drummed on her teeth with the end of her penholder and glanced through the cabin door into the canvas-roofed well, to see Dick earnestly wiping plates, and Dorothea, with a hand luckily small enough to get inside, scooping the tea-leaves out of a little tea-pot. What fun it would have been to take them round the old haunts, away down to Yarmouth and through Breydon Water and up the Waveney to Beccles, where she had been a child herself. . . . And then she looked out of the opposite port-holes, and forward through the children's cabin. There was a port-hole right forward, beside the mast, through which she could see a charming circular picture of the bend of the river upstream. Interesting, she thought, to paint just such a picture. . . . Her mind wandered from Mrs. Callum and her two guests busy in the well, and she thought of canvas and paints, and of what her brother would say to such a subject. . . . And just then, into that picture seen through the port-hole, there came a boy in an old

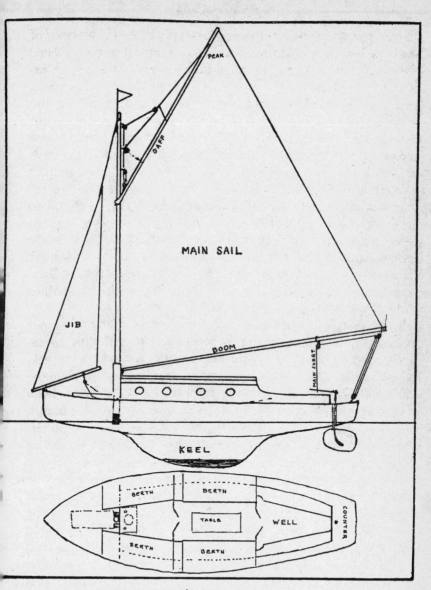

THE *TEASEL* (SAILS AND INSIDE)

tarred punt, shooting round the bend of the river and paddling as if in a race. Instantly Mrs. Barrable forgot everything else.

People in a hurry always interested her. She was always ready to take sides with anybody running to catch a train, and had been known to clap her hands when she saw someone make a really good dash for an omnibus. "Good boy," she murmured to herself, and waited to see him again when he should come paddling past the port-holes on the opposite side of the cabin.

But he never came past those port-holes at all. There was the faintest possible jar as he caught hold of the *Teasel*. There was a sudden, slight list, very slight, for Tom was not heavy, but enough to make Dick and Dorothea in the well wonder what Mrs. Barrable could be doing. Mrs. Barrable leaned forward again and, through that same round port-hole by the mast, caught a glimpse of a rubber sea-boot on the foredeck. There was the faint but unmistakable noise of the opening of the forehatch, a fumbling with ropes, the shifting of a heavy weight, quick steps on the foredeck, a bump, a slow, sucking gurgle, the slam of the forehatch closing, a thud on the bank, the crackle of dry reeds and then, a few moments later, a tremendous salvo of barking from the watch-dog, William, leisurely returning to duty.

Mrs. Barrable pushed away the folding table and hurried out of the cabin. The washers-up looked at her in astonishment. Both were down on their knees stowing things away.

"What's happened?" asked Dorothea.

"What's the matter with William?" said Dick.

"I don't quite know," said Mrs. Barrable. "A boy in a punt . . ." She worked her way out from under the awning, expecting to see that punt, or whatever it was, lying alongside the *Teasel*. But there was no punt at all. It had vanished, like the boy. And from behind the reeds there came the frenzied barking of the pug.

"William!" called Mrs. Barrable. "William! Come here!"

She went forward along the side-deck, steadying herself with a hand on the awning. There was wet on the foredeck. What could that mean? And a rope led from the forehatch over the side. Mrs. Barrable lifted the hatch and looked down into the forepeak. Why in the world, when the *Teasel* was safely moored to the bank, should anybody want to anchor her with the mudweight as well?

"William!" she called again, and William came out of the reeds, stopping on the gang-plank to do a little more barking, over his shoulder, to show people that he was afraid of nobody and that a better watchdog did not exist.

"Quiet, William!"

Dick and Dorothea looked out with wondering faces. They, too, climbed out from the well.

"Quiet, William!" said Mrs. Barrable. "He must have been running away from something. Shut up, William! Listen!"

Yes. They could all hear that something was coming down the river. There was the deep, booming roar of a motor being run at full speed. Another of those motor-cruisers. A very loud loud-speaker was asking all the world never to leave him, always to love him, tinkle, tinkle, tinkle, bang, bang, bang. And beside the loud-speaker there were other voices, loud, angry voices, not singing love songs but shouting at each other. There it was, a big motor-cruiser, coming round the bend.

William was now on the foredeck, but still looking behind him and barking at the reeds on shore. Mrs. Barrable, her eyes sparkling, her mind made up, encouraged him, but pointed towards the motor-cruiser that was roaring down towards them. William was puzzled. Quick work, if that boy in the reeds had managed already to be out there on that noisy thing coming down the river. But he supposed his mistress knew, and any-how he hated that kind of noise. So, with Mrs. Barrable whis-

pering "Cats! William, Bad Cats!" into his ears, William faced
the oncoming cruiser and put into his barking all he thought
about boys who startled honest pugs by lying hid in reeds so
that the honest pugs ran into them face to face on their own
level. There was a good deal of noise, what with William, and the
loud-speaker, and the quarrel going on among the people
aboard the cruiser, who were all shouting to make themselves
heard above the roar of their engine. Old Mrs. Barrable,
hiding her excitement, held William by the fat scruff of his
neck, as if she feared he might leap overboard in his eagerness
to tear to pieces the loud-speaker and its accompanists. Dick
and Dorothea worked their way forward from the counter along
the side-decks. What was happening? Dorothea was trying
one story after another, but none seemed to fit.

Suddenly the quarrel aboard the cruiser seemed to come to
an end. There was a furious shout from the man who was at
the wheel. Everybody was pointing straight at Dick. The big
cruiser swerved towards the *Teasel*. Her engine was put into
reverse and there was a frantic swirl of water as she lost way.

"Whaddo you mean by it?" shouted the steersman of the
cruiser.

But by now another of the Hullabaloos was pointing at
the *Teasel's* little dinghy lying astern of her.

"That's not the boy," he shouted, trying to make himself
heard. "Can't you see the boat, you ass? It wasn't like that.
Bigger boat! LONGER! And that's a white boat. The other
one was dark—a sort of punt."

"It wasn't you turned us loose?" That was the steersman
again.

"I," said Dick. "I . . ."

Mrs. Barrable spoke. "He has had nothing to do with you.
He has been with me, moored here, the whole afternoon."

"Oh. Have you seen a boy go by?"

"In a sort of long black punt."

"Nobody's gone by since the racing," said Mrs. Barrable.

"Eh?" shouted one of the Hullabaloos.

"Do turn that thing off," shouted another.

Everybody aboard the cruiser seemed to be shouting at once, and the loud-speaker was still begging all the world never to leave him, nor to deceive him, bang, bang, bang, tinkle, tinkle, tinkle.

"It must have been one of those three guttersnipes this afternoon." "Bothering us about a beastly bird's nest." "Taking up our anchors and casting us loose." "All right. All right. I'll wring the little brute's neck."

A girl in the gaudiest of beach pyjamas may have thought she was whispering to the man at the wheel of the cruiser, but she had to shout to be heard by him and what she said was just as clearly heard aboard the *Teasel*.

"No good talking to the old woman. He must have gone by."

Mrs. Barrable's eye hardened slightly.

"I shall be obliged to you if you will mind my paint," she said, as the cruiser was coming dangerously near.

"Paint!" said the girl rudely, and then, shouting into the steersman's ear, "Don't waste any more time. Let's buzz along. We'll catch him if you only get on. He can't have got very far."

The engine roared again. The water at the stern of the cruiser was churned into foam. There was a heavy bump as her stern swung in and struck the *Teasel*, and the *Margoletta* went roaring, singing and quarrelling down the reach and out of sight. William, after giving a good imitation of a hungry lion being with difficulty held back from the savaging of helpless victims, turned round towards the reedy bank and barked once more.

Mrs. Barrable also faced the reeds.

"They've gone on," she said, in a very clear voice, though quite low. "Hadn't you better come out and explain?"

There was a rustle and stir among the reeds, and Dick and Dorothea saw the boy they had met in the train come out, looking rather shy and bothered, close by the pug's gang-plank.

"Were you lurking all the time?" said Dorothea.

"You?" said Mrs. Barrable. "We've seen you once before to-day."

"Twice," said Dick. "Once in the train, and once when he was cooking in his boat."

"That was most awfully decent of you," said Tom, "sending them off like that."

"Well," said Mrs. Barrable, "it was five to one, wasn't it? But what was it all about? And what have you done with your boat? And why did you put my mud anchor overboard?"

"It was the only thing I could think of that would be heavy enough," said Tom. "You see, I had to sink her."

"Sink her?" Mrs. Barrable exclaimed. They all looked down into the brown water. "Do you mean to say your boat was here right under our feet all the time those people were talking?"

"She went down all right," said Tom, "once I got her properly under."

"But how will you get her up again?"

"She'll come when the mud-weight's lifted. And anyhow I hitched the painter to your rope. She'll come all right. But I'm very sorry. You know I didn't think there was anybody aboard. There was no pug on deck, and there usually is. And I knew I wouldn't be doing any harm to the anchor. Just for half an hour till those Hullabaloos had gone by. There wasn't time to do anything else. I could hear them already . . ."

"Hullabaloos?" said Mrs. Barrable. "What a very good name for them. But what had you done to them? And don't you think they may be coming back any minute? It wouldn't look well for them to find you here. Come inside and wait till we can be sure they are not turning round again. No, William.

No! Friend! Friend! But what had you done to them? Whatever it was, I expect they deserved it. . . ."

The noise of the *Margoletta* was now far away, but it could still be heard, and it would certainly be awkward if the Hullabaloos came back and found him where he was.

"I can stay hid in the reeds," said Tom.

"But we want to hear about it," said Mrs. Barrable, "and I don't want to have to hide in the reeds while I listen. Much better come inside."

Tom looked anxiously at the anchor rope that disappeared into the water at his feet. It was just as he had left it. The *Dreadnought* was all right down there at the bottom of the river. She could be taking no harm. He followed Mrs. Barrable down into the well.

"And now," said Mrs. Barrable, when they were all in the well and under cover, including William, who was slowly changing his mind about Tom, "do tell us what it was all about. But, of course, you needn't if you don't want to."

"It was birds," said Tom.

"Herons?" broke in Dick, who had spent a lot of time watching one on the opposite bank during the afternoon.

"Coots," said Tom. "You see, the birds are nesting now, and when people like that go and shove their boat on the top of a nest anything may happen. And this is our particular coot. She's got a white feather on one wing. We've been watching the nest from the very beginning. An early one. And the eggs are just on the very edge of hatching. And then those Hullabaloos moored clean across the opening where the nest is, and frightened the coots off. Something simply had to be done."

"I can quite understand that," said Mrs. Barrable. "But what was it you did?"

"Well, they wouldn't move when they were asked," said Tom.

"Who asked them?"

"The Bird Protection Society," said Tom.

"But how did they come to know about it?"

"They were down this way inspecting, because I was up the river and Port and Starboard had to be racing. You must have seen them, I should think. Three of them, in an old black boat."

"We saw them," cried Dorothea delightedly.

"Oh," said Mrs. Barrable. "The pirates . . . turbans, knives in their belts. . . . We all saw them."

"Well," said Tom, "you can't expect them to be Bird Protectors all the time."

"Of course not," said Mrs. Barrable.

"They asked them to go, and they wouldn't, and then, when they found it was no good being polite to Hullabaloos, they came and reported to the Coot Club, the rest of us, at Horning, I mean, and luckily my old punt was in the water. So I came down. They were making such an awful noise, they never heard me put their anchors aboard and push them off. The coots'll be back by now if they haven't been frightened into deserting altogether."

"Um," said Mrs. Barrable, "I'm glad I'm not moored on the top of somebody's nest. I shouldn't at all like to find myself drifting downstream."

"But it wouldn't ever happen to you," said Tom. "You wouldn't be beastly like they were if somebody came and explained that there were eggs just going to hatch."

"I think it was splendid," said Dorothea. "It's just what Nancy would have done. Nancy's a girl we know."

"They sounded very unpleasant people," said Mrs. Barrable.

But Tom was looking rather grim. Somehow it sounded awful, casting loose those Hullabaloos, when Mrs. Barrable said how much she would dislike finding herself adrift. Dorothea had said, "It was just what Nancy would have done."

But, whoever Nancy was, that made no difference to Tom, who knew that he had done the one forbidden thing and got mixed up with foreigners. Why, even now, sitting in this boat . . . But at that moment Mrs. Barrable made this, at least, seem better. It was almost as if she knew what he was thinking.

"You're not altogether a stranger," she said. "Aren't you a son of Dr. Dudgeon?"

"Yes," said Tom eagerly. "Do you know him?"

"In a way I do," said Mrs. Barrable, "though I've never met him. He was very kind to my brother last summer when he was here sailing by himself and cracked his head coming out of the cabin in a hurry."

Well, thought Tom, even that was better than nothing. If not a friend, at least the sister of a victim, not an absolute foreigner. All the same he was in a hurry to go. He answered a lot of questions from Dick about coots and their nests. He explained to Dorothea that it wasn't the *Titmouse* that was at the bottom of the river, but only the old punt. And then he told Mrs. Barrable that he ought to go. They listened.

"They've gone right down the river," said Mrs. Barrable, "or we'd be able to hear them whether their engine was running or not."

Tom hurried along to the *Teasel's* foredeck. Dick and Dorothea hurried after him. Already he was hauling up the *Teasel's* mud-weight. Up it came, with the painter fast to the rope above it, and after it, with a tremendous stirring of mud, the *Dreadnought* herself rose slowly through the water, like a great shark. Up she came, and lay waterlogged, now one end of her and now the other lifting an inch above the surface.

"May I use your peak halyards?" asked Tom.

"Anything you like," said Mrs. Barrable. "But keep the mud off the awning if you can."

Tom, with Dick anxiously watching, unlaced the awning by the mast, freed the peak halyards, used the painter to make them fast to the *Dreadnought's* thwarts, and delighted Dick and Dorothea by asking them to haul away, while he and Mrs. Barrable, who, after one moment's hesitation, seemed not to mind getting her hands muddy, fended off from the deck of the *Teasel.*

"Steady," said Tom. "Don't lift her out of the water. She's very old and the thwarts won't bear it."

Up came the punt, tilting over on one side. Water and mud poured out.

"Lower away," called Tom, and the *Dreadnought*, no longer a submarine, floated with a few inches of freeboard.

Dick, his mind for once on the business in hand, saw what was wanted before anybody had time to tell him, hurried aft, hauled in the *Teasel's* little dinghy, and was back in a moment with a baler.

"Good," said Tom, who was already in the punt, thick brown water sloshing to and fro as he moved. He took the baler and settled down to scooping up the water and throwing it out with a quick swinging motion.

"What would you have done without a baler?" asked Mrs. Barrable.

"Used a sea-boot," said Tom, without a moment's stop in his work. "I'd got water into one already, when I was kicking her under."

"Good boy," said Mrs. Barrable, and then, lightly, as if it was a question that did not really matter, "You are sailing most of the time, aren't you?"

"All the time," said Tom, "except when I have to be at school."

"Could you make anything of sailing a boat as big as ours?"

Tom looked up at the *Teasel's* mast.

"She isn't bigger than the one the three of us sail when Uncle Frank has his holiday. Of course I couldn't manage her all by myself."

"Three of you?"

"Port and Starboard."

Dorothea's eyes sparkled. Always those two seemed to be coming in.

"She'll do all right now," said Tom, handing back the baler and tugging at his paddle which he had firmly wedged before sinking his ship. "And thank you very much. I know I ought not to have come aboard and borrowed that mud-weight. And thank you very much indeed for not minding. Some people would have been pretty fierce about it."

"You can't sit on those wet thwarts," said Mrs. Barrable.

"I'll stand up," said Tom.

"Isn't she very crank?"

"Not if you know her," said Tom. "She's really much steadier than some." And, perhaps just a little because of the spectators watching from the *Teasel*, he stood in the stern of the old punt and drove her up the river, using his paddle as if he were a gondolier or one of the old-time marshmen who, they say, could keep their balance on a floating plank.

*

Mrs. Barrable, Dick, Dorothea and William watched him out of sight.

"That's a very good boy," said Mrs. Barrable at last.

"Wouldn't it have been awful if they'd caught him," said Dorothea.

"He deserved not to be caught," said Mrs. Barrable.

All the rest of the evening, they went on talking of Tom and the pirates, and the Hullabaloos, and the little racing boats they had seen in the afternoon. It was very late that night before Dick and Dorothea were stowed away in their bunks in the little fore-cabin, and Dick had tired of experimenting with the electric light above his head by switching it on and off, and Mrs. Barrable had taken out her letter to their mother, and was sitting at the folding table, finishing it up.

"Do you think we'll see him again?" asked Dick's voice out of the darkness forrard.

"I don't see why not?" said Mrs. Barrable.

"And Port and Starboard, too?" said Dorothea.

"They seem to hang together," said Mrs. Barrable. "Now, go to sleep, both of you." And she crossed out a couple of sentences or so in her letter and added a few more. Then, listening to the quiet lapping of the water under the bows of the dinghy astern, she began drawing pictures as usual, and before she knew what she was doing, she had drawn a little sketch of the *Teasel*, with the awning gone, and her sails set, and a much larger crew than three aboard her, a little old woman at the tiller, Dick and Dorothea at the sheets, two girls on the foredeck, a boy at the mast-head, and a row of three pirates, all with turbans and ferocious knives, sitting on the cabin roof.

CHAPTER VI

PUT YOURSELF IN HIS PLACE

Tom paddled the *Dreadnought* up the river. Considering that she was a flat-bottomed, home-made punt, she really was fairly steady, but, on the whole, he thought it safer not to turn round and wave good-bye. She was very wet and rather slimy after being at the bottom of the river, and Tom was content to be able to keep his balance and to keep her going at the same time. He was still feeling the narrowness of his escape from the Hullabaloos. Things had certainly turned out much better than had seemed likely. How lucky that the *Teasel* had been moored there. How lucky, too, that the little old lady had taken his boarding of her yacht in the way she had. Why, she had played up against those Hullabaloos almost as if she had had a share herself in clearing them away from the coot's nest. Of course, the old lady and those two children were foreigners, too, in a way, but not like the Hullabaloos. And her brother had had his head mended by Tom's father. Anyway, it was very lucky that not even the pug had been on deck. There would not have been time for explanation. If he had not thought the yacht was empty he would never have dared to go aboard, but would have kept on down the river and, as sure as eggs were eggs, would have been caught at the next bend.

The sun had gone down. The tide was on the point of turning, and up-river a calm green-and-golden glow filled the sky and was reflected on the scarcely moving water. A heron came flying downstream with long slow flaps of his great

wings. Only twenty yards away he lifted easily over the tall
reeds and settled with a noisy disturbance of twigs on the top
of a tree in a little wood at the edge of the marshes. The heron
had a little difficulty in balancing himself on the thin, swaying
branch, and Tom, watching him, dark against the glowing
sky, very nearly forgot that he, too, had an uncertain perch.
Balancing like this was tiring, too, and, anyhow, Tom did not
want to be standing up when he came to No. 7. Putting down
his paddle and letting the *Dreadnought* drift, he slipped out of
his jacket, folded it on the wet thwart, sat down on it and
paddled away in good earnest. For a moment he pretended to
himself that he could hear the Hullabaloos far away coming
up the river, but he knew they were not, and no amount of
pretence could make him send the old *Dreadnought* flying
along as he had when it really was a question whether or no
he would get away.

He slowed down as he came near No. 7. One great ad-
vantage of paddling a punt is that you face the way you are
going. Tom, as he paddled, was searching the side of the
river opposite the little opening that the coots had chosen.
He was looking for round black shadows stirring on that
golden water under the reeds. He saw only the broad bulging
ripple of a water-rat. No. At least the coots were no longer
scuttering up and down in terror as he had seen them last.
Quietly he edged the old punt over towards the other bank so
as to be able to look into the opening as he passed it. There
was an eddy here or nearly dead water, and Tom never lifted
his paddle high enough to drip. He slid by as silently as a
ghost. He knew exactly where to look into the shadows.
There was the clump of reeds, and there at the base of them,
among them, the raised platform of the nest. Was it deserted?
Or not? Tom peered through the twilight. No. It was as if
the centre of the nest was capped with a black dome, and on
the dome he had just seen the white splash of a coot's forehead.

And what was that other shadow working along close under the bank? It was enough. Tom did not want to frighten them again. He paddled quietly on. One thing was all right, anyhow. The coots of No. 7 were at home once more.

It was growing dark now. Nobody but Tom was moving on the river, and the only noise was the loud singing of the birds on both banks and over the marshes, whistling blackbirds, throaty thrushes, starlings copying first one and then the other, a snipe drumming overhead. Everything was all right with everybody. And then a pale barn owl swayed across the river like a great moth, and with her, furiously chattering, a little crowd of small birds, for whom the owl was nothing but an enemy. And suddenly into Tom's head came a picture of the *Margoletta* as a hostile owl, mobbed by a lot of small birds, the Death and Glories and himself.

Was that what had really been happening? It looked very like it if you chose to think of it that way. The Hullabaloos, horrid as they were, had only asked to be left alone. What would his father think of it? There were so few rules for the fortunate children of the river-side. They could do what they liked, more or less, so long as they managed to keep out of any trouble with the foreigners. That was the one thing that really mattered. A quarrel with George Owdon, for example, would not matter at all. Everybody knew who George was, and everybody knew what he was. Grown-up people would say something about "Boys will be boys," and think no more about it. But a quarrel with foreigners, with visitors to the Broads, was altogether different. "Don't get mixed up with foreigners" was the beginning and the end of the law. "Help them to set their sails if they ask for help. If they don't know they need help, leave them alone. Show them the way when they ask it. Tow them off when they get themselves aground. Answer their questions no matter how stupid they seem. But do not get mixed up with them."

And Tom, remembering what he had seen and heard while he was lurking in the reeds beside the *Teasel*, knew that the Hullabaloos of the *Margoletta* were very angry indeed. To say that he had got mixed up with them was to put it much too mildly. He had made enemies of them. They had not sounded at all as if they were the kind of people who would forget what had happened or forgive it. And what if they found out who he was and went and made a row about it? The doctor's son casting loose a moored boat full of perfect strangers. . . . His cheeks went hot at the thought. But at least no one who knew him had seen him . . . and then, suddenly, Tom remembered George Owdon lounging on the ferry raft when he had been paddling the *Dreadnought* on his way to the rescue of No. 7. Would George tell? Hardly. George was a beast, but, after all, he was a Norfolk coot, like the rest of them, though, of course, not a member of the Coot Club, which was an affair of Tom and the twins. No, not even George Owdon would do a thing like that.

But, as he paddled on and on up the river, Tom grew more and more bothered about what had happened. It was not a question of being found out. Why, even Mrs. Barrable, the old lady of the *Teasel* who had joined in so splendidly on his side, was a visitor. And those two children he had met in the train and had now met again. . . . Mixed up with foreigners? He seemed to be head over ears in them. And it had all come about so quickly. What ought he to have done? Let No. 7 be ruined at the last moment, after all that watching and the careful way in which the coots had fought the floods by building up their nest? Again he saw those anxious scutterings at the far side of the river. He could not have allowed them to be kept off their eggs until it was too late. What else could he have done? Tom wanted advice, and when he had passed the Ferry, and was coming up towards Horning village, he was very glad to see the glow of a cigarette at the edge of the lawn, and to find his father, resting from victims at last, watching or rather listening to the big bream that come up in the evening and turn over on the top of the water to stir the heart of any fisherman who sees or hears them.

"Hullo, old chap," said his father. "Where have you been? And what have you done with the twins? I thought you had one of your meetings on. Be quiet while you're coming ashore. Your mother says we're to be careful not to wake the monster."

Tom switched his paddle across and held it and turned the old *Dreadnought* neatly into the dyke. Usually he protested when his father spoke of the new baby as "the monster." To-night he hardly noticed it.

Dr. Dudgeon strolled round through the bushes and was there in the dusk beside the dyke, ready to help Tom to moor the punt.

"I thought you'd have given up the old *Dreadnought* altogether," he said, "after last night's sleeping in the *Titmouse*."

"I had something special to do," said Tom, "and, anyhow, there wasn't any wind. . . . I say, dad. . . ."

"All right at your end?"

"Right."

"Your mother says we must keep quiet another five minutes and then creep in to supper."

"Look here, dad, what would you do if the only way to get to our baby was up this dyke, and mother and you and me were all on the other side of the river, and a huge motor-cruiser was fixed right across the opening of the dyke so that none of us could get in, and our baby was all alone, and we knew that if we didn't get to him soon he'd go and die?"

"Do?" said the doctor. "Why, we'd scupper that cruiser. We'd blow it sky high. We'd . . . But what's it all about, old chap? Don't you go trapping me into prescribing before diagnosis. Let's have the symptoms first. Tell me all about it. . . ."

And Tom, walking up and down with his father in the darkening garden, and already feeling a good deal better, poured out the whole story.

*

An hour or so later, when they had had their supper, and Tom and his father had been allowed to go in on tiptoe and see their baby asleep with a purple fist in its mouth, Tom was back in the *Titmouse*, making ready for the night. The awning of the *Titmouse* glowed like a paper lantern, with wild shadows moving on it as Tom pushed things into their places and wriggled himself down into his sleeping-bag.

He heard his father's voice on the bank.

"Tom."

"Yes."

"Thinking it all over, you know, in terms of the monster, and talking it over with your mother, considering her as a coot, I've come to a conclusion. It's a pity it's happened, of course, and I'll be very much obliged to you if you can manage not to let those rowdies catch you, but, looking at the case as a whole, your mother on one side of the cruiser and our baby on the other, I don't really see what else you could have done."

"I won't let them catch me," said Tom.

"I'd much rather they didn't," said his father. "Good night, old chap."

"Good night, dad," said Tom, and blew out his candle lantern.

"Half a minute, Tom, here's your mother coming out."

Mrs. Dudgeon rubbed with her finger on the taut cloth of the awning.

"Still worrying about it, Tom? I don't think you need. You'll have all coots and all mothers on your side. Now, go to sleep. We'll leave the garden door on the latch, so that you can come in early if you want to. Good night."

"Good night," said Tom.

He heard their steps going off along the bank, but before they were round the corner of the house he was asleep. Last night had been his first night in the *Titmouse*. He had had a tremendous day. And now, for the moment at least, his worry about the foreigners was lifted from him. There was nothing now to keep him awake, and he fell into dreamless sleep as suddenly as if he had dropped through a trap-door into a warm, comfortable darkness.

CHAPTER VII

INVITATION

DIFFERENT people in different places woke next morning thinking of what had happened on the river the day before.

Dick and Dorothea, sleeping their first night in the *Teasel*, were waked by a farm-boy who came alongside with a can of fresh milk. Mrs. Barrable was up already, and they heard her tell the boy that she was not quite sure if they would want milk to-morrow, but that they would let him know at the farm if they were still there.

"But I thought she said the *Teasel* wasn't going to move," whispered Dick.

"I know," said Dorothea.

And then, after breakfast, Mrs. Barrable had taken the dinghy and rowed away upstream with William.

"Can we come, too?" Dick asked, eager to have another try with oars.

"Not this time," said Mrs. Barrable. "You and Dot can tidy the boat up, and you'll find lots of birds to look at in the marsh and among those sallows. Put your sea-boots on if you go ashore. I'll be back as soon as I can."

*

Port and Starboard, for once, surprised Mrs. McGinty by being awake when she called them, and downstairs at least a minute and a half before she rang the breakfast gong. The night before they had kept watch until it was time to go in to

82

share their father's evening meal. After that it had been already dark. Port had done some reading aloud while Starboard knitted a row or two on a jersey she had begun the holidays before last, and Mr. Farland had spread a newspaper on the table, taken some patent blocks to pieces and given them a thorough oiling. Every minute the twins had expected to hear a soft tap on the window. . . . Tom, bringing news of No. 7. But there had been none. They woke, wondering what had happened, and, this morning, were almost ready to hurry their father out of the house. It was their daily business to see that he went off with tidy hat and gloves to spend the day as a solicitor. And to-day, of all days, he seemed dreadfully inclined to dally.

"Here you are, A.P.," said Starboard, handing into the car the despatch-case full of legal papers which her father had brought from Norwich yesterday and, as usual, was taking back unopened to the office.

"Half the holidays gone," said he, sitting in the car, gently pressing the pedal with his foot and warming up the engine before starting.

"Two weeks more," said Starboard.

"Two more practice races," he said, "and then, if we get *Flash* tuned up to her best, we'll just show them."

Port used the brown gloves to give a last rub round to the hard hat, and put them in at the window. Mr. Farland set the hat on his head, took it off again to his daughters, tooted the horn and was gone.

"Come on," said Starboard. "We'll know in a minute. Let's go by the drawbridge."

But Mrs. McGinty was standing in the doorway. "Will you bairns be away to the village?" she asked. Precious minutes were wasted while she told them the things that were wanted at the village shop. Starboard scribbled them down on a bit of paper.

"I'm wanting the caulifloors for your denner," said Mrs. McGinty.

"All right, Ginty," said Starboard. And the two of them bolted across the garden and vanished into the osier bushes.

*

Tom, sleeping in the *Titmouse*, was waked very early by hearing a boat brushing through the reeds at the mouth of the dyke. He bobbed up at once to listen and hit his head against a thwart. Was it the enemy coming to look for him? But, of course, it was only the Death and Glories coming to ask what in the end Tom had done about No. 7. He told them and saw that, as boatbuilders' sons, they were a good deal shocked.

"Cast 'em adrift?" said Joe. "Did you oughter 'a done that?"

"Couldn't do anything else," said Tom.

"But how didn't they cotch ye?"

Tom told, briefly, how he had had to make a submarine of the *Dreadnought*. Of that they thoroughly approved.

"Gee whizz!" said Joe.

"That were a real good 'un," said Bill.

"Prime," said Pete.

They wanted there and then to go down the river to have another look at No. 7, but Tom thought better not, and they decided to look at a few upstream nests instead.

"And look here," said Tom, as the *Death and Glory* went off out of the dyke. "Try to find out, if you can, how long those people are going to have the *Margoletta*. I'll have to keep out of the way till they've gone."

He went into the house for breakfast. What was the good of cooking in the *Titmouse* if he could not safely take her down the river? He went to look at the baby. It seemed a hundred years since yesterday when he had come back from Norwich with his hands smelling of tarred rope, planning all kinds of

INVITATION

cruises. His father seemed to think the affair with the Hullabaloos was over. "They'll have forgotten about it themselves
this morning," he said, "unless their livers are badly out of
order." But Tom thought otherwise. His father had not
heard the anger in their voices when they were talking to the
old lady of the *Teasel*. The only real hope was that those people
would presently be giving up the *Margoletta*. A week was
the usual time for which people hired a boat. He would have
to keep out of sight until they were gone. It was hard to lose
even a few days now that he could sleep aboard the *Titmouse*,
but, at least, he could be finishing up those lockers. And as
soon as breakfast was over Tom went back to his ship, and was
hard at work in her when he heard two short blasts on a
whistle and two longer ones, from among the bushes on the
farther side of the dyke.

The twins. They, too, would have to be told how desperately, in the saving of No. 7, he had got mixed up with
foreigners. He scrambled ashore, took an old iron winding
handle from its place just inside the shed, and went along the
dyke to the drawbridge. The handle belonged to a windlass
he had got last summer from a wherry that was being broken
up. The windlass was the most important part of the drawbridge. Tom fitted the handle in place, pulled out a bar that
locked the bridge in its framework, and then slowly unwinding,
lowered the plank with its two handrails, until the end of the
plank rested on the other side of the dyke. The plank was
strong enough to bear even Dr. Dudgeon or Mr. Farland,
both of whom had been known to use it instead of going round
by road.

"Hullo!" said Tom gravely.

"What's the matter?" said Port.

"Couldn't you get them to move?" said Starboard. "Is
No. 7 done after all?"

"Is that why you didn't come and tell us last night?"

85

"No. 7's all right," said Tom. "At least, it was when I came home. And it was pretty dark before I got back. But things went wrong a bit. I've gone and got most awfully mixed up with foreigners. It was the *Margoletta* on the top of No. 7, and I sent her adrift. . . ."

"Good," said Starboard.

"I couldn't think of anything else to do," said Tom. "And the worst of it is they saw me. One chap had field-glasses. And then although I went down river, they thought I was one of the Death and Glories. So I've got the whole Coot Club in a mess."

"The Death and Glories'll be all right," said Starboard.

"Anyway, it isn't your fault," said Port. "One of us would have had to do it."

"But how did you get away?" said Starboard.

"I got mixed up with another lot," said Tom. " I forgot to tell you about a couple of kids I met in the train. Well, they're in the *Teasel*, you know, where that pug's usually hanging about, and there's an old lady in the *Teasel* with them. . . ." And then he told of how he had boarded the *Teasel* and used her mud-weight, and sunk the *Dreadnought*, and hid in the rushes, and how, somehow, after the Hullabaloos had been sent off down the river, he had gone back aboard the *Teasel* by invitation, and had forgotten about these people being foreigners too, and had even told them all about No. 7, and let out something about the Coot Club itself. "You know, she really had been most awfully sporting," said Tom, trying to explain as much to himself as to the twins how it was that he had come to forget the first duty of a Norfolk Coot. "Her brother was a victim," he added, " but I didn't know that until afterwards. . . ."

And at that moment he gave a sudden start and listened. There was the sharp, impatient bark of a small dog, close behind the house. It sounded almost as if it came from the river. Tom had too lately lain in the reeds face to face with William not to know that voice again.

Without another word he crept round the side of the house and peered out through the willows. The others followed him on tiptoe. Yes. Tied to one of the small white mooring posts at the edge of the lawn was a dinghy, and in it, alone, a pug.

"She must be here," whispered Tom, and they slipped quietly back to the shed.

"Come to complain?" said Starboard.

"She was awfully decent yesterday," said Tom.

And then there was a noise of feet on the gravel walk at the river side of the house, and voices talking, and again an impatient bark.

"No, William! You stay where you are. It would make all the difference to those two . . ."

"I don't see why they shouldn't. Tom would love to, and I do believe all three of them are as good in a boat as anybody on the river."

And then Mrs. Barrable and Mrs. Dudgeon came round the corner of the house together.

"Well, Tom," said his mother, "you seem to have made some friends last night as well as some enemies. Mrs. Barrable has a plan to suggest."

"How do you do?" said Tom, dusting the sawdust off before shaking hands.

"And these," said Mrs. Dudgeon, "are Nell and Bess."

"Port and Starboard," said Mrs. Barrable. "We saw you racing yesterday and we all hoped you would win."

"It wasn't daddy's fault we didn't," said Starboard. "If the river'd been a wee bit wider nothing could have saved them."

At that moment there was a determined and rather indignant yelp from "our baby" somewhere upstairs in the house.

"Is he all right?" said Tom.

"Perhaps you'd like to talk it over with them," said Mrs. Dudgeon.

"You run away, my dear," said Mrs. Barrable, just as if
Mrs. Dudgeon was herself only a little girl.

Tom's mother laughed. She did not seem to mind. She
shook hands with Mrs. Barrable and was gone.

"And is that the *Titmouse?*" asked Mrs. Barrable, looking
along the dyke. "You do keep her smart."

"She wants another coat of paint, really," said Tom. "I've
got the paint, but I don't want to put it on till the end of the
hols. You see it won't matter her being wet when I have to
go to school."

"Does she sleep two?"

"There's room for two," said Tom. "One each side of the
centre-board. But I've only had her fitted for sleeping these
last two nights. She isn't really finished yet." He turned back
the awning to let Mrs. Barrable see inside. "Those lockers are
all going to have doors."

And then suddenly Mrs. Barrable turned to the business
that had brought her to the doctor's house. She told them
how her brother had been coming to the Broads for some
years and how this year he had chartered the *Teasel,* meaning
to take his sister for a cruise right through Yarmouth and up
to Beccles, where they had been children together, and round
to Oulton and up the Norwich river.[1] She told them how,
after a week on the Bure and at Hickling, he had suddenly
had to go off, and how she had invited Dick and Dorothea to
come and keep her company in the *Teasel.* "But what I didn't
know," she said, "was that the two of them had set their hearts
on learning to sail ever since they made friends with some
nautical children in the winter holidays. And, of course, they're
dreadfully disappointed. . . . No, no. They don't say so. If
they did I shouldn't feel so bad about it. I'm rather disappointed, too. I'd been looking forward to seeing Breydon
again, and sailing in to Waveney and the Yare. . . . Now,

[1] The River Yare.

how would the three of you care to come and sail the *Teasel* for us? I know Tom knows how to sink a boat."

"Sail her?" said Tom.

"Take her down to the southern rivers and back," said Mrs. Barrable. "Just to let those two children feel they'd seen something of the Broads. And you'd have to teach them a little first, so that they wouldn't feel they were only passengers."

Tom looked down at the *Titmouse*, at the new awning, and the lockers. Black treachery it would be, to leave her for the *Teasel*.

"I've thought it all out," said Mrs. Barrable. "You'd have to bring the *Titmouse* or we shouldn't have enough sleeping room at night. If you could do with Dick in the *Titmouse*, we four will have the *Teasel* to ourselves . . . two cabins, one for the twins, and Dorothea will share the other with me. Two or three days' practice first in the easy waters up here, I thought, and then away for a cruise so as to be back in time to send them home before the end of the holidays."

"The *Teasel's* a splendid boat," said Tom.

For one moment the twins' eyes lit like his at the thought of such a voyage in charge, in actual command, of such a vessel. Then they remembered.

"We'd simply love to," said Starboard, "but we can't . . . really can't. You see there's a race to-morrow, and then another one, and father's entered *Flash* for five races the last week of the holidays, and he's arranging to get back early each day on purpose."

"You try to persuade them, Tom," said Mrs. Barrable.

But Tom knew the twins too well. "It's no use," he said. "They won't be able to come. . . . And I can't either, after last night. At least not so long as those people are about."

But Mrs. Barrable was not to be refused. She had seen the light in Tom's eye and in the eyes of the twins. She knew that all three of them wanted to come.

"They won't know you except in your punt," she said. "And we can always hide you, besides, they'll have forgotten about it by now. . . . Anyhow, come along the three of you this afternoon and see what sort of a crew you think you could make of my visitors. I'll expect you soon after lunch."

"Dick's pretty keen on birds," said Tom. "And he doesn't collect eggs. And I could hop ashore if we heard those people coming."

It was a queer way of accepting an invitation for the afternoon, but what it meant was clear enough.

"We'd love it," said the twins, and then Mrs. Barrable said that she had a few more things to do, was welcomed into her dinghy by a barking William, and rowed away towards the village.

The three Coots stood at the edge of the lawn and watched her rowing up the river, a wrinkled old lady in a little brown dinghy.

"I don't count that getting mixed up with foreigners," said Port.

"She jolly well knows how to row," said Starboard.

"Born in Beccles," said Port.

"Norfolk Coot really," said Starboard. "But, of course, those two children don't sound like Coots at all."

"It's not their fault," said Tom. "Poor little beasts. They've never had a chance of a boat."

"No harm in going to look at them, anyway."

Mrs. Barrable, rowing steadily, with William sitting up in the stern of the dinghy, was almost out of sight beyond the boat-building yards when, suddenly, all three Coots turned and listened.

"The *Margoletta*," whispered Tom.

In a moment there was no one to be seen on the green lawn in front of the doctor's house. The three Coots, crouching among the willows, were looking out through the tall reeds.

INVITATION

A big motor-cruiser had turned the corner above the Ferry and was thundering up the river with a huge gramophone open and playing on the roof of the fore-cabin. Two gaudily dressed women were lying beside it, and three men were standing in the well between the cabins. All three were wearing yachting-caps. One was steering and the other two were using binoculars and seemed to be searching the banks as the cruiser came upstream at a tremendous pace.

"They're looking for the *Dreadnought*," whispered Tom.

The big cruiser roared past them, and from their hiding-place they saw the wash of her swirling along the farther bank and bringing lumps of earth splashing down into the river.

"Beasts, simply beasts, that's what they are," said Tom.

"They'll have Mrs. Barrable over if they don't slow up," said Port.

"They'll probably run right into the Death and Glories up there," said Tom. "Look here, I'd better go along in case."

"You've got to stay hid," said Starboard. "It'll make things ten times worse if they see you."

"You can't do any good," said Port. "Wait and see what happens."

"Yes, but what's happening now?" said Tom. "Their engine's stopped."

"Come on, Twin," said Starboard. "They've never seen us. We'll go and find out. Where's that list of Ginty's? She wants some washing soda and some lump sugar. . . ."

"And a pair o' braw wee caulifloors," said Port. "Come on. Nobody can kill us for going to the grocer's shop."

The two of them raced off round the house and out by the garden gate into the road that led to Horning village and the public staithe.

CHAPTER VIII

THE INNOCENTS

Mrs. Barrable had seen the big cruiser coming and had
made ready for it, but she was nearly swamped when it swept
by her, the people in it turning round to laugh at the sight of
the little dinghy tossing like a cork in the swirling water. She
comforted William, who had not liked being thrown about,
and rowed on to the staithe. The *Margoletta* was already tied
up there when Mrs. Barrable, looking over her shoulder, saw
the *Death and Glory*, the old black ship's boat with its crew of
three small boys, coming round the bend by the Swan Inn.
There was no chance of warning them. She saw the two rowers
turn to look at the *Margoletta*. She saw them hesitate, and then,
as if they had nothing whatever to fear, row calmly on and moor
at the staithe a little above the cruiser. The three men from
the cruiser leapt ashore, and before the small Coots had time to
change their minds and bolt for it, were already within reach.

"That's the one. The biggest of them. We'll teach you to
come casting off other people's ropes and anchors," said a big,
red-haired man, suddenly shooting out an arm and catching
Joe by the collar of his coat.

"That's him."

Mrs. Barrable tied up her dinghy and walked quietly
towards them. But Joe seemed well able to look after himself.
He flung his arms suddenly upward and, with a single wriggle,
left his coat in the hands of the enemy.

"Catch him, one of you," shouted the red-haired man.
"Don't let him go. Grab him, James!"

THE INNOCENTS

"Catch him yourself, Ronald!" said one of the others.

"Look out for my coat," urged Joe, skipping backwards a few yards out of reach. "It's got my rat in it."

The red-haired man dropped the coat and reached again at Joe, who dodged.

"Rat!" shrieked a woman in orange pyjamas who had come ashore to see what was to be done to Joe.

There was a sudden interruption.

"What's all this?" a deep voice asked, pausing between the words. Mr. Tedder, the policeman, had been digging in his little garden by the staithe, and hearing the noise had thrust his spade into the ground and hurried out, putting his coat on as he came.

"It's this boy," said the red-haired man, setting his yachting-cap at a jauntier angle to impress Mr. Tedder, who had seen too many yachting-caps to be impressed. "The biggest of these three. He came along yesterday evening when we were all in our cabins, and unfastened our anchors and set us adrift. Wanton mischief, nothing else."

"Set you adrift?" said Mr. Tedder judicially. "That won't do."

"But I didn't," said Joe. "I couldn't. Why, last night . . ."

Mr. Tedder looked at him. "Why so you was," he said at last. He turned. "And what time do you say the offence took place?"

"Ten past five," said the woman eagerly. "I know it was, because I was boiling eggs, and looked at the clock just when Ronald shouted that we were floating down the river. . . ."

"Ten past five," said Mr. Tedder slowly. "Why from five o'clock all these boys was doin' a bit o' weedin' in my patch, an' gettin' worrams for to make a bab . . . for liftin' eels. . . . Couldn't 'a been this boy cast you adrift. Why, 'twas all but dark when they go home with their worrams. . . ."

"But I tell you we'd had them round earlier with some tale about a blasted bird."

"They was in my patch at ten past five," said Mr. Tedder doggedly.

"It must have been some other boy," said the thin man the other had called " James."

"Not these," said Mr. Tedder. "You skip along, you three. No need to hang about the staithe."

"And my coat?" said Joe.

He came warily forward and picked it up, put it carefully on and then pulled out of an inner pocket a large white rat, which sat on his arm, sniffed the air contemptuously, and looked about it with its round pink eyes.

"Take that thing away," screamed the woman.

"Now then, 'Livy. You don't mind that. Not wearing skirts. . . ." The fat man of the three stopped suddenly as the woman in orange trousers gave him a resounding slap in the face.

"And you, Ronald," she said angrily to the man with red hair. "Come along. You've made us look fools enough already. Last night *and* this morning. That boy down the river was bigger than this one. Anyway, you'll never catch him, letting him go like you did last night."

"Never catch him?" shouted the man they called Ronald. "Never catch him?"

"How are you going to know him when you see him?" said the thin man.

"Bet you five to one I do. I'll know him soon enough."

"Bet you don't. Take you in pounds you don't."

"Done! I'll know him. He's got a criminal face that boy has. What I call sinister. I'll know him when I see him. Casting loose our ropes. What are the police for, anyway? . . . Constable!"

Mr. Tedder pulled out a note-book.

ON HORNING STAITHE

"If you want to make complaint . . ." he was beginning, when a quiet voice close beside him said, "Officer!"

"Ma'am," said Mr. Tedder, straightening his back and turning sharply on his heel, to see a little old lady with a pug. Mrs. Barrable had thought it time to intervene.

"Am I mistaken?" she asked, "or is there a speed limit of five miles an hour through Horning village? I think I have seen the notices."

"No boats to go above five miles per hour," said Mr. Tedder, "not between the board t'other side of the Ferry and t'other board at top of Horning Reach."

"This motor-cruiser," said Mrs. Barrable, "seems to make a practice of disregarding the speed limit as well as the convenience and safety of other users of the river. I have noticed it before, and to-day I think I have been fortunate not to have been swamped by it. Do I lay an information with you, or must I see the Bure Commissioners . . .?"

Mr. Tedder turned again, but he and the old lady and the pug were alone. The people from the cruiser, with their yachting-caps, their berets and their bright pyjamas were hurrying angrily back to their vessel. The three small boys were standing open-mouthed in the *Death and Glory*, wondering at the sudden collapse of the enemy.

"I wouldn't do nothin' about it, ma'am," said Mr. Tedder slowly. "They hear what you say."

"Thank you, officer," said Mrs. Barrable, "I think you're perfectly right. No, William!"

William had felt the quarrel in the air, and, as the *Margoletta's* engine started up and she swung away from the staithe and upstream, he had allowed himself a single bark.

"Least said, soonest mended," said Mr. Tedder, though not thinking of William. "Takes all sorts to make a world, but fare to me as we could do without some of 'em. There's been trouble up at Wroxham with that lot, making such a noise by the bridge nobody in the hotels could get their sleep. But where's the use? Here to-day they are and gone to-morrow. Casting off their moorings? Now who's going to do a thing like that? More likely they forget to make 'em fast."

Mrs. Barrable thought it time to speak of other things. She asked Mr. Tedder what sort of a spring it had been for gardening, and what seeds he had in, and what were the best of the new peas. Constable Tedder told her that, between themselves, she couldn't do better than Melksham Wonder if she wanted peas that would eat well and pod well and not go rambling wild. They walked slowly off the staithe together.

And then they parted. Two people whom Mrs. Barrable thought she knew by sight had just slipped into the grocer's shop after anxiously watching from a distance what had been happening on the staithe. So she looked in there, and found Port and Starboard, still rather out of breath, doing Mrs. McGinty's shopping.

"So we meet again," she said pleasantly. "Thank you. A pound of peppermint toffees, please. For a stand-by. You never know when they may be wanted badly. Oh no, thank you. I'll take them with me. And half a pound of plain chocolate for William. I'll take that, too, and then I'll leave you this list and call for the things on my way back from the Post Office. I have to look in there for letters."

"Does William eat chocolate?" asked Port.

"Doesn't he?" said Mrs. Barrable.

They drifted out of the shop together, and then, at once, the twins, who had been holding themselves in with great difficulty, asked her what had happened.

"We didn't see the beginning," said Port, "but we saw Joe picking up his coat, and then, suddenly, off they went."

"What was it you said to make them go off like that?"

"My dears," said Mrs. Barrable, "I just said whatever came into my head."

"Whatever it was, it worked."

"And was it all right about the Death and Glories?"

"You go and ask them," said Mrs. Barrable.

"You don't think they'll be getting into a row? Tom was in an awful stew about it."

"Tell him their alibis were cast iron."

"Glad I made them weed for the policeman," said Starboard. "I wasn't really sure last night whether it was a good idea or not."

"It was brilliant," said Mrs. Barrable.

"Will those Hullabaloos leave Tom alone about it now?" asked Port.

"If they had any sense at all they would," said Mrs. Barrable, "but they haven't any to start with, and when men begin making bets with each other, there's no end to their foolishness. No, I'm a little afraid this morning has made things rather worse."

Talking it over in the *Death and Glory*, the three small Coots were of much the same opinion.

"Sorry they spoke, they was," said Bill. "Patchin' it on us. We hadn't done nothin', had we? And Mr. Tedder know we hadn't."

"It was worth a week o' weedin'," said the usually silent Pete.

"They didn't like old Ratty, neither," said Bill.

"They've got it in proper for Tom Dudgeon," said Joe.

CHAPTER IX

THE MAKING OF AN OUTLAW

THAT afternoon there was not wind enough to stir the flame of a candle when Tom and the twins rowed down the river in the *Titmouse*. "We'd better all go in one boat," Tom had said, "and then I can hop into the reeds if we hear the *Margoletta*, and you can hang about and pick me up again when they've gone by." That morning's happenings on Horning Staithe had shown the Coots that it was no good thinking that the Hullabaloos were of the kind that forgive and forget. So the three of them together rowed slowly down the river, look-ing at the nests as they passed them, and rejoicing to see that the coot with a white feather, on No. 7 nest, was sitting as steadily as if she had never been disturbed.

"Hullo," said Tom, when at last they came in sight of the *Teasel*, "they've taken the awning down."

"Mustn't let them think us quite incapable," Mrs. Barrable had said when she came back from her shopping, and she and Dick and Dorothea between them had folded up the awning and stowed it in the forepeak, and lowered the cabin roof, and washed down the decks with the mop and generally done their best to make the *Teasel* look as if she were ready for a voyage.

"She's a jolly fine boat," said Starboard. "It's a pity those kids can't sail."

"There they are," said Tom.

Dick and Dorothea had come out of the cabin and were standing in the well. Dorothea was waving. Dick was looking anxiously round the *Teasel*. They had done the best they could, but he felt sure that something or other ought to have been stowed a little differently. Well, it was too late to alter anything now. Dorothea was finding, all of a sudden, that now that these sailing twins were close at hand, she did not know what to say to them. She found it easy enough to make up stories in which everybody talked and talked. Indeed, already, since yesterday, she had gone through half a dozen imaginary scenes in which she and Dick met and made friends with Port and Starboard. And now here they were, and she could not get one single word out of her mouth and was quite glad that William was doing all the talking and doing it very loud.

The *Titmouse* slid alongside.

"How do you do?" said Tom, as Mrs. Barrable came out of the cabin, and William stopped barking, remembered that Tom was a friend, and came and licked the hand with which he was keeping the *Titmouse* from bumping the *Teasel.*

"I am so glad you managed to come," said Mrs. Barrable. "These are Dick and Dorothea. And one of you two is Nell and the other is Bess, and one is Port and the other is Starboard, and the two of you are twins, and I don't know yet which is which."

"It's quite easy, really," said Starboard.

"Once you know," said Port.

"Oh, yes," said Mrs. Barrable. "I remember now. Nell's the one with curly hair."

"And the right-handed one," said Tom. "That's why she's Starboard, and Bess is left-handed and so she's Port. It comes very handy for sailing."

"Not much sailing for anybody to-day," said Mrs. Barrable, looking up the glassy river.

And then, before they had even had time to shake hands, something happened which Dorothea had not imagined in any of her scenes, something which turned them all into old friends working together.

"Why look," said Mrs. Barrable. "Isn't that those piratical bird-protectors?"

Round the bend of the river above the *Teasel's* moorings, just where, last night, Mrs. Barrable had seen Tom racing down in his old *Dreadnought*, and then the *Margoletta* roaring after him, came the old black ship's boat, Joe standing in the stern and steering, Pete and Bill rowing like galley-slaves so that there was a white ripple of bubbling water under her forefoot.

"They're in a mighty hurry," said Starboard.

"Something's up," said Tom.

"It's those Hullabaloos again," said Port.

"Easy," shouted Joe, as the *Death and Glory* swept down the river. The sweating galley-slaves bent forward, panting, over their lifted oars.

"It's that cruiser," called Joe, swinging his vessel round. "A man from Rodley's come down to see my dad, and we ask him. He don't know when that lot's giving up the *Margoletta*. But they're coming down river. Changed a battery, they have."

"They must use a lot of electricity," said Dick, more to himself than to anybody else, "with a wireless like that going on all the time."

"The doctor tell us where you was," said Joe. "Down here any time they may be."

Tom looked at the reeds.

"I'll just have to hide again," he said. "And you three had better clear off, or we'll be getting the *Teasel* mixed up in it too."

"Tom mustn't let himself be caught," explained Port, "because it would be so awful for the doctor."

"It's Coot Club business, anyhow," said Starboard, "and we're just not going to *have* him caught."

"If he's going to skipper the *Teasel*, it's our business, too," said Mrs. Barrable, and laughed when she saw Dick and

Dorothea both staring at her. "We may be going to manage a voyage after all," she said, "if the Coot Club can turn you two into sailors. . . . And this is no place for first sailing lessons, out in the open river. If those Hullabaloos are coming down again, they shan't find any of us. We'll vanish, pirates and all."

"But how?" said Tom.

"Into Ranworth Broad," said Mrs. Barrable.

"No wind," said Starboard, looking up the river on which the only ripple was made by a water-hen swimming across.

"We could quant,"[1] said Tom, "but don't you think I'd better just hide?"

"They can't search the *Teasel*," said Mrs. Barrable. "You come aboard and you can always slip into the cabin. Don't let's lose time. Have you three pirates got a rope?"

"We've a good 'un."

"I'll look after *Titmouse*," said Port. "You'll want Starboard to steer while you quant."

Tom looked doubtful.

"Of course, she's right," said Mrs. Barrable. "They'll take no notice of her. It's not a girl they're looking for. It's a boy with a criminal face, sinister, too. It's no good having either you or Dick there."

"I can't really row," said Dick, "not yet."

Tom and Starboard climbed aboard the *Teasel*. Bill and Pete brought the *Death and Glory* near enough for Joe to throw Tom the long rope they always carried with them in hope of salvage work. Many a time it had come in useful when they had found beginners who had got themselves aground in their hired boats and did not know how to get off. The rope uncoiled in the air. The end fell across the foredeck. Tom had it as it fell and made it fast round the mast.

[1] To quant is to pole a boat along. A quant is a long pole used for quanting.

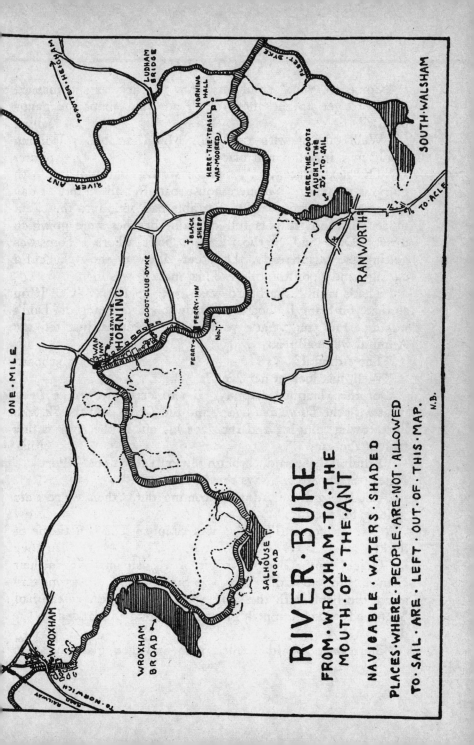

"Come on, you," cried Starboard to Dick, as she jumped ashore to get up the anchors. "And what about the gang-plank?"

"We'll take it with us," said Mrs. Barrable. "William would miss it at the next place."

"The next place. . . ." Simple words, but glowing with glorious meaning. No mere houseboat after all. Here to-day and gone to-morrow. Mrs. Barrable had gone into the cabin to see that no jampots full of paint brushes were going to upset. Dick and Starboard were both ashore. Tom was getting the quant ready. Dorothea, alone in the well, laid a daring hand upon the tiller. This, indeed, was life.

"That's right," Starboard was saying to Dick. "Coil it up so that you bring it aboard all ready to stow. Hang on, half a minute. Hi, you, what's your name, Dorothea, just tell the Admiral we're all ready. . . ."

"The Admiral?"

"Well, just look at her fleet."

Dorothea laughed happily. There certainly was a fleet, what with the *Death and Glory*, and the *Teasel*, and the *Teasel's* little rowing dinghy, and the *Titmouse* out in the river with a twin at the oars.

"Admiral," she said, through the low cabin door. "Port . . . I mean Starboard . . . says they're all ready."

"Good," said the Admiral, coming out, "then we're only waiting for the tug."

"Cast off forrard!" That was Skipper Tom on the fore-deck.

"Quick, you. Give her a bit of a push off. Now's your chance. Hop aboard." That was Starboard, who was moving along the bank with the stern rope amid a great rustling of bent reeds. Dick jumped, grabbed a shroud and landed on the deck.

"Stern warp aboard," called Tom, and then, glancing aft to

see Starboard leap down into the well, where Dorothea eagerly made room for her at the tiller, he waved a hand forward.

"Half ahead!" called the skipper of the tug-boat, *Death and Glory*.

The tow-rope tightened with a jerk. The *Teasel* answered it. She was moving.

"Full ahead!"

Dick and Dorothea looked at the little dinghy brushing the reeds where only a minute ago they had been able to step ashore. Wider and wider was the strip of water between the *Teasel* and the bank. The tow-rope that at first had tautened and sagged, and tautened and sagged again, dripping as it lifted, now hardly sagged at all. With quick short strokes, Bill and Pete, those two engines of the tug, kept up a steady strain. And there was Tom, lifting the long quanting pole, finding bottom with it, and hurrying aft along the side deck, leaning with all his weight against the quant's round wooden head. A jerk as he came to the stern, and back he went on the trot, lifting the quant hand over hand, finding bottom with it and again leaning on it, forcing the *Teasel* along, so hard that if the engines of the tug had eased up for a moment he would have taken the strain off the tow-rope.

"She's moving now all right," said Starboard. "If only we can get round the corner in time."

"Where is the corner?" asked Dorothea.

"You'll see it in a minute," said Starboard.

"But here they are!" said Dorothea. "We're too late."

"That's not the *Margoletta*," said Starboard. "That's only a little one."

A small motor-cruiser, making a good deal of noise for its size, but nothing like the noise of the *Margoletta*, was coming down river to meet them. It slowed up on seeing the fleet, the *Death and Glory* towing the *Teasel* and the little *Titmouse*, rowed by Port, acting as encouragement and convoy.

"Decent of them," said Tom. "Keep an eye on the tug," he added, jerking the quant from the mud and running forward again.

A single, shrill whistle sounded from the *Death and Glory*. It was answered on the instant by a single hoot from a motor-horn on the little cruiser.

"Good for Joe," said Tom.

"What does it mean?" asked Dick.

"He's telling everybody that he's directing his course to starboard," said Tom, "and they're going to do the same."

The little motor-cruiser passed them, and the people on board waved to them, going full speed again as soon as they could see that their wash would not bother the rowing boats.

"They're not all like the Hullabaloos," said Starboard.

"Wouldn't it be awful if they were?" said Dorothea.

"Feathers for Ginty!" called Starboard suddenly. "Pick them up, Twin!" She was pointing at a little fleet of curled white swan's feathers, some in mid-stream, and some close against the reeds. "Mrs. McGinty looks after us," she said, seeing Dorothea's puzzled face. "She always wants swan's feathers. For a cushion or something. She's been collecting them for years." Port, in the *Titmouse*, dropped astern, rowing from feather to feather.

Port was a long way astern of the fleet when, just as they were turning into the long straight dyke that leads to Ranworth Broad, Dorothea heard again the noise of a motor-cruiser. This time she said nothing, but looked at Starboard. Starboard had heard it too. Mrs. Barrable turned round.

Starboard nodded.

The captain of the *Death and Glory* was looking over his shoulder. He, too, had heard.

Tom, for a moment, stopped quanting as they turned the corner.

"They're a long way off," said Starboard.

"They come at such a lick," said Tom, racing forward with the quant. "They'll see us for certain," he panted as he came aft again. "We'll never get to the Straits in time."

Dorothea looked ahead to where the long narrow dyke disappeared among the trees, over which, far away, showed the grey square tower of Ranworth Church. The Straits must be those trees, if the Broad was beyond them.

"*Titmouse* ahoy!" shouted Tom suddenly, but there was no answer, and they could no longer see the river except just where the dyke left it.

"She's all right," said Mrs. Barrable. "They're looking for you in a punt. They aren't looking for a girl. Or for the *Titmouse*."

"We'll be all right too, if we can get to the Straits," said Starboard. "Let me have a go at the quant." But no. Tom would have felt even worse if he had not had the quant to push at, to feel he was doing something in driving the *Teasel* along. As for the engines of the *Death and Glory*, their panting could be heard by everybody.

"If only there were two quants," said Starboard.

"They're simply bound to look down the dyke," said Tom, and they'll see the Death and Glories towing, and if they've got any sense at all they'll come and have a look."

Nearer and nearer behind the reed-beds came the noise of the *Margoletta*. Everybody except Starboard—and even she glanced over her shoulder every other moment—was looking back towards the river, watching for the *Margoletta* to show in the opening at the mouth of the dyke. Who would show there first, Port or the Hullabaloos? And, oh, how far it seemed to those trees.

"There she is," said the Admiral.

"But she's rowing quite slowly," said Dorothea. "She can't not have heard them. And she's not turning in. She's at the other side of the river, picking feathers. . . . But there weren't any feathers there. . . Or were there?"

"Well done, that Port of yours," cried the Admiral. "I should never have thought of it. Dick, where are those glasses? Well done, Port," said Mrs. Barrable again. "Well done! Well done!"

There was the huge bulk of the *Margoletta* passing the mouth of the dyke. The *Teasel* and the Death and Glories were all in full view of them. But not a single one of the Hullabaloos was looking their way. Mrs. Barrable was silently clapping her hands. "They're wondering what on earth that girl is doing. And they can't look both ways at once."

The *Margoletta* passed the mouth of the dyke, and went roaring on down the river. And the crews of the *Teasel* and the *Death and Glory* saw Port in the *Titmouse*, taking short lazy strokes with her oars, disappear behind the reeds as if she were going on upstream.

"Dodged them all right this time," said Tom, "thanks to Port."

In another minute or two the *Teasel* was in the Straits, with trees on either side of the narrow dyke. The dyke bent to the left, and divided into two, one branch blocked with posts and chains, the other slowly widening towards a sheet of open water, still as glass, except for birds swimming and stirring the reflections of the reeds.

"Where do you want to stop?" asked Tom. "The staithe?"

"Much quieter here," said Mrs. Barrable.

"There's a good place for mooring," said Starboard, pointing to a little bay.

"Easy!" shouted Tom. "Casting off the tow-rope!"

Splash! The end of the tow-rope fell in the water, and Joe in the *Death and Glory*, was hauling it in, hand over hand. The *Teasel* slid slowly on in dead smooth water. Tom seemed to be everywhere at once, getting ready anchors and warps.

"Will that do?" called Starboard, as the *Teasel* slid alongside a low grassy bank.

Tom jumped from the foredeck. Starboard jumped from the counter. Dick, Dorothea and the Admiral were, for the moment, passengers only. The *Teasel* was moving no longer. A moment later she was moored in her new berth.

"Well done everybody," said the Admiral.

"Even William," said Dorothea. "At least he didn't bark and he easily might have."

"Narrow squeak that were," said Joe. Bill and Pete were too much out of breath even to speak. They grinned and wiped their foreheads and blinked the sweat out of their eyes.

And then there was the sound of oars from among the trees, and there was Port with the *Titmouse*.

"Well done, Port!" everybody shouted at once.

Port looked happily over her shoulder, steadied the *Titmouse* with her oars and stopped rowing.

"I knew they'd be looking down the dyke if I turned in," she said. "So I dropped a few of Ginty's swan feathers under the other bank and picked them up again one by one. The Hullabaloos nearly swamped me, they came so near to see what it was I was getting. Water-lilies in April I expect they thought."

"They'd have seen us for certain if they hadn't been looking at you," said Tom.

*

"You can't start sailing to-day," said Starboard, when everything had been tidied up. "But what about rowing? Have you done much?"

"Not yet," said Dick.

"Well, what about hopping into that dinghy and seeing what you can do?"

"By the way," said the Admiral, "I suppose he *can* swim?"

"We both can," said Dorothea. "Dick got first prize at school for men under twelve."

"Boys," said Dick, but every one had understood.

Dick, with earnest face, lowered himself into the *Teasel's* dinghy. Starboard untied the painter and dropped it into the bows for him. He found the rowlocks hanging each by its seating. He put them in their places, laid the oars in them, and with little gentle strokes set himself moving. He took a harder pull and the little light dinghy spun round and nosed into a clump of reeds. He got free again. The crew of the tug-boat were looking on. So was Dorothea, dreadfully afraid that he would have that same misfortune that he had had that time when the others had let him row a few yards on the lake in the north.

"Dick," she said anxiously, "'Dip them well in,' Peggy said. Don't catch another lobster."

There was a shout of laughter from the *Death and Glory*.

"You mean a crab, my dear," said the Admiral. "But they're much the same thing. Indigestible on shore and awkward in a boat."

"He's doing jolly well," said Starboard.

"There's more room in the Broad," said Bill, as Dick rammed another clump of reeds.

"We'll come, too," said Joe. "Throw yer arms out straight and you'll be racing us to-morrow."

And Dick paddled away into the open Broad as straight a course as he could, in spite of the horrid way in which the oars slipped in and out so that they seemed to be all lengths at once.

"Poor Dick," said the Admiral. "Three masters at once."

"You want to learn, too?" said Starboard.

"Awfully," said Dorothea.

"Take her in the *Titmouse*," said Tom.

"Your turn, Twin," said Port, and climbed aboard the *Teasel*, while Starboard and Dorothea took charge of Tom's little ship.

Learning if not to sail, at least to row, had actually begun.

When they came back, hot and aching after that first lesson, they found the *Teasel* looking once more as she had looked when first they saw her. Port and Tom had rigged her awning, and William, impatient for tea and the chocolate he expected, welcomed them noisily aboard. The kettle was boiling, and if Mrs. Barrable had twice as many guests as she had asked, she was glad of it, and there was plenty of food to go round.

"It's the most gorgeous lake," said Dorothea. "We've rowed all round it. It's full of good hiding-places."

"And birds," said Dick.

"And there's that place where the chains go across," said Dorothea. "He could escape down that if they came here. And that other place where they're cutting reeds. Anybody could be an outlaw hidden in here for weeks and weeks while people were hunting for him outside."

"You could, you know," said Starboard. "Those Hulla-baloos can't be about for ever, and we could bring supplies."

"It's a good idea," said Port. "They're sure to catch you if you just hang about Horning."

"You'll have disappeared, just like the *Teasel*," said Dorothea.

Tom looked from one to the other. All this romance was rather puzzling. He had got into trouble with some un-pleasant people who had hired the *Margoletta*. He had to keep out of their way because if they caught him it would be hard to prevent his father, the doctor, from being dragged in. It was most unlucky, just when the *Titmouse* was ready for distant voyaging. But somehow this Dorothea, and even Port and Starboard, who were Norfolk Coots and usually as practical as himself, were talking of his misfortune as if it were some kind of exciting story.

"If they did come in here to look for him," said Dorothea, "he could hide among the reeds like a water buffalo, with only his nose above water."

"Jolly cold," said Tom.

"Tell you what," said Joe. "They can't come up this way

without they come by Ludham, or by Acle or by Potter Heigham, and we know chaps in all them places. We'll tell 'em to telephone to Dad's yard, to give us a warning if that lot come through. Then we'll know where they be."

"But we don't know where they are *now*," said Tom. "They may be close to. They may have stopped just round the corner."

"Um," said Starboard. "It wouldn't do to run right into them."

"I must get home, anyhow, and tell Mother what I'm going to do," said Tom.

"Look here," said Starboard. "We've got to get back early. We'll take a passage with the Death and Glories, and tell Aunty you'll be late. Then you can dodge back home when it's beginning to get dark."

"Much the best plan," said Mrs. Barrable.

And presently the *Death and Glory*, with Port and Starboard pulling an oar apiece and the three small Coots taking turns in the steering, disappeared behind the trees. Tom waited in the *Titmouse*, tied alongside the *Teasel*, fitting hinges to locker doors, with Dick and Dorothea watching and passing him screws at the right moment.

At the first hoot of an owl over the marshes he said "Good night" to his new friends. By dusk all yachts and cruisers on the Bure are tied up or hurriedly looking for moorings for the night. But the bye-laws say nothing about little boats, and though there was still no wind, he hoped to get home not too dreadfully late for supper.

"Do you think he'll come back?" asked Dick.

"He simply couldn't find a better place to lurk," said Dorothea.

"He's got a very nice dyke," said Mrs. Barrable, "without stirring from his own home. We shan't see him again to-night. I expect he'll try to get here to-morrow before Hullabaloos wake up in the morning."

But last thing, when they had done their washing up after supper, and Mrs. Barrable had tired of telling them what the Broads had been like in the wild old days of forty years ago, and it had long been dark, and Dick and Dorothea climbed out on the counter, to stand there and watch the stars, and to listen to the night noises in the reed-beds, they caught sight of a pale glimmer away under the trees where the dyke divided.

"He's back," said Dick.

"Far away, at the edge of the marshes," said Dorothea, more to herself than to Dick, "the watchers saw the glimmer of the outlaw's lonely light."

Mrs. Barrable leaned from the well, and herself saw that lit awning of the *Titmouse* reflected in the water under the trees.

"Humph," she said, "I *thought* that mother of his was rather nice. She must be very nice indeed."

The light went out, and there was nothing to show that any other boat was in the Broad beside the *Teasel*.

"He's got good sense, too, that boy," she added. "And you'd better go to bed yourselves, when even outlaws set you such a good example."

CHAPTER X

LYING LOW

First Day

Dɪᴄᴋ and Dorothea in the little fore-cabin of the *Teasel* slept until a Primus stove in the well burst into a sudden roar as Mrs. Barrable set it going to boil the breakfast coffee. They hurried out to feel the side-decks wet with dew and cold to their bare feet, but their first glance across the water towards the other side of the Straits showed them that Tom in the *Titmouse* had long ago begun his day. The awning of the little boat had been turned back at the stern, and they could see the outlaw himself leaning out and washing up a plate.

"Won't he be coming here for breakfast?" asked Dorothea.

"He must have had his ages ago," said Mrs. Barrable. "He was scrubbing his face when I first looked out. Hurry up and scrub yours and then, as soon as you've had something to eat, you can row across and ask him where we get fresh milk. I've opened a tin for now."

Half an hour later, when they had stowed the *Teasel's* awning, and Mrs. Barrable was setting up her easel in the well to paint a picture of the Broad, Dick and Dorothea began their first lesson in sailing. There could not have been a better day for it. Sunshine, a crisp air, and a wind not strong enough to be dangerous, but quite strong enough to send the *Titmouse* flying through the water so that any mistake in the steering showed at once. They beat up to the staithe, took the milk-can to the farm, brought it back filled, went to the little shop and post office and sent off post cards to Mr. and Mrs.

Callum. One sentence was the same on both cards: "We have begun to learn to sail." Then, with a fair wind they flew back across the Broad to the *Teasel*, handed over the milk-can to Mrs. Barrable, heard William noisily exploring among the bushes, fended him off when he arrived at a gallop and wanted to join them in the *Titmouse*, and were off once more to go on with the sailing lesson.

Up and down they sailed in the sunshine, first one and then the other at the tiller, while Tom held the main-sheet so that nothing could really go wrong. They very soon stopped catching their breaths every time a harder puff of wind sent the *Titmouse* heeling over, and Tom said they would do all right as soon as they had learnt that when you are steering you must think of nothing else. He said this after Dick had had a long turn at the tiller. Dick was careful enough when there was nothing to look at, but keen as he was on being able to sail, the sight of a bird was too much for him, and as Ranworth is full of birds of all kinds, the *Titmouse*, with Dick at the tiller, had sailed a very wriggly course.

But it was not much better with Dorothea. Her mind, too, kept slipping away. She was sailing, yes, and all of a tremble lest she should do something wrong, but she could not help thinking of the outlaw and the *Margoletta*, and of the Admiral quietly painting in the well of the *Teasel*, but at the same time ready to give warning of approaching Hullabaloos. How would it be to make a real sentinel's post in one of the taller trees at the outer end of the Straits? What would happen if suddenly, now, this minute, the *Margoletta*, full of enemies, were to come roaring out into the Broad? "The boy outlaw leapt overboard and swam for the reeds, bullet after bullet splashing in the water round his head. . . ."

"Look out, Dot, we'll be aground."

And there was the boy outlaw close beside her, grabbing at the tiller. The *Titmouse* spun round only just in time, and they felt the centre-board move stickily in the mud and then break free again.

Half-way through the morning Port and Starboard came rowing out of the Straits with two bits of urgent news, one that the first of No. 7's eggs had hatched, and the other that while Tom had been busy teaching Dick and Dorothea how to sail, other people had been doing their best for Tom. Far and wide, it seemed, the alarm had been given, and all over the Broads the outlaw's friends were alert and on the watch.

"It's all fixed up," said Starboard. "Joe's taken Bill's bike and gone down to Acle to fix up with a boy there to keep a look-out. Bill's gone up to Potter Heigham on the bus (Coot Club funds, of course), and Pete's got a lift into Wroxham to see what he can find out at Rodley's about how long that lot are going to have the *Margoletta*."

While they were talking, Dick, with Tom's help, was keeping the *Titmouse* sailing to and fro within easy distance of the rowing-boat. At first the twins hardly realised that it was a visitor who had hold of the tiller.

"Jibe her this time," said Tom.

"Jibe?" asked Dick, puzzled.

"Swing her right round toward the side where the sail is. . . . I'll haul in the sheet. . . . Go on. . . . Right round. . . . Till the boom swings over. . . . There it goes. . . . Mind your heads. . . . Steady her again."

"I say," said Port, "you *are* getting on."

The twins had to go back at once, because they had to get the *Flash* ready for a race that afternoon.

"Stick at it," said Starboard as they rowed away.

An hour later, the *Titmouse* was cruising along by the reed-beds in the far corner of the Broad, when a yell from Ranworth Staithe made Tom and his pupils turn round.

"Coots ahoy!"

A small boy with a bicycle was standing at the edge of the staithe and waving . . . the skipper of the *Death and Glory* back from Acle. Tom swung the *Titmouse* round, and they raced back towards him.

"Been down to Acle," said Joe, when they came to the staithe. "Robin think he see *Margoletta* go through for Yarmouth last night, but he ain't sure. He say he'll watch the bridge for us, and I tell him I'll punch his head if he don't, and I leave him fourpence to telephone up to my dad's as soon's he see her coming up again."

"Tell Starboard to open the treasury and hand out that fourpence," said Tom.

"No hurry," said Joe. "Well, I'm off now. Got to see them others, case she go Ludham way or Potter Heigham." He jumped on his bicycle and rode off the staithe to disappear behind the trees by the Maltster's Arms.

In the afternoon they saw Port and Starboard again. The *Flash* had rounded a mark too close and touched it and so was out of her race, and Mr. Farland sailed her into Ranworth to see his daughter's new friends, and to tell Tom that if by any chance the Hullabaloos did get hold of him and talked of the law or anything like that, Tom was at once to refer them to him. "Nothing like letting the other side know that two can play at law as well as one. . . . But you're in the wrong, so you'd much better not let them catch you at all. . . . By the way," he said to Mrs. Barrable, "you mustn't let my girls be a nuisance to you."

"They've been a great help so far," said the Admiral. "I'm left without captain or crew with my brother going off, and Dick and Dorothea are hardly to be counted sailors yet."

"They soon will be with Tom to teach them," said Mr. Farland. "And Nell and Bess know one end of a boat from the other. Anybody like to come for a spin in *Flash*?"

In a minute Tom, Dick and Dorothea had tied up the *Titmouse* and were crowded into the little racing sloop. Dorothea found it hard to believe that only three days before she had been seeing *Flash* for the first time and looking so enviously at those two sailor girls.

The *Flash* had hardly put her passengers aboard the *Titmouse* and sailed out of sight into the wooded Straits before the outlaw and his friends were hailed again. This time it was Doctor Dudgeon, who had escaped from his patients for an hour or two. He had put some cushions in the stern of his old fishing boat to make it comfortable for Mrs. Dudgeon and "our baby" and had rowed them down to Ranworth to call on Mrs. Barrable. "I was so sorry I was out taking people's temperatures when you came yesterday," he said. "Your brother is the most interesting patient I ever had. My patients mostly are as dull as suet puddings. . . . It's safe to say so, for you won't tell them. . . . But your brother is something different altogether, and I'm proud to have plastered his scalp. But what I came to say is how grateful I am to you for aiding and abetting a lawless young ruffian, as I hear you did the other night."

"Horrible people those were," said Mrs. Barrable.

"I must say I should not at all like to have a row with them," said the doctor, " but if Tom's going sailing with you he ought to be safe enough. They've only seen him in that old punt."

Late that night, when sailing was over for the day and the awnings had been rigged, and supper had been eaten in the *Teasel*, and Tom was just setting off to the *Titmouse*, taking Dick with him to bring the *Teasel's* dinghy back. Mrs. Barrable asked him a question. "Well," she said, "and do you think Dick and Dorothea will make a crew?"

"They're doing jolly well," said Tom.

Second Day

Dick wrote in his note-book, "Found two coots' nests in a reed-bed close to Ranworth Staithe. Watched crested grebes fishing. What I thought was a fog-horn last night and the night before was a bittern. There was no fog, and Tom heard it, too, and told me."

Port and Starboard came in their rowing boat to spend the whole day. Dick and Dorothea were taken out by turns first in *Titmouse* and then in the rowing boat, and made to sail and row by themselves, with the elder Coots as mere passengers to tell them what they did wrong. William went hunting, ashore. Mrs. Barrable painted another picture. Port and Starboard and Dorothea did the day's cooking.

In the afternoon the *Death and Glory* came rowing through the Straits with the news that the *Margoletta* had been seen going through Yarmouth to the south the day before. That made everybody feel a good deal more comfortable. All six Coots came to tea in the *Teasel*. Joe brought his white rat, and Dorothea made herself stroke it. They had tea in the *Teasel*, William and the white rat as far from each other as possible, William at the forward end of the cabin and the white rat with Joe at the after end of the well. The *Death and Glory* hoisted her patched and ragged old sail, and Dick and Dorothea went sailing in her, while the Admiral and the three elder Coots held a conference. It was decided that next day, while the twins could be there to help, they should set sail on the *Teasel* and try her on the Broad before venturing out into the river.

Third Day

This plan came to nothing, because in the morning they woke to the steady drumming of rain-drops on stretched canvas. It was no day for a trial trip. Neither Tom nor the

Admiral wanted to get sails wet at the very start. Awnings were left up all day. Dick and Dorothea wore their oilskins and sea-boots and got some rowing practice in the rain. Dorothea planned a story, "The Outlaw of the Broads." Dick helped Tom in the *Titmouse*, and between them they finished up the locker-doors. William, for fear of chills, was given a spoonful of cod-liver oil.

In the afternoon, when the rain was at its worst, Port and Starboard, in oilskins and sou'westers, came rowing into the Broad, bringing letters from the post office at Horning. Dick and Dorothea had a letter apiece that had been written up on the Roman wall and had a Carlisle postmark. Mrs. Barrable had a letter from her brother in London, horrified scraps of which she read aloud.

"Perfectly ridiculous. . . . You can't do it. . . . Taking a boat as big as the *Teasel* down through Yarmouth with nobody to help but a brace of brats who have never been in a boat before. . . . What are you going to do about bridges? . . . What do you know about tides? Tides are no child's play down at Yarmouth. . . . Jolly good chap that doctor, but he ought to put his foot down and tell you to stay where you are. . . ."

Dick and Dorothea listened and said nothing.

"People *will* jump to conclusions," said Mrs. Barrable. "And I told him Tom was coming too."

"He's quite right, really," said Tom.

"What do *you* think?" asked Mrs. Barrable of the twins.

"Yarmouth is an awful place," said Starboard. "And the crew ought to have had some practice going through bridges."

"What are you doing to-morrow?" said Mrs. Barrable.

"We've got to hang about at home to-morrow. The A.P.'s got people coming to tea, and we have to be there to pour out."

"Next day, then?" said Mrs. Barrable. "What about coming with us for a day or so just to help Tom to put us all in the way of handling the *Teasel*?" . . .

"We'll have to be back the night before the first of the championship races," said Starboard.

"We could do a tremendous lot in three days," said Tom.

"Potter Heigham, I thought," said the Admiral.

"Bridge to go through. Two bridges. Just what's wanted," said Tom.

"And then through Kendal Dyke and up to Horsey. It used to be a wonderful place for birds."

"It still is," said Tom.

"Good," said Dick.

"We'll have to ask the A.P.," said Port.

"He won't mind so long as we're back in time," said Starboard. "Anyway, if we can't come we'll get a message to you to-morrow. We've got to get back now."

And then, with the rain pouring off their sou'westers, the twins settled to their oars again and disappeared into the Straits.

*

That night, in the cabin of the *Teasel*, the Admiral, Tom, Dick, and Dorothea pored over the map together. The Admiral, with the wrong end of a paint brush, was tracing the curling blue line that marked the River Bure past the mouth of the Ant and on to the place where it was joined by the Thurne, and the blue line thickened and curled away down the map towards Acle and Yarmouth. Tom's eye followed it down there, thinking of tides and the other dangers of Yarmouth and Breydon which make a cruise on the rivers of the south as exciting an adventure for the children of Horning or Wroxham as a cruise on the rivers of the north is for the children who live down at Oulton or Beccles.

But Mrs. Barrable's paint brush was moving up that other river, the Thurne . . . Potter Heigham . . . "such a pretty little place it used to be" . . . two bridges, road and railway . . . on and on and then sharp to the north-west through the narrow line that marked Kendal Dyke, and into a largish blue blot that meant the widening waters of Heigham Sound, and on again through a narrow wriggling line into another blue blot that was Horsey Mere. At one side of this blot was a short line marking a dyke, and at the end of it the sign for a windmill. "That's where we'll spend the night," said the Admiral, "in the little cut close by that windmill. . . ."

The others leant over the cabin table. Closer and closer they put their heads to the paper. It was very hard to see, all of a sudden. Dimmer and dimmer.

"What's happened to the light?" said the Admiral.

"They looked up at the two little glass bulbs that usually lit the whole cabin. They dazzled no longer. A curly red wire was slowly fading in each bulb.

"The battery must be run down," said Dick at once. He switched off one light, and, for a moment, got a rather brighter glow out of the other.

"Well," said the Admiral, "we've been looking at the wrong end of the map. We can't set out on a voyage with no light. Candles are all right in the well, but I don't like them in the cabin. We'll have to sail up to Wroxham to get the battery renewed."

"It's bad for it to be run down," said Dick.

"Of course, it hasn't been charged since we took the boat over. I forgot about it, with Brother Richard going away. Get out the candlestick for now. And the day after to-morrow, when the twins come, we'll have to go to Wroxham instead of to Horsey."

Dorothea felt a pang of disappointment as she went into the well for the candlestick. They had come from Wroxham that first day and so had seen that part of the river already. Sailing to Horsey would have been sailing into the unknown. Where was that candlestick? She found it and her fingers closed on the matchbox.

"Hurry up, Dot," said the Admiral.

In the cabin the red glowing wires dimmed. "Better turn them out," said Dick, and they sat in the dark, listening to Dorothea striking a damp match that would not light, listening also to the even grunting of the pug, who thought the dark was an improvement. Dick, too, was disappointed. He had been looking forward to Horsey, and to adding reed pheasants and bitterns to his list of birds seen. But, of course, batteries had to be charged.

Help came, unexpectedly, from Tom.

Dorothea lit her candle at last, and brought it into the cabin, setting it on the table where it threw its queer flickering light over the faces round the map. She saw at once that Tom had something to say.

"Wroxham's a bad place for sailing. Specially now that the leaves are beginning to come. Get blanketed altogether in some reaches. It's no good going up there for a trial trip. Much better get it done to-morrow. It's safe enough with the *Margoletta* away through Yarmouth. I'll take the battery up to Wroxham first thing in the morning. I'll be back by tea-time."

The Admiral looked at him in the candlelight, and laughed.

"Tired of lying low?" she asked.

"I'd like to give *Titmouse* a run," said Tom. "And it's perfectly safe now with somebody watching at Acle."

"It certainly would be rather waste of Port and Starboard not to have some real sailing while we've got them," said the Admiral. "And there are no bridges on the way to Wroxham."

"It's stopped raining," said Tom, putting his hand out through a port-hole to feel.

A few minutes later he was baling out the *Teasel's* dinghy for the third time that day. Dick ferried him across to the *Titmouse*. Tom lit his lantern and looked about him. "Bone dry," he said, "in spite of all that rain. That's the first time the awning's had a proper wetting."

He watched Dick vanish into the darkness, listened for his safe arrival aboard the *Teasel*, and turned in for the night, feeling extraordinarily happy. Jolly good that the twins were coming in the *Teasel*, at least to Horsey and back. It was all very well, but he really did not much like the idea of handling a boat as big as the *Teasel* for the first time, with only Dick and Dorothea to help. And jolly good, too, to think that to-morrow, Hullabaloos or no Hullabaloos, the little *Titmouse* would herself be voyaging once more.

CHAPTER XI

TOM IN DANGER

It was a fine clear morning with a north-westerly breeze. Tom was up early, and long before breakfast was ready in the *Teasel* he had come alongside. He and Dick made a double sling with the end of the *Teasel's* mainsheet, and lowered the heavy battery carefully into the *Titmouse*.

"Do you really think it's safe?" said Dorothea. "They may be just waiting to pounce."

"Not they," said Tom. "And we'd know if they were. Joe's got a friend watching at Acle. And, anyway, I'll be back in no time. No tacking. I'm going to row every yard I can't either run or reach."

"It's a very long way," said Dorothea.

"Are you quite sure you wouldn't rather I sent it up from Horning or Ranworth and had it sent back?" said Mrs. Barrable. "It would never do for the skipper to get into trouble the very day before the *Teasel* really starts sailing."

But Tom was sure that everything was all right. The coast was clear, there was a fine breeze and he was in a hurry to be off. Mrs. Barrable handed out a note to the Wroxham boat-letter from whom her brother had hired the *Teasel*. "That's to tell them about the battery," she said. "And then there are these things to buy." She gave him a written list of things, the stock of which was running rather low. Tom took the list, put it in his pocket with the money to pay for the things, and then rowed quickly away between the trees, his sail all ready for hoisting in any reach where he found a fair wind.

It was a dullish morning without him. They washed up. They swabbed the decks. They took William with them as a passenger to Ranworth Staithe when they went to get some fresh water. On the way back they looked in on two coots' nests, and met a pair of crested grebes out fishing, but, with William aboard, they found it harder to come near the grebes than when they were alone. William sat up on a thwart, put his paws on the gunwale and looked out as keenly as Dick, but he could not see a bird on the water without barking. They went back to the *Teasel* at last and found the Admiral busy preparing a canvas. Dick settled down in the cabin, making a fair copy of his roughly scribbled list of birds he had seen in Norfolk. Dorothea tried to write some of the new book that had seemed almost half done when she had put down a list of its chapter headings. . . . The Secret Broad, The Outlaw in the Reeds, The Black Coot's Feather, The Bittern's Warning, and so on. What a book it was to be, and yet, somehow, the first chapter had ended after a paragraph or two, and the second would not go beyond the first gorgeous sentence: "Parting the reeds with stealthy, silent hand, the outlaw peered into the gathering dusk. Away, across the dark water. . . ." Well, what was it that he saw? Dorothea found herself wondering instead what Tom was seeing on his voyage up to Wroxham to change the *Teasel's* battery. Had he managed to see Port and Starboard on his way through Horning? The morning slipped away, and still the outlaw in the book was peering out of the reeds across the dark water. Dorothea had to leave him there, for suddenly it was too late to do any more writing. The Admiral wanted to get dinner over, to have a long afternoon for painting. There was the lighting of the Primus, the choosing of a tin of steak-and-kidney pudding, the timing of its boiling by the ship's chronometer, and then the eating of it, and of some stewed pears, several hunks of cake and some chocolate ("No need to save it now, with Tom bringing a fresh supply").

And all the time the sun was shifting the shadows, and Admiral Barrable hurried through the washing up because with every moment the light was getting better for the picture she had planned of the shadowy Straits, with a little boat coming out of them, its sail just catching the sunshine through the trees.

"There's only one time to paint it," she said, and Dorothea understood that with artists it is the same as with writers, and she hurried Dick into the dinghy to give the Admiral a fair chance, and asked if it would be all right if they rowed up to the main river.

"Don't fall in," said the Admiral. "Better leave William with me. Where *did* I put that turpentine?"

Rowing side by side, with an oar apiece, they paddled away from the *Teasel*. The Admiral absent-mindedly waved a paint-brush at them. They waved back. The trees closed in on either side of them. They were in the Straits and the *Teasel* and the open Broad were hidden behind a curtain of young spring leaves. They paddled steadily on, out of the shelter of the trees into the long straight dyke leading to the river.

"There's a sail!" said Dorothea, looking over her shoulder at a white triangle shining in the sunlight, moving along above a distant line of willow bushes.

"One, two," said Dick. "One, two. . . . You must keep time. Look out! we'll be into the reeds. Not so hard. One, two. One, two. That sail's going down the river. They'll have met Tom, I should think."

"I wonder how far he's got," said Dorothea. "Probably started back. All right, Dick. It's really you forgetting to pull. . . . And they're only water-hens. . . ."

Dick said nothing. He knew he had all but let his oar wait in the air while he watched two water-hens disappear into a shady hole among the reeds.

"Upstream or down?" said Dorothea as they came at last to the mouth of the dyke. "Do you realise we're in a boat by ourselves? Let's go upstream. We might meet Port and Starboard."

"Upstream," said Dick. "Let's try and find No. 7."

"Let's," said Dorothea. "Starboard said the little ones are out of the eggs."

"We'll keep a look-out for a coot with a white feather."

But long before they had come as far as that little reedy drain where the coot with the white feather was looking after her family of sooty chicks, they had other things that to think.

They paddled slowly along, keeping near the bank, past the water-works and as far as the church reach, where they saw two coots, but without white feathers, and dozens of water-hens scurrying to and fro between the rough bushy bank on one side of the river and the green grass that was being clipped short by the black sheep on the other. Dick had a good look at the water-hens, noting their flashing tails, and the bright scarlet of their beaks when they lurked close under the over-hanging bank while he and Dorothea paddled by. A yacht came sailing down the reach with the water bubbling under her forefoot. To-morrow, thought Dorothea, they, too, would be sailing just like that. How very much better things had turned out than had seemed likely when first they came aboard the *Teasel* and Mrs. Barrable broke the news to them that they were not going to sail at all. "And we owe it all to No. 7," said Dorothea. "And the Coot Club, of course."

"What?" said Dick.

Dorothea had spoken aloud without meaning to. But Dick never got his answer. Dorothea had lifted her oar from the water and was listening to a loud drumming from somewhere down the river.

"Another of them," said Dick. "I hope it doesn't make an awful wash like the Hullabaloos. I wonder if we ought to land till it's gone by?"

"It's just as noisy," said Dorothea, and the next moment the cruiser swung into sight round the bend by the water-works. "Dick," she cried. "It's them. The *Margoletta*. They've come back. No, don't look at them. Go on looking at the black sheep. . . ."

With a roaring engine and a tremendous blare of band music from the gramophone on its foredeck, the big cruiser passed them. Its high wash, racing after it, lifted the tiny dinghy so suddenly that Dorothea clutched the gunwale and lost her oar. By the time she had got it again, the *Margoletta* was already out of sight, though the waves were still tearing angrily at the banks.

"They'll get him. He doesn't know they're here. He can't possibly escape. Dick, Dick! What ought we to do?"

Dick's mind could be counted on to work fast as soon as it was interested. The difficulty was to get it interested when it happened to be thinking about something else. The *Margoletta* had done that, and Dick had already come to a decision while the little dinghy was still tossing on that brutal wash.

"Come on, Dot," he said. "We've got to find the others. They'll know what to do." He gave a hard pull. The dinghy swung round. "Come on, Dot, pull for all you're worth."

"And Mrs. B. ?"

"No time to go back there. Come on, Dot. Pull! One, two. One, two."

But it was no good. Paddling easily together, when in no hurry, they could keep the dinghy more or less on its course. But, when the two of them were pulling as hard as they could, first one and then the other got in the stronger stroke, and the little dinghy seemed to be trying to head all ways at once.

"Let me have the other oar."

Dorothea gave it up to him and sat in the stern.

"I'm not going to bother about that feathering," said Dick. He clenched his teeth and pulled, lifted his oars probably rather higher that the Death and Glories would have approved, shot them back, gripped the water with them and pulled again. There was a good deal of splashing, but those days of hard work on Ranworth Broad had not gone for nothing, and the little dinghy pushed through the water at a good pace. By giving a harder tug now and then on one or other oar, he managed to keep her heading up the river most of the time. Not always.

"Look out!" said Dorothea. "You'll be into the reeds again."

"Do like they told us they used to do," he panted back. "Keep pointing always bang up the river. With a hand. Human compass. Then I can just watch your hand without having to turn round to know where I'm going."

Dorothea sat still with her right hand just above her knees pointing straight up the river, so that when Dick's bad rowing made the dinghy swerve, he could see at once what had happened by looking at her pointing fingers. On and on he rowed.

"That coot's got a white feather," said Dorothea.

Dick looked round with eyes that hardly saw. He did not stop rowing. He was breathing hard. He could no longer keep his teeth together. As for looking at coots, he could hardly see Dorothea's pointing hand only a foot or two before his face.

"Swop places," said Dorothea. "Let me row for a bit."

Dick pulled desperately on.

"Scientific way," said Dorothea. "Relay. First you then me, so that we can keep going at full speed."

It was the word "scientific" that persuaded him. With shaking knees he changed places with Dorothea. Try as he would, his hand trembled as he held it out for a compass-needle, pointing the way up the river. Dorothea, with fresh arms, sent the dinghy along faster, but even more splashily than before.

"It's a good thing the Death and Glories can't see us," she said, after a worse splash than usual.

"Don't talk," said Dick. "It makes it worse later if you do."
Dorothea said no more. He was right. In a very few
minutes she was far past talking. She felt as if her arms
would come loose at the shoulder, as if her back would break,
as if something in her chest was growing bigger and bigger
until presently there would be no room for any breath. And,
after all, what was the good? It was too late now. Nothing
could save the outlaw from his fate. And then, suddenly, she
saw Dick's face change. What had happened? What was it
he was saying? "Easy! Dot, go slow! Don't go so fast. They
mustn't think we're hurrying. Look here, let me row."

She glanced over her shoulder. They had passed the little
windmill. Horning Ferry and the Ferry Inn were in sight.
There, tied up to the quay-heading in front of the inn, lay the
Margoletta. Three men and a couple of women were talking to
a boy who was pointing up the river. They were just walking
across the grass towards the inn. The cruiser had stopped.
There was a chance yet, if only they could slip past and up
into Horning, and tell Port and Starboard or the Death and
Glories. The Coots would surely find some way of getting a
warning to Tom.

They changed places again. Dorothea sat in the stern
trying not to pant so dreadfully, and not to look as hot as she
felt. Dick, carefully feathering as Port had taught him,
rowing as if he had nothing to think of but style, pulled
steadily on, past the *Margoletta*, past the Ferry, past the neat
little hut of the Bure Commissioners and the lawn and garden
seat where the Commissioners can sit and watch the river
that is in their charge.

"Did you see that boy," asked Dorothea, "talking to the
Hullabaloos?"

"No," said Dick shortly.

"Sorry! Sorry!" said Dorothea. She had forgotten for a
moment that she was being a human compass, and Dick, who

was pulling away again as hard as he could, had had a narrow shave of ramming the bank through watching a hand that was pointing at nothing in particular.

A hard pull set him right, but he had no breath to waste on talk.

The question now was where to look for the Coots. Dorothea hardly knew what to do. They had only been once through Horning, in the launch on the way from the station. Tom's house, she knew, had a golden bream for a weathercock. The twins' house was next door. But which side? And she knew that if there was any chance of avoiding it, the grown-ups ought not to be dragged in. And then, grown-ups or no grown-ups, the question was settled for her. There was the golden bream swimming in the blue sky above the old thatched gable. That was the doctor's house. That clump of tall reeds must be the opening to Tom's dyke. And there on the doctor's lawn was Mrs. Dudgeon, sitting in a chair and knitting, with the baby's perambulator close beside her.

Mrs. Dudgeon knew them at once, after seeing them in the *Teasel* the day Dr. Dudgeon had rowed down to Ranworth. She waved to them. "Almost like a summer day," she said. "You seem to be doing very well. I thought you had only just begun to learn. My word, you look as if you were in a hurry."

Dick tried to answer, but had no breath. He could not get a word out.

"We're looking for Port and Starboard," said Dorothea, "or any of the Coots. It's that cruiser. The *Margoletta*. They're coming up the river. They're at the Ferry now. And Tom's gone to Wroxham. He doesn't know they're anywhere near."

Mrs. Dudgeon did not seem at all disturbed. "He looked in on his way up," she said, "and had a second breakfast. I don't think you need worry about those people. They'll have forgotten all about him by now."

"Mrs. Barrable said the other day they'd made up their mind to find him . . . you know, when they told the policeman it was Joe and it wasn't."

In her heart, however, Dorothea wavered. Perhaps, after all, there was no need for Tom to be an outlaw. But she remembered the Coots. She knew what they would say. At all costs they would want to let Tom have a warning.

"You'll find Nell and Bess up in the village, I expect," said Mrs. Dudgeon. "They were here a few minutes ago, and then somebody came and honked like a coot, and off they went. I heard them running up the road. 'Sh. 'Sh!" She put out a hand to the perambulator.

"I think we'd better go and find them," said Dorothea.

"They won't be far away," said Mrs. Dudgeon.

Dick rowed on up the village, past the willow-pattern harbours, and the big boat-sheds.

"There's the *Death and Glory*, anyhow," cried Dorothea. The old tarred boat lay against the staithe. A moment later they caught sight of Joe and the twins, all three looking at the notice-board, where people are told not to moor their boats for too long a time.

"Hi!" shouted Dorothea.

"Hullo!" shouted Joe. He ran to the edge of the staithe to catch the nose of the dinghy as they came in. Putting his hand to his mouth, as if that would make a shout more like a whisper, he asked excitedly, "Have you seed that?"

"What?"

"They've papered him," said Joe. "Reward."

"The *Margoletta's* coming up the river," said Dorothea.

"Come and look at this," cried Starboard.

"But there's no time to lose," said Dorothea.

Dick could not speak and the others did not seem to hear her.

"Read what it say," said Joe.

"But Tom's alone up the river," said Dorothea.

"Just look at it," said Port.

"Quick, quick!" said Dorothea.

"Read what it say," said Joe. "It weren't there yesterday, but I see it just now as soon's I tie up."

Dick climbed out on the staithe and hurried across to the notice-board. Dorothea was almost run across the gravel by Port and Starboard, who helped her ashore together.

This was the notice they read:

REWARD

A REWARD WILL BE PAID TO ANY PERSON WHO CAN GIVE INFORMATION CONCERNING THE BOY WHO ON THE NIGHT OF APRIL THE TWENTY-SECOND CAST OFF THE MOORING ROPES OF THE MOTOR-CRUISER MARGOLETTA THEN MOORED TO THE NORTH BANK BELOW HORNING FERRY.

APPLY TO . . . .

(There followed a name and an address, that of Rodley's, the boat-letting firm who owned the cruiser.)

"Well," said Starboard, "nobody'll give them any information, anyway."

"George Owdon might," said Port.

"If he could talk to them," said Starboard, "but even he wouldn't like people knowing he'd done it."

"Anyway, Tom'll have to look out. It's a good thing the Hullabaloos are away the other side of Yarmouth. . . ."

"But they aren't," Dorothea almost screamed. "We've been telling you. They're here."

"Coming up the river," said Dick. "Stopped at the Ferry."

"And Tom's up at Wroxham," said Dorothea. "They can't help catching him if they go on. And there was a boy talking to them."

Joe made half a move towards the *Death and Glory*.

"Pete and Bill away to Ludham," he said. Not with the

best of wills could he by himself get much speed out of the old ship's boat.

"We'll go up the river," said Starboard.

"Where's Bill's bicycle?" asked Port.

"I can get it," said Joe.

"You may catch Tom at Wroxham before he starts back." Joe was gone.

"You two'd better wait here. You can't go really fast in that dinghy. And we've got two pairs of oars. Besides we must have someone on the look out here to know what they do. Come on, Port!"

"Think of some way to stop them, if you can," said Port over her shoulder.

Dick and Dorothea were alone on the staithe.

There was the violent ringing of a bicycle bell. They were just in time to see Joe, head down, legs working like piston-rods, flash across the open space by the post office and disappear behind the inn.

A few minutes later they saw the Farland rowing-boat, long, light and narrow, come shooting past the boat-sheds.

"Go it! Go it!" shouted Dorothea.

The twins hardly glanced at them as they swept by. Round the bend by the Swan Inn they held water with their starboard oars, and then away they went again and were out of sight in a moment behind the houseboats at the corner.

"Mrs. Dudgeon was quite wrong," said Dick.

They read the notice again. Well, they had done their best. They looked anxiously down the river. The *Margoletta* was not in sight. Tom had a chance yet.

UNDER THE ENEMY'S NOSE

IT is a long way to row or sail in a small boat from Horning to Wroxham, but it is not much more than a couple of miles by road. In about half an hour from the time he left them, Dick and Dorothea heard the shrill "Brrr . . . brrr" of Joe's bell as he came flying round the corner by the Swan, jammed his brakes on so that his wheels skidded on the gravel, and flung himself off beside them.

"Missed him," he panted. "By a lot. Tom'd been gone long before. Must be half-way down by now. Has that cruiser gone up?"

"Not yet," said Dorothea. . . . "Two or three others, small ones."

"Four," said Dick.

"And some sailing yachts. . . ."

"Three going up and four going down."

"And a boat full of reeds."

"And a wherry under power."

"Here she come now," said Joe, looking down the river.

With a big spirting bow wave, the noise of some huge orchestra turned on as loud as possible through the loud-speaker, and a wash that was tossing all the yachts and house-boats moored along the banks, the *Margoletta* was roaring up from the Ferry.

"Port said we were to think of a way to stop her," said Dorothea.

Joe, leaning on his bicycle, looked despairingly at the
Death and Glory, lying there against the staithe.

"Short of ramming her . . ." he said.

But they knew, all three of them, that there was nothing
to be done, even in the *Death and Glory*, against that powerful
monster that was making more noise than all the other boats
on the river. And anyhow, they had no time. The next moment
the *Teasel's* dinghy was lifted by the wash and flung violently
against the quay-heading, Joe had dropped his bicycle and
jumped to fend off the *Death and Glory*, and the *Margoletta* was
already swinging round the corner by the Swan. Long after
she had disappeared the three stood listening to the noise of
her. Somewhere up there were Port and Starboard racing
against time. Somewhere up there was Tom in the *Titmouse*
sailing down from Wroxham, knowing nothing of the danger
that was thundering to meet him.

＊

Port and Starboard had no need to talk. For years they had
rowed that boat together. Port rowed stroke and Starboard
bow, each with two oars. Port set a steady rate after the first
minute or two. She remembered that they might have to keep
it up for a long way. Starboard watched a crinkle between her
sister's shoulders, keeping time with her as if they were parts
of a single machine, only now and then glancing upstream
to see that all was clear. Anybody who saw them might have
thought they were rowing rather fast, but there was nothing to
show what a desperate hurry they were in. On and on they
rowed, past the notice that tells you to go slow through Horning, past the eelman's little houseboat, up the long reach to
the windmill and the houseboat moored beside it, on and on and
on. Cruisers came up astern and passed them, kindly slackening speed a little to spare them the worst of the wash. Sailing
yachts met them, sweeping down with a fair wind. And all

the time they were listening for the unmistakable roar of the *Margoletta*, and at every bend of the river Starboard looked upstream hoping each time to see the *Titmouse's* little, high-peaked sail. They passed the private broad with the house reflected in the water. They passed the entrance to Salhouse where, on any other day, they would have looked in to see the swan's nest and the crested grebe's. And then they heard it. No other boat on all the river would try to deafen everybody else with a loud-speaker. No other had an engine with that peculiar droning roar.

"Too late!" said Port.

"But here he is!" cried Starboard.

There, close ahead of them was the little *Titmouse*, sailing merrily down the middle of the river.

"Look out, Tom!" they shouted. "Look out! Hullabaloos! The *Margoletta*! They'll be here in two minutes. . . . And nowhere to hide!"

*

Tom, in the *Titmouse* was very much enjoying himself. He had seen the twins, when he stopped at Horning on the way up. Everything was settled and they were to join the *Teasel* early to-morrow morning and come for a two-day voyage. They would have to be home on the third day for the first of the championship races, but by that time, Tom thought, he and those two strangers ought to be able to manage the *Teasel*, with the Admiral to lend a hand if need be. He had made a fast passage of it, from Horning to Wroxham, by rowing wherever he had not got a fair wind. At Wroxham, the first man he had seen was the man whose business it was to look after the batteries in the boats belonging to the firm that owned the *Teasel*. Not a moment had been wasted, and while the man went off in a punt with the old battery, Tom had hurried to the enormous village store and worked through the Admiral's shopping list, and then ate the sandwiches his mother had given him for his dinner while sitting on the cabin roof of a business wherry, *Sir Garnet*, and talking to Jim Wooddall, her skipper. He had forgotten all about outlawry and Hulla-baloos. He was thinking of the voyage to the south, and Jim Wooddall was telling him how to make the passage through Yarmouth easy even for a little boat by waiting for dead low water before trying to go down through the bridges. Several times while they were talking, Jim Wooddall looked up at a notice that had been nailed that morning on the wall of the old granary where the wherry was lying. Tom never saw it, and Jim Wooddall said nothing about it, though he stepped ashore and read it again, after the man had come back with the new battery, and Tom had said "Good-bye" and was sailing away down Wroxham Reach. If Tom wasn't going to speak of it, Jim Wooddall wasn't. He could put two and two together as well as any man. He had heard of questions asked by that young Bill from Horning about the people in the *Margoletta*. He had just come back from a voyage to Potter Heigham, where another small boy had asked him if he had seen the *Margoletta* anywhere about. He read that notice again, and looked at the disappearing *Titmouse*. Well, of one thing Jim was certain, and that was that if Tom had had anything to do with it, the other people were probably to blame. Foreigners anyway and not pleasant folk. Jim had been in Wroxham when there was that trouble about the *Margoletta* keeping the people in the inns awake all night. And if they were not to blame? Well, Jim Wooddall was Norfolk too. "If a Norfolk boy done it," he said to himself, "those chaps can cover the place with paper before anybody give him away." He was not in the least surprised, some time later, when Joe came panting down to the riverside on a bicycle, and asked anxiously for Tom, to find, after Joe had hurried off again, that the notice had vanished from the wall.

By that time Tom was far down the river. He had used his

oars through the reaches most sheltered by the trees, had
slipped out into Wroxham Broad and found a grand wind
there, had slipped into the river again by the southern entry,
and was sailing merrily along, thinking only of his little ship,
when, suddenly, just as he was coming to a sharp bend in the
river, a rowing boat shot into sight, and he recognised Port and
Starboard, whom he had left at home in Horning, pulling at
their oars as if they were rowing in a race.

"Hullo!" he called.

The next moment they were both shouting at him. "Look
out! . . . Hullabaloos! . . . Here in two minutes. . . . Nowhere to hide! . . ." Whatever was the matter with them?
And then he heard it, too, the droning roar of an engine, and
some tremendous voice shouting a comic song along the quiet
river.

He knew now. He looked quickly up and down the river.
No. They were right. There was nowhere he could stow the
Titmouse. Too late. The noise was close upon them. And that
thing could move at such a pace.

"Turn round!" he shouted to the twins.

He leapt forward and loosed his halyard. Yard and sail
came toppling down.

"Quick! Catch my painter."

He coiled it and threw it aboard. Port made it fast in a
moment. Backing water and pulling, they had the rowing
boat heading downstream.

"Don't row fast," he said, unshipping his tiller and lugging
his rudder aboard. "Nearly forgot that," he said to himself.
"Slowly now. Not in a hurry. And don't look at them!"
He threw himself down and burrowed in under the untidy
sail. The next moment the big cruiser was round the bend,
bearing down on them, towering above them. . . . That man
with field-glasses, standing like a figurehead above her bows,
may or may not have been looking for a boy with a criminal,

HULLABALOOS!

sinister face who had gone up the river. On that reach there was nobody but two small girls, paddling slowly downstream, towing an empty sailing boat. It was amusing to see how violently the mast of the little empty boat swung from side to side, as the big cruiser roared past and left those two small girls splashing and tossing in its wash.

*

Time went slowly on at Horning.

Joe propped his bicycle against the fence, and spent the time putting new whippings on the ends of the *Death and Glory's* frayed ropes.

Dick was watching a pair of water-hens that kept going in and out of a dyke almost opposite the staithe. He could do no good to Tom, so why not watch water-hens?

Dorothea was seeing picture after picture of failure or success. In some the twins were in time to warn the outlaw, and all three of them hid somewhere in the reeds and watched the enemy go by. In others they were too late, and the Hullabaloos met Tom all unsuspecting and had him at their mercy. That was the worst of it. When things went well, it was the outlaw, the romantic figure of a tale, who escaped triumphantly; but when things went wrong it was just Tom himself who was captured, Tom, the skipper of the *Teasel* and the *Titmouse*, Tom, who was teaching them how to sail. And Tom's misfortunes were far harder to bear than those of any hero of a story. Dorothea was doing her best to think of what could be done, in a practical way, to save him.

"I reckon they got him," said Joe at last. "I'll be taking the old bike back to Bill's." They saw him go slowly off, wheeling the bicycle, without the heart to ride it, off the staithe and round the corner into the village street.

"If they've got him we'll have to get help," said Dorothea. "It's dragging in the natives, but I can't help it. We must do it. And Port and Starboard's father is a lawyer. Come on, Dick."

"Those water-hens have got a nest in there," said Dick, "in behind those boats. They must be jolly tame, with people passing all the time, and all that hammering in the boat-sheds."

Dorothea stared at him. She never could get accustomed to Dick's way of letting his mind get filled up by anything he was looking at, no matter what else might be going on.

"We've got to go and tell Mrs. Dudgeon about Tom," said Dorothea. . . . "Tom!" She almost shouted at him.

"It's the best thing to do," said Dick and then went quietly on. "He's sure to know about that nest, right in the village."

It was no good trying to change Dick, and Dorothea said no more. They got into the *Teasel*'s dinghy again, and pushed off from the staithe. Dick took both oars and rowed down past the village, while Dorothea tried to think how best to break the news to Mrs. Dudgeon. Mrs. Dudgeon had been so sure that all was well. Of course she had known nothing about those notices. And now she would have to be told. There was no way out of it. For Mrs. Dudgeon would have to be the one to tell the doctor and Mr. Farland. Those two would surely be able to do something for the captured Tom.

They rowed down the river as far as the doctor's house, with the golden bream still swimming so merrily over the gable, knowing nothing of the sorrow that was coming. But there was no one on the lawn. That made things more difficult. Dorothea did not like having to go to the door and ask. Supposing Mrs. Dudgeon was out, and the doctor, too, she hardly knew what she ought to do in the way of explaining what had happened to anybody else.

"She may be round at the back," she said. "Let's row into the dyke and look."

Dick was thinking about his rowing now, and made a pretty good job of turning in, though the stream carried him down quicker than he had expected. But, with a bit of a struggle, and a pull on a willow branch that was luckily hanging just handy, he worked the dinghy into the dyke. They had never been in there before, but had heard much about the Coot Club stronghold from Tom and the twins and the three small Coots.

They landed and tied up the dinghy. No one seemed to be about. There was the old *Dreadnought*, still rather muddy after her adventure as a submarine. There was the drawbridge. There was the shed where Tom carpentered and the Coot Club held their meetings. The door of the shed was open. There, hanging up, was the Bird Protection Society's map of the river. Dorothea held her breath. It was dreadful to see these things and to know that the outlaw, after all, had fallen into the hands of his enemies.

"If only we'd been a little quicker," she said.

"He's marked that water-hen's nest opposite the staithe," said Dick, looking at the map. "It's No. 27. I thought he'd be sure to know about it."

"I'll just have to go and ring the bell," said Dorothea.

They left the shed and went round the corner of the house towards the river. A pleasant voice called from above them.

"I'm coming down in a minute."

Dorothea looked gratefully up, and there was Mrs. Dudgeon at one of the upper windows. That was all right. No need to explain to a stranger. Mrs. Dudgeon was probably tucking up the baby, after taking him in from the garden. It was only four o'clock, but already not so warm as it had been. And now Mrs. Dudgeon was coming down. The moment had come when the bad news had to be broken to her.

"What shall I tell her?" said Dorothea desperately.

"Just tell her they've got him," said Dick. "She'll know what to do."

There were steps on the gravel path under the windows and

Mrs. Dudgeon came round the house. One look at Dorothea's face was enough to tell her that something was wrong.

"Did you want to see me about anything?" she asked kindly, glancing up at the open window above her. "We won't talk here. I want him to get a little sleep. Let's go and sit down by the river."

But they did not sit down.

Just as they came to the green garden seat, Dick called out, "Here they are!"

And there were Port and Starboard rowing down the river, towing the little *Titmouse* astern.

"Oh! Oh!" cried Mrs. Dudgeon. "What has happened to Tom?"

"They've got him," said Dorothea wretchedly. She was on the very edge of tears. "They've got him. We were too late. I knew we would be. And now they've got him. . . ." She saw Tom a prisoner, in chains probably, locked up, anyhow . . . bread and water . . . the captive outlaw . . . Tom!

But Mrs. Dudgeon was seeing something far worse. There was Tom's boat, a halyard flapping loose about the mast, Tom's boat, towed by the twins . . . towed. . . . But where was Tom? . . . Those dreadful squalls over the marshes. . . . Small boats do capsize so easily. . . . He could swim. . . . Water-weeds. . . . Cramp. . . . No one could ever be sure. . . . "Nell, Bess," she cried out to the rowers. "What is it? Where is he?"

And then Dick, Dorothea and Mrs. Dudgeon saw the loose bundle of sail move in the towed *Titmouse*. A hump rose in the canvas. The yard, one end of which was resting across the gunwale, lifted. Tom grinned at them from underneath it and then made a dreadful face that meant "Keep quiet!" The hump in the sail shrank down. The *Titmouse* looked as empty as before.

"Gee whizz!"

Dorothea turned in time to see a small boy leap joyfully high into the air and disappear round the corner of the house. Joe, too, had thought there was nothing to be done but to get help from the grown-up world. He had come, like Dorothea. to tell Mrs. Dudgeon what had happened. There was no need of that now, and Joe was gone like a flash.

Port and Starboard showed no sign of stopping. Port chuckled, but only for a moment. With grave, serious faces, they rowed steadily on down the river.

Mrs. Dudgeon had turned quite white, but now she laughed, partly at herself for ever having thought that something might be wrong.

"So that's all right," she said. "What was it you wanted to tell me?"

But, like Joe, Dick and Dorothea had now nothing to tell.

"It was just a mistake," said Dorothea. "We thought something had happened and it hasn't."

"So did I," said Mrs. Dudgeon, and laughed again.

She walked back to the dyke with them, and said she hoped they would have a good voyage in the *Teasel* up to Horsey Mere. She steadied the dinghy for them as they got in, and then gave them a good push off. A minute later they were out of the dyke and rowing downstream after the others.

Port and Starboard were rowing down towards the Ferry as if the whole day was before them and they had nothing to do. Dorothea, who felt it was her turn at the oars, had no difficulty in catching them up.

"What happened? What happened?" she asked.

"You'll hear about it later," said Starboard. "Don't look as if you were in a hurry. And don't look so excited."

"And don't keep looking at the *Titmouse*," said Port. "We're towing her down empty. Tom's idea. They may have left someone on the watch down here. And if they think he hasn't come back, then to-morrow, in the *Teasel*, he'll get clean away."

"Tom says we're to look as miserable as we can," said Starboard. "Look out. Better drop astern. Don't get mixed up with our oars."

It was a melancholy procession that passed the Ferry. First there was the Farland rowing boat, with Port and Starboard grimly rowing. Then, at the end of her painter came the *Titmouse*, all untidy, looking indeed as if she had lost her master and owner. And then came the *Teasel's* little dinghy, with Dick looking simply puzzled and Dorothea trying not to lift her oars too high out of the water and at the same time doing her best to remember to look as if she were going to a funeral.

A largish boy leaning on the white railing of the Ferry watched the procession with a good deal of pleasure.

"So they got him," he said. "Serve him right!" and then, almost as if he knew that he had let slip rather more than he meant, turned away and walked off with his hands in his pockets, not looking back.

"Now what did he know about it?" said Starboard.

"That's the boy who was talking to the Hullabaloos when they stopped here," said Dorothea.

"That's George Owdon," said Port.

"He must have told them himself that Tom had gone up the river."

"I wonder if they gave him the reward," said Dorothea.

"They'll want it back if they did," said Port.

Round the bend below the Ferry Inn, out of sight from any of the houses, the twins stopped rowing. Tom bobbed up again in the *Titmouse* and leaned over her stern to hang her rudder on its pintles. He shipped the tiller, and hoisted the sail. The *Titmouse* was herself again. The twins threw him his painter aboard, and turned their boat round.

"But aren't you coming to the *Teasel*?" asked Dorothea.

"Can't," said Starboard. "Tom'll tell you all about it."

"We've got to get home now. The A.P.'ll be back any

minute and wondering whether we've forgotten. There's that party on and we've got to get into pretties and pour out for everybody. 'Two lumps or one?' You know. . . . We'll be early in the morning. Jolly lucky you people had learnt to row. Nothing could have saved him if you hadn't done what you did, or if you'd been one minute later. They'd have been right on the top of him before he could do anything. Specially if that beast George had told them what to look for. . . ."

"Hop in," said Tom suddenly. "You'll have done about enough rowing for to-day. It's a fair wind and we'll tow that dinghy easily."

Almost before Port and Starboard were out of sight, Tom had his passengers aboard, *Titmouse* was sailing, and the dinghy, only a couple of feet shorter than *Titmouse*, was towing astern.

"Of course, the dinghy does rather take her speed off," said Tom. "You really want a bigger boat if you're going to tow a dinghy. You'll see to-morrow, when we get sail on the *Teasel* . . . she'll tow *Titmouse* herself like nothing at all. . . ." He stopped suddenly with a sort of groan, and went on, " If that beast has told them to look for *Titmouse*, it's no good my coming at all. I'll just have to stay hid in the dyke at home till they've gone . . . or till the end of the holidays."

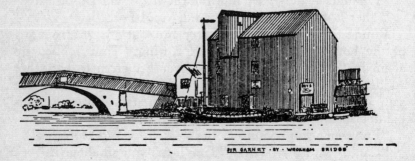

SIR GARNET · BY · WROXHAM BRIDGE

CHAPTER XIII

THE *TITMOUSE* DISGUISED

THE new battery was in its place and Dick had spent happy minutes carefully connecting up the wires. It was almost dazzling to look into the cabin of the *Teasel*. Nobody would have guessed that under those bright and cheerful lamps there was talk of giving up the voyage to the south altogether.

"It's like this," said Tom. "That beast George must have told the Hullabaloos to look for me in the *Titmouse* or he would never have been so sure they'd got me when he saw the twins towing her down the river. It's no good my coming with you. The only thing to do is to slip home and stay hid in the dyke."

"But if you don't come how can the Admiral get to Beccles?" said Dorothea, who thought of the voyage to the south as if its sole object was to take Mrs. Barrable back to her childhood's home.

"The twins," began Tom.

"They can't get away for long enough," said Dorothea.

"And where is Dick to sleep to-morrow night?" said the Admiral. "There's only room for four in the *Teasel*. We'll even have to give up the voyage to Horsey."

"I'll lend you *Titmouse* for that," said Tom. "It won't matter so long as I'm not in her . . . and I shan't be able to use her anyhow."

"Rubbish," said the Admiral. "Why, in another ten days you'll be back at school and not able to sail at all. Now listen to me. First of all, you've promised to skipper the *Teasel*. . . ."

"But the moment they see the *Titmouse*. . . ."

"Listen. Have those people ever seen the *Titmouse* . . . really seen her, so as to know her again? No. What can your George Owdon (horrid name) have told them about her? . . . a small sailing boat called *Titmouse*. But supposing she doesn't exist. . . . Supposing there *is* no *Titmouse* on the river. . . ."

Tom's eye lit up.

"Paint her name out?" he said.

"Disguise?" said Dorothea. "Oh, why not? It'd be simply lovely. Just the thing for an outlaw to do. Mr. Toad got out of prison disguised as a washerwoman. . . ."

"We can't disguise the *Titmouse* as anything but a sailing dinghy," said the Admiral. "But we don't want to."

"The trouble is," said Tom, "there aren't such an awful lot of white dinghies."

"Those people won't be as well up in dinghies as you are," said the Admiral. "They'll look for the *Titmouse*, and if they can't find her name they'll go on looking. I've got plenty of white paint just to cover those black letters. And a little turpentine'll take it off again without making a mess of your boat."

"There's something else we can do," said Tom, jumping up. "Make her look altogether different. The twins won't have gone to bed yet. Botheration! The awning's up in *Titmouse*. May I borrow the *Teasel's* dinghy? There's just time to telephone from Ranworth. I want to tell the twins to bring a bit of rope." A minute later he was rowing away in the dark.

*

Breakfast was over. Washing up was done. The *Teasel*, stripped of her awning, was ready to sail. But William, of all her crew, was the only one aboard. Dick and Dorothea were in the bows of the *Titmouse* cocking her stern up out of the water.

Admiral Barrable was kneeling in the stern of the *Teasel's* dinghy, with her palette on one hand and a paint brush in the other. Tom was in the dinghy with her, holding it as steady as he could. The black E of "Titmouse" was vanishing under fresh white paint, as the *Death and Glory*, with the twins at the oars, Joe in the bows and Bill and Pete in the stern, came out from among the trees.

"Got that rope?" shouted Tom.

"We got him," shouted Joe.

"Whatever do you want it for?" asked Starboard, and at that moment everybody in the *Death and Glory* saw what had happened to the name on the *Titmouse's* transom.

"Gee whizz!" said Joe. "If that don't puzzle 'em."

"You won't know her when we've done with her," said Tom. "Just wait till we've got that rope rigged all round her for a fender."

"Well, Joe," said Mrs. Barrable. "What about that watcher of yours at Acle? He doesn't seem to have been of much use yesterday."

The twins laughed.

"Him?" said Joe indignantly. "I been down to Acle last night. Bill's bike. That Robin never see 'em go through the bridge. And for why? You know that fourpence I leave him for the telephone. His mam keep him in bed with a stomach-ache. You wouldn' think a chap *could* get a stomach-ache for fourpence. But he done it. He go and buy a lot of dud bananas cheap and eat the lot."

"Disgraceful," said the Admiral.

"I'll stomach-ache him when I get him," said Joe.

In a very few minutes the rope had been fixed all round the *Titmouse*, outside, tied to the rings that had been screwed in there for lacing down the awning. The rope was an old warp that Tom had saved when one of the wherrymen was thinking of throwing it away. It was very thick and dark with age, and when it was fastened on, it made the *Titmouse*, with her mast stowed, look like a rather neglected yacht's dinghy. Only those who knew her well could have recognised Tom's smart little sailing boat.

"Poor old *Titmouse*," said Tom, as he made her painter fast on the *Teasel's* counter.

Already the twins were aboard the *Teasel* stowing their dunnage in the little fore-cabin. Dick's blankets had been made into a tight roll and packed into one of the *Titmouse's* new lockers. The *Teasel's* own dinghy had been taken in tow by the *Death and Glory*, to be laid up in the Coot Club dyke until the cruise was over. Joe and Bill were resting on their oars waiting to see the start.

"Look here," said Starboard, coming out into the well. "If you two want to learn quick you'd better start by being apprentices. Come on, Dick. You're with me, and Port'll have Dorothea."

"Come along to the foredeck, Dot," said Port. "We stand by with the peak halyard."

"I've got the stern anchor aboard," said Tom.

Dick and Dorothea did what they were told, and pulled and stopped pulling at the right moment. Up went the *Teasel's* sails, and the apprentices and their instructors coiled down the halyards, and tidied the foredeck.

"I'll just go ashore and get the bow anchor," said Tom, when all was ready for the start.

"You must let the crew do that," said Starboard. "If they make a mistake and don't hop aboard in time, you can always come back for them, but what'll happen if you slip or something, and the *Teasel* goes sailing away with Dick and Dorothea?"

"She's quite right," said the Admiral.

"Your job, Dick," said Starboard.

Dick, in sea-boots, jumped ashore and pulled up the anchor.

PAINTING OUT HER NAME

"That's right," said Starboard. "Coil the warp. Pull her along. Push her out. Jump! . . ."

"She's sailing," cried Dorothea.

Dick, kneeling on the foredeck, was hooking the fluke of the rond-anchor through a ring-bolt. The bushes on the bank were slipping away. Tom, hauling in the main-sheet, headed out into the Broad, went about and brought her racing back for the Straits with the water singing under her bows. In the *Death and Glory* they were hauling up their own old sail as the *Teasel* flew by.

"You're in charge while we're away," Tom called out.

"Back the day after to-morrow," shouted Starboard.

"Right O," Joe called back to them.

"We shan't see Ranworth again," said the Admiral, and Dick and Dorothea looked for the last time at the little Broad where the lurking outlaw had given them their first sailing lessons. In another moment the *Teasel* was slipping along on an even keel in the shelter of the trees. Then she was clear of the Straits and foaming down the narrow dyke. The dyke had seemed long when they were quanting and towing through it in a calm. It seemed very short to-day, as they swept through it, and turned into the wind to beat down the river.

"She isn't much like a houseboat now," said Dorothea exultantly some minutes later, as the *Teasel* swung round close by her old moorings.

"She can jolly well sail," said Starboard.

"Can she no'?" said Port.

"I wish Brother Richard could see her," said the Admiral.

They had a splendid sail to Potter Heigham. Tom and the twins, though they had often sailed with Mr. Farland, had never before been in sole charge of anything quite so big. But she was an easy boat to handle, and presently even the apprentices were allowed to take the tiller in turn, each with an older hand standing by in case of need. Those days in Ranworth had been very useful. There was no need to explain why the *Teasel* had to go first one way and then the other when the wind was against her. The apprentices knew all about watching the flag to see what the wind was doing. Sailing in the *Titmouse* had taught them a lot.

The chief trouble with the apprentices was that with every bend of the river, winding this way and that between reed-beds and wide, drained marshes, there was something new to be seen. But even that had its good side. With everything being new to the apprentices, Tom and the twins, who knew the river by heart, felt almost as if they, too, were seeing it for the first time.

"Hullo," said Dick, as they came to the mouth of the Ant. "There's a signpost. Just as if the rivers were roads."

"Best kind of roads," said Port.

Dorothea was having her first turn at the tiller when they passed the ancient ruins of St. Benet's Abbey, with the ruin of a windmill in the middle of them. The Admiral explained what those bits of old wall and broken grey stone arch had been, and Dorothea, even with the tiller in her hands, slipped headlong into a story. "If only it was still an abbey . . . the outlaw would come panting to the threshold and ask for sanctuary, and the Hullabaloos couldn't do a thing. . . . Sorry, I really didn't mean to let the sail flap. . . ."

The outlaw looked back at the rather large and shabby-looking dinghy towing astern.

"Nobody'd ever know her, poor dear," said Starboard.

"And with three skippers aboard," said the Admiral, "what does it matter if one of them has to hide in the cabin while a motor-boat goes by?"

"We've done them this time, I do believe," said Port. "Even that beast George can't give away what he doesn't know. He'll never think of Tom being aboard the *Teasel*."

And so, rejoicing in their freedom, the outlaw and his

friends sailed on their way, through a country as flat as Holland, past huge old windmills, their sails creaking round, pumping the water from the low-lying meadows on which the cows were grazing actually below the level of the river. Far away over the meadows other sails were moving on Ant and Thurne, white sails of yachts and big black sails of trading wherries. Now and then they met other yachts, running up the river with the wind. Two or three times they met or were passed by motor-cruisers, but not one of them even for a moment made a noise like the *Margoletta's*.

Dick was steering when they came to the mouth of the Thurne.

"Three roads meeting," said Dorothea. "There's another signpost."

"Do what it says," said Starboard. ""To Potter Heigham.' Bring her round. The other way's where you'll be going when you start for the south. 'To Acle and Yarmouth.' Don't we wish we were coming."

"I wish you were," said Tom.

"We all wish you were," said the Admiral.

"But we just can't," said Port. "Anyway, this is gorgeous while it lasts. You must let my apprentice have a go again after we pass Womack Dyke. Just to feel what it's like with the wind free. . . ."

"But it's the beginning of a town," said Dorothea half an hour later, as they came into a long water street of bungalows, built on the banks that have been made by dredging the mud from the river. The little wooden houses took the wind from the *Teasel's* sails and made things difficult. One moment a dead calm, and then, a good wind slipping through the gap between one house and the next.

They came at last to the boatyards of Potter Heigham, and the staithe and the lovely old bridge built four hundred years ago and maybe more.

"We'll never get through it, will we?" said Dick, who was again at the tiller, "even with the mast right down?"

"You wait and see," said Starboard. "Where'll you have her, Tom?"

"Plenty of room close to the bridge," said Tom, who was on the foredeck taking in the jib. "And not so far to tow. Look here. You bring her in. Not Dick. Not just yet. . . ."

Starboard took the tiller, sailed right up to the bridge, and then turned sharply into the wind. With slack sheet and gently flapping mainsail the *Teasel* came up to the staithe. Tom jumped ashore. A moment later, Port and Starboard were taking their apprentices step by step through all the business of lowering the sail, and then the mast.

"Better pretend they've got to do everything themselves," said Starboard. "We'll see nothing goes wrong. Go on, Tom. You go aft to see it comes down all right. Clear away that hatch cover. Now then, Twin, make your apprentice pay out the forestay tackle. Mine'll look after the heel-rope. Are you ready? Let her come. . . ."

Tom, in the stern, gave a gentle pull on the topping lift, and the mast, balanced by the heavy lead weight at the foot of it, came slowly down, while its foot rose slowly up through the forehatch. The mast came down so easily that Dick and Dorothea, though they themselves had paid out the ropes, could hardly believe that they had had anything to do with it.

"Well, who did it, if you didn't?" said Starboard. "All ready for towing now."

"But we're going to land, aren't we?" said Dorothea. What was the good of a voyage if you did not land in the ports you visited?

"Come along, you two, and William," said the Admiral, "We can join them above the bridges."

Both apprentices looked at Tom. They wanted to go ashore, but, at the same time, they wanted to be aboard when the *Teasel* went through that narrow arch.

"She can do with a mop round," said Tom. "We'll wait to tow through till you come back."

*

There was not really much to see at Potter Heigham, and all the serious shopping had been done by Tom at Wroxham the day before. But they had come there by water, under sail, in the *Teasel*, and that made all the difference. They went to the Bridge Stores and bought picture post cards of the old bridge, and the ancient thatched hut beside it, and one of a boat like the *Teasel* actually towing through under the low archway. "This is our first port of call," wrote Dorothea on the card she sent to her mother, "like Malta was when you and father went to Egypt." Mrs. Barrable bought a few buns, and some bottles of lemonade, "to encourage foreign trade," as she said, and they were already on their way back to their ship when, just outside the Bridge Stores, they saw an automatic weighing machine which offered, for one penny, to tell anybody his weight and fortune.

"How can it tell fortunes?" said Dick.

"You stand on the platform," said the Admiral, "and we'll let it try."

"Won't you, too?" said Dorothea, after she and Dick had both been weighed, and little cards had slipped out of a slot in the machine, showing their weight in stones and pounds and telling them that Dick was "Prudent" and Dorothea "Of a Cheerful Disposition," and that Dick "would Amass Great Wealth," and that Dorothea "would Never be Without a Friend."

"Too old for fortunes," said the Admiral, "and I'd rather not know my weight. Now William . . ."

"Oh, *do* let's weigh him. Catch him, Dick. Come on, William. Be good. Sit still."

William rather liked sitting on a platform while everybody looked at him, and the Admiral put in a penny on his behalf.

There was a whirring of wheels inside the machine.

"Here comes his card." Dick took it from the slot. On one

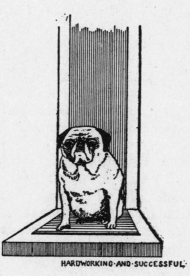

HARDWORKING·AND·SUCCESSFUL·

side of it was printed, "You Weigh 1 st. 3 lbs.," and on the other, "You are a Hard Worker and Should Become Successful."

"Well done, William," said Dorothea.

"But he never does any work at all," said Dick.

"Perhaps he's going to, some day," said Mrs. Barrable, and she gave William a chocolate.

"You see," said Dorothea. "He's being successful already."

"Come along now," said the Admiral, "or those three skippers will be thinking their crew have run away."

"Let's make Tom and the twins get their fortunes told, too," said Dorothea, as they turned back towards the bridge. "Tom's ought to be a beauty now that the Hullabaloos are looking for a *Titmouse* and there is no *Titmouse*, and not even that horrible George knows anything about the *Teasel*."

"Tom's fortune will depend on how many shackles and scout knives he has in his pockets," said the Admiral. "What's the matter, Dot?"

As usual, two or three people were looking down from the top of the bridge watching the boats at the staithe. Among them was a biggish boy, leaning on a bicycle. He was keeping a little way back from the wall of the bridge, as if he wanted to see without being seen. Just as Dorothea noticed him, he turned away with a smile on his face, jumped on his bicycle and rode off.

"Dick," cried Dorothea. "Dick, did you see him?"

"See what?" said Dick.

"George Owdon himself. That boy. There. On the bicycle. The one we saw talking to the Hullabaloos at Horning . . . the one who said 'Serve him right' when the twins were towing the *Titmouse* past the ferry. . . ."

But the boy was already riding away along the road, and Dick could not be sure.

"He'll have seen Tom with the *Teasel*, and he'll go and tell the Hullabaloos where to look for her," said Dorothea. "Just when everything was going all right."

"He may not have seen Tom at all," said the Admiral.

But, as they themselves came to the bridge and looked down, there was the *Teasel* with her mast lowered, all ready to go through, and there were the twins sitting on the cabin roof, and there was Tom himself in full view, never thinking of who might be watching, busy with a long-handled mop cleaning a splash of mud off her top-sides.

"He'll have gone to tell the Hullabaloos already," said

Dorothea, looking up the road, where the bicycling boy was already disappearing in the distance.

"But you've only seen him once," said Starboard, when Dorothea came running down on the staithe with the dreadful news.

"Twice," said Dorothea. "This is the third time."

"George Owdon *has* got a bicycle," said Port.

"Even if he saw you he can't tell them much," said the Admiral.

"And he's got to find them first," said Starboard.

"And perhaps it wasn't him," said Port. "Lots of other boys have bicycles."

"Let's get out of sight of that bridge," said Tom.

*

Tom in the *Titmouse* towed. Starboard steered, standing on the counter. The others sat on the cabin roof, ready to use their hands to fend off when under the arch.

"She'll touch," cried Dorothea.

"She won't," said Starboard.

"Do keep all your heads down " said the Admiral.

"Wough! Wough!" said the hard-working and successful William, and the *Teasel* slipped through exactly under the middle of the arch, with just about a foot to spare.

"I can steer now," said Dick, as they came out on the other side, and he saw the railway bridge ahead of them, crossing the river with a single span.

"All right," said Starboard. "Better learn. Don't look at anything except the *Titmouse*. Keep the *Teasel* pointing at her all the time."

Above the railway bridge they stopped only to raise the mast and set the sails. Tom would not wait for lunch.

"Let's get away from this place," he said. "Can't we have it on the way?"

They sailed on. The sun still shone, and the wind blew, the very best of winds for working through the long dyke into Horsey Mere. But, for Tom, life had somehow gone out of the day. If George Owdon had seen him with the *Teasel*, and told the Hullabaloos, the worst might happen almost any time. Who could tell where those beasts were or how fast they could get about? Lemonade and cheese sandwiches and Potter Heigham buns did not cheer him.

But, of the others, Dorothea alone was sure she had seen George Owdon by the bridge. They grew more and more cheerful as they left the bungalows astern, and turned through the narrow Kendal Dyke into a lovely wilderness of reeds and water, sailed from one to another of the posts that mark the channel, came to a signpost standing not on land but out in the middle of the Sounds, read "To Horsey" on one side of it, reached away through Meadow Dyke, so narrow that they could easily have jumped ashore, and came at last into the open Mere.

This way and that they sailed about the Mere, and, at last, followed another sailing yacht into the little winding dyke, with a windmill at the end of it, just as the map had showed. Here they tied up the *Teasel* and made her ready for the night. Then, while the Admiral settled down to paint a picture, the others crowded into *Titmouse*, and went off to row round the reed-beds and see how many new birds they could find for Dick to put down in his notebook. Dick covered two pages with "Birds seen at Horsey," and began a third. Close by the entrance to Meadow Dyke they found him his first reed pheasants, and, at dusk, as they were rowing back to the *Teasel* he saw his first bittern, unless Tom was mistaken when he pointed it out, just dipping into the shadowy reeds.

After a latish supper Tom and Dick went off to the *Titmouse*, to sleep one each side of the centre-board. The others settled down in the *Teasel*.

"You comfortable?" said Tom when lights were out.

"Very," said Dick.

"Bet you aren't," said Tom. "It's just that one bone that's always a bother. Work round till that one's comfortable and you'll find nothing else matters."

But for a long time after lights were out, people were awake in both boats, listening to at least three bitterns booming at each other, and the chattering of the warblers in the reed-beds, the startling honks of the coots, and the plops of diving water-rats.

It was very late when the Admiral, listening to the steady breathing of the twins in the fore-cabin, leant across to Dorothea. "Why are you not asleep?" she whispered.

"Supposing that boy was George Owdon," whispered Dorothea. "Supposing the Hullabaloos came and found us."

"It's all right, Dot. You needn't worry. An Admiral's boat is her castle, and they'd have to sink us before we'd give him up."

CHAPTER XIV

NEIGHBOURS AT POTTER HEIGHAM

A NIGHT's sleep seemed to have sponged the Hullabaloos from everybody's mind. Even Dorothea was thinking less of the dangers threatening the outlaw than of the coming voyage of the exiled Admiral home to her native Beccles. To-day and to-morrow with the twins to help, and then she and Dick would have to take their places. The *Teasel* that morning was training ship and nothing else. Sails were set and furled three times over, just for practice. And then, hour after hour, the *Teasel* flew to and fro on Horsey Mere, beating, running, reaching, jibing, one thing after another, with the apprentices taking turns at tiller and mainsheet, each with a lecturing skipper.

Everything went extremely well, and when they tied up in the mouth of Meadow Dyke for their mid-day meal, the Admiral left Dorothea in charge of the cooking, and settled down in the cabin to write a rather boastful letter to her brother.

"Yes," she wrote. "You may well look at the postmark. Too late to stop us. I am leaving this to be posted after we have left for the horrors of Yarmouth. So the best you can do is to wish us a good voyage. The doctor's son is an excellent skipper, and if you could see the hard work that is being done in turning my visitors into tarry seamen, you would know you had nothing to worry about." Here was a picture of her brother the painter frantically tearing his hair. "The whole lot of them are far better sailors than you and I were when we were young." Here was a picture of a small girl with frilled drawers showing beneath her longish petticoats, and a small boy with a very wide-brimmed sailor hat. "And if you could only see the three young pirates who hover round and make themselves useful, you would know why I wish the *Teasel* were a little bigger. Too big for children to handle, you say? Brother Richard, I wish she were twice the size."

"Look here," said Starboard when the washing up was over. "This wind is just right for getting through Meadow Dyke, and fine for the Thurne. We'll only have to quant through Kendal Dyke. What about pushing on now, and sailing down to Thurne Mouth so as to be safe for getting home to-morrow?"

"We ought to get home to-morrow before the A.P. comes back from Norwich," said Port. "There may be lots of things to do getting ready for next day's race. It would be awful if we got stuck with a calm and couldn't get back to Horning at all."

"And we'd better be giving the apprentices some practice in 'the rule of the road.' We can do that much better in the river."

"Let's just get one more bird for the list," said Dick.

"No time for birds to-day," said Starboard. "But we'll take one more turn across the Mere if that'll do."

They swept across the Mere to the far reed-beds, turned and were half-way back when, almost in a shout, Dick cried, "There's our one more bird. Look! It's a hawk. Yellow head . . ."

"Marsh Harrier," said Tom. "Jolly rare."

"There's another," said Dick. "Two of them."

One bird was high above the reeds. The other, the larger one, was rising towards it. Dick tried to see them with the glasses. "Better without," he said. "They're moving too quick. Not like stars. What's that top one got in its claws?" The two birds were flying one above another and no longer so far apart. Suddenly the first hawk dropped or threw from it the small bird it was carrying. The other turned almost on its back in the air and caught the quarry as it fell.

"Oh, well held, sir," said Tom, as he would have said on seeing a good pass at a football match.

"Why not 'madam'?" said the Admiral.

"It ought to be 'madam,'" said Port. "It's the cock bird feeding his Missis."

"She's a jolly good catch," said Tom.

"My goodness, Dick," said Starboard. "It's a good thing you weren't steering when you saw that."

But Dick did not hear her. He was already busy with his notebook.

They sailed away now, straight through the long narrow dyke and back through Heigham Sounds. Here the wind headed them. The Sounds grew narrower and narrower. Port took the tiller from her apprentice, who was glad to give it up in this place where the *Teasel* had hardly left one side of the channel before she was already at the other.

"We can't tack through here," said Tom. "We'll have to quant."

"Do let me," said Dick. He was still glowing from the excitement of seeing those hawks, but he had been wanting to quant ever since that day when he had seen Tom doing it while the *Death and Glory* was towing the *Teasel* into Ranworth Broad.

"Do you think he can?" asked Tom.

"Current's with us, what there is of it," said Starboard. "He's only got to keep her moving. It's a good chance to learn. Come on, Dick. I'll give her a shove or two and then you be ready. Hi, you people, get the main-sheet hard in. We don't want the boom swinging about."

Twice Starboard, standing by the shrouds, held the long quant upright, let it slip through her hands until it found the bottom, and then leaning on it walked aft along the side-deck, freed the quant from the mud with a sharp twist and jerk, and ran forward again.

"Now then," she said. "Ready to take it?"

The quant was in Dick's hands, and Starboard was out of the way, behind him, on the foredeck.

"That's right. Look out for fouling the shrouds. Let it go down."

Funny, thought Dick. No chance of being able to lean on the end of it. The thing was nearly upright.

"Better next time."

"Keep her moving," said Tom.

Dick galloped unsteadily forward along the narrow deck. More of a slant. That would do it. Down went the quant. There was the mud. Now push. Push. He walked aft, pushing with all his force. The next time was easier, and the next.

"She's moving beautifully now," Dorothea encouraged him, as he came aft a fourth time, leaning on the quant in the most professional manner.

The longer the push the better she moved, thought Dick. He walked to the very end of the counter and turned to hurry forward again. But what was this? The quant would not stir. He pulled. The *Teasel*, still moving beautifully, was leaving the quant behind. Dick hung on, pulling desperately. The counter was going away from under him.

"Grab him!" cried Tom, but it was too late.

For one moment, Dick hung between the quant and the departing *Teasel*. The next he was struggling in the water.

"Dick!" cried Dorothea, and the Admiral, hearing the splash, came hurrying out of the cabin.

Tom was already casting off the *Titmouse*.

"Don't try to turn the *Teasel*," he shouted. "Not room."

Bother those rowlocks. What a time it seemed to take to get them into their seatings. But it was only a second or two really before Tom was backing the *Titmouse* towards Dick who had, too late, let go of the quant, and was trying to swim and at the same time to do something with his spectacles.

"They got off one ear," he spluttered. "Lucky I didn't lose them. I got my cap all right. I say, I'm awfully sorry. I don't know how it got so stuck. Pouf. Pouf." He spluttered out a lot of water, and grabbed hold of the *Titmouse's* stern.

"You all right?" asked Tom.

"Yes," said Dick.

"Well, don't waste time trying to come aboard. We've got to have that quant."

The quant was loose enough now, and Tom freed it with a single tug, while Dick, blinking through his wet spectacles, trod water and held on by the transom.

"Quant's too long," said Tom. "We'll have to tow it. Can you just hang on with one hand and hang on to the quant with the other, till we can let them have it again? They'll be in a mess if we can't let them have it quick."

The quant was back aboard the *Teasel* before the apprentice who had lost it. They were very glad to have it, for already the *Teasel*, helpless in the narrow channel, had drifted against the reeds and was held there between wind and current. The twins, Port at the tiller, and Starboard with the quant, had her going again before Dick had scrambled in over *Titmouse's* stern. A moment later he was kneeling, dripping on the *Teasel* counter. He was astonished to find that everybody was very pleased with him.

"Well done, Dick!" said Starboard.

"Jolly good bit of work," said Port.

"But I tumbled in," said Dick.

"Everybody does that some time or other," said Tom, making fast the *Titmouse's* painter. "But you'll make a sailor all right."

And then the Admiral, who had watched the rescue without

DICK OVERBOARD

a single word, let go Dorothea's hand, remembered Dick's mother, and made him take off his wet things.

"Well," she said. "It's a good thing you're not drowned, but I really don't know how we're going to get you dry."

"That's easy," said Port. "The boat-yards at Potter have got a hot room for airing mattresses and things. The people there'll dry them for us. They'll do it in no time."

"I've got a spare pair of bags," said Dick.

"I can lend him a jersey," said Tom.

"Oh," said Dick. . . . "How awful. I've got my notebook wet, the outside of it . . . and some of the inside, too."

"But you ought to be pleased," said Dorothea. "Think of explorers swimming tropical rivers. This notebook'll be the best you've ever had."

"I bet Kendal Dyke wasn't very tropical to-day," said Tom with a grin.

"Do the best you can, Dick," said the Admiral.

Dorothea was already in the cabin, digging out a vest and drawers for him. "You can wear your pyjamas over the top," she said, "just till your things are dried."

They got through the dyke, Dick himself, in flannel shorts and a pyjama jacket over a jersey much too big for him, quanting the last few yards after Starboard had shown him the twist and jerk that frees a quant from all but the most obstinate mud. Once in the river they could sail again. They swept down to Potter Heigham, lowered the mast, quanted through the bridges and tied up.

"We'll have to wait till those things are dry," said the Admiral. "We can't dry them in the *Teasel*, and it's no good starting on a voyage with wet clothes."

"We're all right now," said Starboard. "If there's any wind at all we can get from Potter to Wroxham to-morrow, and if there's a calm we can take a bus. It's not like being miles away from anywhere like we were at Horsey."

The people at the boat-yards told the Admiral it was not the first time they had had clothes to dry for a quanter who had been pulled in by his quant. They said a few hours would do the trick, and if she would wait till evening, she could have them back as dry as a bone. So, thanks to Dick, the *Teasel* and the *Titmouse* settled down to spend the night at Potter Heigham.

The Admiral painted a picture of the old bridge. The others took William for a walk, and, on their way back met a "Stop me and Buy one" ice-cream boy on his tricycle. They stopped him and bought seven, of which one was wasted because it was strawberry and William decided that he did not care for any but vanilla. The Admiral wanted to take them to have a hot meal at the inn, but the twins were longing to play with the Primuses and they and Dorothea had an orgy of cooking instead . . . steak and kidney pies, suet and ginger puddings, green peas, and mushroom soup, all out of tins but none the worse for that, and beautifully hotted up.

But they were not allowed to forget the Hullabaloos altogether. Tom and Dorothea, as soon as they had tied up, had looked to see if George Owdon was among the idlers by the bridge. He was not, but, as time went on, they noticed that, though other people came and went, a small, tow-haired, scrubby little boy seemed unable to tear himself away.

The funny thing was that he seemed to take no interest in sailing yachts. But every time a cruiser came to the staithe the small boy left the bridge and came strolling along the bank, whistling and looking in all directions except at the cruiser, until he was near enough to be able to read her name.

"I wonder if that's Bill's friend," said Dorothea. "He said he had one here, watching, and that boy was here yesterday when we went through."

"Soon find out," said Starboard. "Hallo, you. Looking for someone?"

"Only for a cruiser. . . . Leastways not exactly. . . ."

"*Margoletta?*"

The small boy goggled at her.

"You lookin' for her, too? Don't say as I tell ye," he whispered.

"That's all right," said Starboard. "Your friend's name is Bill."

The small boy came a little nearer and pulled one hand from his breeches pocket. Looking about him to see that no one was watching, he opened his fingers, and showed a folded bit of grubby paper in which could be seen the shape of something flat and round.

"Telephone money," he whispered darkly. "You got it too?" but sauntered off without waiting for an answer. Another cruiser was coming up, and they saw that as if by accident the small boy was in the right place to meet her and ready to lend a hand with her warps. A minute or two later he was on his way back to the bridge.

"That's not her neither," he said, as he passed close by the *Teasel*.

"A much better sentinel than Joe's stomach-ache boy down at Acle," said the Admiral.

Not until dusk did the small boy leave his post.

"She won't come now," he said, as he passed them, pretending to look the other way, and presently disappeared behind the first of the bungalows, along the bank of the river.

"Well," said the Admiral, "that's all right. Nothing to worry about until to-morrow. Here's the man with Dick's clothes. Very nice of him to take the trouble of getting them out for us so late. And now, to bed, everybody. Poor old William's snoring already."

*

It was perhaps an hour and a half after that, or even more, when Tom, in the bottom of the *Titmouse*, snug in his sleeping-bag, first heard the distant throbbing of a motor-boat.

It was quite dark, long after the time at which all hired cruisers are supposed to be moored for the night. For a moment, Tom thought that worry about the *Margoletta* had made him dream of her. But there it was, a steady, thrumming noise, and it seemed to be coming nearer. Yes. There was no doubt about it. A motor-cruiser was coming up the river. Tom lay listening.

"Tom!"

That was Dick's voice, very low, from the other side of the centre-board case.

"Yes."

"Do you hear anything?"

"Yes."

The noise was coming nearer and nearer.

Dick whispered, "Is it them?"

"It's the noise they make." Nobody could mistake that loud rhythmic thrumming.

"No wireless this time."

"They oughtn't to be moving after dark, anyway. That's why they aren't using it. Unless . . ."

"What?"

"Perhaps they want people to think it isn't them."

"What can we do?"

"Don't talk."

The noise came nearer and nearer, and suddenly lessened. An engine had been throttled down. Whatever it was, it did not want to rouse all Potter Heigham in the dark. Tom and Dick lay, silent. The awning above their heads paled for a moment as the beam of a searchlight swept across it. Tom held his breath. If they had spotted him that light would come again. It did not. Yet he could hear the cruiser close at hand. The noise of the engine changed again. Stopping. Reversing. Swinging round. Waves from the wash lifted the little *Titmouse* and slapped up under the counter of the *Teasel*.

Were any of the others awake? At any moment William might start telling those people they had no right to be about. The cruiser was going ahead again. No. Again they heard her put into reverse. There was a bump against the wooden quay-heading. Someone landed heavily on the grass. Orders were being given in a low voice.

For a long time Tom and Dick listened. If it was indeed the Hullabaloos, they had tied up somewhere very near them. There was a faint murmur of talk, but not louder than might have come from any other boat. There was not a sound from the *Teasel*. The Admiral, the twins, Dorothea and William were all tired out and solidly asleep.

Time went on and on. The murmur ceased. There was no noise at all but the gentle tap tap of a rope against the *Teasel's* mast, and the quiet lapping of the water against the quays on the other side of the river. The inn had closed long before and it had been an hour at least since the last motor car had crossed the bridge.

A breath of cold air touched Dick's face. He woke suddenly to find that Tom was no longer lying beside him, but had got up and turned back a flap of the awning.

"Tom."

"Keep quiet."

"What are you doing?"

"Going to see if it's them or not."

Dick felt the *Titmouse* sway as Tom leaned out and took hold of the wooden piling along the edge of the staithe. He felt her lurch as Tom scrambled silently ashore. He fumbled for his spectacles, found them, and put them on. There wasn't much go left in that torch of his, but it might come in useful. He wriggled himself out from under the thwart. Whatever happened he must make no noise. Ouch! That was his hand between the *Titmouse* and the quay. Everything was pitch black out there. He scraped a shin on the gunwale, and bumped a knee on the top of a pile, but, somehow, found himself crawling in wet grass. He waited a moment. His eyes were growing accustomed to the dark. He could see dimly the shape of the *Teasel* covered with her awning and not so dark as the darkness all about her. He could see the broken line made against the sky by the roofs of bungalows and boathouses. And there, just beyond the *Teasel*, was a huge mass, and something pale creeping towards it in the grass. Dick stood up and the next moment stumbled over a mooring rope.

There was a long silence.

Dick lay still, and so did that other creeping thing that was now close to the bows of the *Teasel*. In that strange moment, Dick heard the boom of a bittern far away over the marshes, but hardly noticed it. He felt his way forward, found the next mooring rope by hand instead of by tripping over it, and, at last, was close beside Tom, looking up at the dim high wall of a big cruiser's stern.

Tom whispered, "I can't read the name."

Dick said nothing, but found Tom's hand and pressed his torch into it.

Tom pointed the torch down towards the black water at their feet, covering the bulb with his hand so that when he switched it on, it gave out nothing but a faint red glow. He let a little more light out between his fingers. That was no good. He held the torch close against the dark stern of the cruiser and lifted it inch by inch, until it showed them the name. One half second was enough to let them know the worst—

"MARGOLETTA"

And there was Tom, as near to the cruiser and its sleeping Hullabaloos as he had been on the evening when for the sake of No. 7 he had turned himself into a hunted creature.

There was the *Margoletta* within a few yards of the *Teasel's* bows. Their mooring warps crossed each other. There was hardly room between them for the *Margoletta's* dinghy. Aboard the *Teasel*, everybody was asleep. It was the same aboard the *Margoletta*. Even Hullabaloos must sleep sometimes, and there they slept while Tom and Dick crept home along the bank and shut themselves in once more under the *Titmouse's* awning.

"But what are you going to do?" whispered Dick. Tom was thinking.

"There's only one thing to be done," he said at last. "But we've got to do it without waking the others. . . . If William wakes he'll wake everybody. . . . And it's no good trying to do it until it's light enough to see."

And so, keeping awake as best they could, Tom and Dick waited for the dawn. In the end, of course, they slept, and woke in panic remembering who were their neighbours. Silently they stowed the *Titmouse's* awning, unstepped her mast and made her a dinghy once more. It was already light, but everybody slept about them. The little wooden houses slept, and the boat-yards, and the moored yachts, and the great threatening bulk of the *Margoletta*. Only the morning chorus of birds sang as if impatient to stir the sleepers.

"They'll go and wake William," whispered Dick. It was not at all the way in which he usually thought of the songs of the birds.

The worst moment was when Tom had to unlace a bit of the *Teasel's* awning, so as to lift a leg of its framework and get the tiller amidships. Then, in spite of all his care, he heard someone stir in the cabin. But there was no barking.

"Look here, Dick," he whispered. "You never *have* steered with a foot. But it's quite easy. You've got to steer standing on the counter, so as to see over the top of the awning."

Silently the mooring ropes were taken aboard. Silently Tom pulled the *Titmouse* out into the river. The tow-rope

IT WAS THE *MARGOLETTA*

tightened. The *Teasel* was moving. Dick, steadying himself with a hand on the boom, steered as well as he was able.

"'Sh! 'Sh!" he whispered, as the flap of the awning was flung back, and Dorothea, like Dick, in pyjamas, looked sleepily out in time to read the dreaded name on the sleeping cruiser's bows, as the *Teasel* slipped downstream, only a yard or two away.

CHAPTER XV

PORT AND STARBOARD SAY GOOD-BYE

Port and Starboard, sleeping in the fore-cabin of the *Teasel*, missed the excitements of the night. All was over, and Tom and Dick had moored the *Teasel* at a staithe three-quarters of a mile down the river, when Port, hearing their voices, leaned across from her bunk, tugged at Starboard's blankets and began, in the best Ginty manner, "Time for the bairrns to be stirrin'. It's a braw an' bonny mornin'. . . . What? . . . What's happened? Where are we?" She had caught sight through a port-hole of a bungalow that had certainly not been there the night before.

"'Sh!" whispered Dorothea. "Don't wake the Admiral. She's been awake and gone to sleep again, and so's William."

She squeezed through into the little fore-cabin and told them how the *Margoletta* had come up in the dark and moored just below them, almost touching the *Teasel's* bow, and how Tom and Dick had slipped out early, and, towing and steering, had taken the *Teasel* into safety, out of sight and hearing of the enemy.

"But that was in a dream," said Port. "I dreamt I heard their beastly engine."

"I don't believe it," said Starboard.

"It wasn't a dream," said Dorothea. "I saw the *Margoletta* myself. And the Admiral says we're all to get to sleep again. She and William are asleep already."

But nobody could sleep for very long. Even Tom and Dick,

who had lain awake half the night, could not settle down. It did not seem worth while to rig the *Titmouse's* awning all over again, and, Tom in his sleeping-bag and Dick in his blankets in the bottom of the open boat, they dozed off only to be waked again, by a gentle bump against the staithe, or by the sun which had begun to find its way wherever it was least wanted. The twins could not help whispering. Dorothea could not help hearing them, and, herself, was lying awake trying how best to fit the story of that night into the framework of "The Outlaw of the Broads." In the end even the Admiral gave up hope of sleep, and, long before the usual time, was about in the well, stirring the Primus stove to action.

Dorothea was the next to be ready. She was in the cabin getting into her clothes, and at the same time looking at the map spread on the cabin table, to see what ways of escape were open to the outlaw in case the *Margoletta* came down the river in pursuit of him.

"Do you know what this place is called?" she said suddenly, and took the map out of the cabin with her to show it to the Admiral.

"Why so it is," said Mrs. Barrable. "There, William, you never knew you were going to a place called Pug Street, did you? You can't be the first of the hard-working and successful pugs. There must have been another to have a street called after him."

There was a tremendous noise of splashing astern, where Tom and Dick were doing their washing in a tin baler.

"Your turn for the wash-basin," Starboard was saying in the fore-cabin.

Presently everybody was ready to begin the day, even those who were now beginning it a second time.

"Somebody take pug for a walk along his street," said the Admiral, "and see if it's too early to get milk. There must be a farm over there."

"Come on, pug," said Dorothea. "It's more like a lane than a street, but anyhow, let's go and have a look at it."

"Come on," said Tom. "Hear that yellow-hammer?"

"Let's try to see him," said Dick.

Mrs. Barrable handed out the milk can, and off they went past the old barn and along the narrow green lane that leads to Repps.

By the time they came back, after stopping to watch the yellow-hammer flitting through the branches of the pollarded willows, so that Dick could fairly add its name to the list in his notebook, they found breakfast waiting in the cabin, the awning stowed, the cover taken off the mainsail, and Port and Starboard swilling down the decks.

"Well," said the Admiral, when they had crowded into their places on the bunks at either side of the cabin table and she was passing Tom his mug. "Are you going to make a habit of casting off people's moorings without telling them anything about it? And *we* weren't moored over a coot's nest."

"It was the only thing to do," said Tom.

"Like last time," said the Admiral, laughing at him.

"But he didn't send you adrift," said Dick. "He just towed you into a safe place."

"I do think you might have waked us," said Starboard.

"I didn't want to wake anybody," said Tom. "They were almost touching us. One bark from William and we'd have been done."

"Let's slip back along the bank and have a look at them," said Port.

"What for?" said Tom, who wanted never to see them again. "Let's get on. They may wake any minute and come charging down the river."

"I wonder," said the Admiral. "Now, supposing somebody happened to know we'd gone up through Potter Heigham, and supposing the somebody told your Hullabaloos, they may very well have come along just to wait at the bridge and make sure of Tom when he came back."

"Look here," said Starboard. "It may really have been George Owdon Dorothea saw on that bicycle."

"If the twins hadn't been in such a hurry to get back, we'd have been coming down this morning," said Tom. "I'd have come rowing out from under the bridge towing the *Teasel*. They couldn't have helped seeing me, and I wouldn't have had a chance of getting away."

"And now," said the Admiral, "they'll be sitting there all day, watching the bridge and waiting for the criminal to come through."

That was a very pleasant thought and lent an extra relish to the eggs and bacon.

*

It was turning out another fine spring day. The south-easterly wind was freshening up again. "Just the wind," Starboard said, "to take us back to Horning. And we needn't be there till afternoon." Now that they were no longer worried about being held up by a calm, the twins wanted to make the very most of the *Teasel's* last day as a training ship. To-morrow she would be sailing south without them, and they were determined that she should sail with as good a crew as could be trained in the time. "Train them?" Port had said. "We're simply going to cram them." And on this last day, the moment breakfast was done with, they got Dorothea so muddled with questions first from one side and then from the other about the rule of the road that, when asked what she would do if, running before the wind, she met two boats beating on opposite tacks, she said, "I should ask the captain," which the Admiral said was a very good answer indeed. The twins simply had to keep themselves busy, so as not to feel too sad to think that they were not coming too, to help in sailing the *Teasel* in the big rivers of the south. It could not be helped.

Their A.P. was counting on them. But the good wind, and the brisk spring day made staying at home and sleeping in beds instead of in bunks a very gloomy prospect.

There was no doubt that the *Teasel*, as a training ship, had been a great success. Neither Dick nor Dorothea hesitated for a moment now when asked to touch their port cheeks or starboard shoulders, though the mischievous Port had them both muddled when suddenly she ordered them: "Now, quick; no waiting! Touch your starboard noses." They knew the names of all the ropes and could find the right one if not too desperately hurried. They had begun in Ranworth learning to handle the little sail of the *Titmouse*. They had gone on to dealing with the big mainsail of the *Teasel*. They had hauled on rope after rope in the actual business of sailing. They had coiled down halyards again and again, trying to learn the trick of getting the same length of rope into each round of a coil. Already they had been seen comparing hands. "What are you doing?" the Admiral asked. "Only wishing Captain Nancy and the others could see our hands," said Dorothea. "They are so beautifully horny."

On this last day of their training, Tom and the twins made Dick and Dorothea sail the *Teasel* almost by themselves, of course, after lending weight on halyards to get the sails properly set. They slipped away from Pug Street and left the last of the Potter Heigham bungalows, and reached past the Womack Entry, and beat down to Thurne Mouth, and ran before the wind when they turned by the signpost into the Bure, without a hand on the tiller other than the beautifully horny ones, while the Coots stood by, giving a word of advice sometimes, and easing out or hauling in the mainsheet. Nothing went wrong, except that just once a pair of reed buntings very nearly made Dick steer into the bank.

When they came to the entrance to the Fleet Dyke it seemed too good a chance of going into South Walsham to be missed, as the wind would let them reach in and out again without tacking. So they sailed down the narrow dyke into that beautiful little broad, and through the pass between the trees into the inner broad where they very nearly got stuck on a shallow. They anchored in the outer broad, not tying up to the staithe, but lowering the mud-weight that had last been used to sink Tom's *Dreadnought*. Then, while Dorothea and the Admiral were making ready a dinner (steak and kidney pie again, and a lot of fruit tartlets bought in Potter Heigham) the others went sailing in the disguised *Titmouse*, and found a crested grebe on her nest in a clump of reeds not thirty yards from the staithe. They sailed silently by, and she let them come to within a few yards before she quickly covered her eggs with some rotted reeds and slipped off into the water. She was back again on the nest before they had gone far, and, after they had had dinner, when they brought Dorothea to see her, she let them sail close by without stirring from her nest, sitting with neck and crest erect, following them with her eyes and moving nothing but her head.

After that they set sail in the *Teasel* once more, and sailed down the Fleet Dyke into the river again. Dick, for the first time in his life, went up the mast, using the mast-hoops as footholds, to look out from the masthead ("It would never do," said Dorothea, "to sail out and meet them in the river before Tom had time to hide in the cabin"). But there were no signs of the *Margoletta*, and Dick, under orders from the Admiral, came down. Dorothea herself, though proud to see him up there, was glad when he was safely on the deck. In the main river they had a grand wind to help them, and they sailed home at a great pace, past Ant Mouth, and Horning Hall Farm, and the *Teasel's* old moorings and the entry to Ranworth where the outlaw had laid low. They swept by too fast to see much of No. 7, but they all saw the coot with the white feather, and Dick, who had the glasses, thought he could see the sooty young ones in the nest. As soon as they passed the Ferry, Tom hauled the *Titmouse* close up to the counter.

"I can't take her up to the staithe," he said. "Anybody who knows her would be sure to see her name's been painted out. I'll hide her in our dyke, and come along at once."

The wind was already not so strong, and Tom slipped easily down into her, and the *Teasel* sailed on up the village without a dinghy towing astern of her while the disguised *Titmouse* with the rope fender round her and Mrs. Barrable's oil paint over the letters on her transom, disappeared behind the reeds, and was tied up once more beside the ancient *Dreadnought*.

"Well, and how did you get on?" asked his mother, when Tom ran in just to have a look at our baby before running up the lane to join the others at the staithe. "I hear dreadful stories about you and the twins up the river."

"Oh, that was all right," said Tom, "but we had a narrow squeak last night. Those people moored next door to us at Potter in the dark, but we got away before they woke this morning."

"Trust you," said his mother. "But what about your crew? Do you think you and Mrs. Barrable will really be able to sail her yacht with only those two children to help?"

"They're coming on like anything," said Tom. "We'll manage all right. But I wish the twins were coming too."

The twins meanwhile had brought the *Teasel* up to the staithe in style, and swung her round and laid her alongside so tenderly that if Dick and Dorothea had been holding fenders packed with valuable eggs instead of with scraps of old cork, not an eggshell would have been broken. Then, teaching to the very last, they put their apprentices through the whole routine of stowing jib and mainsail. When that was done, they did some good work with the mop, and then helped in getting in stores, reminding the Admiral of several things, such as matches and candles, which they knew by experience were only too often forgotten. It was on their advice that the Admiral bought three new electric torches, one each for Dorothea, Dick and Tom. Even to help in getting ready was something.

They were back aboard the *Teasel* when Tom joined them and asked if they had seen the Death and Glories. They had not, but they had hardly said so before the old black boat herself came round the bend from up-river, hauling down her ragged old sail as she came to meet the wind.

"Have they dropped one of them overboard?" said Mrs. Barrable.

"There's Joe stowing the sail," said Starboard, "and Pete steering, but where's Bill?"

A bell sounded, and brakes put on hard brought a bicycle up with a scrunch. Bill, hot, and out of breath, jumped off. He had been riding his own bicycle for once.

"I thought they'd cotched ye," he panted. "I get word they gone up to Potter last night. Laying for you below the bridge. So I biked up there. Thought I'd get above bridges and tell ye to keep out. They been there, but they're not there now. How d'ye get by 'em?" He could hardly get his words out.

"Good man, Bill," said Tom, and told of what had happened in the early morning.

"How far is it to Potter Heigham by road?" asked the Admiral.

"About six miles," said Starboard.

"Twelve altogether," said the Admiral. "Well done, Bill. And what were the others up to?"

"We had to have someone on the river," said Bill

"What it is," said the Admiral, "to be a member of the Coot Club."

Joe and Pete had tied up the *Death and Glory* and came along, eager to hear how yet again the elder Coots had dodged the enemy. They reported all well with all nests both up and down the river.

Tea was made in the *Teasel*, and drunk in the well, and on the cabin roof, by apprentices, teachers of seamanship and thirsty pirates. Then, with everybody helping, the awning was put up for the night.

It was very jolly to be making ready for a real voyage, with so many active helpers, but, after the younger, piratical Coots had gone off to their homes, sadness came down over the others. Port and Starboard, who were so busy seeing that everything was just right, and had just swilled down the decks for the last time, were going to be left behind.

"It's an awful pity you aren't coming," said Tom.

"Change your minds," said the Admiral. "We shall be wishing you were with us all the time."

"You'll be all right," said Starboard. She spoke to Tom, somehow not trusting herself to say it to the others. "You'll be all right. Look at the way you and Dick managed everything this morning and let us go on sleeping."

"It wasn't that," said Tom. "You know it wasn't. It wasn't that I didn't want to wake you. William was the one I was afraid of waking."

"The puir wee doggie," said Port, turning suddenly and looking out of a port-hole. It was not of William she was thinking.

And then Mr. Farland, back from the office in Norwich, strolled along the staithe to fetch his daughters.

He thanked Mrs. Barrable for being so kind to them, and then turned to Tom.

"Well, Tom," he said, "the whole river seems to know about your feud with those motor-cruisers."

"But I haven't told anybody but the Coots," said Tom.

"You've got a lot of very active friends," said Mrs. Barrable, who thought it was not surprising that secrets slipped out with the pirates and their allies (with or without stomach-aches) inquiring in all directions about the *Margoletta*.

"It's those people in the cruiser," said Mr. Farland, "boasting about what they're going to do and about some bet they have among themselves. And Norfolk folk can use their ears as well as most. They've got hold of the story of my two girls towing a dinghy that wasn't exactly empty right under the noses of those fellows when they were looking for you. There's been a good deal of laughing about it. People keep asking them when they think they're going to catch that boy."

"If only people would leave them alone," said Tom.

"Somebody must have told them Tom went up to Potter," said Starboard. "They came up there last night after dark."

"I shouldn't have thought any of the local people would have given Tom away."

"We think we know who," said Starboard.

"Your dear friend George?" said Mr. Farland, laughing. "Oh well, Tom'll be out of his way when he gets down south. Nobody'll look for a Horning boy down there. You'll be safe enough as soon as you're the other side of Yarmouth. What are you going to do when you get there?"

"Oulton, Beccles, Norwich," said Tom. "All over the place, like we did when you took us last summer."

"We're going to Beccles first," said Dorothea. "You see, the Admiral was born there."

"How far do you think you'll get to-morrow?"

"I thought we'd get down to Stokesby," said Tom, "and then we can watch our tide and make sure of getting through at low water the next day."

"Much the best plan," said Mr. Farland. "Down at Stokesby anybody'll tell you when to start to get down to Yarmouth at the right time. Let me see, if the wind's like this, you'll be leaving here soon after nine to carry your tide down to Stokesby. Well, you two, have you packed your dunnage?

Sling it ashore and say good-bye to the ship. They'll be off in the morning before you've done your breakfasts. They never wake, these two," he added, "before Mrs. McGinty calls them."

Port and Starboard stepped ashore with their knapsacks and rugs. They too were ready to say good-bye now. It would be more than they could bear, to come in the morning, and wave handkerchiefs, and see the *Teasel* sail away without them.

"Good-bye! Good-bye! And thank you ever so much, Admiral."

"Good-bye, and good luck to your racing."

"And thanks most awfully for showing us how to do things," said Dorothea.

"Touching starboard noses for instance," said Port.

At the last minute it was hard to go. The twins stood there on the staithe, as if there was still something they wanted to say if only they could remember what it was.

"Come along," said their A.P., picking up both their knapsacks. "You must get a good sleep to-night. Remember you've a championship race to-morrow."

*

"Funny," said the Admiral after they had disappeared. "I got the impression that Mr. Farland doesn't know his twins could have been sailing south with us."

"He doesn't," said Tom. "They didn't tell him. Port said that if they did he'd have made them come with us, and then he'd have had to scratch *Flash* out of the championship."

"And, of course, they'd rather win those races than come with us," said the Admiral queerly.

"It isn't that," said Dorothea. "They don't want him not to be able to sail. You see he counts on them. . . ."

"They don't want to let him down," said Tom. "It's never any use trying to persuade them when it's like that. I've tried before."

"Well," said the Admiral, "I hope they get the first gun in every race. They deserve to."

        *

Everything was ready now for to-morrow's start. Dick was again to share the fore-cabin of the *Teasel* with Dorothea, leaving the main cabin to William and the Admiral. Tom was to go home to supper, and to sleep in the *Titmouse*, safely hidden in the Coot Club dyke.

Last thing before he left, Dick and Dorothea came ashore on the staithe with him, to look at the weather. The wind from the south-east had dropped. Small wisps of cloud very far overhead seemed to be moving the other way. Tom watched them carefully.

"I do believe the wind's changing," he said. "If we get it from the north-west we needn't bother about Stokesby. We could get right through Yarmouth in the day and down the other side of Breydon. But we'd have to start jolly early. How early *could* you be ready?"

"We'll go to bed *now*," said Dorothea.

"Stick your head out the moment you wake," said Tom, "and have a sniff at the wind. If it's north-west I'll be along first thing, and we'll get off right away."

BOOK TWO

IN SOUTHERN WATERS

NOTE

From now on, readers who want to know where they are should use the map of the southern rivers which makes the final end-paper.

CHAPTER XVI

SOUTHWARD BOUND

Tom woke, remembered that the *Titmouse* was in the dyke at home, looked at his watch, saw that it was close on six o'clock, and, a moment later, had wriggled out of his sleeping-bag and was scrambling ashore bare-footed and in his pyjamas to have a look at the weather. The grass, wet with dew, promised well. Already there was a stirring in the leaves of the willows. Tom looked up at the gable of the house. The golden bream above the thatched roof sent him hurrying back into the *Titmouse*. It was heading north-west. There could not be a better wind for the voyage. North-west would be a fair wind all the way to Yarmouth, not bad for Breydon Water, and a fair wind again for most of the Waveney. With that wind, if only it held, and if they got down to Yarmouth by low water, there was no knowing how far they might not get before night. In two minutes he was dressed, stowing his dew-soaked awning, and unstepping his mast. Then he tiptoed round the house and looked up. Everybody was asleep. Good-byes had been said the night before, but he listened almost hopefully. If our baby happened to be kicking up a row his mother would be awake, and he could softly call her to the window. But our baby was asleep. There was not a sound except from the starlings who had, as usual, picked their way in and made a nest in the thatch. Tom poled the *Titmouse* quietly out of the dyke, and paddled silently upstream through the rising mist. The last of the flood tide was holding up the stream. The sooner the *Teasel* was off the better, to make use of the whole of the ebb. What about the others? Would young Dick have had the sense to look out at the weather and wake them up?

Presently he looked over his shoulder and saw the *Teasel* moored against the staithe. One look was enough. A flag was fluttering at her masthead. He had seen it taken in the night before. It was up now. One, at least, of the *Teasel's* crew must be awake. And then, as he came nearer, he heard voices aboard her.

"Well, he did say we were to get up early if the wind was north-west," Dorothea was saying.

"You'd better both of you run along down the village, and you'll find Tom's still fast asleep."

"*Teasel* ahoy!" said Tom softly. What a good thing it was he had happened to wake.

A flap of the awning was flung back and Dick looked out.

"Good! Good!" he said. "Here he is. Wouldn't it have been awful if he'd come and found us still in bed?"

"Come along, Skipper," said Mrs. Barrable. "Breakfast's ready. I don't believe Dick's really been to sleep at all. He was up on deck in the middle of the night."

"I just had one look out," said Dick, "but I didn't go on deck till I went to put the flag up. . . ."

"Hoist it," said Dorothea.

"Hoist it," said Dick, "and by then the sun was up. I could see the sunshine on the tops of the trees sticking up out of the mist."

"He didn't give us much chance of oversleeping," said Mrs. Barrable. "So breakfast's ready. Come along in."

Tom climbed aboard from the *Titmouse* and made her painter fast to a ring-bolt on the *Teasel's* counter. The *Titmouse* was a yacht's dinghy once again. He looked up at the *Teasel's* flag. The flagstaff was already a little askew. The morning sun was drying and slackening the halyards which had been

194

very wet when Dick had sent the flag to the masthead. He would put that right presently. The halyards would dry a lot more yet. He took one look round, thinking already of how best to get the *Teasel* under way.

"Fill his mug, Dot," said the Admiral. "Slip in here, Tom. Two eggs, Dot, and have a look at the watch when you put them in."

Tom slipped in between table and bunk and settled down to breakfast. William, curled up on that bunk, laid his chin on Tom's lap.

"Look here, William," said the Admiral, "you're *my* dog."

Tom took hold of the scruff of William's neck and gently moved it up and down, while William, his pink tongue hanging out, looked up at Tom with eyes that seemed to bulge with adoration.

"And to think of the way he barked at you when first he met you," said the Admiral.

Tom laughed. Ever since that first day, he and William had had a liking for each other. But, though he rumpled William's scruff for him, he was thinking all the time of the routine of making sail. Dick had certainly done very well in waking everybody early. Blankets had already been rolled up and stowed. Below decks nothing needed putting away except the cooking things. It was as if they had merely tied up for a meal and had rigged the awning only to keep the wind from the Primus.

"We women'll wash up," said Mrs. Barrable, the moment breakfast was over. "And you and Dick can be getting on with things on deck."

It was not what the Admiral called a full-dress washing up. By the time the awning was folded and doubled into a neat bundle and stowed away in the forepeak, all hands were ready for the hoisting of the sails. It seemed queer to be hoisting sail without Port and Starboard to help, but by not hurrying, and by taking a little longer about it, everything was done without mistakes.

"Good for you, Dick," said Tom, when all was ready for the start. Dick had seen for himself those slackened flag halyards and was making them taut again, so that the flagstaff stuck proudly up into the sunshine, and the little flag fluttered out above the masthead.

The Admiral, in spite of herself, was looking worried. The river is so narrow up there by the staithe, and there was a hardish wind blowing. The thought of Yarmouth was in her mind, too, and in spite of her cheerful letter to Brother Richard, she could not help thinking of what he would say if anything went wrong. But Tom did seem to know exactly what he meant to do.

"All ready?" said Tom. "Push her head off, Dick. Come aboard." The *Teasel* was moving. Close-hauled across the river, into the wind, round again, and there she was, heading downstream. Dick was on the foredeck making a neat coil of the mooring rope. Dorothea, in the best Port and Starboard manner, was easing out the jib sheet. The staithe was left astern. They were passing the deserted boat-yards. Nobody was there to see them go.

"They folded their tents like the Arabs," quoted Mrs. Barrable, "and silently stole away."

"But she's making a beautiful noise," said Dick hurrying aft along the side-deck and stepping quietly down into the well.

She certainly was. The water was creaming under her forefoot. The wind exactly suited her. Tom said nothing, but that noise was a song in his ears. If only Port and Starboard had been with them! The boat-sheds were astern of them, the willow-pattern harbour, and now his own home, still asleep in the early morning sunshine. There was the entrance to his dyke, between willows and brown reeds. There, behind bushes, farther back from the river front, was the twins' house. He looked at the windows. . . . No. . . . There was not a sign of them. Everybody was still asleep.

"It's an awful pity they couldn't come," said Dorothea, and Tom started, at hearing his own thought spoken aloud. But it was no good thinking it. He set himself again to the business in hand. There must be no mistakes. He knew that the success of the voyage and the safety of the *Teasel*, and of the little *Titmouse*, too, towing astern, depended on him. Mrs. Barrable was very good in a boat, but, talking it over among themselves, the three elder Coots had decided that the Admiral, though a good sailor, was inclined to be a little rash. And then there were the new A.B.'s. Well, they were certainly shaping like good ones. As soon as they were in a reach where there was less chance of an unexpected jibe, he would have them at the tiller, standing by, of course, in case of accident. They had managed very well with the hoisting of the sails. And there had been nothing to be ashamed of in the actual start. He wished the twins had been there to see how well their pupils had remembered what they had been taught. And now the *Teasel* was sweeping past the Ferry, where George Owdon had exulted too soon, and betrayed that he knew rather more than he should of the plans of the Hullabaloos. The next bit would be easy sailing.

"Come on, Dick. Take over for a minute or two."

Dick was ready, clutched the tiller as if he thought it might get away, watched the burgee fluttering out, and glanced astern to see how badly the *Teasel's* wake betrayed the unsteadiness of his anxious steering.

"Never mind about the wake," said Tom. "You're doing jolly well."

He looked into the cabin, to see what had become of the Admiral. She was sitting on her bunk with William beside her. William had decided that it was still too early for pugs to be out-of-doors. Seeing Tom, the Admiral held up some sheets of paper she had folded so that they made a little book. On the outside page she had drawn a little sailing yacht, and under that picture she had written, in very gorgeous printed letters:

"LOG OF THE TEASEL."

"I forgot all about the log," said Tom.

"Sailed 6.45 a.m.," said the Admiral. "Within a minute or two. Anyhow, I've put it down."

"Thank you very much," said Tom.

Then, leaving Dick and Dorothea alone in the well, Dick at the tiller, and Dorothea at the main-sheet, and both of them rather horrified at being left there, he went forward and stood on the foredeck, listening to the water foaming below him, and feeling somehow even more responsible than when he had the tiller in his own hands. The Admiral in the cabin noting things in the log, the two new sailors looking after the steering, and the *Teasel*, trembling beneath his feet with this good wind to drive her on and on towards the dangers of Yarmouth and the big rivers of the south . . . it was a wonderful feeling, and, anyway, it wasn't as if he had deserted the *Titmouse*. There she was foaming along astern. She was coming, too, and he would be sailing her in all kinds of strange places. If only Port and Starboard could have been there to share it. Hullo, there was No. 7 that had upset all plans and made this voyage possible. How fast the *Teasel* was moving, although the tide, such as it was, was against her. One after another the familiar things went by. There were black sheep. Good-bye now to Horning, and the Coot Club and the Death and Glories, our baby, father and mother, and all those nesting birds . . . he would not see them again till the voyage was over and he had either made a mess of things or carried it through to success. He glanced up at the flag. They would be having the wind on the other side in the Waterworks reach, and he had better help them with the jibe. Jolly well they were doing, those two, but it was no good expecting too much of them.

The jibe, even with Tom to help, was not one that anybody aboard would have liked the twins to see. The *Teasel* took charge when the boom swung across, and Dick was not quick enough in meeting her with the helm. There was a wildish lurch before she settled down again, and William, who had been standing on the leeward bunk, stretching himself and yawning, was shot suddenly on the cabin floor when that bunk became the windward one. He gave a startled yelp, and came out into the well as if to warn people that things like that must not happen again.

Mrs. Barrable came out, too, after marking down in the log the time at which they passed the Waterworks, but she did not seem to have noticed that fearful lurch across the river.

"We're getting on very well," she said. "We'll be down at Stokesby in no time."

"There's a man at Potter Heigham," said Tom, "who sailed a smaller boat than the *Teasel* all the way from Hickling to Yarmouth and right down to Oulton in one day with a north-west wind like this."

They swept past the entry to the Ranworth Dyke, jibed again, more successfully, and again, not quite so well, as they turned from one reach into another in this winding bit of the river. Smoke was rising from the chimneys of Horning Hall Farm, and they saw someone moving beside the dyke.

"What about stopping and getting milk?" said Dorothea. "We used what was left of last night's milk for breakfast, and we haven't any now."

"Mustn't waste a fair wind," said the Admiral, "must we, William?" And William, who would have disagreed if he had understood, licked her hand most trustfully.

"We can get milk all right at Acle," said Tom. "We'll get it from the Provision Boat."

"Provision Boat?" said Dorothea.

"You'll see," said Tom.

At first the *Teasel* seemed to be the only vessel moving on the river. The few yachts and motor-cruisers they passed were all moored to the banks, covered with their awnings, still asleep. But not far from Horning Hall they came round a bend in the river to find an eel-man in his shallow, tarred boat, going the rounds of his nightlines. He was a friend of Tom's, and lifted a hand like a bit of old tree root as they swept past him, calling out their "Good mornings." Then they met a wherry quanting up with the last of the flood.

"Hallo, young Tom," called the skipper of the wherry, seeing Tom at the main-sheet of the *Teasel*. "Have you seed Jim Wooddall?"

"He's lying above Horning," shouted Tom. "I saw old Simon on the staithe last night."

"Do you know everybody on the river?" asked the Admiral.

"I know all the wherrymen," said Tom. "You see, they all come past our house."

Just past St. Benet's somebody in a moored yacht stuck out a tousled head from under the awning, and Dorothea wondered how the *Teasel* must look to him, sails set, flag flying, racing along in the sunshine while he had only just poked his nose out of a stuffy cabin. She looked at Dick, who was steering again and thinking only of his job. She looked at Mrs. Barrable. How must she be feeling? "Day after day, week after week, the ship sailed on, and the returning exile watched till her (or his . . . better his) eyes grew dim for the white cliffs of home." But perhaps Beccles was without white cliffs. It was only too probable, and as for the returning exile, she was as usual busy with some coloured chalks, making notes for a picture. She looked more hopefully at Tom, the outlaw, flying from his

OFF AT LAST

home to a far country overseas. But Tom was not looking back with a tear in his eye at the country he was leaving. He seemed to be interested in nothing at all but the small bubbles or scraps of reed that were floating near the banks.

"Tide's turning," he said at last. "She's done all right so far. We'll have it with us now." His mind ran on, calculating. Horning to Ant's Mouth. . . . Then to Thurne Mouth . . . then to Acle. . . . How long would it take to lower the mast, get through the bridge and hoist again? . . . Two miles to Stokesby . . . and then ten miles of the lower river . . . no trees down there, and the wind looked like holding. "Slacken away the jib-sheet a bit more, Dot," he said. "Let's get all the speed we can out of her."

"I don't believe even the *Flash* goes faster than this," said Dorothea.

Tom knew better. A cabin yacht like the *Teasel* would be lucky indeed if with her small sails she could keep up with a little racer like the *Flash*. The thought of the *Flash* saddened him again by reminding him of Port and Starboard. What a pity it was that the twins were not aboard.

But there was not much time for sorrow. Already there were sails moving far away over the fields towards Potter Heigham, and they were coming to the mouth of the Thurne and the sharp turn of the Bure down towards Yarmouth, where the signpost on the bank points the way along the river roads.

Tom hauled in on the main-sheet.

"Round with her," he said. "Steadily, right round."

Dick pulled the tiller up. The jib flew across. There was a flap and a violent tug as the mainsail followed it. Tom paid out the sheet hand-over-hand. It was a beautiful jibe. The *Teasel* was in waters where Dick and Dorothea had never been. The outlaw, the exile and the new A.B.'s were southward bound at last.

CHAPTER XVII

PORT AND STARBOARD MISS THEIR SHIP

At the moment when the *Teasel* was sailing down the river past their house, and Tom was looking at the windows and thinking they were still asleep, Port and Starboard were lying awake in bed. They were both thinking of the voyage of the *Teasel*, and had been awake for some time.

"They're sure not to get off as early as they meant to," said Starboard.

"Nobody ever does," said Port.

"It'd be awful hanging about to see them go," said Starboard.

"We've said good-bye once," said Port.

There was a long silence, except for the birds and for a growing rustling noise in the trees.

"Which way *is* that wind?" said Port at last.

Starboard rolled out of bed and ran to the window. One moment earlier and she would have seen the *Teasel* sailing by. She leant out so that she could see Dr. Dudgeon's roofs beyond the dyke and willow bushes, and, high above the nearer gable the big flat-sided golden fish he had set up there for a weather-vane.

"North-west," she said.

"Um," said Port, propping herself on her elbows. "Fair wind. They won't have to hurry. That'll blow them down to Stokesby in no time. It'll be ages before they start."

"Let's go to sleep again," said Starboard. She got into bed and pulled the sheets in under her chin, but found that running barefoot across the bedroom floor had made her less sleepy than ever.

"Bother, bother, bother," said Port suddenly. A new idea had come into her head. "Won't they think it rather funny if we don't turn up to cheer?"

"I wish they'd gone straight on yesterday," said Starboard. There was another long silence. It was broken by Mrs. McGinty coming in with a big can of hot water. The twins after lying awake so long had got to sleep again just before she came to call them. They pushed their noses into their pillows. The hot water stood there cooling. The next thing they heard was the banging of the breakfast gong, when they shot out of their beds, one to port and the other to starboard, tubbed and dressed without more than half drying, and raced downstairs.

"Good morning. Sorry we're late."

But the A.P. was not there.

"An' well you may be sorry," said Mrs. McGinty. "Mr. Farland's had a letter the noo and I'll be keepin' his buttered eggs warm. . . . So help yoursel's while ye can."

"Good old Ginty," said Starboard. They both knew that Mrs. McGinty was never as cross as she sounded.

"A letter?" said Port, looking at the pile by her father's plate. "But he's had lots."

"Well, he's ta'en this yin to the telephone," said Mrs. McGinty, and then they heard their father's voice through the open door of the study.

"Never mind about keeping things hot, Mrs. McGinty. I'll have to be gone in a minute. . . . Hallo! Hallo! Hallo! Is that Norwich Ten-sixty-six? Norwich. . . . One-owe-double-six. . . . Hallo! Yes. I said so. Engaged? Can't be engaged. Private exchange. Please ring them again. Give them another ring. A long one. Hallo! Hallo! Is that Norwich One-owe-double-six? Oh. Wrong number. Ring off please. . . . Hallo! Exchange? Oh, *please* ring off. Exchange? . . . Hallo! Hallo! . . . Bring me a cup of coffee out here, some-body. . . . Hallo! Exchange! Gave me a wrong number. No. No. Not one-double-six. One-owe-double-six. Thank you, Bessie. Take care, Nell. Don't make me take too big a mouth-ful. I've got to be able to talk to these dunderheaded nincom-poops. Hallo! Oh, is that you, Walters? Thank goodness for that. Nip round to the office and get me all the papers in that Bollington business. Consultations on it this week. Yes. . . . All in the folder. And the deeds. . . . Yes, yes. Bring the whole lot down to the station. Coming in by car. You'll get it garaged after I've gone. I've got to catch the nine-one. Right. Good man. Everything on the case. . . ." He hung up the receiver, took another mouthful of buttered egg from Star-board, washed it down with a drink of coffee offered him by Port, and hurried back to the dining-room.

"What is it, A.P.?" asked Starboard.

Mr. Farland looked at his watch and compared it with the clock on the mantelpiece, a clock won by the *Flash* at Wrox-ham Regatta the year before.

"Seven minutes for breakfast. . . . Yes, Mrs. McGinty, if you will be so good. The small suit-case. Everything for a week. . . ."

"You aren't going away?" said Port.

"These things will happen," said Mr. Farland. "I didn't expect this business to come on for another two months at least. . . ."

"But what about *Flash* and the championship? Couldn't you put it off for a week?"

"Impossible," said Mr. Farland, scooping the last of the buttered egg off his plate. "Better peddle whelks and mussels than follow the law. At least you're your own master."

"But the first race is to-morrow."

"I've got to scratch for it," said their father. "I've got to scratch for the lot. And with old *Flash* properly tuned up she'd have shown them her heels in every race."

"Oh, A.P. How awful! And when you'd got everything ready."

"I'll have to telephone to the secretary right away, and get him to explain to the others. Never mind, *Flash* shall challenge the winner as soon as I get back. I'll tell him so at once."

"Are you going to-day?"

"Didn't you hear me say so? Going this very minute. Pass that toast-rack, will you . . . and the marmalade."

Somehow, with the head of the house galloping through his breakfast, his daughters did the same. It was as if all three of them were off to catch that early train. Overhead, they could hear drawers being pulled out and pushed in, and the steady murmur of Mrs. McGinty loudly remembering the things that must not be forgotten. "Half a dozen collars for the blue. . . . Bless the man, if he hasna been stirrin' a puddin' wi' the ties . . . an' where's the sense in a body layin' out shirts braw an' neat if . . ." Mr. Farland, his mouth full of bread and marmalade, caught his daughters' eyes and winked solemnly at the ceiling. "She doesn't mean exactly 'Bless'," he said.

In the hurry and bustle of getting him off, it was not until the very last moment that the thought came to Starboard that the A.P.'s going changed everything, and that now there was nothing to keep them at home.

"I say, A.P.," she said. "If you're going away, and *Flash* won't be racing, what about us sailing in the *Teasel* with Tom and Mrs. Barrable and those two children?"

"But you haven't been asked, have you?"

"Oh yes," said Port.

"We said 'No'," said Starboard.

"But if *Flash* isn't racing we'd like to."

"Consolation prize, eh?" said Mr. Farland, stowing his suit-case in the back of his car.

Nothing was said by either twin in reply to that.

"I don't see why you shouldn't, if Mrs. Barrable'll have you," he went on, throwing himself into the driver's seat, and starting the engine.

"Tell Ginty," said Port.

"You'll be quit of all three of us, Mrs. McGinty," said Mr. Farland, as Mrs. McGinty came running out with a spare pair of chamois leather gloves. "These two are going off sailing with Tom and his friends. . . ."

"Don't say anything about clothes, Ginty. We shan't want any besides what we've got on and sweaters. . . ."

"Well, if a body mauna pit a worrd in . . ." began Mrs. McGinty. But the car was moving. Mr. Farland had just caught sight of the clock on the dashboard.

"Good-bye." "Good-bye."

Mr. Farland waved with his left hand, steered with his right, swung out of the gate and was gone.

"Come on," said Starboard.

The two raced for the house and upstairs again into their bedroom. The knapsacks, unpacked with such melancholy last night, were taken once more from the hook behind the door. The twins' packing was less orderly than Mrs. McGinty's. Drawers were pulled out and left out. Shoes were tossed under the bed and rubber sea-boots put on. Sweaters, sand-shoes, washing things and night clothes were crammed into the knapsacks, rugs rolled up, and, by the time Mrs. McGinty had climbed upstairs, the twins were already rushing down.

"But look at yon room," said Mrs. McGinty.

"Fair awfu'," said Port. Starboard was already leaping down the last flight of stairs. "Leave it till we come back,

Ginty. We'll tidy up then. There simply isn't time now. We're in a worse hurry than father."

"Ye're aye that," said Mrs. McGinty.

*

They kept up a steady trot all through the long lower street of Horning.

"We'll be in time to help them up with the sails," said Starboard jerkily. "Those two . . . not very strong."

"Shan't have any breath," panted Port.

"Keep it up," said Starboard.

At last they swung round the corner at the end of the boat-yards and came out on the staithe where, last night, they had said good-bye to the *Teasel*.

The *Teasel* was there no longer.

"They've shifted her," said Starboard.

"They've gone," said Port.

The staithe was deserted. Even the old *Death and Glory* that had been tied up close by the Swan had disappeared. The twins ran to the water's edge, and looked down the river. Not a boat was stirring.

"Too late," said Starboard.

"And with this wind there was no need," said Port. "They'll be at Stokesby with hours to spare before the tide turns against them."

"Of course, they didn't think we were coming," said Starboard.

An old wherryman, Simon Fastgate, came to the end of the staithe with his arms full of parcels, and a big bottle of milk. He untied an old boat that was lying at the end of the boat-sheds, dumped his parcels into it, pushed himself off, and paddled away upstream.

"Ask Simon," said Port.

"Hullo, Simon. Do you know when the *Teasel* sailed?"

"Been gone before I come ashore," said Simon. "And that's an hour and more." He pulled away as hard as he could.

An hour already. Perhaps more. If only Tom had not been in such a hurry. The twins looked miserably at each other. It was one thing to give up a voyage to Beccles in order to help the A.P. to win his races. It was a different thing altogether to miss it for no reason at all. A whole week's voyaging lost for nothing. And after the A.P. had himself given them permission to go.

"We can't do anything," said Starboard.

"Go back to Ginty," said Port.

And just then, they heard the splash of a quant, and looked up the river. A wherry with mast up and sail ready for hoisting was coming into sight round the bend. They knew the wherry, *Sir Garnet*, and they knew the skipper, Jim Wooddall, when they heard him shout at his mate, who was already scrambling aboard and making fast his boat to a bollard in the stern.

"Simon, ye gartless old fool. Ye've missed us this tide. We should'a been gone two hour since."

There was no reply. Simon was already hurrying to the winch and the big black sail of the wherry began to lift. Jim Wooddall had indeed been in a hurry, to start quanting his wherry round to the staithe to look for his mate, and old Simon knew that hoisting sail was better than excuses.

Suddenly Starboard dropped her knapsack and her rug and shouted at the top of her voice.

"Jim! Jim Wooddall. *Sir Garnet*! Ahoy! Jim. JIM!"

The wherryman waved a hand to her. He was already laying his quant down, and going aft to the tiller. *Sir Garnet* would be sailing in a moment.

"Jim!" shouted Port.

They both waved their arms at him, until Jim Wooddall, in a hurry as he was, saw that there was something urgently needed.

"Half a minute, Simon!" he called. The clanking of the winch pawl stopped. The gaff had been lifted not more than a couple of feet. *Sir Garnet* was hardly moving, except with the stream. But she had steerage way, and Jim brought her round close by the staithe. The twins, picking up their knapsacks, ran along the staithe to meet him, and then walked with the wherry, explaining as she drifted down.

"Can't wait," said Jim. "Simon's lost us a tide down to Gorleston."

"But we want to get to Stokesby," said Starboard. "Tom's taken the *Teasel* down there, and they're going on to-morrow."

"We're going too," said Port. "Only we missed them."

"You see, we didn't know till this morning we could go."

All this time the wherry was moving. Another few yards and they would be at the end of the staithe, so that they could walk no further.

"Ah," said Jim. "So Tom don't know he left you."

"That's just it," said Port.

"Ain't supposed to take passengers," said Jim Wooddall. "Let's have them bags. . . ." The knapsacks and rugs were swung aboard. "Now then!" Port and Starboard leapt from the staithe after their knapsacks. "Pierhead jump," said Jim Wooddall. "I'll take you down to Stokesby. But you'll have to work your passages. Peelin' potatoes. Now then, Sim!"

The winch clanked again. The huge black sail climbed up and spread above them, and the wherry, *Sir Garnet*, late with her tide, gathered speed and stood away down the middle of the river.

CHAPTER XVIII

THROUGH YARMOUTH

A LITTLE brown heron flew low over the reeds on the Upton side of the river.

"Isn't it a bittern?" asked Dick. Dorothea was steering and Dick was free to look at birds.

"It's a bittern all right," said Tom, but just then he was not interested in bitterns. As he himself had once said of the Death and Glories, "You can't expect them to be bird protecting all the time." The *Teasel* was sweeping down towards Acle, and at Acle, he knew, would come the first real test of her crew. Never before had they lowered the mast and raised it again without the help of Port and Starboard. And at Acle Bridge there are always lookers-on, waiting to enjoy the misfortunes of the unskilled. Tom could give none of his mind to birds. But Admiral Barrable pleased Dick a good deal, by reaching into the cabin for the log of the *Teasel* and writing in it: "Sighted bittern over Upton Marshes." The Admiral, after that one nervous moment at Horning, seemed to have no worries at all. It seemed to Tom that she must have forgotten that every minute's sailing was bringing them nearer not only to Acle but to Yarmouth and Breydon, racing tides and every kind of possible disaster. Tom felt like the newly appointed captain of a liner on his first voyage in a new ship approaching a coast long noted for its dangerous shoals.

But the passing of Acle Bridge was a most comforting success. True, in rounding up to the northern bank, to lower sail, the *Teasel* hit the bank a little harder than Tom intended, but the bank is soft mud, and a great many people hit it harder still. And Dick, on the foredeck, was not flurried by the bump, but jumped ashore and stamped the rond anchor well in, as if he had been doing it for years. Dorothea fished the crutches up out of the *Titmouse* before he had had time to tell her. The sails came down without any trouble. Tom put a tyer round the jib so that it would be all ready for hoisting again. He untied the parrels[1] and laid the gaff on the cabin roof beside the boom.

"Sure you can manage?" asked the Admiral.

"I'm taking the heel rope," said Tom, "and Dick's going to pay out the forestay tackle. It'll be all right." And it was. Even with Port and Starboard instead of Dick it could not have been done better. The mast swayed slowly down and rested in the crutch.

Tom looked down towards the bridge, much narrower than usual, because of a lighter moored under it to serve as a platform for workmen.

"There's that provision boat," said Dorothea, as a small motor-boat with a roof fixed over it came up through the bridge and tied up in a little opening in the bank. The motor-boat was a regular floating shop.

"We'll do our shopping after we get through," said the Admiral.

"It's only a few yards to quant," said Tom, and Dorothea looked doubtfully at Dick. Tom laughed. "I'll do it," he said, "if the Admiral will steer close down this side. Shove the anchor aboard, Dick, and skip along the bank to meet us under the bridge. Dot had better go forrard and be ready with a fender."

Dick gave the *Teasel* a good push off. Tom, with the quant, managed to get her moving just enough to let the Admiral steer her as she drifted down with the stream. Dick ran along

---

[1] Parrels are wooden beads threaded on a loose string between the jaws of the gaff. Until this string is untied the gaff is held to the mast.

the bank, round the provision boat's little bay, and waited for the *Teasel* on the narrow tow-path under the bridge, ready to take the anchor.

"Nearer in," said Tom, hurriedly stowing his quant. He went forward, stepping carefully among the shrouds that lay along the side-decks. "Stand clear, Dick!" He threw the anchor ashore. Dick had hold of it in a moment, and walked along with it, waiting the word.

"Hang on, now!"

Dick hung on, and the *Teasel* swung slowly round. Tom took his chance and jumped ashore. Dorothea was ready with her fender. The anchor was forced into the ground. The *Teasel* was safe below the bridge, and the first of their difficulties was already behind them.

"Now then," said Tom, stepping aboard again. "Come on, Dick. Up with the mast. Everything the other way round. You haul on the forestay. I'll haul on the heel. Dot'll watch to see the shrouds don't catch on corners of the cabin roof. Ready? Haul away!"

The balanced mast lifted easily, foot after foot, as the two of them hauled away on the foredeck. Dot was in time to free the only shroud that looked like getting itself caught. The very flagstaff at the masthead stood up as if it had been newly hoisted, as the weighted heel of the mast swung into place.

"That were well done," said an old sailor, looking down at them from the bridge, when, at last, all was ready for making sail once more. Tom with a cheerful smile wiped the sweat from his forehead. Dick sat on the cabin roof cleaning his spectacles.

"Seven minutes," said Admiral Barrable. "I've put the times down in the log."

"Nearly half an hour," said Tom, "from the time we moored above the bridge."

"What about dinner here?"

"Let's have it under way," said Tom.

"Very well," said the Admiral, "you can be making sail, while Dot and I slip back along the towpath and see what they've got in that provision boat. Yes. You, too, William. Come along."

The man in the provision boat was selling almost everything anybody could want, fresh vegetables, tinned foods, chocolates and toffees, oranges and apples and bananas, and milk out of a huge milk-can with a brass tap. Mrs. Barrable bought milk for tea. . . . "My dear Dot," she said, "I'm dying for some as soon as the skipper will let us stop for long enough to boil a kettle. . . ." She also bought four bottles of lemonade, a dozen bananas, of the smaller and more tasty kind, four pork pies, four apple pies, and a large slab of the chocolate cream of which William was particularly fond. A small boy was hanging about on the bank, looking greedily at the provision boat. Dot pulled Mrs. Barrable gently by the sleeve.

"Admiral," she whispered. "I wonder if that's the sentinel, you know, the boy who ought to have sent word about the Hullabaloos."

"The boy who got a fourpenny stomach-ache," said Mrs. Barrable, and turned to the boy.

"Is your name Robin?" she asked.

"Yes," said the boy.

Mrs. Barrable bought another big slab of chocolate cream and gave it to him. "I should not think," she said, "that you could get a stomach-ache from eating this. But you might like to try."

They hurried back to the boat leaving the boy taking his first bite and looking, wondering, after them.

Tom and Dick between them, going slowly and carefully about it, had hoisted the sails.

"We saw the sentinel," said Dorothea. "Joe's friend; the Admiral gave him some chocolate."

"He jolly well deserves another stomach-ache," said Tom, "and I expect he'll get one as soon as he meets Joe. Greedy little beast."

In another minute they were off again, sailing down the river and feasting as they sailed.

Tom, with his eye always on the time and the tide, felt better now. He was steering because, alone of his crew, he could manage the tiller with one hand and a pork pie in the other without danger of running the *Teasel* into the reeds. Sitting on the coaming that ran round the well, he could even manage to hold a bottle of lemonade between his knees. Acle Bridge was left astern. The tide had still a couple of hours to run down, and already they were nearing Stokesby where, at first, they had planned to spend the night. They were going to be able to do much better than that.

The Admiral, however, would have been content to stop.

"What about it, Tom?" she asked, as Stokesby windmill came in sight, and then the houses of the little village. "Have we done enough for the first day?"

"We'll be down at Yarmouth in time for low water," said Tom, "with the wind holding like this. We could get right through Breydon. . . ."

"Wouldn't it be lovely if we got to Beccles," said Dorothea.

"It would certainly be very pleasant," said the Admiral, "to know that we were through Yarmouth."

"Well," said Tom, "of course it *is* much the worst bit. It'd be jolly nice to get it over."

And just then they saw something that made them decide at once that wherever they might stop for the night it would certainly not be at Stokesby.

Dorothea went suddenly quite white. She stammered. "L-l-look! . . . T-t-tom! . . ."

"What's the matter, Dot?" said the Admiral.

"We must turn back," gasped Dorothea.

"I can steer her," said Dick quickly.

"Take the tiller somebody," said Tom, and dived head first into the cabin.

A big motor-cruiser was lying moored to the quay by the inn at the lower end of the village.

"You'd better let me have her," said the Admiral. "But are you sure that's the one? There are lots of them about, and they are very much alike."

"I can read the name," said Dick, who was looking at it through the glasses.

All three of them could read it now, and Tom, lurking in

the cabin, could read it, too, looking through a port-hole. There it was, " MARGOLETTA," in big brass letters on the cruiser's bows. They drove past with wind and tide and read the name again, across the stern of the cruiser, as Tom and Dick had read it at Potter Heigham by the light of a pocket torch. The gramophone and loud-speaker were silent and there was no sign of anyone aboard.

"Probably in the inn," said Mrs. Barrable.

And as they watched, the door of the inn opened, and the whole party of the Hullabaloos came out and sauntered across the grass to the *Margoletta*. They took no notice of the little white yacht with the rather large dinghy sailing down the river. There are plenty of such little yachts on the Broads, and if George Owdon or anyone else had told them Tom was sailing in the *Teasel* with Mrs. Barrable and those two children, the very last place they would have expected to meet them was below Acle Bridge in the strong tides of the lower reaches.

"It's all right now," said Dorothea when the *Teasel* had rounded the next bend and left Stokesby out of sight.

"Well, we can't possibly stop here," said Tom, coming back into the well.

"All right, skipper," said the Admiral, "but I do count on being able to make some tea before very much longer."

"I wonder if they're coming down, too," said Tom. "Oh well, we'll hear them coming. But I shan't be able to hide while we're going through Yarmouth bridges."

He took the tiller again, and soon forgot the Hullabaloos in the excitement of steering the *Teasel*. With this good wind, and the tide under her, she seemed to be going faster every minute, and he could almost see the river narrowing as the tide ebbed. This was not at all like steering in the gentle streams and easy tides that run above Acle Bridge.

"Deepest water round the outer side of the bends," Tom murmured to himself, after cutting a corner too fine, and feeling the *Teasel* suddenly hesitate and then leap forward again as her keel cut through the top of a mudbank.

Dick, who, now that he was not steering had his mind free, was looking at some birds taking flight with drooping pink legs and splashes of white on wings and tail.

"Redshanks, aren't they?" he asked.

"Plenty of them," said Tom. "I say, if we do get stuck we'll stay stuck, with the tide racing out like this."

Mile after mile the *Teasel* and the *Titmouse* flew down those dreary lower reaches of the Bure. Windmills slipped by one after another, and the rare houses called by their distance out of Yarmouth, "Six-Mile House," "Five-Mile House," and so on. And still the ebb was pouring down, and the mud was widening on either side of the channel. Were they going to reach Yarmouth too soon? Tom knew well enough that many a boat had been carried down and smashed against the bridges after getting there too soon and not being able to stop in the rush of the outflowing tide.

Chimneys and church spires were in sight. Already, across Scare Gap, they had caught a glimpse of Breydon Water. Now, right ahead of them, they could see a row of houses.

"What's that moving above the roofs?" asked Dick.

It was a triangle of brown topsail. The next moment, through a gap between the roofs they saw the peaks of a mainsail and mizen.

"Trawler," said Tom.

"The sea must be just the other side of those houses," said Dorothea.

"It is," said the Admiral. "That trawler must be running up the coast close to the shore."

On the left bank now was a low wall of cement shutting in the river.

"It wouldn't do to bump into that," said Dick, remembering the harmless reeds and mud of the upper waters.

Tom did not answer. The *Teasel* was sweeping round the bend, heading down for Yarmouth and its bridges, and he could see by the way the flecks of foam were being swept along that there was a lot of the ebb to run out yet before low water. "A dolphin on the right bank going down. . . ." Jim Wooddall had told him exactly what to look for, and he had been down here before with Mr. Farland and the twins. Tom looked anxiously down the river for the group of heavy piles standing out into the channel, so that boats can tie up to them and wait in safety. With wind and tide together, the *Teasel* was moving dreadfully fast.

"Too early," he said quietly to the Admiral. "We'll have to turn round and hang about a bit . . . if we can. We're going too fast to make sure of catching the dolphin. Ready about!"

There was sudden bustle in the well of the *Teasel*. Nobody had expected this, and even Dick could feel that Tom was worried. Dick and Dorothea fumbled together at the jib sheet.

"No. No," said Tom, "just be ready to harden in when she's round."

The *Teasel*, still being carried down by the tide, swung round into the wind.

"Main-sheet," said Tom.

Hand over hand the Admiral hauled it in. The *Teasel* was sailing again, but heading up the river the way she had come. She could point her course and was moving fast through the water, but Tom was looking not at the water but at a little stump on the bank. Would she do it or not?

"She's going backwards," said Dorothea, almost in panic.

"Give her a little more main-sheet," said Tom.

Slowly, slowly, inch by inch, though the water was foaming under her bows, she began to move up the river. The stump on the bank was level with her mast, was level with Tom at her tiller, was left astern.

"She can do it," said Tom exultantly. As long as the wind held like that they were safe.

And then a man appeared on the bank.

"Take you through Yarmouth, sir?" he said.

Tom glanced at him.

"Fetch her in here and I'll come aboard," said the man.

But Tom was no visiting stranger but a Norfolk Coot. He had heard about the wreckers of Yarmouth who are always ready to lend a hand and, a little later, to do a bit of salvage work. He knew that the Yarmouth Corporation itself warns visitors to apply for help at the Yacht Station and nowhere else. And the Admiral had not forgotten the tales of years ago, when she had been a little girl. She gave one look at Tom.

"No thank you," said Tom, "we're in no hurry."

"You just throw me a warp then," said the man, "I'll make you fast."

"We don't mind sailing till the ebb slackens," said Tom.

All this time the *Teasel* was slowly creeping up the river again, and the man was keeping pace with her, moving foot by foot along the cement wall.

"Bit o' soft mud just here," said the man. "You head her in for me, and you'll be all right."

"I'll try it next year," said Tom.

The man threw out his hands as if to signal that he had failed. Instantly three other men bobbed up from behind the wall and joined him, and all four of them settled down to play cards while waiting for an easier victim.

"Those were the ones who were going to save us when he had got us into a mess," said Tom.

"Real wreckers," said Dorothea. "How lovely."

"Not for us," said Tom, "if we'd let them get a foot aboard."

At last the tide began to slacken and the *Teasel* moved faster past the stumps and stones Tom noticed on the banks.

"We can do it now," he said. "Ready about!"

Once more the *Teasel* swung round and a moment later was flying downstream again towards the bridge.

"Phew," said Tom. "Sorry. I ought to have thought of it before. We'll want the anchors off their ropes. The anchors will be in the way for tying up."

"Don't tumble off, Dick," cried Dorothea. Dick was again sailor and nothing else, and had darted forward. It was an easy job, slipping the loop at the end of the rope clean over the anchor and then pulling it out through the ring on the shank. Dick was back in a moment with an anchor in his hand. Dorothea was unfastening the stern anchor in the same way.

"Shove them anywhere," said Tom.

"Now," said Mrs. Barrable quietly, watching the dolphin as they swept down towards it.

"I'll go forrard to make fast," said Tom. "Could you steer? I'll bring her round, and then you just edge her over and I'll grab the dolphin and hang on. . . ."

The *Teasel* swung round in the stream.

"She'll do it," said Tom, and ran forward. "A wee bit nearer," he called. There was the dolphin, huge, above him, a great framework of black piles, with a platform. He got hold of the platform, and with the other hand flung the warp round a pile. He caught the end of it again. Safe. "Hi! Look out. Fend her off." The *Teasel* was swinging hard in against the piles. "All right now." He made the warp fast and lowered the peak. In another moment he had the jib in his arms, brought it down on deck, pulled a tyer from his pocket, and made sure that it would not blow loose. And now, comfortably, without hurry, the mainsail was lowered, and Tom looked happily at the brown water still pouring past them, and at the bridge below them, and at a few small boys who were critically watching.

"All right now," said Tom. "We've just got to get the mast down ready to go through as soon as it's dead low water."

"Let's have the mast down now," said the Admiral, "and then we'll be ready when the tide's ready for us, and we can have our tea while we're waiting for it."

"Come on, Dick," said Tom, "Acle over again."

"Nine minutes," said the Admiral, watch in hand, when the mast, after coming slowly down, rested beside the boom.

"It's always a wee bit quicker getting it up," said Tom, gathering all the shrouds and halyards with a length of string round them and the mast, so that they did not hang in festoons over the well.

Tea was ready and the whole crew of the *Teasel* were enjoying it in the well, when they were hailed from the shore. They looked up to see a little old sailor man with a white beard standing on the bank.

"Wanting a tow through the bridges?" he said. "They know me at the Yacht Station," he added, but there was no need. Anybody could see in a moment that he was not one of the wreckers.

The Admiral looked at Tom.

Tom, just for a moment, thought how pleasant it would be to take a tow and have no more to worry about. And then he thought of Port and Starboard. He would like to be able to tell them that the *Teasel* had got through alone.

"It's just as you like," said the Admiral.

"No thanks," said Tom. "We're going to wait for slack water."

"You'll be all right," said the old man cheerfully. "Tide be setting up Breydon already.[1] But you'll be coming back another day. If you want a tug then to pull you through Yarmouth, you ring up the Yacht Station from Reedham or St. Olave's and say you want the *Come Along* to meet you on Breydon. They'll give me the word."

"The *Come Along*," repeated Mrs. Barrable.

"What a lovely name for a tug," said Dorothea.

"She's a lovely tug," said the old man. "Motor-boat, she is. Take you up no matter how the tide run. When she say come along, they have to come."

Mrs. Barrable scribbled down the name in the log of the *Teasel*.

"You wait for slack water and you'll come to no harm," said the old man, and went off along the bank.

"We're in for it now," said Tom, "but I know it's easy enough if you don't start down too soon."

"All right, Skipper," said the Admiral. "We've done very well so far."

*

[1] The flood tide begins to run up the Yare while the ebb is still pouring out of the Bure.

TIED UP TO THE DOLPHIN

All the earlier part of the voyage they had been sailing as hard as they could, because they were afraid the tide would turn against them before they came to Yarmouth. Now that they were there, it seemed as if the ebb would never stop. Tom, dreadfully wanting to get it over, felt as if they had been lying there a week, when Dick said, "The water's stopped going down the piles," and, almost at the same moment, Dorothea said, "That last crumb's sailing very slowly."

"Let's get along," said Tom

"Quanting?" said Dick hopefully.

"Not if we can help it," said the Admiral. "We don't want anybody o.b. down here, even if they can swim like porpoises."

"I'm going to tow down in *Titmouse*," said Tom, "with the long rope. There's only one thing, Admiral. We've got to tie up again at the mouth of the Bure, and all the dolphins are on the right-hand side. We'll have to keep well over this side when we're through the bottom bridge." He pulled up the *Titmouse*, dropped into her, worked her forward and made fast the end of the long tow-rope that, so far, had never been used.

"Hang on with the stern warp," said Tom. Standing in the *Titmouse* he cast off the *Teasel's* bow warp. There was still enough current to swing her slowly round.

"Cast off stern warp!" They were doing jolly well, those two, but, at a moment like this he could not help wishing for the twins.

"Everything's loose," said Dick.

"Everything's loose. . . ." Port and Starboard would hardly have put it like that. But Tom knew what Dick meant. Slowly, easily, he settled to his oars. The dolphin was slipping away astern. The *Teasel* tugged at her tow-rope, tugged half-heartedly once again, but presently came more willingly.

"Is she steering all right?" Tom asked.

"Beautifully," said the Admiral.

"There's one bridge gone already," said Dorothea.

The *Teasel* slipped down between the high quays, and the little houses that seemed to rise out of the river mud. There was a dreadful smell of dead fish. Moored to ring-bolts in the walls of the houses and lying on the mud beneath them were little fishing boats, some with brown nets spread to dry. It was strange, coming from the lonely marsh lands up the river

THE · OLD · FIGUREHEAD

to hear the noises of a town, and the hooting of steamers talking to each other in the harbour. In a backyard close above the river, the Admiral, Dick and Dorothea, saw the figurehead of a sailing ship, a huge carved and painted figure of an old gentleman, looking out over clothes drying on a line, as long ago he had looked out over spirting foam and blue water while his ship drove southward in the Trades.

"What's his name?" asked Dorothea.

"What's his name?" called Mrs. Barrable. But the old gentleman and the ship called after him had long been forgotten, and a boy looking down over the wall told them he did not know.

But Tom, steadily rowing in the *Titmouse*, had no eyes for all this. It had seemed to be nearly dead water up above the bridges, but the further he got the faster the stream was pouring out between the mud-banks. Had he, after all, made the mistake he had been warned against, and in spite of all that waiting, started down too soon? There could be no going back now. It would be all right if only he did not miss the dolphin when they came out from under the third bridge where the rivers meet at the top of Yarmouth Haven. The second bridge was gone. A motor-bus roared across the third close behind him. Now was the time. Keep close to the right bank. He edged nearer, and began to wonder if he had better make fast to the dolphin with his own painter or with the tow-rope itself. Better with the tow-rope if he could. The shadow of the bridge fell across him. He was through. He glanced over his shoulder. There was a steamer coming up out of the lower harbour. A schooner was moored against the quay on the left bank. There were the dolphins, black and white, and beyond them open water, miles of it, and the long white railway bridge over Breydon, with the swing bridge in it open for the passing of the steamer. And the Admiral and Dick and Dorothea, looking at all these things, were steering gaily down the middle of the river.

Tom yelled: "Starboard! Head her to starboard! This side!" Oh, if only the twins had been aboard.

He pulled as hard as he could across the stream and towards the dolphins. There was one that would do if only he could get to it and make fast in time. Over his shoulder he saw the iron bar flecked with green weed, fixed upright on the pile for people to pass their warps round. But it was more than he could do with the *Teasel* heading straight downstream.

"This side!" he shouted again. At last they understood. The *Teasel* headed after him towards the dolphin. The tow-rope slackened. Another stroke, another, and his hands were clutching at the slippery pile. "Go through, you beast!" he muttered to the spare end of the tow-rope as he pushed it in behind the iron bar. It was through at last. He freed the rope from the thwart of the *Titmouse* and hung on. The *Teasel* drifting down with the stream tautened it, stretched it, stopped and swung. A moment later he was alongside her bows, and had given the end of the rope to Dick to make fast. They were safe.

"Well done, Tom," said the Admiral as Tom came aboard and tied the little *Titmouse* to the *Teasel's* counter. "Sorry about our steering."

"The steering was all right," said Tom. "Only that last

MOUTH·OF·THE·BURE

bit. I was afraid there wouldn't be time to make sure of the dolphin. But it was all right. Come on, Dick, let's have the mast up and get away."

The mast went slowly up, and the jib, and Tom and Dick and Dorothea were being very particular about the set of the mainsail. Tom wanted it exactly right for sailing up Breydon.

"That man's shouting at us," said Dorothea.

A sailor on the schooner away by the quay was giving them a friendly warning. "Ahoy there. Best stir yourselves. They'll be closing the bridge."

"Cast off," cried Tom, and Dick let go one end of the tow-rope, and began hauling in hand over hand on the other as it came slipping round the bar on the dolphin. The foredeck was all a clutter of tow-rope and halyards, but no matter.

The *Teasel* was sailing.

"Close-hauled," called Tom to the Admiral. "We've got to tack up through the bridge."

"You'd better come and take her, Tom."

"You deal with these ropes, Dick. Sit on the roof when she goes about. But tidy up as well as you can." Tom ran aft and jumped into the well.

The Admiral seemed glad to let him have the tiller. Dorothea was anxiously watching Dick, who was busy on the foredeck, trying to coil down the ropes exactly as he had seen them coiled by the Coots.

"The tide'll take us through," said Tom. "We've just got to keep her moving and head her in between the piers. And once we're through and round the corner we'll have a free wind up Breydon."

"They seem in a bit of a hurry on the bridge," said the Admiral. High on the bridge, someone was leaning from a signal cabin and waving.

"Ready about!" sang out Tom. "Sit down and hang on, Dick!" The *Teasel* had gone almost as far as the opposite shore of the Yare. She swung round now on the port tack, but not for long. "Ready about!" Tom sang out again. Again Dick sat down on the end of the cabin roof and took a firm grip of the mast.

"She'll do it now," said Tom, and headed in between the piers. Railway men up on the bridge looked down on the little *Teasel*. The crew of the *Teasel* looked up at great iron girders above them on either side. The sails flapped. Tom was heading straight into the wind, counting on the tide to carry him through. Another ten yards. Another five. There was the clang of a changing signal, and the noise of levers slipping into place. They were through and already the huge swinging span of the bridge was closing astern of them. Presently a train roared across.

Dick finished tidying up the foredeck and joined the others in the well. William barked at the train. Tom gave a little flourish with his hand, without really meaning to do anything of the sort. "We've done it," he said. "Got through Yarmouth, anyway."

"Chocolate all round," said the Admiral. "We've done it without letting the *Teasel* get a single scratch."

"I do wish Port and Starboard were here to see," said Dorothea.

"They'll be just finishing their race," said the Admiral.

BREYDON · BRIDGE

CHAPTER XIX

SIR GARNET OBLIGES FRIENDS

THE twins had missed their ship, but what of that? They were aboard the fastest wherry on the river, and would catch the *Teasel* at Stokesby if they did not catch her before. They were extremely cheerful. Everything had been saved at the very last minute, and after all, they too would share in the voyage to the south, for which they had been training the Admiral's eager crew.

They looked at the windows of the doctor's house as the wherry slipped past it. "Our baby" had not yet been moved into the garden. They caught a glimpse of somebody in a white apron in one of the upper rooms, but nobody looked out. Dr. Dudgeon's golden bream, high above the brown reed-thatching, was still swimming merrily north-west.

"Couldn't have a better wind," said Starboard.

"We'll need it," said Jim Wooddall shortly. He could not forgive old Simon for dawdling ashore and making him late in getting away.

Only the upper windows of their own house showed above the willows. But at the edge of the river, under the low boat-house roof, they could see the *Flash* with lowered mast, waiting all unconscious that she had been deserted by her skipper and her crew.

"Poor old *Flash*," said Starboard. "Hullo! Ginty's waving at us."

"Only shaking out a duster," said Port. "Of course she isn't waving. If she saw us going down the river on a wherry she'd be throwing fifteen different kinds of fit."

They were relieved to see the duster disappear.

"She'll have spring-cleaned the whole house by the time we come back."

And then Jim Wooddall was asking them about the races, and they told him how it was that *Flash* was out of them, and that as soon as Mr. Farland came back they were going to challenge the winner. *Grizzled Skipper*, Jim Wooddall thought, was the likeliest of the lot, "And I'd like to see her an' *Flash* fight it out," he said. And then they talked of sugar-beet, that was keeping wherries busy at one time of the year, going round to Cantley on the Norwich River, and of other cargoes, such as grain, of which there was less than ever, and of the bungalows that were sent down by water all ready-made and needing only to be set up ("Card houses, I call 'em ") and cargoes of planks for quay-heading and cut logs for piles. And all the time they were talking, Port and Starboard were looking eagerly down each reach of the river as it opened before them, until, at last, Jim Wooddall noticed it and laughed.

"He've a long start of us, Tom have."

Old Simon was steadily working away, making beautiful flat coils of the warps on the top of *Sir Garnet's* closed hatches. He came aft now, and went into the little cabin, and came out with a bucket of potatoes and a saucepan half full of water.

"Better give him a hand," said Jim Wooddall. "Workin' yer passage, you are." And old Simon sitting on the hatch with the bucket between his knees made them laugh by opening an enormous clasp knife and offering it to Starboard.

But they had knives of their own, of a handier size, and were soon hard at work, though old Simon peeled four potatoes to every one of theirs, and did not think much of them as cooks.

"Look ye here, Miss Bess," he said, "if you takes the top-sides off that thick, what sort of a spud'll ye have left for puttin' in the pan?"

They were close to the mouth of the Ant when they heard and saw the *Margoletta*. She was coming up the river against the tide, and the wherry with wind and tide to help her was sweeping down. They were close to each other when the *Margoletta* swung round and into the Fleet Dyke, where, only yesterday, the *Teasel* had been.

"Lookin' for him in South Walsham, likely," said Jim Wooddall with a grin.

The assistant cooks of *Sir Garnet* stared at him.

"But how do you know about it?" said Starboard.

"Easy," said Jim Wooddall, puffing at his pipe. "Them cruisers talk enough. There's only one boy down Horning way what have a black punt and paddle her from the stern. Tom Dudgeon and his old *Dreadnought*. Tom say nothin' about it to me that day he come to Wroxham, and there was me, readin' that notice over his head. And after he go, up come that lot in *Margoletta* asking for a boy in a sail-boat. . . . Tom Dudgeon and his *Titmouse* for certain sure. And you missies know somethin' about how they didn't cotch him that day." And he grinned again.

"Look here, Jim," said Port. "Nobody but George Owdon would have told them Tom was gone up the river in a sailing boat. And the night before last they came up to Potter Heigham, and we think George must have told them Tom was gone up the Thurne."

"They as good as said someone tell 'em, that day Tom come to Wroxham."

"But what we don't understand is this," said Starboard. "If George wants them to catch Tom, why doesn't he send them straight to Doctor Dudgeon?"

"Simple," said Jim Wooddall. "Fare to me that George he want 'em to cotch young Tom, but he nat'rally don't want to be in it hisself. So he send 'em where he think they can't fail for to meet him. If they meet young Tom and know him, how

232

be George Owdon to blame? But if them cruisers go to the doctor and ask for his son, why, how do they know the name of a boy they seen once in their life? Somebody must 'a told 'em. And everybody in Horning'd know who 'twas."

"Phew!" said Port. "I wonder if they met Tom sailing the *Teasel* to-day."

"They didn't cotch him," said Jim Wooddall. "They'd be going to Horning or Wroxham to raise a bobbery else. Eh, Simon," he broke off, looking at his huge old watch, "we'll never get to Gorleston on this tide. They'll be laughin' at us when we go through Acle Bridge."

Jim Wooddall, late with his tide, was as much in a hurry as the twins, and he was sailing *Sir Garnet* as if in a race, trimming her huge black sail, keeping always in the fastest water. Presently they came to Thurne Mouth, where the two rivers join, and had to jibe round the corner just as Tom had jibed in the *Teasel*, as they turned south for Acle. The huge black sail swung across with a clap and a creak of the gaff jaws, and a clang as the big blocks of the main-sheet shifted. Port and Starboard, themselves accustomed to racing in the little *Flash*, knew just how well their friend the wherryman was handling *Sir Garnet*.

"She jolly well *can* sail," said Starboard.

"She can fly when she've a mind to't," said Jim.

And still there was no sign of the little white yacht they were looking for, the little white yacht with a white dinghy a good deal too large for her.

The potatoes were peeled now, and old Simon went down into the cabin.

Jim, half laughing, half serious, pushed out his chin at him as he passed.

"Can we go in, too?" asked Port.

"Ye'd better. He'll ferget the salt else, the gormless old lummocks!"

233

"Sing out as soon as you see her," said Starboard, and they slipped down to join old Simon, who was busy with the stove.

It was very pleasant, just for a while, to be down below in the dusk of the cabin. A wherry is a heavy boat to push through the water, and fast as *Sir Garnet* was moving, the twins were wanting her to go faster still and pushing at her in their minds. Down below they could not see what was happening and were no longer trying to see round the next bend in hope of finding the *Teasel*, moored perhaps, or just starting again after stopping for a meal. It was pleasant, too, to hear the noise of the water under another boat coming upstream, and Jim's cheerful "Marnin'," and other voices giving him "good day," while, sitting on one of the narrow bunks in the little cabin they could see just a bit of blue sky now and then, and Jim's sea-boots, and now and then his gnarled hand on the tiller, and, sometimes, a little floating cloud of blue tobacco smoke.

Old Simon stowed away some of the stores he had brought aboard at Horning. Port and Starboard were sitting on Jim's bunk, and he made room for himself on his own, beside an *Eastern Morning News*, wrapping up a parcel of thick rashers of bacon, a big block of plug tobacco, two loaves of bread, a packet of matches and a bottle of milk. On the floor between the bunks was the small sack of potatoes into which he had already dipped. He set the potatoes on the little stove, altered the draught of it, and put more coal on, until Jim bent down and told him it was a good thing they had a black sail with all the smoke he was making.

"He'll have his joke at me all day," said old Simon quietly, "along of me keepin' *Sir Garnet* waitin' at the top of the tide."

The potatoes were done to old Simon's liking and were simmering in their pot. Port was prodding them to see how soft they were. Starboard was busy with the bacon and the frying-pan. Old Simon was digging in the back of the locker for a spare knife and fork when he sniffed suddenly at the good smell that was filling the little cabin.

"Hi," he said, "missie, you be spilin' good bacon."

Starboard, turning the rashers quickly over, lowered the pan towards the flames.

"Gingerbread, I tell ye," almost screamed the old man. "Who wants that stuff crackin' and fiddlin' down to nothin'." He took the pan from her and turned the well-cooked browned rashers out. "Not half what it was," he said. "Now you mind me," he went on, slapping a few more rashers down on the pan, "and then when you get husbants they'll have a good word for yer cookin'. Thick an' soft an' jewsy, that's what's good in bacon."

"But we like it the other way," said Port, defending her twin.

"Jim don't," said old Simon.

And sure enough when Jim came down into the cabin for his dinner, letting his mate take the tiller, he was on the point of throwing the well-cooked rashers overboard. "Wasters," he said. "Don't eat 'em. We've plenty more. Old Sim's not hisself to-day. Crossed in love, that's what he is. An' we'll be lucky, too, if we don't have the tide against us before we come to 'Six-Mile House.'"

"We cooked them," said Starboard, "and we like them that way."

"Well," said Jim, "ye can have 'em an' welcome."

There was no time to finish that dinner in the cabin before old Simon called the skipper on deck. *Sir Garnet* was in the last reach before Acle, racing down towards the bridge with her great black sail full of wind.

"Can ye hold her steady between ye?" said Jim, "an' I'll give old Simon a hand."

Port and Starboard knew what was going to happen, but never before had they been aboard a wherry when actually shooting a bridge.

"We'll manage all right," said Starboard. "They must have gone through," she added.

"No sign on 'em here," said Jim.

"They may have gone through and tied up below the bridge," said Port.

There was the bridge, a single span across the river, and with wind and tide alike helping her, *Sir Garnet* was sweeping down towards it.

"They'll be too late to get it down," said Starboard. It did seem impossible that the mast would be lowered before it crashed into the bridge. But Simon and Jim, without a word to each other, seemed not to be hurrying at all. There was a long rattle of the winch paying out the halyard. The huge sail was down. And now, so near the bridge that the twins felt like screaming, the huge mast was dipping towards them, down and down.

"Right O, missie," said Jim Wooddall, and his brown hand closed on the tiller.

"Overslept, eh?" said an old man looking down from the bridge as *Sir Garnet* shot through.

"That's with our bein' late on the tide," said Jim.

And then Jim let them have the tiller again. The mast was lifting the moment they had cleared the bridge. The big black sail rose bellying in the wind. *Sir Garnet* had left Acle Bridge astern of her, and was sailing once more. And never a sign of the *Teasel*.

"He'll have gone right through to Stokesby," said Starboard, and went on steering the wherry, while the wherrymen finished their dinner, and old Simon made some very strong tea. The twins had had all the bacon and potatoes they could eat, but Jim would not be satisfied until he had made them huge sandwiches of bread and cheese and seen the sandwiches eaten. "I would'n have Mr. Farland think we starved ye," he said.

Almost sooner than they expected, the windmill and the roofs of Stokesby showed above the reedy banks.

"What about putting us ashore?" asked Starboard.

Port dived down into the cabin and handed up the rugs and knapsacks that had been stowed there out of harm's way.

"Anything to break in these?" asked Jim.

"No."

"That's lucky," said Jim. "We'll heave 'em ashore, an' give you an easy jump an' a soft landin'. Can't stop now."

"But where are they?" said Port. "Tom said he was going to moor at this end, by the windmill if he could. The wind's just right for it, but he's not there."

"By Stokesby Ferry, likely," said Jim.

But *Sir Garnet* swept on round the long Stokesby bend, past the windmill, and the farm, past the village, past the inn, past the ferry. Stokesby was astern of them, and one thing was clear to both of them. It was no use going ashore at Stokesby, for the *Teasel* was not there.

And now, for the first time, it came into the heads of the twins that nobody but themselves and the wherrymen knew where they were. Ginty and the A.P. thought they were aboard the *Teasel*. Aboard the *Teasel* everybody thought they were at Horning. It was one thing just to take a lift on a friendly wherry as far as Acle, or even as far as Stokesby, but here they were sailing on farther and farther from home with every minute and not knowing what was before them. What if the Admiral had changed her mind and put off going south, and Tom and the *Teasel* had gone up the Ant to Barton and Stalham, or made another trip to Potter Heigham? Some word might have reached Tom about the *Margoletta* and given him a reason for a change of plan.

The wherrymen were troubled, too. The one thing on which a wherryman prides himself is making the best use of the tides. There is no sense in sailing against the tide when an hour or two earlier or later you might be sailing with it. A wherryman sailing with the tide is always ready to laugh when he meets another struggling against it. Bad seamanship is what it seems to him. And now here was *Sir Garnet* leaving Stokesby with ten miles to go to Yarmouth, and Jim and his mate knew that if they had been an hour earlier they would not have been a minute too soon. Jim kept taking a look at his big watch, and at the mud that was showing below the green at the sides of the river. Once the tide turned it would be a long time before they could get down to Gorleston against it. And besides all this, Jim was thinking that perhaps he had been a bit hasty in taking Mr. Farland's twins aboard. "If Tom Dudgeon hadn't knowed they was coming, why should he stay waitin' for 'em? That boy'd use his tides right, and not go foolin' 'em away like some folk, darn it."

Things grew more and more grim aboard *Sir Garnet* as the old wherry hurried on her way down those desolate lower reaches of the Bure. Before they got to "Six-Mile House" the ebb had slackened. At Runham Swim it was beginning to flow the other way. They met two sailing yachts coming up with the first of the flood. From Mautby down to Scare Gap there was a hardish stream against them, and Jim and his mate had stopped talking together. At Scare Gap, the twins thought that far away beyond the narrow neck of land and the mud-flats on the other side a white sail moving on Breydon Water might have been the *Teasel's*. They knew already that if Tom had come this way at all he must have got right down to Yarmouth. The mud was showing on both sides of the river, and the wherry was twisting this way and that to keep in the narrow channel. There was no place here for a little vessel like the *Teasel* to bring up snug against the windward bank.

The good wind and her big black sail kept *Sir Garnet* forging through the water. But she moved more and more slowly past the banks as the flood strengthened against her.

Yarmouth chimneys were in sight, and rows of houses, and they could hear the steamers down by Gorleston where Jim could no longer hope to take the wherry till the tide turned again. Slowly *Sir Garnet* drove round the big bend by the racecourse. Clear ahead of them was the first of the Yarmouth bridges. Twice the twins had their hopes raised at the sight of other little yachts. Twice their hopes fell again. The *Teasel* was not there.

"We can't go no further," said Jim Wooddall at last, as he brought *Sir Garnet* quietly alongside some mooring-posts. "This'll do for us." For a few minutes Simon and he were busy stowing the big sail. Then he stood, rubbing his chin and looking at the worried faces of the twins.

"Tom may be down by the Yacht Quay," said Starboard.

"Sure he come this way?" said Jim.

"They said last night they were going down to Stokesby."

"If he come this far, he'd be taking the flood up Breydon," said Jim. "You can't catch him. . . . Best be takin' a bus to Horning if ye can get one."

What would Mrs. McGinty say if they came home with a tale like that, or even Mrs. Dudgeon . . . sailing off on a wherry to Yarmouth to look for a boat that might be anywhere?

"We've simply *got* to find them," said Port.

"Ye'll be gettin' me into trouble with Mr. Farland."

And then, suddenly, Starboard saw that old Simon was pointing down river towards the bridge. A yacht with lowered mast was coming through, towed by a little motor-boat with a big red-and-white flag.

"Ye're right," said Jim suddenly. "If young Tom go down here, old Bob see him. Comin' and goin', old Bob see all."

The *Come Along*, with the tide to help her noisy little engine, was soon passing close by the wherry. Port and Starboard saw a little old sailor in a blue jersey, by himself in the little tug, looking back every now and then over his shoulder because the people in the yacht he was towing were not steering very well. It needs practice to steer well standing on the counter of a yacht and reaching the tiller with a foot through a lot of shrouds and halyards draped about the lowered mast.

"Ahoy!" shouted Starboard. "Have you seen the *Teasel?*"

"Hi!" shouted Jim. "Half a mo', Bob."

The little old sailor could not hear a word because of the chug-chugging of his motor. But he saw that he was wanted, and he made a signal with his hand, up the river and down again, to show that he would be casting off his tow and would be coming back.

"Old Bob'll know," said Jim.

"He'll know," said Simon.

Those few minutes of waiting after *Sir Garnet* had been moored were much worse than all the hours of hurrying down the river. Then, at least, they had been moving. Now they were keeping still, and, perhaps, at that very moment, Tom might be hoisting sail below the bridges ... if, indeed, he had not gone some other way and never come down the Bure at all. It was horrible to see how far up the river that yacht was towed, how slow her crew were in making fast, and then how unwilling they seemed to say good-bye to the old sailor. Someone was paying him. Good! They were hoisting the yacht's mast. And still the little motor-tug waited alongside. Why couldn't he hurry? What could there be to talk about? And then, at last, they saw a bow wave flung suddenly out on either side of the tow-boat as she started off towards them.

"Eh? What's that?" The little old sailor was trying to quiet his engine without stopping it altogether.

"Friends of ours," Jim was explaining. "Joinin' a little yacht, the *Teasel*, with Tom Dudgeon from Hornin' aboard. Seen her go through?"

"Boat full o' children with an old lady an' a dog? I see 'em. Went through at low water, they did. Wouldn't take help from no one. Last I see of 'em they was away through Breydon Bridge."

Jim bent lower. The old man shut his engine off.

"They *got* to do it," Port heard Jim say. "Can't send 'em back now."

The old man looked at the twins.

"Hop in," he said suddenly. "I got to go up Breydon to fetch a yacht down what's missed her tide. Hop in. We'll catch that *Teasel* for you if she've not gone too far. Easy now."

In another two seconds the twins and their knapsacks and their rugs were aboard the *Come Along*. Jim and Simon were wishing them good luck. The twins were thanking the wherry-men. The old man had started his engine again and they were off once more, chug, chug, chug, chug, against the muddy tide that was pouring up under the town bridges.

CHAPTER XX

WHILE THE WIND HOLDS

A STRANGE peace filled the well of the *Teasel*. There was a good wind, and they felt it more on the open water of Breydon than sheltered between the banks of the river. But that was pleasure only, and the good wind was helping them on their way. The thing that Tom had been worrying about for a week was safely over. They had got through Yarmouth. Everybody felt the same. It was as if by passing Breydon railway bridge they had passed from a turbulent day to one of settled weather. They began looking at things afresh, with the eyes of people who have no longer a care in the world. There was the enormous sheet of Breydon Water, spreading up over its wide mudflats. There were the great wooden posts marking the channel, black on the northern side, red on the southern, almost every post with its perching gull, who flapped off as the *Teasel* sailed by. Here and there, far away over the mud, were the little black tarred houseboats of fishermen and fowlers. Far ahead of them they could see a steamship, the same that had gone through the bridge before them, pouring out a long whirling feather of black smoke. A small motor-boat, with a big red and white flag in its bows, was coming to meet them, towing a yacht with lowered mast. A woman was sitting on the cabin roof of the yacht, and a man was standing on the counter leaning on the lowered mast and steering with his foot. But it was not at them that the crew of the *Teasel* were looking.

"That must be the *Come Along*," said Dorothea.

"I can read it," said Dick, who had again got out the glasses.

"There's our friend," said the Admiral.

The little old sailor with the white beard was sitting in the stern of his little tow-boat, and waved as he passed them.

It was somehow very pleasant to see him again, now that they had come through Yarmouth by themselves.

"Come down all right?" he shouted to them, but they could hardly hear him above the loud chug, chug of the *Come Along's* motor. They waved back joyfully.

Mrs. Barrable was looking eagerly about her, and had pulled out her sketch-book and was making little rough notes in coloured chalks. She had never been on Breydon since the building of the railway bridge across it, and she was remembering the old Breydon of forty years ago, and old regattas, and boats with bowsprits as long as themselves racing round a mark-buoy close above Yarmouth harbour. Dorothea was feeling she was at sea, looking forward over that great sheet of water at the distant smoke of the steamship. Dick, busy with the binoculars, was looking at the birds on the mudflats, watching the herons paddling in the shallows as the water rose, and the gulls, who felt the place belonged to them, mobbing the herons. Tom, too, was free to think of birds once more. And even William, now that the bustle was over, had come out of the cabin, climbed on a seat and was looking out with both forepaws on the coaming. It was as if the voyagers were beginning a new day instead of coming to the end of one that had started very early.

Nor was it only getting through Yarmouth that gave them so light and holiday a feeling.

"The Hullabaloos would have come through by now if they were coming," said Tom.

Dorothea looked back towards Breydon. There was not another boat to be seen.

"Of course, they may come to-morrow," said Tom, "whatever they do to-day. Those beasts can get about so fast. But we're all right for now. What I was afraid of was their coming down while I was towing in the *Titmouse*."

"It seems to me," said the Admiral, "that we get about pretty fast ourselves." She shaded her eyes to look over the water ahead of them towards the evening sun. "What do you think, skipper? Where shall we tie up for the night?"

"Let's go on sailing for ever," said Dorothea. "We could take turns in being awake."

"Let's go on as far as ever we can," said Tom. "While the wind holds. . . . That man at Potter Heigham got all the way from Hickling to . . ." He dived into the cabin for the map.

"All right, Dot," said the Admiral. "You take the tiller. Keep as near the middle of the channel as you can. Not too near the red posts."

Tom came out again with the map and glanced at the long line of red posts on the port side, and the long line of black posts on the starboard side, leading away into the distance. All was well. He opened the map and ran his finger along the Waveney River. "We can't get as far as Beccles," he said doubtfully. "Nobody could. . . . There's St. Olave's Bridge to go under. . . . Mast has to come down again. . . . But we're getting pretty good at that . . . then two swing bridges . . . we may get held up by some beastly train. . . . But we've got a grand tide with us, and the wind's holding, and it won't be dark for a long time yet."

"We'll see what we can do," said Mrs. Barrable.

"You'll be at Beccles to-morrow, Admiral," said Dorothea. "Won't she, Tom?"

"Depends on the wind," said Tom. "Look here, Dot, keep away from the red posts. We don't want to have to tack if we can help it."

"I say," cried Dick suddenly. "Isn't that a spoonbill, there, with hunched-up shoulders, and another, dipping in the mud where that trickle is? . . . White, like storks."

"They must be," said Tom. "Let's have the glasses a minute. I've only seen them once before. This goes down in the Coot Club book."

"And in the log," said the Admiral.

"And those are curlews," said Dick. "Aren't they? Or are they whimbrels? I say, can't we anchor here and stay the night?"

"We may have a dead calm to-morrow," said Tom. "And the *Teasel's* doing far too well to stop."

"Anyhow," said Dorothea, her eyes fixed on the row of posts with the water swirling past them, "we must try to get somewhere so that we can send off post cards to tell Port and Starboard where we've got to. Am I far enough away from the posts now?"

The *Teasel* sailed on up the broad channel of Breydon Water. The rising tide was spreading farther and farther over the mud flats on either side. Herons were stalking about knee-deep far away by the embankment. One rested for a moment on the top of a red post and then, as the *Teasel* came nearer, floated away with steady flaps of its long wings and a sharp indignant squawk. There was a constant chatter of quarrelsome gulls, besides the warning calls of the nervous greenshanks, the long whistling cry of the curlew and the restless shrilling of the sandpipers.

It did, indeed, seem a pity to be leaving that wild place, but, as Mrs. Barrable said, they would be seeing it again on their way home. And now the channel began to bend to the south, Tom was able to ease off the main-sheet, and the shores, closing in, showed that they were nearing the upper end of Breydon. They were reading the numbers on these big red and black beacon posts, and had already reached the forties. Away to the right was a long wall of tarred piling. More black piles stood out into the water at the mouth of the Norwich river (the Yare). There was a lonely inn, the Berney Arms, standing above the river. Far away over the land they could see the smoke of the steamship.

"Which way do we go?" asked Dorothea at the tiller.

"Up the Waveney," said Tom. "Follow the red posts round."

There were still mudflats away to the left, and behind them, on a lump of rising ground, Mrs. Barrable pointed out the ancient remains of the Roman fort of Burgh. But nearer at hand was something that interested them still more. An old sailing vessel with no masts, just the hull of her turned into a sort of houseboat, was resting on the mud against the spit of land that divided the two rivers. There was a notice, "Breydon Pilot," and there walking up and down his deck was the pilot himself, watching the shifting channel and ready to tell people where the deep water was as they went up or down. He signalled with a wave of his arm to tell the *Teasel* not to cut the corner too fine. Tom put his hand out towards the tiller, but drew it back again. Dorothea had understood and was steering across to pass close by the houseboat.

"Silted a bit over there," the pilot called to them.

"Thank you," shouted Tom.

"Grand evening," said the pilot.

"Look, look," said Dick, still hankering after stopping within reach of those birds on Breydon. "There's a notice, 'Safe Moorings for Yachts,' and another one, 'Yachts repaired.'"

"But we don't need repairing," said Mrs. Barrable.

"And we'll get miles farther yet," said Tom.

"If we do get wrecked, we'll come here to be mended," said Dorothea.

"Where are ye bound for?" asked the pilot.

"Beccles."

"Ye've a good tide yet if the wind don't fail ye," said the pilot, turning round and looking away towards the north-west.

Once in the river, with the tide helping them and the wind still strong, they seemed to be going much faster than when on

Breydon, because, with the banks so near, they could not help seeing how they were rushing by. High banks they were now, with reeds growing on them, and great caves of mud below the reeds, filling up as the tide rose.

"We can't tie up here, anyway," said Tom.

By the time they reached St. Olave's, where a road crosses the river by an iron bridge, they were tired, but hardly knew it. They moored there, lowered the mast, towed through under the bridge, tied up, hoisted the mast and sailed on almost in a dream.

"Is that another river?" asked Dick, just after they had left St. Olave's. Looking back, they could see another little bridge, and water beyond it.

"That's the New Cut," said the Admiral. "Between the two rivers, so that people can go from one to the other without having to go down to Breydon, or under St. Olave's Bridge. That one opens."

"Why is it called 'New'?" asked Dick.

"I suppose they called it 'New' when it was new, a hundred years ago."

Tom at that moment was a little worried. Just ahead of them was the Herringfleet swing bridge, where the railway crosses the river, and up at the signal-box by the station a red flag was flying to show that the bridge was closed, as Tom could see for himself. Had the signalman not noticed the white sail of the *Teasel* coming round the bend from St. Olave's? Or was there a train coming so that he could not open the bridge?

"I think I'll take the tiller," said Tom, looking about him for somewhere to tie up in case they had to wait, and then deciding that he would do as he had done on the Bure, and turn round and sail the other way, if the tide were not too strong. It would never do to be swept up against the bridge . . . lose the mast that way. . . . Oh, couldn't that man give them a signal if he wasn't going to open?

"That flag's going down," cried Dorothea. "What does that mean?"

"Bridge opening," said Tom, glad now that he had not yet done anything to show that he was in doubt.

The *Teasel* sailed on and through the opened bridge. Up in his signal-box they could see the signalman working his levers. Already the bridge was closing. The red flag was again flying from its tall flagstaff.

"Thank you!" they shouted, and waved, and the signalman high up there in his box put his head and shoulders out of the window and waved back.

From the Herringfleet bridge to the bridge at Somerleyton is only a mile and a half. But by the time they reached it, the Admiral knew that they were tired. A small yacht was moored to the bank below the Somerleyton Ferry. The yacht was ready for the night, with her awning up, and the Admiral, looking at her, said that if the bridge was closed they might as well moor there, too, and go on next day.

"Oh, Admiral!" said Dorothea, who was standing by while Dick was steering, in case he should see a heron or some other bird. "Oh, Admiral! Just when she's going so well."

But the bridge was opening as she spoke.

I think I can steer her through," said Dick.

"All right," said Tom.

Somerleyton was left behind them, and there seemed to be no point in stopping now.

The sun had set, the wind was dropping, but the *Teasel* was still gliding on, so smoothly, so easily, that it seemed impossible to stop. On and on they sailed. A sunset glow spread over the sky, and the reeds stood out black against it. On and on. They could hardly see where the reflections ended and the banks began. Nothing else was moving. Windmills, dark against the darkening sky, seemed twice their proper size. At last, peering forward, they could see that the river was dividing in two.

TIED UP FOR THE NIGHT

"Oulton Dyke," said Tom, hardly above a whisper. For some time now he had been at the tiller.

There was hardly enough wind to give the *Teasel* steerage way as she bore round up the Waveney River. It died altogether. The boom swung in. The main-sheet dipped in the water.

"Have you got a torch?" said Tom. "Mine's in the *Titmouse*." Dick was into the cabin and out again with his torch.

"Will you take her, Admiral?" Tom hurried forward and stood waiting with the rond anchor in his hand, flashing the light of the torch along the bank.

"We'll try here," he said. "Bring her in. She's hardly moving. Will she steer?"

Gently the *Teasel* pushed her nose towards the bank. There was a thud and a squelch as Tom jumped ashore. He had the anchor fixed in a moment and was back aboard again as the dying tide swung the *Teasel* slowly round. Aft, in the well, they heard the faint rattle of the block as the jib came down. The peak of the mainsail came slowly, and with difficulty, for the halyard had swollen with the evening dew. By the light of their torches they stowed the sails. By the light of their torches they rigged the awnings, first over the *Teasel* and then over the *Titmouse*.

"Well, it isn't the furthest anybody's ever done in a day," said Tom, "but she really has come a jolly long way."

"It seems a pity," said the Admiral, "but I suppose we must try to keep awake, just until we've had our supper."

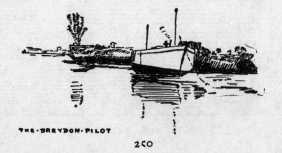

THE·BREYDON·PILOT

CHAPTER XXI

COME ALONG AND *WELCOME*

The twins had been very near despair when the wherry had tied up above Yarmouth and the wherryman had told them that the best they could do was to go home. Suddenly, Old Bob and his *Come Along* had filled them with hope once more. With a motor-boat like the *Come Along* they felt sure they would be overhauling the *Teasel* in a minute or two.

"She's a splendid little tug," said Starboard. "SPLENDID TUG," she shouted, seeing that the old man had not heard her.

Old Bob, sitting snugly in the stern with his arm over his tiller, agreed with a smile.

"She's a good 'un," he shouted back. "When she say 'Come along,' they have to come, and no mistake about it. Many a hundred she've pulled off Breydon mud."

Both Starboard and the old man had been shouting to make themselves heard, but now, perhaps just to show what she could do, Old Bob opened the throttle and let her out. It was no use even shouting. Port and Starboard looked astern at the following wave racing along the quays. Somehow it seemed quite different from the wash of a motor cruiser. It simply gave them a pleasant feeling that they were really moving through the water. It was a cheerful promise of catching up the *Teasel*. They settled down to enjoy the chase.

Old Bob, too, was enjoying himself. All through the summer the *Come Along* had plenty of work to do, but now, so early in the year, when the season had not fairly started and only a few of the visitors were afloat, every job was worth having, and Old Bob was pleased with his day. At low water he had taken three yachts up through the bridges, and now, thanks to that message from the Yacht Station, he was off again to meet another coming down the Waveney from St. Olave's. That would mean a long tow back to Yarmouth against the tide, and money well earned. Old Bob hunched himself contentedly in the stern of the *Come Along* and steered down the narrow river between the Yarmouth houses, with the air of a man who knew he had a job waiting for him as soon as he could get to it.

The *Come Along* passed the first bridge, and a goods engine went slowly across it just above their heads. A man on the Corporation Yacht Station waved to Old Bob and Old Bob lifted a hand in return. The second bridge was coming nearer as the little tow-boat, with her steady chug, chug, chug, chug, forced her way down over the incoming stream. That bridge was gone, too. Brown nets hoisted to dry in a blue fishing boat, boys perched on walls looking down, a wherry with lowered mast coming up at a great pace, little spirts of smoke from her stern showing that she had a motor tucked away below, two boys in a rowing boat also going up with the flood, and then the bridge that carries the road to Acle and Norwich, and beyond it widening water, the quays of Yarmouth on the left, big black and white dolphins on the right, the long Breydon railway bridge, and the broad inland sea where the *Teasel* had gone before them.

Suddenly, as old Bob cut a corner between the outer dolphins and headed for Breydon Bridge, they seemed to be going four times as fast as before. There was no difference in the noise of the engine, and they were going no faster through the water, but instead of forcing their way down against the tide flowing up the Bure they were moving with the tide flowing up Breydon. It seemed no time at all before they were racing under the bridge and out on Breydon Water, looking eagerly ahead of them for the *Teasel's* white sail. Chug, chug, chug, chug . . . the *Come Along* hurried up the middle of the marked channel, with its red posts on one side and black posts on the other. There was not a sail to be seen. Old Bob pulled a pair of binoculars from under a thwart and looked into the distance ahead of them.

"Where was they bound?" he shouted into Starboard's ear.

"Beccles," shouted Starboard.

The old man looked back over his shoulder and seemed to settle himself closer to his tiller.

Port looked at Starboard. Starboard looked at Port. Each knew what the other was thinking. They had no need to shout. They had been sure that the *Teasel* would be in sight as soon as ever they were out on Breydon Water. Already they could see the line of beacon posts bending away to the left. That house dimly seen on the low ground above the shining water must be the Berney Arms on the Norwich river. And where was the *Teasel*? They had left Jim Wooddall, who knew them and knew the A.P. There they were, the other side of Yarmouth, in strange waters where no one knew them. How far would the old man take them? And, if they had lost the *Teasel*, what could they do? It would soon be evening. There could be no getting back to Horning now, even by bus.

They looked back. There was nothing in sight but a Thames barge, with topsail set over her mainsail, driving up Breydon astern of them, in from the sea.

"Bound for Norwich likely," shouted Old Bob, glancing over his shoulder. "Or Beccles. . . . Corn to Beccles. . . . Malt to London. . . . CORN," he shouted in Starboard's ear, thinking she had not heard, and Starboard nodded hard for fear he should shout again.

They came to the top of Breydon Water and the long wall of black piling that guards the Reedham marshes. They passed the point of the spit that divides the Norwich river from the Waveney. Ahead of them, moored against the bank, was the old white hulk of the Breydon pilot.

"He'll have seed 'em," shouted Old Bob, above the chug, chug of his motor. He leaned forward and shut down his throttle. The *Come Along* seemed almost quiet.

The pilot, hands in pockets, was walking up and down the deck of his hulk, and stopped, and stood at the rail and waited for them, when he saw that Old Bob meant to have a word with him.

"Evenin', Bob," he said.

"Evenin'," said the old man. "Ha' you seed a little yacht, with some children aboard, an' a dog an' an old lady?"

"The *Teasel*?" said the pilot. "They'll be through St. Olave's by now, the way they was going. Aimin' for Beccles, they said."

"I got two first-class passengers what missed the tender," said Old Bob, and then, suddenly, "Is that a sail beatin' down river?"

For one moment Port and Starboard were full of hope, but the pilot said, "Yes. Tide's too strong for her. She've been beatin' there these last twenty minutes and makin' nothin' of it."

"That'll be my tow," said Old Bob, opened the throttle and sent the *Come Along* racing up the river to meet her.

"But what are we to *do*?" shouted Starboard.

"I reckon we've missed 'em," the old man shouted back. "Gone too *far*. I got to take that *tow*. . . . You'd best give up and come back to Yarmouth wi' me. . . . If there's no bus I reckon my missus'd . . ." And then, seeing Starboard's face, he stopped short. He looked back over his shoulder at the Thames barge coming up Breydon. He looked forward at the white triangle of sail showing above the banks far up the river. "My tow won't have seed me yet," he shouted with a grin, swung the *Come Along* round and headed back the way they had come.

"He isn't taking us back to Yarmouth now?" said Port. But nobody heard her.

Back they went, past the place where the two rivers join and there by the Reedham marshes at the top of Breydon they met the barge, forging grandly along with a curl of white water under her bows. They could see a big old man standing at the wheel, a woman busy with some knitting close beside him, and another man sitting on a hatch and playing a mouth organ. They could see his hand move to and fro across his mouth, but could hear nothing at all but the chug, chug of Old Bob's engine. Just as they met, Old Bob swung the *Come Along* round, came alongside, and closing the throttle of his engine reduced speed until the *Come Along* was keeping pace with the barge.

"*Welcome* of Rochester," said Starboard, reading the name on a lifebuoy.

With the engine quietening, they could hear the noise of the barge rushing through the water, and the creaking of blocks and gear. The old skipper of the *Welcome* had turned over the wheel to his mate and came to the side.

"Hullo, Bob," he said.

"Hullo, Jack. Bound for Beccles?"

"Beccles Mills," called the skipper.

"Friends o' mine," said Old Bob, "joinin' a boat gone up just ahead o' ye. Will ye give 'em a lift?"

The skipper of the *Welcome* hesitated a moment, looking down with a puzzled face at the two small girls in the little tow-boat, but before he could speak the woman who was knitting was standing beside him.

"Don't you be so slow, Jack," she said. "Of course 'e will, and welcome."

"But . . ." began Port.

Old Bob was edging his little boat nearer to the barge. The two were touching now, with only the tow-boat's fenders between them.

"Can you make it?" he shouted.

"Give me a 'and, missie."

"Up she goes. And the next . . ."

The two boats, the little tow-boat and the big barge were moving fast through the water. But there was no time to think. There were strong arms to help them. Somehow or other, both twins found themselves aboard the barge. Their knapsacks and rugs came flying aboard after them. Old Bob's engine roared again, and the *Come Along* had sheered off and was racing up the river.

"I say," said Port. "We've never thanked him."

Aboard the barge, moving under sail, there was quiet. The woman was speaking to them, not shouting, and her voice sounded queer to the twins, whose ears were still throbbing from the chug, chug of the *Come Along*.

"Where's 'e off to? Going upriver in a 'urry. Why don't 'e take you wiv 'im if 'e's going that way?"

"He's meeting that boat," said Starboard, pointing to the white triangle of sail still in the same place.

"They'll be glad to see 'im," said the skipper. "If they're trying to beat down over this tide. And where's this craft o' yours?"

"She's going to Beccles," said Starboard. "She can't be very far ahead. But which way are you going?" she asked, as the *Welcome* of Rochester turned up the Yare instead of keeping round to the left up the Waveney.

"We go up to Reedham and through the New Cut," said the skipper. "Same thing in the end."

"But what shall we do if they stop at St. Olave's or somewhere?"

"They won't stop if they're bound for Beccles," said the skipper, "not before they 'ave to."

GETTING A LIFT

There was nothing to be done about it. Bob and the *Come
Along* were already out of sight and in the other river. And
anyway this was better than going back to Yarmouth.

"And what about a nice cup o' tea?" the woman with the
knitting broke in. "I was just going to make tea for my
'usband, that's Mr. Whittle. I'm Mrs. Whittle. And the
mate's name is Mr. 'Awkins."

"Our name's Farland," said Starboard. "I'm Nell and this
is Bess."

"Well, now we know each other," said Mrs. Whittle.
"That kettle should be on the boil now, if you'll come this
way with me. I'll go down first, seeing as 'ow I know the way.
And mind that bottom step."

For the first moment after stepping off the steep companion
ladder, Port and Starboard could hardly see. Then, gradually,
their eyes grew accustomed to the twilight below decks. There
was Mrs. Whittle, bending over an oil-stove and turning up
the wick so that flames flickered out from under the kettle.
"The cooking stove's forrard," she was saying, "but we 'ave
this 'ere for convenience. That? That's Jack's darling in there.
That's the engine-room. Spoilt our state-room it 'as, putting
that in. And taken most of the light. Jack's darling, I call it.
The time 'e spends on that engine polishing and oiling, you
wouldn't believe. Use it? Not 'im. 'E's bin in sail all 'is life,
Jack 'as, and 'e makes it 'is pride to use no petrol what 'e can't
'elp. But polishing and oiling, 'e's at it morning, noon *an'*
night."

"May we look?" said Starboard.

"'E'll show you," said Mrs. Whittle. "When they put that
in, I 'ad a partition wall (it ain't a bulk'ead, not really) put
right across 'ere, so we 'as no smell of engine, which I can't
abide. But you should 'ave seen the stateroom as it was.
All this was in it and that spare bunk we use for stores. It's a
bit cramped now, but snug."

She opened a door, and let them peep into a tiny sleeping-cabin filling the extreme after end of the barge. There were two bunks in it, and a very small table with a lace cover on it held in place by brass-headed drawing-pins. There was a clock and a barometer fixed to the wall and a blue velvet frame with a picture in it of a young sailor with a big curl across his forehead. "That's our Jacky," said Mrs. Whittle. "'E's in the *Iron Duke*."

From a locker in this inner cabin, Mrs. Whittle took a red-and-white checked table cloth. This she spread on a table that when not in use folded flat against the wall of the engine-room. When it was open people could just squeeze in round it to sit on a low fixed bench.

"I like things what I call nice," said Mrs. Whittle, who was clearly very pleased to have the twins to talk to. "It ain't no life for a woman aboard a barge. Nothing to keep clean. Not even a doorstep you can take a pride in. They won't let you do nothing on deck. Everything must be their way, no matter 'ow much better it might be done. But I 'ave things my way in 'ere." She poured out a huge mug of tea and going up two steps of the ladder reached out and put it on the deck.

"Jack," she said. "You give this to 'Awk, and tell 'im to take the wheel while you come down and 'ave a cup o' tea."

A moment later the light from the companion-hatch was blotted out by the descending skipper.

"Now you two missies slip in there," said Mrs. Whittle. . . . "Twins, did you say. You're not as like as some twins I've seen. Like as peas, some of 'em, and you 'ave to dress 'em different to know 'em apart."

The twins squeezed together along the bench. Mr. Whittle took off his billycock hat, worked himself round the corner of the table and sat down, smoothing his moustache with his fingers. Mrs. Whittle liked to be handy for the kettle and the stove. And presently the twins were eating bread and strawberry jam, and drinking their tea, listening to the water sluicing past them on the other side of the planking, and to the short clank of the steering gear above their heads when Mr. Hawkins spun the wheel this way and that as the *Welcome* of Rochester nosed her way up the river.

"And 'ow did you 'appen to miss 'im?" asked Mr. Whittle.

"Well, you 'ave 'ad a day of it," said Mrs. Whittle, when they had told about finding the *Teasel* gone from the staithe, and how Jim Wooddall had given them a lift down to Yarmouth, and how Old Bob had taken them up Breydon in the *Come Along.*

"It was very lucky he knew you," said Starboard.

"'E didn't," said the skipper.

"But he called you Jack,"

"They calls all sailormen Jack."

"And you called him Bob," said Port.

"Is 'is name Bob? I didn't know. I 'ad to call 'im something."

"Then why did you take us?" asked Starboard.

"It was jolly nice of you," said Port.

"And why not?" asked Mr. Whittle. "It's dull for the missus being the only lady aboard."

"Coming to the Cut." Mr. Hawkins called from up on deck.

The skipper emptied the last of his deep mug and went nimbly up the ladder.

"And this Mrs. Barrable?" said Mrs. Whittle. "She's your aunt, I s'pose?"

"Oh no."

"Tom's aunt then?"

"She isn't any relation to any of us."

"And you said there was two others with her as well as your Tom?"

They set off again, first one and then the other, explaining how it happened that the Admiral had gathered such a crew.

Suddenly there was a great noise overhead, the squeaking and groaning of blocks, the flap of heavy canvas, the clank of steering gear. The whole barge shook with a sudden jar as the great sprit swung across and the mainsail filled again. Running footsteps sounded on the decks.

"What's happening?" said Starboard.

"May we go and see?" said Port.

"Give 'em 'alf a mo' to settle down," said Mrs. Whittle.

After waiting a minute or two, everything seemed quiet, and the twins went up on deck. The *Welcome* had left the Yare, had swung round into the New Cut, and, with the skipper at the wheel, was sailing between high banks that stretched away into the distance where the Cut was crossed by a bridge. The bridge in the distance looked so small that it was hard to believe there would be room for the barge to go through even if it opened.

"Have you been this way before?" asked Starboard, hardly liking to suggest that they might not be able to get through the bridge.

"Many a time," said Mr. Hawkins. "It ain't no trouble, not if them lazy scuts is on 'and to lift the bridge."

On and on they sailed down that straight, narrow cut, feeling all the time as if there was scarcely room between the banks for the barge and her own bow wave, which rushed along the piling on either side of her. Beyond the little bridge they would be coming into the Waveney again, and the twins were doing their best to catch sight of the *Teasel's* sail.

They were close to the bridge before there was any sign of its opening. The twins looked at Mr. Whittle. He seemed at ease though the big barge was racing down the narrow Cut, and there was certainly no room to turn her.

"'Ere y'are, 'Awk," said Mr. Whittle, putting his hand in his trouser pocket. "'Ere's the money for the butterfly net."

Almost as he spoke, the bridge seemed to split in half,

and both halves cocked up in the air. Two men appeared, one of them with a little bag at the end of a long pole. Mr. Hawkins went to the side. The barge swept through, and as she passed the bag was held out and Mr. Hawkins, holding his hand high above it, dropped two shillings in it.

"Keep the chynge," he said. "There ain't none," he added, turning with a wink to the twins.

The barge was through.

"P'raps they haven't got so far," said Starboard to Mr. Whittle.

Mr. Whittle shouted out to a man in a blue jersey and sea-boots who was digging in a potato patch just where the New Cut joins the Waveney River.

"Say, mate, you seen a little white yacht, wiv a white tender to 'er? Lot o' kids aboard."

"They was by here half-hour ago. From Hornin' they tell me. Pushing on to see how far they could get afore dark."

Half an hour ahead. Only half an hour. It almost seemed to the twins that they were in touch with the *Teasel* at last. Evening was closing in, too. The Admiral would soon be mooring for the night. Any time now they might see the *Teasel* tied up to the bank, with the *Titmouse* astern of her, and Tom and Dick and Dorothea hard at work getting the awnings up.

The twins went forward to the bows of the barge, and stood there, looking out. Mrs. Whittle and Mr. Hawkins came forward to join them.

"She's the finest ship we've ever been in," said Starboard to Mr. Hawkins.

"There ain't many barges afloat to touch 'er," said Mr. Hawkins. "Carries 'er way, and 'andy, too. You should see 'er in the London River."

"She's been foreign many a time," said Mrs. Whittle. "Gives you quite a turn, coming up out of that companion after a night at sea to find yourself in a foreign 'arbour and everybody talking Dutch."

But the tw ns were really thinking less of the *Welcome* than of the *Teasel*. They had remembered that half an hour ahead at the end of a day might be a very long time.

The railway bridge at Herringfleet was closed, and a red flag was showing by the signal-box, but the flag came fluttering down, and a moment later the bridge was swinging. It was open just in time to let the *Welcome* through.

At Somerleyton it was the same. Nothing happened delay them for a moment.

"They simply can't have gone much farther," said Starboard.

"Isn't that a sail?" said Port. "You can just see it over the reeds."

"I can't," said Starboard.

"They will be 'appy when they sees you," said Mrs. Whittle. "Getting almost too dark to knit," she added. "Cold, too."

And then, suddenly, the wind failed them. It had been weakening for some time. Now it died utterly away. Flat shining patches showed on the river astern. A windmill was reflected as if in glass. The skipper's eye noted some old mooring posts standing up above the reeds.

"Topsail, 'Awk! Foresail! Brails!"

As if by magic the foresail came down and the other sails shrank away against the mast. The great sprit towered bare into the sky.

"Dead water," said the skipper. "Tide's turning."

The *Welcome*, hardly moving, slid nearer to the reeds.

"Couldn't 'ave let us down 'andier."

The next moment he had left the wheel and he and Mr. Hawkins were busy with creaking warps, mooring the *Welcome* for the night.

"But they aren't going to stop here?" said Starboard in despair.

"No wind," said Mrs. Whittle. "Getting dark, too."

"Won't he use the engine?" suggested Port.

"Not 'im," said Mrs. Whittle. "We ain't due in Beccles till to-morrow, and you won't catch 'im wasting owner's petrol."

"What's sails for?" said the skipper. "Dark coming, too. We've a good berth 'ere, and we'll be in Beccles to-morrow before they want us."

"But what about Tom and the *Teasel*?" said Starboard.

"'E ain't expecting you," said Mr. Whittle. "So 'e won't worry. And you'll give 'im a 'ail in the morning and startle 'im out of 'is skin."

"Jack's right," said Mrs. Whittle, "and now what do you say to a nice fresh 'erring for your supper, and then I'll make the two of you snug in that spare bunk? I'll 'ave the stores out of it in no time."

"You wouldn't 'ave us going on, and maybe passing 'em or running of 'em down in the dark," said Mr. Hawkins by way of comfort. "And we'll all be in Beccles to-morrow." He pulled his mouth organ from his pocket, and played just a bar or two from *The bonny bonny Banks of Loch Lomond*. "There's no high road and low road to Beccles," he said. "So you can't miss 'em."

The dark closed down over the marshes and the river. A light was hoisted up the forestay, for even in inland waters the *Welcome* of Rochester did not forget that she was a sea-going vessel. Down below, under a lantern hanging from a beam, her crew and her passengers ate fresh herrings and bread and butter. And there was talk of London River and Rochester Bridge, and of Rotterdam and other foreign ports. And Mr. Hawkins brought out his mouth organ and gave them a tune when invited to do so by Mrs. Whittle.

At last Mr. Whittle was spoken to by his wife for yawning. Mr. Hawkins covered his own mouth with a huge and tarry hand, said "Good night," and went off up the ladder and away in the darkness to his berth forward. Port and Starboard climbed the ladder, too, and walked up and down the deck as Mrs. Whittle told them to, while she cleared that spare bunk for them. They came down again to find that Mr. Whittle had disappeared. Already a steady snore came through the partition wall.

"Up at five 'e was," said Mrs. Whittle. "It's been a long day for 'im. You mustn't take no notice of 'is snoring."

"We don't mind it," said Starboard.

"We like it," said Port.

"You won't feel lonely, any'ow," said Mrs. Whittle. "Well, good night, everybody, as they say." And she, too, was gone into the tiny stateroom, after turning the lantern low.

In a minute or two the twins had stuffed themselves into the bunk, and rolled their rugs about them. All was quiet, except for the skipper's easy snore. Presently Mrs. Whittle started snoring too, in a slightly different tone.

"My word," said Starboard just before she fell asleep. "Just think what Ginty would say if she knew."

"A dinna ken juist whit she wudna say," murmured Port.

CHAPTER XXII

THE RETURN OF THE NATIVE

Wᴵᴸᴸᴵᴬᴹ had waked the *Teasel* early. He had gone ashore by his private gang-plank and met a terrier. He had not exactly run away, but he had waited to bark until he was safely back aboard, and after that nobody had been able to sleep another minute. Tom, still thinking of record passages, had called out from the *Titmouse* that the wind was just right and the tide running up. They had moored in the dusk quite close to a little ancient church, with a tower built in steps, like a pyramid. "Burgh St. Peter," the Admiral had said. As soon as they were dressed she had sent Dick and Dorothea off along the bank to the Waveney Inn near by to get the milk for breakfast. Tom had stowed both awnings by the time they had got back. They had sailed on after a hurried breakfast. Trees on the banks had bothered them a little, but Dick had been allowed to do some quanting, this time without even looking as if he were going to fall in. And now, for a long time, the tower of Beccles Church had been in sight, and Dorothea had been expecting the Admiral to make some memorable remark.

"At last. At last. The town of his birth lay before him in the evening sunshine. The exile tottered, leaning on his stick. For a moment towers and houses and long-memoried trees vanished in a mist of tears." Something like that, Dorothea thought, the return of a native ought to be. "Long-memoried" pleased her a good deal. It was better than "well-remembered," and did not mean the same thing either. Or course, really, it was going to be morning, not evening, and the returning native was Mrs. Barrable, and not an aged man. But for Dorothea the main thing was that there would be a good deal of feeling about it. And somehow the Admiral seemed hardly to realise that she was coming home at last. She was making studies of trees in her sketch-book. "In spring," she said, "one has a chance of seeing their bones."

It was not until they had passed through Aldeby Swing Bridge that she put her sketch-book away and began to talk a little as a returning exile should. There was a hill rising from the water's edge, with fine old trees on it here and there, and patches of thick undergrowth, and steep slopes of fresh green grass.

"That's Boater's Hill," she said, "where we used to go for picnics, just the right distance out of Beccles on a summer afternoon. My brother Richard caught a grass snake there and got beaten afterwards for taking it to school with him and letting it get loose in the middle of a lesson."

"What did he feed it on?" asked Dick.

"Frogs, I believe," said Mrs. Barrable.

"He wouldn't mind being beaten for its sake," said Dorothea.

Beccles was very near. They sailed past houseboats moored to the bank, with smoke blowing from their chimneys. A young man came tacking down the river in a little racing yacht like the *Flash*, and set them wondering if the twins and their A.P. had won their first race. And then, sweeping slowly round a bend, they came in sight of the tall Beccles mills, and the public staithe, and a dyke full of boats still at their winter moorings, and a road bridge, with a railway bridge beyond it. Under the bridges they could see the curving river, houses almost standing in the water, rowing boats tied to the walls, and a flock of white ducks swimming from one back door to the next.

"Brother Richard was quite right," said the Admiral. "This is much the best way to see it again."

The next moment they were rounding up by the staithe. Dick jumped ashore. Tom turned to the Admiral with a grin.

"We've got to Beccles," he said. "Now for Oulton. And then we may have time to get right up to Norwich before we start back."

"Oh, but Tom," said Dorothea. "It's the Admiral's old home. She won't want to start again at once."

"I want to do a little shopping first," said the Admiral.

"And we must send off post cards to the twins," said Tom. "Just to let them know how far the *Teasel's* got."

Sails were lowered. The *Teasel* was moored fore and aft. Tom looked her over critically and decided that she was neat enough, and all five of them made ready to leave her and go up into the town.

"What's that big boat?" asked Dick, looking at a brown topsail moving above the trees far away over the meadows.

"Thames barge," said Tom. "You can see her sprit. She'll be here by the time we get back, the way she's moving."

"I expect I shall hardly know the little place again," said Mrs. Barrable. Dorothea looked at her hopefully, but romance died as Mrs. Barrable went on, "Better bring both shopping baskets, Dot. I don't know what your mother would say if she knew how badly I've been feeding you. Fresh vegetables we want, and something not out of a tin. The butcher's name used to be Hanger, but I suppose he's gone long ago. What do you think about fried chops if we can get them?"

Romance came to life again as, after a last look at the *Teasel* and the distant barge, they left the staithe and walked up the long street into the town. After all, thought Dorothea, even if the Admiral was altogether too light-hearted for a returning exile, they had come a long way. They walked up the middle of the street like travellers in a strange country, come for to see and to admire. And, though the Admiral did seem to be mostly thinking about chops, she kept looking about her,

SHOPPING IN BECCLES

remembering this and that. She delighted Dorothea by recognising between two houses the little alleyway through which, as children, she and her brother Richard used to slip down to the river. From the street they could see between the houses right down to the water, and tied at the foot of some steps was a boat that might have been the very boat they learned to row in, so the Admiral said.

They found the post office, with the mail van waiting outside it, so, to Tom's delight, they were able to get their post cards off by the early post. They sent pictures of Beccles to the twins, to Mrs. Dudgeon, and to the three small Coots of the *Death and Glory*. "Burgh St. Peter last night. Beccles this morning, 8.45 a.m.," wrote Tom triumphantly, on his post cards to the twins. "Wish you were here," he added, finding there was a little room left on each card.

"And I must send one to Brother Richard," said the Admiral.

Dorothea chose one for her, showing the river flowing close under the old houses.

"Tell him when we left and when we arrived," said Tom, remembering the letter Brother Richard had sent warning the Admiral not to sail south with children. A long time ago it seemed now since she had read those bits aloud in Ranworth Broad.

The Admiral wrote her post card and held it out for Tom to see what she had written. "Left Horning yesterday. Beccles to-day. Look at the postmark. *And not one scratch on her paint.*"

They saw their cards stamped, put into a bag and carried out to the van. "Good," said Tom, as the van drove off. "They ought to get those cards this afternoon."

From the post office they went to a shop with a sign hanging out over the pavement, "Ye Olde Cake Shoppe."

"Hmph!" said the Admiral, "it wasn't 'ye olde' when I used

to buy buns there, but I daresay the buns will be none the worse for it."

Here they bought a large fruit cake and some buns. Then they found the butcher's, and bought some chops that the butcher said would be very good ones. He had had one that morning for his own breakfast. They bought onions, a cauliflower and some oranges from the greengrocer. Dorothea wanted to see the house where the Admiral had been born, but it had long ago been pulled down, and where the old garden had been was a big new shop with enormous plate glass windows. Mrs. Barrable went in, quite heartlessly, Dorothea thought, and bought a new BB pencil. Then they went to have a look at the church, which is built, so to speak, in two bits, the tower in one bit and the rest of the church in another. They had a fine view out over the country from the wall of the churchyard. Then, tired with wandering round, they went back to "Ye Olde Cake Shoppe" and had coffee and biscuits, after which, with most of the morning gone, they set off back to the *Teasel*.

"Where shall we sail for next?" the Admiral was saying, as they turned the corner and came out on the green grass.

"But we've only just got here," said Dorothea. "There must be heaps more things in Beccles that you want to see again."

"That barge has got here all right," said Tom, "and tied up at the mill just opposite the *Teasel*. Come on, Dick, let's get a good look at her. You never see one of them in the North River. What a beauty. . . ." His face suddenly changed. . . . "Why! . . . There can't be. . . . There is. . . . There's somebody aboard the *Teasel*. Hi! You!" And he set off at a run to turn out the invader.

"Wait a minute," called the Admiral, but he did not hear her.

They saw him take a flying leap into the *Teasel's* well from the edge of the staithe.

"He didn't wipe his shoes," said Dick, who was always being reminded by Tom to wipe his before coming aboard.

"Something must really be wrong," said Dorothea. "Hullabaloos, perhaps, lurking in the cabin. Come on, Dick. . . ."

All three of them hurried to the rescue as fast as they could, with William galloping among them and nearly sending them headlong by getting mixed up with their feet.

"Tom," called Dorothea.

Just as they came to the edge of the staithe there was a burst of laughter from the *Teasel*'s cabin, and Port and Starboard and Tom came tumbling out together.

"But however did you get here?"

Port and Starboard, bursting with pride, pointed across the river at the *Welcome* of Rochester moored by the mill.

Everybody was talking at once. "But that's a Thames barge." "Not at Horning." "Jim Wooddall took us in *Sir Garnet*." "But the championship races . . ." "The A.P. going off in a rush and Ginty packing." "Awful when you weren't at Stokesby or Yarmouth." "Hullabaloos?" "Nosing into Fleet Dyke looking for you." "Needn't be back for a week." "Yes. In a cupboard bunk." "Oh, three million cheers!"

And then the twins wanted to know all about the voyage of the *Teasel*.

"Those apprentices must have done jolly well." "Should think they did." "How was it at Yarmouth? Did you take a tug?" "Came through by ourselves." "Good for you." "And the bridges?" "Lowering the mast?" "Nobody could have done better." "You won't really want us as well." "What rot!" "Of course we do." "Ten times the fun with all of us together." "And we were jolly lucky with weather." "We couldn't have managed without you if it had come properly blowy."

"Well," said the Admiral when the hubbub had subsided

a little and not more than three people and William were talk-ing at once, "with two spare skippers we can go almost any-where. But we must at least have dinner. And somebody must go back into the town and buy another couple of good big chops."

"We'll all go," said Starboard.

"I'll stay in the *Teasel*," said the Admiral, "and get the cook-ing started. I want to feed you properly for once. Specially if we're sailing for Oulton this afternoon. . . ."

"The Admiral's an explorer by nature," Dorothea explained to Port as they went off with the others to see the butcher again. "She isn't like a returning native, not really. . . . Coming home means nothing to her at all."

•

But there was no getting away from Beccles that day. The morning had gone in shopping and cooking, and when dinner had been eaten and the things washed up, the Admiral had to be ferried across in the *Titmouse* by the twins to thank the *Welcome* of Rochester for giving a passage to the *Teasel's* missing skippers. Mrs. Whittle was very pleased to have a visitor, and for a long time she and Mrs. Barrable sat talking of foreign parts, such as Antwerp and Rotterdam. Then, as the *Welcome* was not to begin discharging her cargo until next morning, Port was sent back in the *Titmouse* to bring the rest of the ship's company, who had been sitting on the *Teasel's* cabin roof looking at the barge. They all crossed the river together. William liked the barge very well, and liked the mill staithe even better, and rummaged in the straw there as if he were interested in rats like any ordinary worldly dog. Dick, Dorothea and Tom were shown all over the *Welcome* by the twins, who felt, after spending a night aboard her, that they were members of her crew. Mr. Whittle smoked his pipe and listened. And when Dick explained that the others were teaching him and Dorothea to be sailors, Mr. Hawkins, the mate, asked him if they had shown him how to throw a bowline on a bight. The instructors in seamanship said that they did not know themselves, and he got some rope and did it for them like a conjuring trick, so quickly that they could not see his hands working. And then he settled down on a hatch and showed them all kinds of knots and other things that can be made with rope, Bowlines and Fisherman's and Carrick bends, Rolling, Blackwall, Timber and Handspike hitches, Cat's Paws and Sheepshanks, Eye splices and Long splices, Grommets and a Selvagee strop. They had not heard half the names, and long after Mr. Hawkins had made four Grommets for them, and had shown them how to play deck quoits, the ones who were not actually playing were still wrestling with bits of rope, trying to remember what they had been taught. And old Mr. Whittle sat by, smoking his pipe and thinking of new things for Mr. Hawkins to show them. "What about a Turk's 'Ead, 'Awk?" he would say, and "'Awk, you ain't showed 'em 'ow to use toggles." Then, as the afternoon was wearing on, Mrs. Barrable invited Mrs. Whittle and Mr. Whittle and Mr. Hawkins to come across the river and have a cup of tea in the *Teasel.*

"Do come," said Starboard. "We've seen your ship, and you ought to come and see ours."

And Mrs. Whittle came, but her husband and the mate said they didn't really like to leave the ship in port, even if the port was as quiet a place as the quay by Beccles Mill.

Mrs. Whittle brought her knitting with her, and very much admired the electric light in the cabin which Dick turned on so that she could see better. She told how once going down Channel to Falmouth she had been knitting on deck and her ball of wool had dropped overboard, and how the faster she tried to pull it in again the faster the ball unrolled, and all the time her husband was telling her to go below because it was so rough. And at last, just when she came to the end of the wool, hauling it hand over hand till she had it all aboard, a sea came rolling along the decks, and another on the top of it, and she had to grab something not to go overboard herself. "And what 'urt me was to think 'ow I'd pulled in miles and miles of good green wool just to see it picked up and carried away and 'alf a knitted tea-cosy with it and a set of knitting needles. 'Now, Mrs. Whittle,' says my 'usband, 'you go below.' 'But my knitting,' says I. 'We can't go about to pick it up,' says 'e. 'It'll fetch to France some time next week.' 'And my tea-cosy?' says I, for it was a real 'andsome cosy. 'One o' them Frenchy fishermen'll wear it for a berry,' 'e says. 'They'll know what to do with it.'"

By the time tea was over, it seemed too late to start. Nobody was very sorry. Tom, privately, had a sort of feeling that it was hardly loyal to the *Titmouse* after she had pretended all the way from Horning to Beccles to be nothing but a dinghy, not to let her do a little sailing for herself. So, during the short spring evening, while the Admiral was painting a picture of the *Welcome* of Rochester (which now hangs in Mrs. Whittle's stateroom), Tom, Port, Starboard, Dick and Dorothea all crowded into the *Titmouse*, rowed through the bridges, stepped the mast and sailed away. They sailed through the fleets of ducks, close by the houses that climb the hill beside the river, close under the walls below the church, which look like castle bastions. Up there, of course, the returning native ought to have leaned on the stone parapet and looked out with dim eyes over the country from which he (or she) had been absent for so long. But it could not be helped that the Admiral was not like that, and Dorothea regretted it only for a moment. There was a rickety old houseboat moored down there, and on the open deck at the stern an old man was sitting with a big bucket at his side fishing with a stout bamboo rod. Dorothea forgot returning natives when she saw him lift his rod and bring two eels at once hanging from a big reddish lump at the end of his line. He held them over his bucket. The eels dropped in and he lowered his red lump over the side again.

"Babbing," said Tom.

"That red thing's nothing but worms," said Port.

"Made like a cowslip ball," said Starboard, and Dorothea was very nearly sick.

"But how do the eels get hooked?" asked Dick.

They were close by the houseboat, and the old man heard that question. "Bless you," he said, "they don't get hooked. You feel 'em, nuzzling the worrams, an' then when they've properly fanged 'em, you lifts 'em gently, so," and as he spoke up came another eel biting hard into the lump of worms, and letting go when he found himself in the air only to drop into the eel-babber's big bucket.

They sailed on until they had left the town behind them, and they had meadows and grazing cattle on either hand. Then with hardly wind enough to move them they turned back. It was dusk when Tom paddled the *Titmouse* through the bridges to the staithe, and they had only just time to rig the *Teasel's* awning before dark and to do the same for the little *Titmouse*, where Dick was sleeping once more.

That night everybody was ready to go early to bed. Nobody asked to have the light for another minute or two. From across the river came the cheerful little noise of Mr. Hawkins, sitting on the *Welcome's* forehatch and playing his mouth organ as quietly as he could. But they did not hear it long.

CHAPTER XXIII

STORM OVER OULTON

The twins had joined the *Teasel* none too soon. All the way from Horning to Beccles there had been nothing too difficult to be managed by Tom with no one to help him but the Admiral and a most inexperienced crew. But when they were waked in Beccles by a milkman bringing the morning milk down to the staithe, they saw, as soon as they put their heads out, that the weather did not look so kind as it had been. There was a sulky feeling in the air, and the sky was dark in the east.

"Thunder coming," said Tom, when he and Dick went aboard the *Teasel* for breakfast.

"Looks as if it's going to blow," said Starboard.

"Rain, too," said Port.

"Let's get away quick," said the hopeful Admiral, "and we'll be in Oulton before it starts."

The moment breakfast was over they were off. With a full crew once more, two to a halyard and one to spare, not counting the Admiral and William, the *Teasel* set sail in record time, while Mr. Whittle and Mr. Hawkins, smoking their pipes, watched from the deck of the *Welcome* at the other side of the river.

"You've got a smart ship, you 'ave," said Mr. Whittle as the *Teasel* headed towards the big barge, swung round close by her and was off, racing down the river with the wind abeam.

Mrs. Whittle came up the companion to shake a duster just in time to use it to wave farewell.

"You'll be wanting a reef later," called Mr. Hawkins, pointing at the dark clouds in the eastern sky.

No one was on the staithe when they sailed, but just before they lost sight of it, Dorothea looking back at the town the returned native was leaving once more, saw a boy on a red post office bicycle ride across the staithe to the water's edge. No one else saw him. The Admiral was tidying the cabin and filling in the time of sailing in the ship's log, which, as usual, everybody else forgot in the bustle of getting away. Tom and Dick were busy with main-sheet and tiller. Port was swabbing the decks round with a mop, to clear off any mud brought aboard from the shore. Starboard was washing a muddy anchor over the side. The boy jumped off his bicycle and stood on the edge of the staithe, waving. Dorothea, thinking it was rather nice of him, waved back. The next moment they were round a bend in the river and could see the staithe no more.

*

The wind was easy enough at first, and when they had got through Aldeby Bridge, Dick was being allowed to steer when, without a moment's warning, a squall came whistling over the marshes, and the *Teasel* swept suddenly round as if she wanted to charge the bank.

"Keep her going," said Tom, who was on the foredeck tightening up the flag halyards.

Starboard steadied the *Teasel* with a quick, helping hand on the tiller. The squall was gone as suddenly as it had come, but the three Coots looked anxiously over the marshland at a threatening wall of cloud.

"I wonder if we ought to," said Port.

"Reef?" said Starboard. "We'll have to if it gets worse."

"We may get through to Oulton before it really comes on," said Mrs. Barrable cheerfully.

The Coots looked at each other. That was the Admiral,

being rash. But everybody is glad of an excuse not to reef, and Tom and the twins were happy to put it off. They were happier still when they sailed into the shelter of the trees and, so far from wanting to reef, would have been glad of a little more wind than found its way through the leaves.

"The leaves are getting thicker every day," said Starboard.

"It must be rotten getting through here in summer," said Tom! "nearly as bad as Wroxham."

They let Dick and Dorothea take turns in steering, as the *Teasel* tacked along that reach under the tall trees just breaking out into their summer green. First to one side of the river and then to the other, watching the *Teasel's* wake to see how well or badly they had brought her about. The *Teasel* was a training ship once more.

"Not so hard," Port kept saying. "Let her come round gently, and she'll get a little bit for nothing."

"For nothing?"

"If you bring her hard round, the rudder stops her, and you lose. Gently. . . . Gently!"

They came out of the trees at last, and, just as they reached the open, they heard again that wild, hissing, whistling noise over the marshes.

"A Roger[1] coming," said Port.

"A Roger," laughed Dorothea. "Give him some chocolate. The Roger we know's always ready for some."

But the Coots hardly heard her. Things were much too serious.

"Better take the tiller, Tom," said Starboard. "We'll look after the sheets. Look out! Here it comes."

A sudden violent gust of wind hit the *Teasel*. She heeled over. Port and Starboard eased the sheets, just a little. She lifted, and again heeled over. Tom, clenching his teeth, held

---

[1] A Roger is the Norfolk name for a sudden squall which makes a loud hissing noise as it comes sweeping over the reeds.

her firmly on her course. If only the gust would slacken before he had to go about. But the river was narrow. The *Teasel* was foaming towards the bank. "Ready about!" he called. The yacht churned round with flapping head-sail. The wind dropped as suddenly as it had come.

"Now's our chance," said Tom. "Jam her nose in by those reeds. I'll skip forrard. Let go jib-sheet."

The Admiral, Dick and Dorothea were utterly disregarded. This was an affair for experienced seamen. The three Coots knew that the *Teasel* was carrying too much sail if the squalls were going to be as hard as that one. They were going to take a reef in at once. In a moment Port had the tiller and was bringing the *Teasel* up to the bank, Tom was on the foredeck with the rond anchor in his hand, and Starboard was standing by to let go the sheets. There was a gentle swish as the *Teasel's* bows pushed into the reeds, and a squelch as Tom jumped.

"What's going to happen?" asked Dorothea.

"Reefing," said Starboard.

"It'll hold all right," said Tom, and was aboard again and busy at the mast. Port ran forward to help. The jib was coming down, the boom was lifting, the peak was dipping, and all at once. The mainsail came quickly down. The boom was lowered into the crutches that Starboard had fished up out of the *Titmouse*.

"I suppose you're right," said the Admiral.

"More squalls coming," said Tom.

The next twenty minutes were full of hard work. Everybody had something to do, and William, feeling the excitement, cheered them on at their work with one of his barking fits. Just as they had finished neatly rolling up the reef, and lacing it along the foot of the sail, down came the first large spots of rain.

"Never mind," said the Admiral "we've all got oilskins, except poor William." But William was not going to let himself get wet. While other people were struggling into oilskins, and those who had been wearing sand-shoes were changing them for sea-boots, William decided that it was not the sort of day he liked, went into the cabin and made himself comfortable on the Admiral's bunk.

"What about your *Titmouse*?" said the Admiral. "How are you and Dick going to sleep in her if she gets all wet?"

"Come on, Dick," said Tom, who was beginning to regard Dick as the mate of the *Titmouse*, even if, in the *Teasel*, he was only an apprentice. "We'll use the awning as a hatch cover. We'll lace it all round over everything. It'll keep things pretty dry."

The *Titmouse* was covered all over. She was pulled up alongside so that the last bit of the lacing, round the stern, could be done from the deck of the *Teasel* after Tom and Dick had scrambled out. They looked down at her, with her mast and sail making a sort of mountain range between two valleys in the awning.

"There'll be a lot of water in the hollows," said Dick.

"We can empty it out by lifting the awning in the middle," said Tom.

"She'll be dry enough inside," said Starboard.

A few minutes later the *Teasel*, with a reef in her mainsail, was off again, and there was hardly enough wind to give her steerage way.

"That's what it always does," said Port. "It makes you reef and then it drops away altogether and makes you wish you hadn't."

"Not for long," said Tom, looking ahead of them at the dark sky behind the rain.

They were just moving with the stream, while the rain poured down on them, dripping off the sail on the cabin roof and off the cabin roof on the side-decks. Already there were lakes in the valleys of the *Titmouse's* awning. Then, gently at first, the wind came again, and they worked round the bends by Black Mill and Castle Mill, and were able to reach the rest of the way down the Waveney to Burgh St. Peter and the mouth of Oulton Dyke. Here the wind headed them. They had long ago stopped wishing they had not reefed. Squall after squall had made them wish they had taken in two reefs instead of only one. It was really hard work sailing, and in a wind like this, that found its way through everything, not even oilskins seemed able to keep the rain out.

"I can feel it trickling down my collar," said Dick. "And, oh, my beastly spectacles!"

"It's gone right up my sleeves," said Port, who had been looking after the mainsheet.

Tom said nothing. His were old oilskins, and the proofing had cracked across the shoulders, and all the top part of him was wet. While steering he had not noticed until it was too late that water was running off the oilskins straight into one of his sea-boots. Every time he moved his right foot he could feel the water seeping round it. But this was no time to think of things like that. The wind was growing harder and harder, and backing to the east. If it was as bad as this between the banks of sheltering reeds, what would it be like when they came out into Oulton Broad?

"It isn't very much farther," said the Admiral, "and it really does look rather fine."

"Thunder," said Dorothea.

"I thought it must be coming," said Starboard.

There was a distant rumbling, and then a sudden crash, followed by a clattering as if an iron tea-tray ten miles wide was tumbling down a stone staircase big enough to match it.

"Look!"

"And over there!"

Threads of bright fire shot down the purple curtain of cloud into which they were beating their way. There was a

tremendous roll of thunder. And then, just as they were
coming out of the Dyke into the Broad, the rain turned to hail,
stinging their hands and faces, bouncing off the cabin roof,
splashing down into the water. In a few moments the decks
were white with hailstones. The noise of the hail was so loud
that no one tried to speak. It stopped suddenly, and a moment
later the wind was upon them again. The *Teasel* heeled over
and yet further over, till the water was sluicing the hailstones
off her lee deck.

"Ease away mainsheet," shouted Tom. "Quick!"

There was a crash somewhere close to them, in the *Teasel*
herself. They looked at each other.

"Water-jar gone over," said Port.

"Ready about!"

Crash.

"There goes the other jar."

"Ease out. In again. Must keep her sailing."

"Look *out*, Tom, you'll have her over."

"Sit down, you two. On the floor," said the Admiral. "My
word," she murmured, "Brother Richard ought to see this."

It was a gorgeous sight. There was that purple wall of
cloud, with a bright line along the foot of it, and against this
startling background, white yachts and cruisers afloat at their
moorings in the Broad shone as if they had been lit up by
some strange artificial light. The green of the trees and
gardens looked too vivid to be real, wherever it was not veiled
by a rain-squall. It was a gorgeous sight, but not for the Coots,
who were finding it all they could do to keep the yacht sailing
and yet not lying over on her beam ends. It was a gorgeous
sight, but not for Dick and Dorothea, who began to think
that they had not yet learnt much about sailing after all. And
it was not at all a gorgeous sight for poor William, who was
thrown from one side to the other whenever the *Teasel* went
about, and was shivering miserably on the floor of the cabin,

sliding this way and that with the sand-shoes that had been
thrown in to keep dry.

They were half-way down the Broad now, looking at the
Lowestoft chimneys, and the Wherry Inn, and a great crowd
of yachts at their moorings. Tom kept telling himself to
think only of keeping the *Teasel* sailing, and not to bother
about the yacht harbour until they came to it. But he could not
help wondering all the time what he would find. He knew it
had been changed since he had been there with the twins and
their father. He would soon have to be making up his mind
where to tie up. With the wind that was blowing he did not
think the *Teasel's* mudweight would hold her if they were to
try to anchor in the open Broad. And all the time they were
getting nearer. The *Teasel* was crashing to and fro, beating
up in short tacks nearer and nearer to all those boats, and the
road beyond them, where motor-buses were driving through
the rain. Suddenly to starboard he saw a wooden pier with a
tall flagstaff at the farther end of it, where the opening must be.
Behind it was clear water . . . a stone quay . . . little grey
buildings . . . a moored houseboat. And there was a man in
oilskins running out on the quay and waving. To the *Teasel*?
It must be to her. There was no other boat sailing.

Tom headed for the flagstaff. The *Teasel* flew past it, round
the end of the wooden pier, and was in the yacht harbour.
The harbour seemed much too small, as a squall sent her
flying along between the pier and the quay. Tom swung her
round, judging his distance from the beckoning man. How far
would she shoot, going like this? He had never before had
to moor her in such a wind, and against a stone quay, too.

"Let fly jib-sheet! Slack away main! Fenders out!"

"Not you, Dick!" But Dick was already out of the well,
and hanging the fenders over the sides.

"Look, out of the way, Dick." Port was hurrying forward.

Nearer and nearer. Tom looked up at the high stone quay.

LEE RAIL UNDER

Would she fail to get so far? Would he have to bring her round and get her sailing again? Nearer and nearer. And then, close alongside the quay, the *Teasel* stopped, without even touching. That man in oilskins was holding her by the forestay. Port was already on the foredeck, handing him up the mooring warp, rond anchor and all. The rain was stopping. The wind had suddenly dropped now that the *Teasel* had escaped it. Tom, rather shaky in the knees, went forward to help in lowering the sails. The man was talking.

"Good bit of work you did then," he was saying. "Didn't think you'd make it as neat as that with the wind blowing as it was. She had all she wanted coming up the Broad. The *Teasel*, is she? Are you Mr. Tom Dudgeon? I've a telegram for you sent on from Beccles."

"A telegram?"

"I've got it in the office. I'm the harbour-master."

He ran across the quay and was back in a moment with a red envelope. Tom tore it open. He had never had a telegram in his life. But there it was, plain on the envelope, and again on the telegram form:

"TOM DUDGEON YACHT TEASEL BECCLES
ARE TWINS WITH YOU TELEPHONE IMMEDIATELY
MOTHER."

Tom read the telegram aloud, and took it to the well to show it to Mrs. Barrable.

"Why does she want to know about us?" said Port.

"How did they know at Beccles we'd gone here?" said Tom.

Dorothea remembered the boy with a red bicycle on Beccles staithe. "It only just missed us," she said. "I saw the boy waving, but I never thought he wanted to stop us. He probably asked the barge people, and they knew we were going to Oulton because we told them."

"You can use the telephone in my office," said the harbour-master, and Tom, dripping as he walked and squelching in his sea-boots, one of which was half full of water, hurried with him across the wet quay.

"We'd better go, too," said Starboard.

"Yes," said the Admiral, and the twins, shaking the water from their sou'westers as they ran, hurried after Tom.

"I do hope something isn't wrong," said the Admiral.

The harbour-master left the Coots at the telephone in his office and came back to the *Teasel* to lend a hand with the soaking wet sails. He came aboard and took charge and had the sails down in no time, while Dick and Dorothea did their best to help.

"Don't tie them up," he said. "We'll be having sunshine after this and getting them dry. But it's wet you are, and no wonder. Will you be having hot baths, and I'll be having your wet clothes dried the while?"

"Hot baths!" exclaimed Mrs. Barrable, and there, on the quay, by the harbour-master's office, Dorothea saw the notice and pointed it out, "Hot baths, 1s."

"We *have* fallen on our feet," said Mrs. Barrable, and then hesitated, looking across the quay towards the office where the ringing of a telephone bell suggested that Tom had got through to Horning. "We must wait till we know what that telegram means."

*

In the harbour-master's little office, all three Coots wanted to use the telephone at once. Tom was talking to his mother.

"But they're here. . . . They caught us up at Beccles just after we'd sent off those post cards. . . . Jim Wooddall gave them a lift . . . and then a barge. . . . They're here now." He turned to speak to the twins. "It's those post cards we sent to you first thing in the morning. They got the early post. And Ginty went flying round to mother. . . ."

287

Starboard grabbed the receiver. "Good morning, Aunty. . . . Oh, no. . . . We're as good as gold, really. . . . We always are. . . . Rather wet. . . . Come on, Port. . . . Your turn. . . ."

Tom got the telephone again. "Hullo, mother. No. I've shut them both up. Oh, Ginty wants to talk to them. All right. What did Joe say? . . . I can't hear. . . . Sorry. . . . Beasts. . . . Stuck in Wroxham? Three cheers. . . . Awning for the *Death and Glory*. . . . Good. . . . I thought they would. . . . I'll telephone from Norwich. Somewhere, anyhow. Everything's going fine. The *Teasel's* a beauty. Oh, no. The storm wasn't so awfully bad. We got through it quite all right. What? Ginty waiting? Oh, all right. Good-bye, mother. Love to our baby and dad. Come on, Port, Ginty's coming to the telephone to give you what for. . . ."

Port took the telephone and waited. There was a short pause. She frowned and signalled to Tom and Starboard to keep quiet. Tom was bursting with good news.

Then: "Yes. Hullo. It's a braw mornin', Ginty, and we're all well the noo, and hoping your ainsel's the same."

"Oh, Port, you idiot," said Tom. "What did Ginty say?"

"Ye young limb. . . . All right, Ginty. . . . I'm only trying to tell them what you said to me. . . ."

*

The anxious watchers in the *Teasel* knew the moment the Coots came out of the office that the telegram had not brought bad news.

"It was only those post cards," Tom explained to Mrs. Barrable from the edge of the quay. "Ginty couldn't think what had happened when those post cards came for the twins saying how much we wished they were with us. So she shot round to mother, and wanted to send telegrams all over the place. It's lucky mother didn't let her send one to Uncle Frank.

And the Hullabaloos are stuck at Wroxham for repairs. They bust someone's bowsprit, and got a hole in old *Margoletta* at the same time, charging across the bows of a sailing yacht . . . big one, luckily. And Joe's been making an awning for the *Death and Glory*. I thought he would when he'd seen *Titmouse's*. I've promised to telephone again from wherever we go to next."

"Stupid of me," said the Admiral. "I ought to have thought of telephoning myself."

"It would have been much worse if you'd telephoned before we arrived," said Starboard.

"It's all right now, anyhow," said Port.

"Everything's going righter and righter," said Dorothea. "First, Port and Starboard coming, so we're all together. And now no more Hullabaloos."

"They were bound to have a smash sooner or later," said Starboard, "charging about and expecting all sailing boats to get out of their way."

"Well," said the Admiral, "Tom's worries are over at last. And everybody is soaked through, and perfectly happy. Hot baths all round come next. Oilskins for dressing-gowns. And a hot meal at the Wherry Hotel with no cooking to do. And then we'll take the bus to Lowestoft and see the fishing harbour. But first of all I must give William a dose of his cod-liver oil. He mustn't catch a chill, poor little dog."

The rain had stopped, and the sun was coming out as the harbour-master had said it would. Dorothea climbed up on the quay and shook the wet from her oilskins.

"It feels rather nice to be on land just for a change," she said, and wanted to know if the Coots counted what they had been through that day as a proper storm.

"Quite proper enough for the *Teasel*," said Starboard.

Tom looked at her. "Good bit of work," the harbour-master had said. But what would have happened if he had not had the twins to help?

CHAPTER XXIV

RECALL

THE *Teasel* carried a light-hearted crew next day when she sailed from Oulton for the Norwich river. No need now to think of Hullabaloos. If the *Margoletta* was safely out of the way being patched up in a Wroxham boat-yard Tom, for the time, was outlaw no longer. Even Dorothea stopped looking anxious at the sight of every motor-cruiser, no matter whether large or small. That storm on the Waveney had given them a good deal of confidence, and they were all looking forward to sailing in the Yare where every day may be seen big steamers bound for foreign ports or coming in from sea. The Coots had been there before with Mr. Farland. But then Mr. Farland had been skipper, and his daughters and Tom had been eager crew. In the *Teasel* things were different. The Admiral simply left the sailing of the ship to them, and did not seem to trouble her head about it. She seemed to think that they could make no mistakes, and spent all her time with her sketch-book.

"That's all right," she said, when Tom suggested that they had all had a turn and that it wasn't fair never to let her steer her own boat. "That's all right. Admirals never do take the wheel. They just hang about and try not to get in the way. Brother Richard always says that's how you can tell a good one. He knows, because he was in the Navy during the War."

They sailed from Oulton in the afternoon, to catch the last of the ebb through the New Cut. The harbour-master stood by to give them a hand, but there was no need. Everything went well, and their voyage out of Oulton with a light south-westerly wind was very different from that mad crashing to and fro in the storm as they were beating their way in.

As they were sailing along Oulton Dyke, they caught sight of the topsail and mainsail of a big barge far away over the marshland, moving towards the queer little church with the steeple built in steps.

"The *Welcome*," said Port.

"Can't be anyone else," said Starboard.

Soon after they had left the dyke and were in the Waveney river, the barge swept grandly by with a loud noise of swirling water, her huge brown sails towering high above the little yacht. Captain Whittle was at the wheel. Mrs. Whittle was beside him with her knitting. Mr. Hawkins was making an elaborate coil of rope on the top of the hatch. Somehow they had found time to go ashore after all, or perhaps, as Dorothea suggested, Mrs. Whittle had taken her chance and gone for a country walk while they were loading, for both captain and mate were wearing big bunches of primroses in their button-holes.

"Get your telegram?" bawled Captain Whittle.

"Yes, thank you," shouted Tom.

"Where 'r ye bound for?"

"Norwich."

"Where's *Welcome* going?" shouted Starboard.

"London River."

"Going out to sea," said Port, as proudly as if she were still aboard her.

"Out to sea," said Dorothea.

There she was, sailing now between reedy banks, stared at by grazing cows, and in a few hours she would be at sea . . . Yarmouth . . . the lightship . . . trawlers . . . liners out of Harwich. . . . The Thames at night with the big ships home from the East. . . . The crew of the *Teasel* watched her wistfully.

The Admiral, with a few strokes of a pencil, noted how high she was compared with a windmill ashore.

"Not forgotten them knots?" shouted Mr. Hawkins, stirred by an afterthought that came a little late.

"Funny to think we sailed in her," said Starboard.

"And slept in her," said Port.

Long after the *Welcome* herself was out of sight, they could see her topsail moving above the reeds.

"Oh well," said Tom suddenly, "the *Teasel's* come a jolly long way herself. And we've got another four days. . . ."

"Yo ho for Norwich," said Port. "There's nowhere else left to go to."

*

But they never got to Norwich.

No one can count on the wind, and that afternoon, when they had passed Somerleyton and Herringfleet, and Dorothea had dropped the money into the butterfly net for the men who open the road-bridge on the New Cut, the wind was dying away to nothing. They drifted out of the New Cut into the Norwich river, but there was not wind enough to carry them up through Reedham Bridge against the stream, and Tom had to jump into the *Titmouse* and do some hard towing. They tied up for tea above the bridge, and sailed again later in the evening, past Hardley Cross and the mouth of the Loddon, past Cantley, where a foreign-going steamship was loading at the wharf, and moored for the night a mile or so higher up. Next day the wind was not much better, and they cruised slowly on, coming to Brundall in the afternoon. There was so little wind that no one minded when the Admiral suggested tying up while she made a sketch of that lovely bend of the river. They found a good mooring-place at the mouth of a dyke, close to an old sailing ship that was being dismantled and turned into a houseboat. The Admiral settled down in the well of the *Teasel* to make her sketch, and the others went ashore, and

climbed a ladder to the deck of the dismantled ship, and
watched a man who was cutting through the old iron-work
with a jet of hissing, white-hot flame.

Tom had watched this for some time when he remembered
his promise about telephoning home.

"Now's your chance," said Starboard. "They're sure to
have a telephone at the inn here, and we'll never get up to
Norwich to-night."

"We'll come, too," said Port, and the three Coots left Dick
and Dorothea watching the flame-cutter, and strolled slowly
along the dyke and so to the Yare Hotel.

Mrs. Dudgeon had hardly answered the telephone before
the twins, watching Tom's face, saw that he was getting
serious news.

"I'm so glad you rang up," Mrs. Dudgeon was saying.
"I've an urgent message for the twins, and for you, too.
Which day were you meaning to start back?"

"Day after to-morrow."

"Uncle Frank's written to say he's coming back by the
early train the day after to-morrow, and the twins must be here
by then, because he's racing *Flash* at eleven. You'll have to
come through Yarmouth to-morrow if the twins are to be in
time. Do you think you can manage it? . . . If not they'd
better come by train or bus. Brundall, you said, didn't you?"

"We were going on to Norwich to-morrow."

"Better not. We've had a call from a friend of yours, one
of the wherrymen."

"Jim Wooddall?"

"Yes. He thought we ought to know that those people in
the *Margoletta* have been boasting that they knew the boy
they were after had gone south. This was in some inn, up at
Wroxham. They even knew the name of the *Teasel*. You
were right about George. Someone's seen him talking to them.
And Bill's here, waiting for a word with you. He says the

Margoletta will be only two more days at Wroxham getting mended. So come through Yarmouth to-morrow if you can. Your father doesn't want you to leave the *Teasel* in the lurch, specially with the twins having to leave too, but he thinks the sooner you're safe home the better. . . . Hang on now while I call Bill in. He's been weeding all day just outside, so as to be able to talk to you if you rang up. Mischief of some sort, I've no doubt. *Bill!*"

Tom passed on the news.

"I say," said Starboard. "There's jolly little wind. Do you think we can get down to Yarmouth in time?"

"If we can't," said Tom, "you'll just have to take the train at Cantley or somewhere."

"Tide's all right to-morrow," said Port, "if we do get down. And if we get up to Acle before dark, we can easily get to Horning next day, before breakfast if somebody wakes us up."

"If those beasts know about the *Teasel* being down south," said Tom, "it's no good waiting to be caught by them. Once they leave Wroxham they can get anywhere in no time. And they'd only have to hang about Breydon to make sure of catching us on our way through."

"Come on," said Port. "We'll just slip home and diddle them again."

"Yes. . . . Yes. . . . Hullo!" Tom had the telephone receiver at his ear, and waved at the others to keep quiet.

"That you, Bill?"

"Hullo. . . . That Tom Dudgeon? . . ." Tom could hear Bill's anxious puffing and blowing at the other end. "The grebe's nest in Salhouse Entry been robbed. Rest all right. We thought No. 7 had lost a chick but it was only Pete counted wrong. . . . Er. . . . See here. . . ." There was a long pause. Tom heard, more faintly, his mother's voice. "All right, Bill, if it's a secret I'll go out of the room." There was more anxious puffing. Then Bill's voice came again. "Say, Tom. Which day you comin' through? . . . Ter-morrer? . . . Afternoon tide? . . . Can ye hear? Joe's mended our sail, and made a crutch, and we got a tarpaulin, so's we can sleep under like you . . . see? . . . Joe an' Pete's took her down-river . . . down to Acle. . . . I'm bikin' down now. . . . An' a boy at Rodley's is going to telephone about the *Margoletta.* . . . So we'll have the news for ye. . . ."

"Will you pay for another three minutes?" the indifferent voice of a telephone operator broke in from the Exchange.

"No, no," said Tom hurriedly. What was the good of throwing money away like that when it could be spent on ropes and other really useful things? "Good-bye, Bill. See you at Acle to-morrow night. . . ."

"At Acle?" said Port and Starboard together.

"They've fixed up their awning for the *Death and Glory,*" said Tom. "Those three kids are going down to Acle, and someone's going to let them know when the Hullabaloos are going to leave Wroxham."

"Jolly good," said Starboard.

"Let's get away at once," said Port. "We ought to get as far down the river as we can before dark. Buck up."

They ran along the dyke to the *Teasel.*

Tom stopped just before they reached her. "I say," he said, "the others'll be awfully sick at having to start back."

"Well," said Starboard, "it can't be helped. We've got to get home for the A.P.'s race. You've got to get home because of the Hullabaloos. It'd be much worse if they came down here and caught you in the *Teasel.* And anyway we can't leave the Admiral and those two to get home by themselves."

But, for various reasons, Dick, Dorothea and the Admiral were as ready to start as the Coots.

The Admiral was for sailing at once. "We've done so well," she said, "we don't want anything to go wrong now and spoil it."

"Good," said Dick. "We'll be seeing Breydon again to-morrow. These spoonbills may still be there. And Norwich is only a town anyhow."

"Let's start now," said Dorothea. "The warning came and the outlaw bolted for his lair. It would be too dreadful if he got caught after all. We've had a splendid voyage. . . . And the Admiral's done her sketch. . . . Or haven't you?"

The Admiral laughed. "Luckily, I've done it," she said.

"And the man who was using that flame-cutter has stopped work for the day," said Dick.

Ten minutes later, sails were set, and the *Teasel* drifted out of Brundall, homeward bound, with hardly wind enough to stir her. They sailed her as long as they could, and tied up at dusk not far from Buckenham Ferry.

"I'll tell you what," said the Admiral. "We're a set of seven donkeys not to have bought more food at Brundall. The larder's very nearly empty."

"It isn't William's fault," said Dorothea. "He'd have bought some if he could."

"Six donkeys," said the Admiral.

They had a rather hungry supper and made up their minds to call at Reedham and do some shopping in the morning. Then Tom and the twins spread the map on the cabin table and got themselves thoroughly muddled about the tides. In the harbour-master's office at Oulton, Tom had copied on a bit of paper the times of low water at Yarmouth for each day of that week. He was trying to work out a time-table for the voyage, so as to be sure of getting to Breydon Bridge at exactly the right moment.

"It's no good," he said. "Not really, because we can't tell what sort of wind there'll be."

"Awful if there's a calm," said Dorothea.

"We had no trouble coming the other way," said the Admiral.

"It's much worse getting back," the three Coots all began explaining at once.

"You see we've got to get to Yarmouth at low water in the Yare, and then hang about to go up the Bure, because low water in the Bure is about an hour later."

"But why?" asked Dick.

"It just is," said Starboard.

"Sometimes it's more and sometimes less," said Port.

"Well," said the Admiral at last. "Put all those figures out of your heads and get to bed. Good-night, Tom, and you, Dick. Listen to William grunting. He hasn't got a head for mathematics, poor dear, and you're keeping him awake."

"The only thing to do," said Tom, "is to start early and make sure."

"Better whistle for a wind," said Starboard. "We'll never get anywhere if it's like this."

Somewhere, away over the marshes, a belated curlew gave his long whistling cry.

"Thank you," said Port. "Did you hear him? Whistling his best for us, because he knows we've got no time to lose."

HADDISCOE·BRIDGE

CHAPTER XXV

THE RASHNESS OF THE ADMIRAL

"THAT wretched curlew must have been whistling the wrong tune," said Port.

The morning had brought them an easterly wind.

"Fine for going up the Bure," said Starboard.

"But we've got to get down to Yarmouth against it first," said Port.

Tom and the twins began their calculations over again. How long must they allow to get down to Yarmouth against the wind so as to be at Breydon Bridge exactly at low water?

Meanwhile the Admiral and Dorothea were looking through the larder and calculating how to make four eggs (all that were left) do for six people. There was fortunately plenty of butter to scramble them, but when breakfast was over, nobody would have said "No" to a second helping.

"We don't know what time we're going to get down to Reedham," said the Admiral, "but we'll get all we want there."

"We'd better keep the tongue to eat on the voyage," said Dorothea. "It's only a very little one anyway."

In the end the navigators gave up all hope of making their figures agree. There were too many things to think of, the speed of the current, the speed of the *Teasel* when tacking, the speed of the *Teasel* when reaching, how much of the river would be tacking, and how much of it would let them sail with the wind free, and, on the top of all that, the wind itself seemed very uncertain.

"There's only one thing to do," said Tom. "We'll sail

right down to Reedham straight away. People will know there what the tide's doing."

"So long as we're not too late, nothing else matters," said Starboard.

All down those long reaches by Langley and Cantley they sailed the *Teasel* as if she were a China clipper racing for home. Tom and the Coots were for ever hauling in or letting out the sheets to get the very best out of the wind. Dick and Dorothea took turns with the steering whenever the wind was free, but gave up the tiller to a Coot whenever it was a case of sailing close-hauled and stealing a yard or two when going about. The little tongue was eaten while they were under way, cut by the Admiral into seven equal bits, for William was as hungry as everybody else. Indeed, he did not think his bit was big enough, and the Admiral promised him that as soon as the *Teasel* came to Reedham he should have some more.

But as the *Teasel* turned the corner into the Reedham reach, and Tom was looking at the quay in front of the Lord Nelson, thinking where best he could tie up, above or below a couple of yachts that were lying there, they saw that the railway bridge was open, and that the signalman was leaning out of his window.

"He's beckoning to us to come on," said Dorothea.

"He's probably going to shut it for a long time," said Starboard.

"Two trains, perhaps, or shunting," said Dick.

"Well, I'm going through now, to make sure of it," said Tom. "It'd be awful to be held up."

"What about our stores?" said the Admiral..

"Let's hang on till Yarmouth," said Tom. "We'll have to stop there anyway."

It was no use arguing. Tom had other things to think of. Beating against the wind, and carried down with the tide, he had to work the *Teasel* through Reedham bridge. Just as he came to it he had to go about and the tide swept the *Titmouse* round quicker than he thought it would. The *Titmouse* bumped hard against one of the piers. Tom glanced wretchedly over his shoulder, and winced as if he had been bumped himself.

"She's got that rope all round her," said Dorothea. "The bridge won't have touched her really."

"Bad steering," said Tom. "My own fault."

The bridge closed behind them. The red flag climbed up, and they knew that they might have had to wait a long time before it would be opened again. They were beating on towards the New Cut. Just for a moment they could see right down it, a long narrow lane of water, and, in the distance, the little road bridge, where the porters who open it catch their two shillings in a long-handled net.

"Couldn't we have stopped below the railway bridge?" said Dorothea.

"We can't turn back," said Tom.

On and on they went, beating down the Yare against the wind but helped by the outflowing tide. And then, after being afraid of being too late, they began to be afraid of being too early. The Coots kept looking anxiously at Tom's watch and at the Admiral's, which she lent to Starboard because, as she said, she was tired of being asked the time. They kept looking at the mud that showed how far the level of the river had dropped since high water. It had dropped so little that anybody could see that the ebb must last for a long time yet.

They had just passed the three windmills, a mile and a half before the meeting of the Waveney and the Yare at the head of Breydon Water, when they had to change their plans once more.

"It doesn't look as if the ebb's nearly half done," said Starboard.

"We mustn't get down there while it's still pouring out."

Last night they had been talking of what this might mean, and Dorothea saw the *Teasel* and the little *Titmouse* swirling, helpless in the tide, being swept down to sea under the Yarmouth bridges.

"We'll have to stop somewhere," said Tom.

"The banks look unco' dour," said Port.

"Fare main bad to me," said Starboard, who talked broad Norfolk because of her sister's talking Ginty language.

"I'll tell you what," said Tom. "We'll go round into the Waveney and tie up by the Breydon pilot. He'll tell us when to start again. . . ."

"It said 'Safe Moorings for Yachts'," said Dick. "And there'd be lots of waders to look at, with the tide going out."

"Why not?" said Starboard.

"Wind's easterly," said Tom. "We'll easily be able to sail that bit up to the pilot's against the tide."

"All right," said the Admiral. "But what about stores? William and I are starving. And we can't expect the pilot to have food for seven. Eggs? Who said eggs? We ate the last four. There isn't an egg in the ship. And no bread. And both water-jars are empty. . . ."

Dorothea was looking at the map. "There are two houses marked near the mouth of the river," she said.

"We could get milk and eggs at the Berney Arms," said Tom. "Water, too, probably."

On and on they sailed. Already the wind seemed colder coming over Breydon, and they could hear the calling of the gulls. A red brick house came into sight on the bank, close above them.

"That looks like a farm," said the Admiral. "Let's tie up and ask here."

"I daren't," said Tom. "Not with the *Teasel*, and the tide going out. No good getting stuck. Come on, Starboard. You take over. I'll slip ashore in *Titmouse*. You sail round the corner. The pilot'll tell you the best place to moor. I'll be along with the stores by the time you get the sails down."

He hauled *Titmouse* alongside, and dropped carefully into her, while Starboard took the speed off the *Teasel* by heading her into the wind. Port and Dick between them gave him the big earthenware water-jar. Dorothea handed down milk-can and egg-basket. The Admiral gave him the ship's purse and told him to take what was wanted out of it.

"Coming, too, Dick?" Tom was bursting to have a little voyage in the *Titmouse* in these strange waters, and thought that Dick would be delighted at the chance.

But Dick was all for sticking to the *Teasel*. He wanted to get to the pilot's. There might be another chance of seeing those spoonbills. He remembered the mud-flats opposite the pilot's hulk. He wanted all the time there that he could get.

Tom let go, and, as the *Teasel* sailed on, was left astern, fitting his rowlocks and getting out his oars. As they turned the bend, they saw him already rowing in towards the bank.

*

"My word," said Starboard, "she sails a lot better without *Titmouse* to tow."

"*Titmouse* is very useful," said Dorothea.

"All right," laughed Starboard. "We couldn't do without her, but the *Teasel* does like kicking up her heels without a dinghy at her tail."

"There's the Berney Arms," said the Admiral, and then, as they began beating down the last reach of the river, "And there are the Breydon posts."

Ahead of them was black piling and a tall post marking the place where the two rivers met. Beyond it they could see where open water stretched far into the distance, with beacon posts marking the channel. They were at the mouth of the river. There, round the corner, was the old hulk of the Breydon pilot's houseboat.[1]

"We've never seen Breydon with the water all over everywhere," said Dorothea.

[1] See map on page 311 and picture on page 250.

"Just look at the birds," said Dick.

"Can't we just go down a little way to have a look at it?" said Dorothea.

Port looked back up the river. There was no sign of Tom.

"It'll take Tom a long time to come round in *Titmouse*," said Dorothea, "and the *Teasel* sails awfully fast."

Starboard was already bringing the *Teasel* round the end of the piling, and heading her up towards the Breydon pilot's moored hulk.

"What do the Coots think?" said the Admiral.

"We'd be able to get back all right with the wind as it is," said Starboard. "You can see by the way she's going now."

"Do let's," said Dorothea. "It must be all right if they used to have regattas on it."

"It *is* all right, really," said the Admiral. Far-off days were in her mind when Breydon Water was gay with yachts and she was listening for the crack of the winning gun in the commodore's steam launch. She was seeing frilled parasols and rowing skiffs, and young women with little sailor hats, and spreading skirts and sleeves most strangely puffed above the elbows.

"I don't think we could possibly get into trouble if we went down as far as the end of the piling."

"Hurrah," said Dorothea.

"Good," said Dick, who had the binoculars all ready in his hands in hopes of seeing the spoonbills.

"All right," said Starboard. "In with the main-sheet. Ready about."

The *Teasel* swung round into the wind, went about, and, with the tide helping her once more, beat down into Breydon Water.

"Tom'll see us all right," said Dorothea.

"We'll turn back in plenty of time," said the Admiral, and leaning on the top of the cabin roof, looked far ahead, seeing crowded boats, and remembered figures aboard them, where now was nothing but the salt lake, the posts marking the channel and the wild birds moving over the mud-flats following the outgoing tide.

"Just a little farther I think we might go," she said, when they came to the end of the piling that protects Reedham marshes from the river. "It isn't really Breydon till it's clear on both sides."

On they sailed, beating slowly to and fro, against the north-east wind, but hardly noticing how fast the ebb was carrying them with it.

"She can jolly well sail," said Starboard. Even the twins, though doubtful about what Tom would think of it, could not help enjoying themselves, sailing in this wide channel, leaving a red post on one side, and turning again when they came near a black post on the other, although, with the tide as it was, the water on both sides stretched far away beyond the posts.

"There they are, I do believe," whispered Dick, looking through the glasses.

"What?" said Dorothea.

"Spoonbills," said Dick. "They're a long way off. But they can't be anything else."

"Fog at sea," said Starboard, as they heard the foghorn of a lightship off the coast.

"It really *is* just like the bittern," said Dick.

"We'd better turn back now," said Port.

"Just a wee bit farther," said Dorothea.

"Two more posts and then we'll turn," said the Admiral. "Wonderful it is, with that low bank of haze over Yarmouth."

"It isn't as clear as it was," said Starboard. "Ready about." They came close up to a red post, sending a gull screaming from the top of it, went about, and stood away towards a black post on the other side of the channel.

Dorothea shivered, and laughed. "Cold wind," she said. "But isn't this lovely sailing?"

"I can't see those spoonbills," said Dick, rubbing the lenses of the binoculars with his handkerchief.

'It's getting foggy over there," said Port.

"It's rather foggy here," said Dick. "It *is* like a bittern, that horn."

And suddenly, almost before they knew it was coming, the fog was upon them. Yarmouth had disappeared, and the long line of those huge posts seemed to end nearer than it had. They could see only about a dozen . . . only six . . . and some of those were going . . . had gone. . . .

"Turn her round," said the Admiral sharply. "We must get back to the river as quick as we can."

But it was too late. The fog bank had reached them and rolled over them. The *Teasel* turned in her own length, and began driving slowly back over the tide, with the boom well out and the wind astern. But, already, her crew could not see the mouth of the river. They could see nothing at all except a black post close ahead of them.

"Leave the post to starboard," said Port.

"Teach your grandmother," said her sister.

"Don't lose sight of it until you see the next one," said the Admiral.

"Not going to."

"We'll just have to sail from post to post."

There was something terrifying in sailing quite fast through the water with nothing in sight but a dim, phantom post that seemed hardly to move at all. That was the tide, of course, carrying them down almost as fast as they sailed up against it. It was quite natural, and nobody would have minded if only it had been possible to see a little farther. But now, alone, in this cold, wet fog, with everything vanished except that ghostly post, it was as if they had lost the rest of the world. The long deep hoots from the lightship out at sea and the sirens of the trawlers down in the harbour made things worse, not better. The fog played tricks with these distant noises, making them sound now close at hand and now so far away that they could hardly be heard. Dorothea knew that the Admiral was worried, and she listened anxiously for the note of fear in the voices of the others. She could tell nothing from their faces as they stared out into the fog.

"I'm going forward," said Dick. "Even a few yards may make a difference in looking through the fog for that next post."

He was gone, clambering carefully along the side-deck with a hand on the cabin roof. On the foredeck, holding on by the mast, it was as if he were a boy made of fog, only of fog a little darker than the rest.

"Keep your eye on that post," said the Admiral again.

"It's going."

"I can see it."

"Can't see anything at all." Dick's voice came from the foredeck.

Starboard was not accustomed to steering in the dark. And this pale fog was worse than darkness. Dimly, away to her right, she could see that post, but she had a lot of other things to remember. There was the tide trying to take the *Teasel* down to Yarmouth, and the wind blowing her the other way. What if the wind were dropping. She glanced over the side at the brown water sweeping by. The little ship was moving well, but oh how slowly she was leaving that post. She must not lose sight of it, until she had another to steer for. Was the wind changing? If it did change, why, anything might happen. Funny. There it was on her right cheek. She could feel it on her nose. A moment ago it was not like that. . . . Why, it wasn't dead aft any more. . . .

"Haul in on the sheet, Twin. She isn't going like she was."

"The post's moving," said Dorothea. "It's going. Dick, Dick, can't you see the next ? We've passed this one. It's gone. . . . No. . . . I can still see it. . . ."

"Something's wrong with the wind," said Starboard in a puzzled voice.

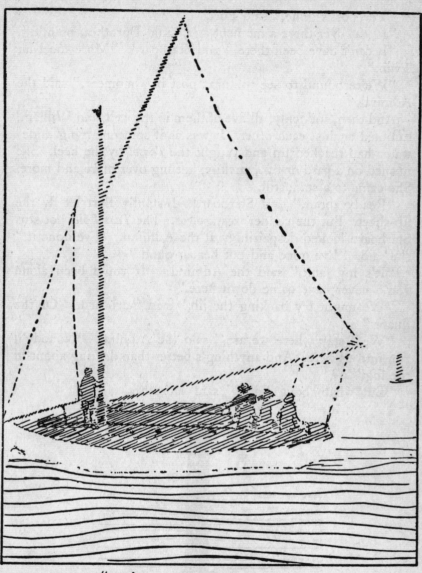

"DON'T LOSE SIGHT OF THAT POST!"

"The post's gone," said Port.

"It was over there a moment ago," said Dorothea, pointing.

"It can't have been there," said Starboard. "More sheet in, Twin."

"We're bound to see the next post in a moment," said the Admiral.

And then, suddenly, all five of them in the well, and William, tumbled against each other. It was as if someone lying under water had reached up and caught the *Teasel* by the keel. She pushed on a yard or two, stickily, heeling over more and more. She came to a standstill.

"Ready about," said Starboard. Instantly Port let fly the jib-sheet. But the rudder was useless. The *Teasel* did not stir. Starboard looked despairingly at the Admiral. "I've done it," she said. "I've gone and put her aground."

"It's my fault," said the Admiral. "If you'd been alone you'd never have come down here."

"We might try backing the jib," said Starboard. "Or the quant."

"We'll stay where we are," said the Admiral. "Nobody'll run into us here. And anything's better than drifting about in the fog."

"But what about Tom?" said Dorothea.

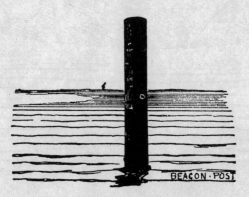

BEACON·POST

CHAPTER XXVI

THE *TITMOUSE* IN THE FOG

Tom pulled in towards some quay-heading, tied up the *Titmouse*, and went up the bank to the house. There was no one about. He wandered round to the back, but there was no answer to his knocking, the windows were all closed, no smoke was coming from the chimneys and he soon made up his mind that everybody was away from home. He hurried down the bank again to the *Titmouse*, saw that the river had fallen several inches in those few minutes, and was presently drifting downstream with the tide.

He was no longer worried about getting through Yarmouth. The only difficulty now was to make sure of getting there at exactly the right time, and the Breydon pilot would know to a minute when they ought to start. He was perfectly happy about the *Teasel*. The twins would sail her round to the pilot's just as well as he could himself. Why should the little *Titmouse* not have her turn of sailing? He stepped her mast, hoisted her sail, lowered her centre-board and tacked down-river to the Berney Arms. Here he chose his moment, dropped the sail again, pulled up the centre-board, and brought the *Titmouse* alongside what seemed to him the best landing-place. He made fast her painter round the top of an old pile, and went up the bank to the inn, taking with him basket, milk-can and stone water-jar.

A cheerful young man met him at the door.

"Two dozen of eggs? And a quart of milk? And I daresay

we can find you a loaf. But where's your ship? You won't be eating all this in that little boat."

"She's gone round to the Breydon pilot's," said Tom, looking away towards Burgh over the strip of land between the two rivers, and wondering why he could see nothing of the *Teasel*. Afloat in the *Titmouse* he had not been able to see beyond the banks.

"Not that little yacht gone down Breydon?"

"Gone down Breydon?"

That certainly did look very like the *Teasel's* sail, tacking away down there towards the open water. But what were they doing? Could they have made a mistake about the plan? Port and Starboard knew what they were about, surely.

"You'll have a job to catch her."

"They'll be turning back in a minute," said Tom, but kept his eyes on that white sail, growing smaller and smaller, while a girl was sent off to collect eggs, and, after she had brought his basket back full of eggs, had to go off again to fill his milk-can. The young man took the big water-jar and filled it with fresh water at the pump.

"Main heavy this," he said, as he brought it back. "I'll give you a hand with it down to your little boat."

He carried it down and put it in the *Titmouse*, and then after Tom had stowed milk and eggs and bread, and had gone aboard and was all ready to sail, the young man unfastened the painter but did not let it go. He just stood there smiling down at Tom and talking, asking Tom where he and his friends had come from, and how many they were aboard, and if they had been that way before, until it was all Tom could do to keep from begging him to have done. Tom thanked him several times, and at last the young man dropped the painter into the *Titmouse* and gave her a push off. If Tom had been asked what the young man had been saying he could not have answered. His mind was all with the *Teasel*. What could the

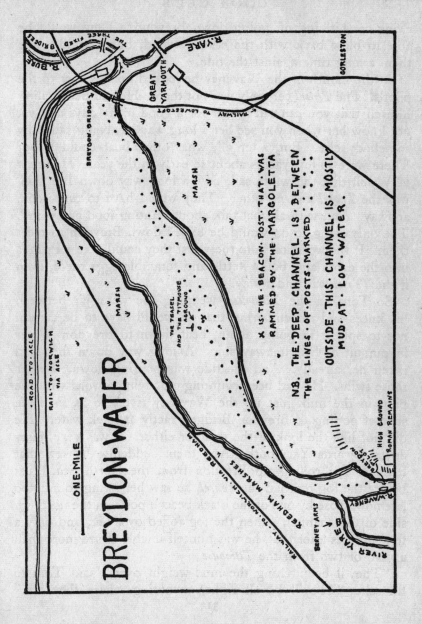

BREYDON·WATER

ONE·MILE

·ROAD·TO·ACLE·

RAIL·TO·NORWICH·VIA·ACLE

MARSH

THE·THREE·FIXED·BRIDGES
R.BURE

BREYDON·BRIDGE·

GREAT·YARMOUTH
RAILWAY·TO·LOWESTOFT

R.YARE

GORLESTON

MARSH

THE·TEASEL
AND·THE·TITMOUSE
AGROUND

X·IS·THE·BEACON·POST·THAT·WAS
RAMMED·BY·THE·MARGOLETTA

N.B.·THE·DEEP·CHANNEL·IS·BETWEEN
THE·LINES·OF·POSTS·MARKED : : : :

OUTSIDE·THIS·CHANNEL·IS·MOSTLY
MUD·AT·LOW·WATER.

RAILWAY·TO·NORWICH·VIA·REEDHAM

REEDHAM·MARSHES

BURNEY·ARMS

R.YARE

R.WAVENEY

BREYDON·PILOT

HIGH·GROUND
ROMAN·REMAINS

ι.vins be thinking of, going down Breydon? They would be able to blow back with the easterly wind, but it would take them a long time against the tide.

At the mouth of the Waveney he looked up the river to the pilot's. The *Teasel* certainly was not there. He had been telling himself that you can sail a boat for a good many days and yet not know her when you see her a long way off, being sailed by somebody else. But, after all, what other boat could it be? There were so few yachts about so early in the year. He knew very well that the white sail, now a long way down Breydon, was the *Teasel* and no other. They would have to turn soon, anyway. And with all that talk about wanting food and drink. The only thing to do would be to sail down Breydon to meet them. If the worst came to the worst they could take a Primus into the cabin and boil a kettle and scramble eggs there, even if the *Teasel* was under way.

So Tom, in the *Titmouse*, wedging the water-jar between his knees and remembering that he would have to be careful not to spill it in going about, beat down to Breydon Water in pursuit of his runaway ship. A long way down they had taken her already. And the tide was pouring down. Bother those twins. He had been counting on having a word with the pilot in the hulk just up the Waveney river, so as to make sure of getting to Breydon Bridge exactly at slack water. He did not like the look of the weather either. It was very misty down towards Yarmouth. And then, suddenly, he saw that bank of fog rolling up Breydon from the North Sea. Just before the fog reached the *Teasel*, he saw her swing round, too late now, close by one of the black beacon posts on the northern side of the channel. Then the fog rolled over her, and only a few minutes after that, he was himself unable to see more than a yard or two from the *Titmouse*.

"They'll be pitching the mud-weight over," said Tom to himself. "They'll be all right, anchoring where they are."

He never guessed for a moment that this was the one thing they had not thought of doing.

His first idea was to do the same for the *Titmouse*. These sudden fog banks that on a day of easterly wind sometimes sweep up from the sea over the lower reaches of the tidal rivers seldom last long. He had only to take the *Titmouse* to the side of the channel, anchor her and wait till the fog rolled away. He could see nothing, but, at the moment, he knew where he was, and feeling the cold wind on his right cheek-bone he kept the *Titmouse* close-hauled, until the black tarred piling by Reedham marshes loomed suddenly close ahead. He headed into the wind and lowered his sail. The black piling, dim in the fog, was sweeping by as he drifted down with the tide. He would anchor, light his oil-stove in the bottom of the boat, and do a little cooking.

He was just going to throw his mud-weight over, a lump of iron, painted green to keep the *Titmouse* clear of rust, when his own hunger reminded him of the *Teasel's* empty larder. It was all very well for him to sit comfortably in the *Titmouse* and make himself a pot of tea and boil an egg or two, but the crew of the *Teasel*, anchored away in the middle of Breydon, with nothing to do, would have to go on starving until the fog had passed.

Standing in the drifting *Titmouse*, looking into pale fog and at the ghostly piling at the edge of the marshes, Tom changed his mind. Somehow or other he had to bring food and water to the *Teasel*. Could it be done? Why not? The *Teasel*, he had seen, was on the northern side of the deep-water channel down Breydon. He, too, drifting past the piling, was on the northern side of the channel. If he could manage to keep close along that side of the channel as he drifted down, the tide itself would take him within hailing distance of the *Teasel*. Suddenly the piling ended. He was out on Breydon now, with nothing to look for but the big black beacon posts which seem near enough together in clear weather but ever so far apart in a fog. Yes, only the posts to look for above water, but what he had to follow was the bottom, where the shallow Breydon mudflats drop steeply into the deep dredged channel. He pulled up his centre-board. *Titmouse* with centre-board down was no joke to row. What was that? A huge black post loomed suddenly beside him, and was gone. Phew! Wouldn't have done to go bumping into that. He got out his oars, and spun the *Titmouse* round, and began paddling her stern first, the better to keep a look out for the next post.

But the next post seemed long in coming. Tom paddled harder. Then he stopped paddling altogether, and did a little thinking. He prodded down over the side with an oar, and

could not touch the bottom. His mud-weight had only a short rope, but longer than the oar. He lowered it over the side, using it as a sounding lead. It touched nothing. He must be well out in the dredged channel. He could see nothing but fog and a yard or two of brown water all round the boat. But all that water, though it looked still, was sweeping down to the sea, with the *Titmouse* upon it. Which way? Unless he could see something, or touch the bottom, he could not tell. The cold wind gave him some idea of the direction in which he was moving. But the wind might have changed. Tom looked blindly round him in the fog.

Suddenly he jumped to his feet. What an idiot not to remember his compass. He opened the after locker of the *Titmouse* where the compass lived in a little box of its own, hooked under the stern-sheets so that it could not get thrown about. Uncle Frank had laughed at him for taking a compass with him when sailing in the Bure. It was going to be useful now. As a general rule a compass is not much use for navigation unless you have a chart. But Tom's trouble was a simple one. All he wanted to do was to get back to the north side of the channel. The compass would make that easy enough. He laid it carefully on the floor of the *Titmouse*, in front of the water-jar, which, now that he was no longer sailing was standing in the stern. North? What? Over there? He paddled the *Titmouse* stern first, due north as the compass showed him. Good. There was another of those posts, dim in the fog, with the water swirling round it.

He found bottom with his mudweight. The *Titmouse* swung round, giving him, roughly, the direciotn of the tide. He hauled up the weight again and paddled on. Every now and then he saw the ghost of a beacon. Every now and then he dipped over the side with an oar, and, sounding and paddling, with the tide to help him made his way along the edge of the channel. He grew a little over confident, and paddled for a long time without sounding at all. Then, when he sounded, he found deep water again. He paddled northwards. Another of those posts showed for a moment and was gone. Worse than blind man's buff, thought Tom. How far had he come by now? The *Teasel* could not be very far away. No harm in hailing. He rested on his oars, drifting silently and listening. Gulls chattering. Foghorn. A steamer's siren. He gathered his breath and shouted, "*Teasel!* Ahoy . . . oy!"

There was no answer. Probably the fog made it hard to hear. He hailed again, "*Teasel!* Ahoy . . . oy . . . oy!"

That did sound almost like an answering hail, faint, far away. He glanced at the compass. Yes. East-north-east. Tom paddled away, straining his eyes into the fog and listening. He was almost sure he had heard them.

He hailed again, and listened.

"Ahoy. . . . Ahoy. . . . Ahoy!"

There they were. No doubt about it. But still far away. He paddled on.

Suddenly he heard the barking of a dog. He pulled his oars in and stood up, letting the *Titmouse* drift.

"*Teasel!* Ahoy . . . oy!"

The barking broke out again, and a chorus of shouts. There they were. He had done it. Come down Breydon in a fog and found them. No need to worry about compass now, or mud-weight. They would be anchored at the side of the channel, and he had only to join them.

"Ahoy!" he shouted, settling to his oars, spinning the *Titmouse* round and heading directly towards William's welcome barking.

"*Titmouse*, ahoy!" That was Dorothea. Too shrill for either of the twins.

"All together," he heard Starboard's voice. And then there was a really splendid yell from the whole of the *Teasel's* crew, "*Titmouse! Ahoy!*"

Tom rowed as if in a race, quick strokes and as hard as he could, fairly lifting the *Titmouse* along. "Good old William," he said to himself. William seemed almost to have guessed how useful it would be, and kept up excited barking all the time.

"Ahoy!" panted Tom, and the next moment his oars were scraping on mud, the *Titmouse* had come to a standstill, and he had tumbled backwards almost as if he had caught one of Dorothea's "lobsters."

He was up in an instant and frantically digging at the mud with an oar. The oar sank in as he pushed. He felt the *Titmouse* stir beneath him, and then settle again as he pulled to get the oar unstuck.

And then, too late, the fog began to clear. Twenty yards

away over the wet grey mud he saw a ghostly *Teasel* heeled over on her side, with her ghostly crew crowded together in her well. The *Titmouse*, drawing only her inch or two, was stuck fast. The muddy water was already creeping away from her.

"I say," he gasped. "I'm aground."

"So are we," said Starboard.

"And some of us are very hungry," said the Admiral.

"I've got the water," said Tom, "and the eggs and the milk, and they gave me two loaves of bread."

And then, prodding into the mud with his oar, he realised that with only twenty yards of it between them, the *Titmouse* and the *Teasel*, until the tide rose once more, might just as well be twenty miles apart.

CHAPTER XXVII

WILLIAM'S HEROIC MOMENT

"Idiots we are, idiots," said Starboard. "We ought to have shouted to him to keep away."

But, at such times as these, no one can think of everything. There had been a desperate struggle to get the *Teasel* afloat, which, of course, had failed. Then everybody had been wondering what would Tom be thinking when he found that they were not tied up at the pilot's moorings in the Waveney. That first distant call out of the fog had told them that Tom had come down Breydon to look for them, and they had thought of nothing but of letting him know where they were.

And now there was Tom aground as firmly as themselves. And though they had forgotten their hunger for a time, they could not forget it now that bread and eggs and milk and water for making tea had come so near and yet were out of reach.

The fog was still thick. But it had cleared enough to let them see what had happened. From the stern of the *Teasel* a little creek ran across the mud to drain into the channel not far from one of the beacon posts, probably the very post they had sailed round while trying to keep it in sight. The *Teasel* had sailed thirty or forty yards up this creek before taking the mud at one side of it. The *Titmouse* had headed towards her out of the channel about midway between that beacon and the next, so that Tom had seen neither. He had grounded on the ridge of mud between the *Teasel's* creek and the main channel. They could see him rocking the *Titmouse* on the mud. If only

318

he could get afloat he could come much closer to the *Teasel* by rowing round and up the creek in which there seemed still to be a little water. But he could not stir her. Already mud was showing all round her, and they could see the tide slipping away from her towards the beacons that marked the channel.

"Can't shift her," he shouted to them.

"We're done until the tide comes up again," said Starboard.

"I say," said Tom. "We shan't be able to get down to Yarmouth even then. Wind and tide'll both be against us. It comes up at a terrific pace."

"If only we'd stopped at Reedham we could have telephoned for the *Come Along* to meet us," said Mrs. Barrable. "But it's no good saying that. And it's my fault. Disobeying the skipper. If we'd gone straight to the pilot's everything would have been perfectly easy. No, William, it's no good asking. There simply isn't any food. Not even for you."

"I'd better try to get across the mud with some of the grub," called Tom.

"No," said the Admiral. "You're not to try. . . . If you did sink in we couldn't do a thing to save you. . . . And we wouldn't be any nearer having anything to eat."

"You couldn't chuck a rope?" shouted Tom.

"Too far."

"I daren't try to buzz a loaf."

"What about mud shoes?" suggested Port. "Fastening boards under our feet, and waddling across like ducks."

"No tools," said Mrs. Barrable.

"And no boards," said Starboard, "unless we pull the *Teasel* to bits."

"Is the tow-rope long enough?" asked Dick. "The big coil in the forepeak. The one we used at Yarmouth."

"It's long enough," said Starboard, "or jolly nearly. But we can't get it across."

"There *is* one way we could do it," said Dick. "If William

helped. But he wouldn't like it. And I don't suppose you'd let him, really."

"William?"

And then Dick explained his idea, and, as they listened, even the twins cheered up a little, wretched though they were at having to wait on the mud. Would it work, or wouldn't it?

"Of course he doesn't weigh much, and if only he keeps going pretty fast."

"He'd feel the string pulling him back."

"It needn't be string. It doesn't matter how light the first thing is. We could start with cotton, and then string. There's a huge ball of string in the stores."

"I've got a reel of cotton," said Dorothea. "Mother put it in, in case buttons came off Dick."

"And if it unrolls on one of the Admiral's pencils," said Dick, "William wouldn't feel it at all. Is the hole through the middle big enough?"

Dorothea slipped into the cabin sideways and worked herself along it to get at her little suit-case. The cabin was on such a slant that walking through it was impossible.

"Poor old William," she said, looking at him. Disliking the fog, he had made himself comfortable on the lee bunk.

"Get his harness," said the Admiral. "In the cupboard under the looking-glass."

Good! The Admiral must really be going to let him try. It was in moments like these that Dick had his best ideas, and Dorothea did not feel that the twins half understood how useful he could be.

The Admiral poked a pencil through the cotton reel, and made the reel spin by patting it.

"He'll never feel the pull of that," said Dick.

"William," said the Admiral, suddenly making up her mind.

There was no answer.

"William," she said again, and leant down and put her head into the cabin.

William snuggled down on the port bunk. The next moment he felt his mistress take a firm grip of the scruff of his neck. He was plucked forth, out of the cabin into the cold fog and dumped in the well, which, like the cabin, seemed to have taken a permanent slant. William made a half-hearted attempt to get back into the cabin, but found people's legs in the way. And after all it was his mistress who had plucked him out. He pretended he had meant to come, and, slithering on the bottom of the floor of the well, scrambled up on the port seat, and, with his paws on the coaming, looked out into the fog and down at grey-green mud with trickles of water winding across it.

Mrs. Barrable was putting his harness on him.

"What about it, William?" she said.

William looked up at her with a hint of doubt in his goggling black eyes. His green leather harness with the silver bells on it usually annoyed him, but he knew that he never had to wear it unless out walking in a town, or in someone else's garden. Anyhow, on dry land that knew its place and did not tip up sideways like this horrid boat. He decided that harness meant going back to sweet-shops and civilisation. For once he made no difficulty about having it put on.

"Hullo, William," called Tom, and William barked back.

"He'll do it," said Dorothea. "He always does do what Tom tells him."

"Have you got the cotton ready?" said the Admiral over her shoulder.

"Here's the end of it," said Dick. "I'm going to hold the pencil at each end so that the reel won't slip off. If only he'll go. . . ."

"Now, William," said the Admiral, tying the end of the cotton to the ring in the harness to which the leather lead was clipped. "This is your moment. It comes to everybody, just once, the moment when he has to be a hero or not think much of himself for the rest of his life. Are you ready, Dick? Luckily it's good stout cotton. . . . Good little dog. Clean, tidy little dog. . . . Never gets his feet muddy. . . ."

"You be ready to call him, Tom," shouted Starboard.

"Call who?" said Tom, his voice coming queerly from the shadowy little boat away over the mud. Tom had been busy stowing his sail. It would be needed no longer, and he was making a neat job of it.

"William," called Dorothea. "He's bringing a cotton across."

"A life-line," called Port. "He's a pug-rocket."

And then, suddenly, William's own mistress lifted him up and lowered him over the side of the *Teasel* down to the Breydon mud, keeping firm hold of his lead for fear the mud should be too soft even for pugs. The next moment she was wiping the mud from her eyes. William made a desperate, splashing effort to get back aboard the *Teasel*. But he could get no hold for his fore-paws. In half a minute he was more like a little grey, muddy hippopotamus than a dignified and self-respecting pug.

"Quick," said the Admiral, reaching down again to unclip the lead from the harness. "The mud'll bear him." William was free on the mud, held by nothing but the thread of cotton.

"Now!" everybody shouted at once. "Call him, Tom. Call him."

"Good boy," called Tom. "Come on, William! William! Come on, boy! Come on! Chocolate, William. . . ."

"Is there any chocolate?" asked Dorothea.

"There's a scrap in his box," said Dick. "I left a bit when I gave him his breakfast."

'Go on, William," said the Admiral. "I can't help it. You've just *got* to be a hero. Go on! Go to Tom!"

"William!" Tom's voice came again. "Good old William!"

William stopped struggling to get back aboard the *Teasel*. He looked over his shoulder. Never in all his life had he been so badly treated. Dumped into sticky grey mud. Green slime, too. And after all this talk about wiping paws on the mat. William barked. His bulging black eyes looked as puzzled as he felt.

"We'll have to let him come back," said Starboard.

"Don't be a donkey, Starboard," said the Admiral, though tears were in her own eyes as she looked down at the unhappy, muddy little dog.

"Come along, William!"

"He's going," said Port.

William set out towards the *Titmouse* and his friend. He stopped and turned back.

"Don't let him get the cotton round his legs," said Dick.

"Go away, William. Get out, we don't want you. Go to Tom! Tom! Go to Tom! Fetch him!"

William gave a last disgusted look at the crew of the *Teasel* and waddled off across the mud.

"The reel's unrolling perfectly," said Dick.

The others watched it spinning on the pencil that he held by both ends.

"It's stopped. Tom! Tom! Do make him go on!"

But William had hesitated only for a moment. He had gone more than half-way. The reel spun once more as the cotton unrolled.

"He's got there."

"Tom's yanked him aboard."

Tom's voice suddenly changed its tone. He had been calling to William, begging him to come on, but now in the *Titmouse* William was shaking himself, and Tom was doing his best to save his sail. "Shut up, William! Keep still! I'll wipe it off for you! *Do* keep still."

"Have you got the cotton?" called Dick.

"I've got it! Steady, William!"

"Haul it in gently. Very gently!"

"Sure you've made the string fast to it?"

The ball of string leapt from side to side in the well as they paid it out over the side, and Tom hauling in the cotton dragged the end of it across the mud.

"Got it," shouted Tom. "Well done, whoever thought of that! Do keep still, William."

"Now for the rope," said Dick, "and then we can get the things across. The string won't bear anything. . . ."

"Haul in again, Tom," called Starboard, who without cutting the string had made it fast to the end of the big coil of rope that had not been used since they came through Yarmouth. A snake of rope crept away over the mud as the twins paid it out from the foredeck, while the string went on unrolling in the well.

"Got it," shouted Tom. "Now what?"

"We must haul our half of the string back," shouted Dick. "Hang on to your end of it. Then we can use it for pulling things each way along the rope."

"You'll want a shackle to run on the rope," shouted Tom. "There's a spare one in the forepeak. Right in the bows."

"I've got it," said Port.

"Splendid," said the Admiral. "But, oh, I do hope poor William won't have caught his death of cold."

"We'll send across his bit of chocolate."

"Cod liver oil," said the Admiral, "is what he ought to have."

"We'll send that across, too," said Dorothea, wriggling into the slanting cabin. "Tom'll have a spoon, won't he?"

"William always likes to have his own," said the Admiral.

So the first parcel ready to travel by the rope railway that now stretched between the *Teasel* and the *Titmouse* was a scrap of chocolate, a bottle of cod-liver oil, and his own spoon for

William, the pioneer, who had crossed the mud and made the railway possible.

"It'll get awfully muddy going across," said Dorothea.

"Couldn't we hoist it up at both ends?" said Dick.

"Of course we could," said Starboard. "Hi! Tom! Hoist your end of the rope up. . . . Top of the mast. . . . Keep things out of the mud. . . ."

That was easy. Tom fastened *Titmouse's* halyard to his end of the rope and hauled it up as if he were hoisting a sail. The

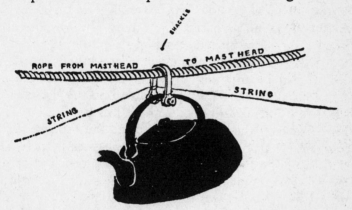

twins, aboard the *Teasel*, did the same. A moment later the rope was no longer lying on the mud, but stretched from masthead to masthead. The shackle, loose on the rope, had already been made fast to the string, and William's parcel had been tied to the shackle.

"All ready now," called Starboard.

Tom hauled in on the string. The parcel, amid cheers, left the masthead of the *Teasel* and moved slowly out. The rope sagged a bit in the middle, but the parcel was well above the mud. When it had reached the masthead of the *Titmouse*, Tom slacked away his halyard and a moment later had the parcel in his hands.

"Send us across a drop of water," called the Admiral, "and we can pour it into our kettle and put it on to boil. Don't try to send too much at once."

"Does William have his oil after chocolate or before it?" asked Tom, as the *Titmouse's* kettle went on its way, sloping a little from the spout in spite of Dick's trying not to jerk it as he hauled in on the string.

"Chocolate always comes afterwards," called William's mistress.

"Now, William," said Tom, carefully balancing the brimming spoon, as he gathered the muddy William in one arm and made him sit as he had seen him sit on the Admiral's knee that wet day at Ranworth and again at Oulton Broad. And William, glad of anything to which he was accustomed, sat on Tom's knee in the *Titmouse*, aground on the Breydon mud, and lapped up his cod-liver oil as if he had been at home.

Then back by the rope railway came the little kettle to be filled again. Three or four times it went to and fro. Already, in the *Teasel* the Primus was at work, propped in a corner of the well, with a paint-box under it at one side to keep it level. Then a loaf of bread was sent across. The eggs, for fear of accident, were divided into two lots, and travelled in the basket, a dozen at a time. The milk, too, was sent over in small lots, in the *Titmouse's* milk-can. "Don't you bother about making tea, Tom," called Mrs. Barrable when she saw that Tom was lighting his oil-stove. "We'll send yours as soon as it's ready, but if you could manage some bread and milk for William. . . ."

As soon as the big kettle had boiled, the *Teasel* sent the little milk-can, full of hot tea, by rope railway to the *Titmouse*, together with two boiled eggs tied up in a handkerchief, and a big bread and butter sandwich to eat with them. Meanwhile, Tom, in the *Titmouse*, had warmed a little milk in his frying-pan because he had not got a saucepan. He had chopped up some bread and added it to the milk, and William, though he would rather have had it from his own saucer, had decided to make the best of things. In both ships everybody was settling down to the first good meal that day. They were aground on the mud. They had missed their tide. They had lost their chance of getting through Yarmouth that day. Everything was going wrong. But, at least, thanks to Tom to Dick, and to the heroic William, no one was any longer in danger of starvation.

THE HERO

CHAPTER XXVIII

WRECK AND SALVAGE

"Tide's begun coming up again," called Tom at last. "It'll be turning in the Bure in another hour, and boats going south'll be coming through."

Slowly the water came licking up over the edge of the mud-flats, little thin waves hurrying over the mud and going back to meet other little waves that spread wider and wider. Herons were fishing knee-deep, ready for small fish coming unsus-pectingly up with the tide. With the change of the tide the fog lifted. Pale sunlight made its way through. The crew of the *Teasel* could see far down Breydon to the railway bridge, and up to the meeting of the rivers at the head of it. Away to the north a big black wherry sail showed above the low-lying land. The shallow creek through which the *Teasel* must have sailed before she stuck, filled with water. Water rose slowly round the big black posts that marked the deep-water channel. Water crept over the mud, nearer and nearer to the *Titmouse*. It was time to get ready. Tom's plans were made. As soon as the *Teasel* floated he would tow her out into the deep water, and then they would sail back to the pilot's moorings to wait for the morning tide.

"Anything else to go across?" he shouted.

"Couldn't you send William back by the railway before you take it down?" suggested Dorothea.

"Too heavy," said Tom. "He'd drag in the mud and make the *Teasel* as dirty as poor old *Titmouse*. He's fairly clean now."

"You keep him," said the Admiral, looking up at the mention of William's name. She was sitting on the upper edge of the sloping cabin roof, and making a sketch of Breydon at low tide, with the little *Titmouse* reflected in the pearly shine of the mud almost as if in water.

"I'm going to cast off my end of the rope," said Tom. "So that I can get my mast down. *Titmouse* 'll be wanted as a dinghy pretty soon."

He unfastened the rope from the halyard and dropped it on the mud. "Haul away!"

"Coil it down, Twin. In with it."

Port and Starboard, miserably thinking of to-morrow's race, and of the A.P. without his crew, were cheered at having something to do. For a few yards they hauled in the tow-rope hand over hand, and then stopped short as they came to the part of the rope that had dragged over the mud.

"Pretty smelly," said Starboard. "Look out. Stop pulling. We can't stow it in the forepeak till it's had a bit of washing."

"Keep it off the cabin roof," said Port "Don't let the mud get on the sails. Shove that jib out of the way, somebody with clean hands. Lucky we rolled it up at once."

"Come on, Dick," said Dorothea, and Dick gave up looking for the vanished spoonbills, and helped her to take the jib, rolled up round its short boom, and stow it in the cabin out of danger.

"Hi," called Tom. "Don't try to stow that rope in the forepeak. I'll be using it to tow *Teasel* out into the channel, and that'll wash the mud off it."

The rope was coiled down on the foredeck, just as it was, grey with mud, and green with scraps of twisted weed, while Dick was busy winding up the string that had been used for hauling the shackle to and fro.

"The water's right up to me," called Tom. "I'll be afloat in another ten minutes."

"It's all round us already," Dorothea shouted back.

The water spread slowly over the mud between the *Titmouse* and the *Teasel*. Anyone who did not know that it was mostly only an inch deep might have thought they were afloat, except that the *Teasel* was leaning over on one side.

"There's the first boat through," called Dorothea.

Everybody looked down Breydon water and those two long lines of beacon posts stretching away to Yarmouth. Down there, far away, a small black spot was moving in the channel. If they had not been so busy, they would have noticed it before.

"Only a rowing boat," said Starboard. "Probably a fisherman coming home with the tide. The water's really coming up now. Let's try to get afloat before he gets here."

"Anyway that one's not a rowing boat," said Dorothea a few minutes later.

"Motor-cruiser," said Port, glancing over her shoulder.

"It's a jolly big one," said Starboard.

All work stopped aboard the *Teasel*. There was something in Starboard's voice that held even the Admiral's chalk in mid-air, and stopped Dick in winding the string into a ball, though he had just found the scientific way of winding it so that the turns did not slip off. Tom heard nothing. He was busy tugging at his mast, which was always rather hard to work out of its hole in the bow thwart.

"But it can't be," said Starboard. "Bill said yesterday they wouldn't be able to leave Wroxham for another two days."

"He must have got it a day wrong," said Port. "I'm sure it's them. Tom! Tom! Hullabaloos!"

"Oh, hide! hide!" cried Dorothea.

Tom turned round and stopped wrestling with the *Titmouse's* mast. There could be no doubt about it. The cruiser had passed the rowing boat now, and came racing up Breydon, foam flying from her bows, a V of wash spreading astern of her across the channel and sending long bustling waves chasing one another over the mudflats. Even in the dark Tom had known the noise of the *Margoletta's* engine. He knew it now, and the tremendous volume of sound sent out by her loudspeaker.

He looked this way and that. If those people had glasses or a telescope they might have seen him already. Anyhow, there could be no getting away. He felt like a fly caught in a spider's web, seeing the spider hurrying towards it. There they were, *Teasel* and *Titmouse*, stuck on the mud in shallow water, plain for anyone to see. If only the water had risen another few inches and set them afloat. But even if it had, where could they have gone? There was only one thing to be done. It was a poor chance, but the only one. Tom made one desperate signal to the others to disappear, and, himself, slipped down out of sight on the muddy bottom-boards of the *Titmouse*, and, holding William firmly in his arms, told him what a good dog he was and begged him to keep still.

Aboard the *Teasel* no one saw that signal. Their eyes were all on the *Margoletta*. It was not till several minutes later that Dorothea whispered, "Tom's gone, anyway."

The little *Titmouse*, now that the water had spread all round her over the mud, looked like a deserted boat, afloat and anchored.

On came the *Margoletta*, sweeping up with the tide, and filling the quiet evening with a loud treacly voice:

"I want to be a darling, a doodle-um, a duckle-um,
    I want to be a ducky, doodle darling, yes, I do."

"Indeed," muttered Port, with a good deal of bitterness.

"Try next door," said Starboard.

They spoke almost in whispers, as the big motor-cruiser came nearer and nearer, though no one aboard it could possibly have heard them.

"We ought to have done like Tom and hidden," said Dorothea. "Let's."

"Keep still," said the Admiral. "It's too late now. They're bound to notice if we start disappearing all of a sudden."

"Good," whispered Starboard. "They're going right past." And then the worst happened.

William, still slippery with mud in spite of Tom's pocket handkerchief, indignant at being held a prisoner while this great noise came nearer and nearer, gave a sturdy wriggle, escaped from Tom's arms, bounded up on a thwart and barked at the top of his voice.

"Oh! William! Traitor! Traitor!" almost sobbed Dorothea.

"They've seen!" said Port.

The man at the wheel of the cruiser was looking straight at the *Titmouse* and at the *Teasel* beyond her.

"Here they are," he suddenly shouted, to be heard even above the loud-speaker and the engine. He spun his wheel, swung the *Margoletta* round so sharply that she nearly capsized, and headed directly for the *Titmouse*. . . .

"Ow! Look out!" cried Starboard, almost as if she were aboard the cruiser and saw the danger ahead.

"They've forgotten the tide," said Port.

The next moment the crash came. Just as the rest of the Hullabaloos poured out of the cabins, startled by the sudden way in which the steersman had swung her round, the *Margoletta*, moving at full speed towards the *Titmouse*, and swept up sideways by the tide, hit the big beacon post with her port bow. There was the cracking of timbers and the rending of wood as the planking was crushed in. Then the tide swung her stern round and she drifted on.

The noise became deafening. The loud-speaker went on pouring out its horrible song. All the people aboard the *Margoletta* were either shouting or shrieking and something extraordinary had happened to the engine which, after stopping dead, was racing like the engine of an aeroplane. Nobody knew till afterwards that the steersman had switched straight

THE WRECK WAS DRIFTING AWAY

from "full ahead" to "full astern," had wrenched the propeller right off its shaft, stalled his engine, started it again and was letting it rip at full throttle, pushing his lever to and fro trying to make his engine turn a propeller that was no longer there.

Everything had changed in a moment. That crash of the *Margoletta* against the huge old post on which Tom had been watching the falling and the rising of the tide brought him up from the bottom-boards of the *Titmouse* in time to see the wreck go drifting up the channel with a gaping wound in her bows and the water lapping in. No longer was he hiding from the Hullabaloos. They were shouting at him to come and save them, shouting at Tom, whom only a few moments before they had thought was a prisoner almost in their hands. And Tom was desperately rocking the *Titmouse* in an inch or two of water, trying to get her afloat so that he could dash to their rescue.

The three Coots, Tom, Port and Starboard, knew at once how serious was the danger of the Hullabaloos. Just for a moment or two the others were ready to rejoice that Tom had escaped them. But soon they, too, saw how badly damaged the *Margoletta* was. They saw, too, that the Hullabaloos, instead of doing the best that could be done for themselves, were making things far worse. The *Margoletta* had been towing a dinghy. Two of the men rushed aft and tried to loose the painter and bring the dinghy alongside. They hampered each other. One pulled out a knife and cut the rope, thinking the other had hold of it. The rope dropped. They grabbed at it and missed. The dinghy drifted with every moment farther out of reach. They seized a boat-hook, tried to catch the dinghy and lost the boat-hook at the first attempt.

"She's down by the head already," said Starboard. "Oh can't they stop that awful song?"

The crew of the *Teasel* watched what was happening, hardly able to breathe. There was the cruiser drifting away with the tide up the deep channel. With every moment it was clearer that she had not long to float. Were the whole lot of the Hullabaloos to be drowned before their eyes? Would no one come to the rescue?

They looked despairingly towards Yarmouth. That rowing boat was coming along. But so slowly, and so far away. Too late. They would be bound to be too late, with nothing but oars to help them. But something was happening in that boat. They could see the flash of oars, but surely that was a mast tottering up and into place in the bows. And then, in short jerks, a grey, ragged, patched old lugsail, far too small for the boat, rose cockeye to the masthead. The sail filled, and the oars stopped for a moment while the sheet was taken aft.

"Hurrah!" shouted Port as loud as she could shout. "Hurrah! It's the Death and Glories!"

Nobody else in all Norfolk had a ragged sail of quite that shape and colour. How they had got down to Breydon nobody asked at that moment. It was enough that they were there, while the *Teasel* and the *Titmouse*, still fast aground, could do nothing but watch that race between life and death. The wind was still blowing from the east, and the old *Death and Glory*, her oars still flashing although she was under sail, was coming along as fast as ever in her life. She might do it yet. And then the watchers turned the other way to see the drifting cruiser, her bows much lower in the water, the Hullabaloos crowded together on the roof of her after-cabin.

"She'll go all of a rush when she does go," said Starboard under her breath.

"Deep water, too," said Port.

Minute after minute went by, and then the *Death and Glory* swept past them up the channel, her tattered and patched old sail swelling in the wind, Bill and Pete, each with two hands to an oar, taking stroke after stroke as fast as they could to help her along, while Joe stood in the stern, hand on tiller, eyes fixed on the enemy ahead who had suddenly become a wreck to be salved.

"Go it, the Death and Glories!" shouted Starboard.

"Stick to it!" "You'll do it!" "Hurrah!" "Keep it up!" shouted the others. And William, not in the least knowing what it was all about, jumped up first on one thwart of the *Titmouse* and then on another and nearly burst his throat with barking.

*

The noise of the engine had stopped. The shouting of the Hullabaloos was growing fainter as the *Margoletta* drifted up the channel with the tide.

"It's going to be a jolly near thing," said Starboard, who was looking through the glasses at the sinking cruiser already far away.

Far away up the channel the *Death and Glory* had drawn level with the *Margoletta*. Her ragged old sail was coming down. From the *Teasel* nothing could be heard of what was being said, but it was clear that some sort of argument was going on. They could see Joe pointing at the *Margoletta's* bows. They could see the five Hullabaloos, crowded together on the roof of the *Margoletta's* after-cabin, waving their arms, and, so Starboard said, shaking their fists. The two boats were close together, drew apart and closed again. A rope was thrown and missed and coiled and thrown once more.

"But why don't they take those poor wretches off?" said Mrs. Barrable.

Starboard laughed.

"Boat-builders' children," she said. "They won't be thinking about people when there's a boat in danger. All they're worrying about is not letting the *Margoletta* go down in the fairway. You'll see. They'll tow her out of the channel before they do anything else."

She was right. *The Death and Glory* moved towards one of

the red beacon posts on the south side of the channel, towards which the cruiser had drifted. The cruiser, at the end of the tow-rope, was following her, stern first, her bows nearly underwater. *The Death and Glory* left the channel, passing between one red post and the next. The *Margoletta* followed her. She stopped.

"Aground," said Port.

"Safe enough now," said Starboard. "Well done, Joe."

They saw Joe jump aboard the wreck, moving on the foredeck almost as if he were walking in the water. They saw him lower the *Margoletta's* mudweight into the *Death and Glory*. They saw the *Death and Glory* pulling off again, to drop the weight into the mud at the full length of its rope. Then, and then only, when the *Margoletta* was aground on the mud in shallow water and safe from further damage, were Joe and his fellow salvage men ready to clutter up their ship with passengers. "Idiots!" said Starboard, watching through the glasses. "All trying to jump at once."

"Well," said Mrs. Barrable, as the distance widened between the salvage vessel and the wreck, and she saw that all the Hullabaloos were aboard the *Death and Glory*, "I'm very glad that's over."

"Of course," said Dorothea, "in a story one or two of them ought to have been drowned. In a story you can't have everybody being a survivor."

"If it hadn't been for the Death and Glories," said Port, "there wouldn't have been any survivors at all. The *Margoletta* would have gone down in the deep water and the whole lot of them would have been drowned. What's Joe going to do with them now? It looks as if he's putting up his sail."

"He can't do anything against the wind," said Starboard. "The *Death and Glory* never could. And with the tide pouring up. . . . Hullo! Tom's afloat!"

"Get the tow-rope ready on the counter," shouted Tom.

All this time the water had been rising. Just as the last of the Hullabaloos had left the wreck of the *Margoletta* Tom had felt the *Titmouse* stir beneath his feet. He had her mast down in a moment. Her sail had been stowed long ago. Tom got out his oars and paddled her round to the stern of the *Teasel*. William, welcome in spite of his muddiness, scrambled back aboard his ship. Tom made the tow-rope fast.

"Try shifting from one side to the other," he said.

The *Teasel's* keel stirred in the mud. The creek by which she had left the channel in the fog had filled, and Tom with short sharp tugs at his oars made the tow-rope leap, dripping, from the water.

"She's moving," said Dick.

"She will be," said Starboard, pushing on the quant, while Port hung herself out as far as she could, holding the shrouds, first on one side of the ship and then on the other, and Mrs. Barrable, Dick and Dorothea shifted first to one side and then to the other of the well.

"She's off."

The *Teasel* slid into the creek. A moment later the tow-rope had been shifted to her bows and Tom was towing her back towards the channel. In a few minutes she was once more on the right side of the black beacons, drifting up with the tide, while Port and Starboard were hoisting her mainsail. The tow-rope, now more or less clean, was hauled in, hand over hand. Tom came aboard, and the little *Titmouse* became once more a dinghy towing astern.

"Let's just see if she'll do it," said Starboard, looking away down Breydon to the long, railway bridge. If only they could get through that bridge they might, after all, be home in time for to-morrow's race.

Port was busy with a mop. "Foredeck's clear of mud," she said. "What about that jib?"

Dick and Dorothea were already bringing it carefully from the cabin, while the Admiral was keeping a firm hold of the muddy William, for fear he might print a paw upon it.

Up went the jib, and the *Teasel* went a good deal faster through the water, away across the channel to a red post on the further side. Round she came and back again. She had not gained an inch. Once more Tom took her across the channel. Once more he brought her back. No there was no doubt about it. This time she had lost ground. The wind was dropping, and the tide pouring up was sweeping her further and further from Breydon Bridge.

"It's no good," said Tom. "We'll just have to go back to the pilot's and have another shot at getting through Yarmouth to-morrow."

"We're done," said Port. "It's too late now. We'll never get home by land to-night."

"And the A.P.'ll have no crew," said Starboard.

The *Teasel*, a melancholy ship, swung round and drove up with the tide to meet the *Death and Glory*.

The *Death and Glory* was desperately tacking to and fro across the channel, losing ground with every tack, even though Bill and Pete were rowing to help her sail. On the southern side of the channel, beyond the red posts, the tide was rising round the after-cabin of the *Margoletta*. A black speck in the distance, the *Margoletta's* dinghy was drifting towards the Reedham marshes.

"Joe," shouted Tom, when within hailing distance of the *Death and Glory*, "you can't get down to Yarmouth against this tide. We can't, either. Going back to the pilot's?"

And at that moment Dorothea looking sadly back towards Yarmouth saw something moving on the water far away.

"There's another motor-boat," she said.

"Hullo," said Starboard, "I do believe it's the *Come Along*. Where are those glasses?"

Well above Breydon railway bridge a yacht was hoisting the peak of her mainsail. The *Come Along* must have brought her through from the Bure, for there, already more than half-way between that yacht and the *Teasel*, there was the little tow-boat, with the red and white flag, coming up Breydon at a tremendous pace. Old Bob had seen that something was amiss.

Joe saw the motor-boat, too, and was afraid his salvage job would be snatched from him when all the work was done.

"Them Yarmouth sharks," he said, and looked at the wreck. But the tide had carried him too far away already. Even with the help of those stout engines, Bill and Pete, he could not get back to stand by the wreck before this boat from Yarmouth reached it.

The *Come Along* seemed to be close to them almost as soon as they had sighted her. She circled once round the wreck, and then made for the *Death and Glory*, probably because Old Bob saw that the old black boat was carrying the shipwreck d crew.

"You leave her alone," Joe was shouting at the top of his voice. "She ain't derelict. Don't you touch her. You leave her alone!"

"Take us into Yarmouth," yelled the Hullabaloos.

"She ain't derelict," shouted Joe. "She's out o' the fairway. We've put her in shallow water, an' laid her anchor out. She belongs to Rodley's o' Wroxham, an' you leave her alone."

Old Bob shut down his engine to listen. He laughed. "All right, Bor," he called. "She'll take no harm there. I'm not robbing you. Good bit o' salvage work you done. And where're ye bound for now?"

"Down to Yarmouth," shouted the man who had been at the wheel of the *Margoletta*. "We want to get ashore."

The *Come Along* swung alongside the *Teasel*.

"Good day to you, ma'am," said Old Bob to the Admiral. "Was you going down to Yarmouth, too? And so you found your ship all right?" he added, seeing Port and Starboard smiling down at him.

"I suppose there's no chance now of getting through Yarmouth until to-morrow morning," said the Admiral. "The tide seems to be running very hard."

Old Bob laughed again. "Take ye through now," he said. "Tide or no tide. When the *Come Along* say 'Come along,' they *got* to come along. I'll be taking this party down to Yarmouth and I'll be taking you at the same time. If you'll be ready to have your mast down for the bridges. You'll have the tide with you up the North River."

"They'll be in time," cried Dorothea.

"We'll do it yet," said Starboard.

"Never say dee till ye're deid," said Port.

"Perhaps we ought to pick up that dinghy for them," said Tom, pointing it out in the distance.

"You be getting ready," said Old Bob. He was off again, chug, chug, chug, chug, to catch the *Margoletta's* dinghy before it had drifted ashore.

"Oh, can't you let the blasted dinghy go?" shouted one of the Hullabaloos. But Old Bob did not hear him.

All was bustle aboard the *Teasel*. Tom sailed her to and fro close hauled, waiting for Old Bob to come back. Port and Starboard were ready on the foredeck to lower the mainsail. Dick and Dorothea were stowing the jib once more in the cabin. Presently the *Come Along* came shugging back, bringing the *Margoletta's* dinghy. Old Bob brought the *Death and Glory's* long tow-rope and threw it to Tom aboard the *Teasel*. Then he threw the end of *Come Along's* tow-rope across the *Teasel's* foredeck. Starboard caught it and made it fast.

"All ready?" shouted Old Bob. "Mind your steering."

Slowly he went ahead. First the *Teasel* and the *Titmouse* felt the pull of the little tug. Then the *Death and Glory* swung into line astern of them. They were off.

Down came the *Teasel's* mainsail.

"Come on, Tom," said Starboard. "What about getting the mast down? You'll want to take the heel-rope, won't you? Port'll take the tiller."

Tom went forward. And then, for a moment, he forgot that he had a mast to lower. He was looking at the after-cabin of the *Margoletta*, a melancholy island in the water. For some minutes they had heard nothing of the loud-speaker. Now, suddenly, they heard it again.

"We now switch over. . . . The Hoodlum Band. . . . Relayed from . . ." There was a pause, and then a sudden torrent of noise that broke off short almost as soon as it had begun. "Blaaar. Taratartara. . . . Tara. Tara. . . . Blaaaaaar!" And then silence, except for the loud chugging of the *Come Along*.

"Who's turned it off at last?" said the Admiral.

"I expect it's the water," said Dick. "It must have come as high as the batteries and made a short circuit. . . ."

"Thank goodness it has," said Starboard on the foredeck close beside Tom. They settled down to the business of lowering the *Teasel's* mast, while Breydon Bridge, once so impossibly out of reach, came nearer and nearer.

CHAPTER XXIX

FACE TO FACE

"Come on and take the tiller, Tom," called Port.

Tom heard her. He was standing on the foredeck, with an arm over the foot of the lowered mast, looking at the *Come Along*, at old Bob hunched up in the stern of her hugging his tiller, at the dinghy of the wrecked *Margoletta*, and ahead at the long iron railway bridge and Yarmouth town. But he hardly saw the things he was looking at. He had failed after all, and the others did not seem to know it. All this time he had kept out of the way of those foreigners and now, in the end, there could be no escape for him. The others aboard the *Teasel* were thinking of wreck and rescue and getting through Yarmouth and up the river in time for to-morrow's race. But he could think of one thing only. With every yard they made down Breydon they were nearer to the moment when the Hullabaloos would have to know whose son it was that had cast off their moorings and sent them drifting down the river. His father had told him to keep out of their way, and now there they were, all being towed down Breydon together. He could not bring himself to look at them. But, through the back of his head, as it were, he could see them, towing astern, in the *Death and Glory*, too, after all that those three young bird preservers, pirates and salvage men had done to help him to keep clear. Well, he could not exactly wish the Hullabaloos had all been drowned. He himself would have gone to help them if he had been able to get *Titmouse* off the mud.

"Come on, Tom," said Port.

He went aft, and stood there, steering with a foot on the tiller. He could not help glancing down into the little *Titmouse*, spattered all over with the mud poor William had brought with him after heroically taking the life-line from ship to ship. Close astern of the *Titmouse* was the *Death and Glory*. He wondered if the Hullabaloos, crowded together in the old black boat, could see the name that had been painted out on the *Titmouse's* stern. It seemed now that he might just as well have left it as it was.

"Look! Look!" cried Dorothea. "Joe's got his white rat on his shoulder."

In spite of himself, Tom had to look round.

Right in the bows of the *Death and Glory* were Bill and Pete, looking over at the flurry of foam from her fast towing. In the middle of the boat were the Hullabaloos, and in the stern, steering, with a face of simple happiness and pride, was Joe. His white rat crawled slowly from one shoulder to the other round his neck, but Joe's eyes never shifted from the stern of the *Teasel*, and his steering was as steady as Tom's own.

The Hullabaloos were far past minding being in a boat with a white rat. Men and women, looking all the more wretched for their gaudy clothes, they huddled together in the *Death and Glory*, miserable, angry, and silent after all that frantic shouting. Far away up Breydon a speck on the silver water at the side of the channel was all that could be seen of the *Margoletta*.

After all, even if while they had her they had used her to make things uncomfortable for other people, upsetting old ladies in their houseboats, throwing dinghies against quays and tearing down the banks with their wash, even if they had carried their horrible hullabaloo into the quietest corners of the Broads, they now were shipwrecked sailors. They had lost their ship. And, in a way, Tom felt it was his fault. If only

THE *COME ALONG* SAYS "COME ALONG!"

he had not been there in the *Titmouse*, if he had not let William get loose and bark, indeed, if only he had not managed to dodge them for so long, they never would have sent their vessel crashing into a Breydon beacon.

Tom began to think how awful he would have felt if he had wrecked the *Teasel* in such a way ... or the little *Titmouse*. The thought was so upsetting that he gave the *Teasel* a sudden sheer that surprised young Joe in the *Death and Glory*, and made old Bob in the *Come Along* look reprovingly over his shoulder.

Through Breydon Bridge the *Come Along* towed them, and round the dolphins and into the mouth of the North River, where the tide was running up. Old Bob signalled with his arm. He was swinging round to bring them head to tide alongside the quay. The moment was very near now when Tom would have to meet his enemies face to face.

"It's all right," said Dorothea, who seemed, alone, to guess what was in his mind. "The outlaws rescued their pursuers and everything was all right."

But was it? There was only one thing to be done, as far as Tom could see. As soon as they were tied up to the quay he went and did it.

The Hullabaloos had come ashore from the *Death and Glory*. They were standing on the quay, explaining. Old Bob was explaining, too, to some fishermen, and telling a friend to telephone up to Rodley's at Wroxham, to say what had happened to the *Margoletta*. A lot of other people seemed to be there, which made it rather worse for Tom.

He went straight up to the Hullabaloos, to the red-haired man who had been steering when the *Margoletta* crashed into the post.

"I've come to say I'm very sorry. I'm very sorry about the wreck, of course. Anybody would be. But I mean I'm very sorry about casting off your moorings that time. I wouldn't have done it if only the nest hadn't belonged to a rather special bird. But I oughtn't to have done it at all. . . ."

The man stared at him, turned as red as his hair, and suddenly shouted at him, "Blast your special bird . . . and that friend of yours at Horning who sent us wild-goose chasing up and down . . . the two of you laughing in your blasted sleeves. . . . You may think it a joke. . . ."

Tom did not think it a joke, and he could not understand what the man meant about a friend of his at Horning. Surely not George Owdon? But, before he could answer, while the man was still raging on, one of the older fishermen cut him short.

"Stow that now," he said. "What ye shoutin' about? Fare to me that if it hadn't a been for these young folk ye'd be too full o' Breydon water to be talkin' to 'em like that. Let be, say I, and be thankful for a dry skin. . . ."

"Shut up, Ronald," said one of the other Hullabaloos. "You've made a mess of things, and the less said the better."

"Isn't there a hotel in this beastly place?" said one of the two women, the one who had been rude to Mrs. Barrable that first day. "Need you keep us waiting here to be stared at by everybody?"

A boy on the quayside led them off, a melancholy, cross procession, in their white-topped yachting caps and gaudy shirts, and berets and beach pyjamas. "Rammed a post on Breydon, they did," the boy explained again and again to the people they passed, as he piloted them off the quay and along the crowded streets.

Not one of them had thought of saying "Thank you" to the Death and Glories.

Not that that mattered to the Death and Glories. Fishermen and sailors who had listened to old Bob were looking down at them from the quay and saying what a good job they had done. Presently news came that somebody had got through to

Wroxham on the telephone, and that Rodley's were sending a man down to see what could be done with the *Margoletta* when the tide went down.

"They'll float her again easy," said Old Bob. "Couldn't have beached her in a better place myself."

"You'll have saved someone a pretty penny," said a sailor on the quay to the three small boys fending off their old black boat below him. "It'll be worth a new mast and sail to you, likely, if you're wantin' 'em in that *Death and Glory* o' yours."

At that moment salvage was the thing, and Joe, Bill and Pete decided there and then to give up piracy for good and all.

The *Margoletta's* dinghy was left in charge of a friend of Old Bob's until Rodley's man should arrive. Then the Admiral and the skipper of the *Come Along* had a word or two together, and the Admiral told the others something of what she meant to do. "It'll take those three far too long to get up the river in that old boat. We'd better give them a tow."

Once more Old Bob settled down over his tiller and the *Come Along* said "Come Along" to the *Teasel* and the *Titmouse* and the *Death and Glory*. The whole fleet went up the river together, with cheers for the three small boys from all the people on the quayside and in the moored boats. News like that of the wreck and salvage of the *Margoletta* is very quick in getting about.

"What about yanking our mast up?" said Starboard, as they left the last of the three Yarmouth bridges astern.

"Better wait till we get through Acle," said the Admiral.

"Acle?" said Starboard.

"Acle?" said Tom.

"It won't take long with the tide and the *Come Along*," said the Admiral. "And I should never forgive myself if Port and Starboard were to miss to-morrow's race after all."

As for the Death and Glories, their faces looked more and more surprised as they were towed up the river, past Three-

Mile House, past Scare Gap, and Runham Swim, and Six-Mile House, and the Stracey Arms, and Stokesby Ferry. Was it never going to end?

At last they were through Acle Bridge, and there moored for the night. The Admiral settled up with Old Bob, and Port and Starboard thanked him again for taking them up Breydon from *Sir Garnet* and putting them aboard the barge.

"We'd have missed everything if you hadn't," said Port.

"Good night to ye," called the old man, and set off, chug, chug, down the river, back again to Yarmouth. He left the Death and Glories with bursting hearts, for, just as he was going, he had said, "I'll see ye're not put upon. I'll tell Rodley's myself about that salvage job o' yours."

And then, when masts and awnings were up, and the Death and Glories had shown just what could be done in that way with a sheet of old tarpaulin, the Admiral put the kettle on, and sent the crew of the *Teasel* off with a message to the inn below the bridge. The provision boat had stopped business for the night. They came back with fresh milk and two big slabs of chocolate and two cold chickens cooked that day.

"They might almost have known we were coming," said Dorothea.

"Back in home waters," said Starboard as they walked along the bank, picking their way in the dusk.

"We've had a gorgeous voyage," said Dorothea, "and we can tell Nancy that we've been in a storm and been in a fog, and even if we haven't been shipwrecked ourselves, not properly, we've seen a real shipwreck, which is the next best thing."

"Half a minute, Dot," said Dick. "Do listen. . . . There it is again. . . ."

"Boom . . . boom . . . boomm . . . boom . . ." The call of the bittern sounded over the marshes in the quiet May evening.

"I'm very glad I heard it to-day," said Dick. "The same

349

day as the fog-horns. It's very like the fog-horns, but not quite."

"All right," said Port. "Give me the milk, if you're trying to get at that pocket-book of yours."

The kettle was boiling when they reached the *Teasel*, and they all crammed into her for supper. Joe's white rat was given bread and milk and kept at a safe distance from William, who had his fill of chocolate.

Then, free from all fears of Hullabaloos (and after all he had not had to give his name), Tom and the others heard how it was that the Death and Glories had come sailing up Breydon in time to save the *Margoletta*. They heard how, at Acle, Joe and Pete had learnt that Bill had made a mistake about the day, and that the *Margoletta* was coming down to Yarmouth at low water on the very day that the *Teasel* had planned to come through. There was only one thing to be done if they were to save the elder Coots. They set out at once, and with the tide to help them and a lucky tow from a friendly wherry going down under power they came to Yarmouth just as the ebb ended. There was no sign yet of the *Margoletta*, held up, perhaps, by the fog. Tom and the *Teasel*, they were sure, must be waiting at the dolphins at the mouth of the river for the tide to turn up the Bure. There was still time to warn Tom to slip ashore. They rowed down through the Bure bridges. It was dead low water and quite easy. Then, finding no *Teasel*, they thought they might as well go on through Breydon Bridge to see if she were in sight. That they found easier still, for the tide was already sweeping up the Yare. They were just thinking of turning back for fear it would be too strong for them, when they caught sight of the *Teasel* on the mud, far away in the distance. And, at that very moment, the *Margoletta* had come roaring past them and they had known they were too late. They had watched the big cruiser racing up Breydon towards the helpless outlaw and then, suddenly, they had seen her swing round, ram the post, bring up short and drift away. Pete's long telescope had shown them that they had a real wreck to salve at last. The rest everybody knew.

"And now," said the Admiral, "those poor Hullabaloos have lost their ship, and are having to explain at the hotel how they had to leave her in such a hurry that they haven't even got their tooth-brushes. And all because they moored on the top of a coot's nest, poor things. . . ."

"They wouldn't go when they was asked," said Joe.

"I tell 'em it was our coot," said Pete.

"They only got themselves to thank," said Bill. "Yes, please, I'd like another bit of that chocolate."

POSTSCRIPT

THAT is really the end of the story. But those who like to be quite sure about everything may want to know a little more. The fleet set sail from Acle to Horning after a very early breakfast, and the twins had *Flash* all ready for the race before their A.P. came home. Tom moored the *Teasel* at Horning Staithe, where Jim Wooddall in *Sir Garnet* was moored too. The Admiral, Tom, Dick, Dorothea, and William aboard the *Teasel*, and Jim and his mate aboard the wherry, had a splendid view of the end of the race, which *Flash* won by the length of a short bowsprit. Dick and Dorothea went off home with proper discharge certificates, signed by three skippers and an admiral, to say that they could fairly be counted able-bodied seamen. The Admiral's Brother Richard came back from London and sailed off again in the *Teasel* with the Admiral, and she rather enjoyed telling him, whenever things went a little wrong, that he ought to take some lessons from the Coots. The Admiral and he went to see the Dudgeons, and he pleased the doctor and his wife and Tom too, by painting a portrait of "our baby," which was admired by a great many people when it was exhibited at Burlington House. Nothing more was seen of the Hullabaloos. They had had enough of the *Margoletta*, went straight home to town and had their wet luggage sent after them. Old Bob kept his word and explained to Rodley's how much they owed to the salvage men of the *Death and Glory*. And Rodley's were so pleased that they took the *Death and Glory* out of the water and scraped her and gave her a new coat of paint, and a new sail and spars, and an awning as good as the *Titmouse's*, and something over in the way of pocket-money for all three members of her crew.

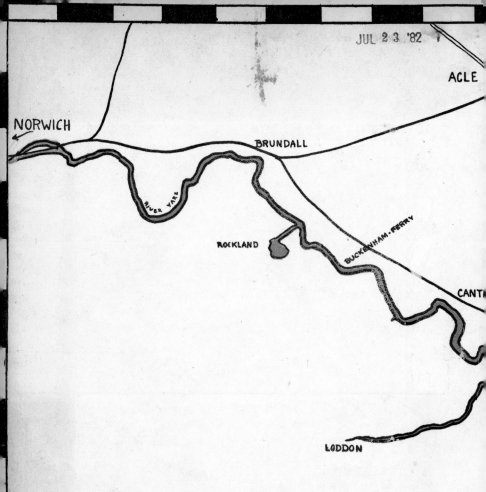

ACLE

NORWICH

BRUNDALL

RIVER YARE

ROCKLAND

BUCKENHAM · FERRY

CANT

LODDON

NORFOLK · BROADS
SOUTHERN · RIVERS
[NAVIGABLE · WATERS]
ONE · MILE

BUNGAY